MY TURN
A Novel by Jill Baker

A Winchester Cottage Print Book
Published by LSI
WinchesterCottage Print
A Division of Winchester Cottage Fine Art and Print
618 Main Street, #184
New Harmony, Indiana 47631

Cover design by Jill Baker
Illustrations by Jill Baker

Printed in the United States of America

Copyright 2009

MY TURN

A Novel by

JILL BAKER

A Winchester Cottage Print Book

Insulated in dreams

I move in a world I make.

A slow boat

Rowing through the mist.

FLIGHT

Camille walked very quietly along the shadowy hall, holding a piece of paper in her hand. Her heart was thudding, making even more noise than her feet on the creaking boards in the hall. What she had to do was very important. It meant her future.

She was trembling and hot as she stood outside the door and looked in. She could see John's profile, as he sat typing at his desk as usual. If he heard her, he did not look up. Supper was long over. John had washed the dishes and gone into his workroom. The humidity and growing dark brought a false hope that the hot, August evening in Texas would cool down.

John continued pounding away at the typewriter. The clacking noise was extraordinarily loud. Camille stood in the doorway looking at him until he became aware of her presence and the noise stopped. The room around him was almost as dark as his hair, straight and shiny in the light of the single lamp on the desk. The thick, black beard he sported was trim and neat, framing striking white skin and dark eyes, but his heavy body sat like a lump in the worn desk chair. He stared straight ahead and did not turn his head, though his hands were still and poised over the keys. When he turned to look at her, his huge, sad eyes peered over his glasses and said as clearly as if he had spoken aloud, "What torture will you inflict on me now?" She felt an urge to turn away, to say "never mind;" but that's what he was hoping for.

It could be put it off no longer. There was only one week left and she had to know. But Camille could not make her voice come out of her throat, and felt her face flush pink as a result. In spite of her inner trembling, she willed her body to be rigid. If he saw she was shaking, she would be put at a disadvantage. She had to remember what she was doing; that it was the only thing to do, and now was the time to do it. She walked into the room, reached out and laid the sheet of paper, full of figures, down carefully beside John's typewriter, on top of a pile of white papers he had there. His eyes stayed on her face, but then moved to the alien, new page on top of his stack and he frowned as if he saw something crawling on it. His thin mouth tensed in preparation for disgust. He picked it up and began to read, mumbling, "What is this?"

"I was wondering, John," she began quietly, scratchily, cleared her throat, tried to remember the words she had rehearsed, "I was wondering. . . well, I will need an allowance to live on – you know – while I am going to school in New York. You know. I will need about two hundred dollars. . . . A month. . . I have to buy food and, and ride the bus. . . . and school supplies. . . ."

As he turned a cold stare on her she could not remember what else she had planned to say. There were more things that she needed money for in order to live, but from the look on his face she wondered if he was going to hit her. If he did she would have a good reason to get mad, she thought. In response, she felt herself becoming angry. If he hit her, it would be good to feel the cleansing force of her anger overriding fear. But he had already steeled himself, looked down and was reading the white paper in his hand again. His feet scraped the floor as he prepared to stand up.

"I can only give you one hundred a month," he said as he stood, the chair making a loud screeching noise as it skidded backward. She realized suddenly that he was taller and heavier than she, even though hunched over. She was backing up out of the room in case he should come at her, but he was not even looking at her any more. He carefully laid the paper down on the far side of the table, dismissing it.

Camille stopped and stood still in shock. A hundred dollars? There was a long silence while Camille assimilated the information.

"But what about. . . ?" This was worse than she had imagined.

Had he said a hundred dollars? She could not believe he would give her only a hundred dollars a month to live on while she went to school. It would be impossible to live in New York on one hundred dollars a month. But he was already turning away from her. She stepped forward into the room, as if she was going to attack him. Everything was red. His white shirt had turned red, the light over the typewriter was glowing intensely. The whole room was bloody. Driven forward, she advanced until she was at his back. Then he turned and faced her, daring her.

"What about the time I supported you, us, when you were attending graduate school?" She said, in a voice that came out in a scratchy whisper.

"That was different." His deep, certain voice was so cold it could have frozen the sun.

"Different?" Her voice rose, needing to know exactly why he thought that. "How was that different? You were going to school and I was working. For six years I worked. I gave up everything and came out to Texas with you, for you. I gave up children for you. I gave up everything for you! I worked for six years to put you through school and have worked at home since then, doing nothing but serving you. Now you won't even give me a couple hundred dollars a month?"

"I came home every evening. You are going away to school. You won't be coming home every evening. Don't you think that's different?" He glared into her eyes, his pupils shrinking so fast she could see them, his mouth so close to her the spit hit her in the chin, challenging her. She glared back at him, looking him straight in the eye. Now she was so full of hurt and anger and fear that she could feel her face contorting. Everything had been planned for months. He had known she was going away and had said nothing until now. His eyes were dark and glaring and his movements, as his large body hunched over her, standing so close to her, were threatening. But she did not back off. Her determination and absolute rage made her hold her ground, even to advance. She stood as close to him as she could, facing him, yet he still seemed far away across the room.

"You can't even afford to give me two hundred dollars to live on, out of all you make? I certainly earned more than two hundred dollars a month when I worked to put you through school, when we first married. And you got all of that!"

"I can't afford it now. You can have one hundred. That's all I can afford." His voice was becoming loud and adamant. He raised his hand, but as she shrank back she saw it held the paper she had given him.

"I pay the bills. I know how much you can afford," she said, trying to remain calm. Anger was gradually consuming her. He was no longer her husband, he was the enemy. He had decided to only give her a hundred dollars a month, knowing she could not live on it. If he didn't want her to leave, he was telling her in this way that she couldn't go back to school. He was going to try to force her to stay at home.

She did not care what happened now. There were no words to say how angry she was, and as she turned to walk away, she heard him behind her.

"Oh no, you don't! You're not going." His hand struck her arm and whirled her around. "You think you're so deserving, such a victim!" he shouted. Now anger was pouring out of him, rolling over her. "Poor little you? You haven't even thought about me? I'm left with all this, the car payments, the house, the insurance, all your art debts."

"What debts?" she challenged, turning back to him. "I've told you we have no debts. We have no debts, except for the house. Your mother gave us the car. My paintings earn their own way, since I sell them. I don't buy any supplies that I haven't paid for by selling a painting. Now what else are you going to do with your money, John? I've scrimped and saved to pay everything off so I could go to school. I saved coupons and bought things at sale prices to save on food, even though you ate well. I never bought clothes for myself until this month. I've sewn our curtains and pillows and everything else, instead of buying them. I saved money a million ways. You've known I was counting on this. I've talked about it for three years! You knew I wanted to go to graduate school after you finished your degree. You've known I was going, and now you won't let me go?"

"Oh! They told me this would happen!" said John, striking his forehead with both hands and twirling around. "Phil. His wife did the same thing – ran off after she finished college, to go to graduate school." And now he turned slowly to face her, his white skin turning dark red and his eyes becoming darker. "You don't just graduate from life, you know. You don't just up and leave the house, as if you were a teen-ager. We're married, remember? You don't graduate from marriage and go away!"

"I gave up everything to do this. I gave up my art to go to work. Remember? I worked to put you through school? I waited till you were sure of your salary before I quit working at the office.

"But I intend to come back and teach at the University with you when I finish. I'm not leaving you for good. I'm coming back on the holidays."

"I've been working to help you, and I finally was able to quit because you said you would spend time with me, once you finished school and had a job. But where have you been for the past four years? Writing. Writing for four years, in this room! We moved here four years ago and I've been waiting for you do something else ever since. You said we would spend time together in the summers. Well here I am. . . . I've been waiting and waiting for you to spend time with me, waiting for you to talk to me . . . like you used to . . ." Tears came to her eyes at the memory and the pain. She coughed and cleared her throat. She could not afford to cry now.

"Camille, we spend our vacations together. I spend a lot of. . . I spend time with you. . ." He said it in a harsh way. He was furious. He moved around the room, waving his arms like the professor he was.

Camille stood still, "What vacations? The only vacations we take are to your mother's house. You call that a vacation? You never ask me if I want to go, we just go. You've never asked me if I wanted to go on vacation. And I can't stand your mother's house!" She said this last too loudly. She shouldn't have said that. She didn't want to dishonor his mother, poor thing. Camille found herself shaking again, and tried to speak as calmly as she could. She could not help it; it had just come out. She wanted to leave and not say another word. It was useless to talk to him. And now she had said too much.

"What's wrong with my mother's house?" he asked, turning, quiet and hurt.

"Nothing." she said, abashed. His mother had nothing to do with this. "Absolutely nothing." His face was again the face of a martyr quietly accepting his horrible fate, his sad eyes peering out

5

over his glasses in deep, questioning pain.

She knew she shouldn't say anything else. She should quit now.

He had already decided. He had made the decision for her. Only it wasn't the decision she wanted him to make. There was nothing else to do but leave.

She turned and stumbled back through the dark hall to her studio, closed and locked the door and sat in the sudden silence alone, staring at the wall in front of her, beaten and battered. No tears came to her eyes. This was deadly serious. A life decision had been made.

There was silence from John's den as well.

Eventually the wall in front of her came into focus. On the wall was her big cork bulletin board with photos, sketches for paintings, and magazine clippings. She looked at the photograph of the sleek girl in a leather suit she had cut from <u>Vogue</u> magazine two years earlier, wanting to look like her, and she saw the sayings she had cut out or written out in large letters and pinned there: "You're only young twice," and "By the Street of By-and-by one arrives at the House of Never – Cervantes," and "One of the most puzzling characteristics of the human brain is its ability to rearrange reality."

THE STREET OF BY-AND-BY

Nine months earlier, the arched front door of the Tudor-style house had opened slowly. It creaked in the silence of the icy day. Holding her arms tight, Camille shrugged her shoulders against the cold, ran out of the house and across the white lawn. Her shoes slid, cracking the surface of ice on the sidewalk. She was in such a hurry that when she grabbed the mail out of the mailbox she dropped half of it into the depression beside the road. She bent down to look at the letters lying there, and saw the one she had been waiting for, the letter from Pratt Art Institute, Brooklyn, New York. She forgot the cold and tore it open on the spot. Her lips curved into a smile as she read the first line beneath the salutation. "We are happy to inform you. . . ."

It was winter, and everything frosted white and silent. Even the big lawns across the street were eerily white and empty of students.

Winter in Texas was colder than usual this year. Even though it should have been warm, they had a sudden freeze. On Camille's quiet street, ice shone in the morning sun, polishing the frozen surfaces glazed over what would have been green lawns, and heated by the sun, mist rose through bare trees. Camille saw black icicles hanging from the roof above the black crossed beams on the front of her house. Smoke drifted from the chimney above them, mingling with the rising mist from melting ice and giving the air a woodsy odor. The sky above was as pale and white as the frozen puddles below. It might have been cold and hard outside, but in Camille's heart the sun shone.

Pratt Institute had accepted her application to begin graduate school next fall! Camille suddenly jumped up and down in delight, letter in hand, eyes closed in disbelief, yet praying it was true. Then she ran back to the house across the yard, hugging the precious letter.

Now she could go to graduate school herself! She had researched schools carefully, applying to the top colleges first. She wanted to get the best degree, to be qualified to teach art. One school had already turned her down. But now Pratt had accepted her! Pratt had actually been her first choice, since it was located in New York.

She had worked and painted all during the ten years she and John had been married, and turned to painting more as her husband sequestered himself in his study to write his thesis, course outlines, and now scholarly books.

In Billington, it was absolutely crucial that John spend time studying to prepare lesson plans and lectures for the classes he taught. A year after he received his Ph.D. he secured a contract from a publisher to convert his doctoral thesis on the philosophy of the monk Justinian into a book for lay readers. Now, years later, he was still consumed by writing, pondering the inscrutable and trying to solve the problems of the universe.

She had to admit John was an ivory-tower-type of philosophy professor. He hid his physical and social awkwardness behind ten-dollar words, a beard and glasses. When Camille met him, she was attracted to him for his scholarly looks, accomplishments and then, when she knew him better, by the fact that his intellectualism and silence actually hid an intense loneliness. His loneliness provoked sympathy and his silence romance. She was Eve in the Garden during the first year of their married life, as she explored his mind and world. He was a true philosopher and, though his strength was not logic, he could argue his beliefs convincingly.

He was a Gestalt philosopher. As they discussed one morning over breakfast during their first year together, communication exists as a matter of signs. Camille thought she understood signs to be a symbol that one displayed to other people when you were trying to get them to understanding their meaning. But John said signs were the "meaning" of meaning itself. He quoted Aristotle to her, "spoken words are symbols of mental experience and written words are the symbols of spoken words. Just as all men have not the same writing, so all men have not the same speech sounds, but the mental experiences, which these directly symbolize, are the same for all, as also are those things of which our experiences are the images."

"I agree!" Camille exclaimed, realizing she had found a common belief with Aristotle.

"But that concept is wrong!" John explained, "There are no

common meanings shared by all, regardless of the signs we use. Everyone sees different meanings in a sign, depending upon their background. A triangle to an Egyptian is a pyramid; to a mathematician it is a formula, to an Amish man it is what he puts on the back of his wagon. You are a Jungian," John said accusingly.

As time passed, Camille realized John's Eden was his den, his passion the research he did, and he hid behind his beard and his books because he was truly naive in the ways of the real world. Still, she was proud of him and proud to be part of his life, believing that some day his great intellect would be recognized. Then they would spend time together as they did when he was courting her, talking about philosophy, history and religion. They would roam the world together, and with his intellect and her gregarious skills, would enjoy the company of famous people. Philosophy was an important and worthy pursuit for a husband and it would earn both of them a lifetime of wealth and happiness.

As a student, John had gone to classes when she left to go to work as a secretary. She would come home in the evening to make supper and do housework; then, worn out from physical labor, she would fall sleep while John continued working into the night on his studies.

She had given up a normal life with children and a home life, to support a student husband for six long years. While she worked to support them, he finished up his Master's degree and earned a Ph.D. She had added typing to her evening duties when John's Master's and then doctoral thesis needed to be typed and they could not afford one. She typed his thesis in a typewriter, triple carbon copy. When he graduated and accepted a teaching position at the state college in Billington, Texas, she felt relieved and rewarded as well. She would at last be able to relax and enjoy life with him; they would have lots of time to travel and talk together.

As John's salary and income from his books became more than sufficient for the two of them, she looked for a house and found a quaint stone cottage near the college to remodel and decorate. John could walk to work. He was a professor and she unwillingly began to play the role of Professor's Wife in the social makeup of the town and the college.

It took a year for the house to become completely remodeled and comfortable and then, since she was no longer occupied with decorating, Camille began to paint again. Her undergraduate degree was in Fine Art.

Now John was working as hard as he had while studying for his degrees, only he was studying to prepare for speeches, lectures for new classes and the books he was writing. With these important projects to preoccupy him, he spent even less time talking with her than he had when he was a student. Time became more and more precious to him and with its scarcity the tension grew. There were deadlines for research articles, deadlines for chapters of the book he was writing. Courses were demanding and special studies took up his spare time. He was also head of the University Philosophical Society and worked long hours with graduate students.

Two years passed since she had quit work. Camille knew John had written two books in that time. So intense was his seclusion, he often neglected to mention what he was working on, and then forgot to tell her his new book had been published, much to her embarrassment when a fellow professor greeted them in public and asked her what she thought about it. John had to explain that he had not told her about it.

After ten years of marriage, Camille realized John's life was not getting any easier; there was less time than ever for them to do anything together. Even though things were different now than when they had been students, John continued on the same demanding schedule he had as a student. They had enough money, they had a nice house and did not have to scrimp and save for special things. But they lived almost separate lives. The house was bigger, but he was doing the same things he had always done; he just did not do it in the same room with her any more. Now, after supper, John went in his den and Camille cleaned up, played the piano for an hour, and then went into her studio to paint.

The little Texas town of Billington was supposed to be a friendly town, but Camille found herself alone and isolated. She had few friends and only a speaking acquaintance with the women in church. Her closest companions were the other wives in the faculty wives' group. Sometimes, in her loneliness, she thought about children, but John adamantly insisted he did not want them yet. She did not want to work outside the home any longer. She loved to paint, and John's salary was sufficient. She kept the books, balanced the checkbook and spent money frugally to make up for not working. Not only that, surprisingly, her paintings had begun to sell, and from time to time she proudly added some money to their mutual budget. She bought her first vacuum cleaner with the sale of one of her paintings.

Camille began showing her paintings in local shows in the small college town they lived in, and then in neighboring towns around, until she grew bored with the limited expectations for her art. She became depressed over her prospects. Had it only been a few years ago she had dreamed of showing her work in New York, as most young artists dream? In a sudden decision last year, she decided to go to New York, visit an old girlfriend there and take her work around to galleries.

"The sunlight fell like a lightning bolt on my closed eyes. I turned over to face the wall and slept a shallow sleep. I dreamed a little dream of hawks flying in the shadows of some great mountain, glowing and floating against the dark rocks with the sun shining on their feathers. One ray split a wing and pierced my eyes and I cried out. The cry awoke me."

When Camille could finally open her eyelids, she saw around her the familiar shapes of the bedroom. The cries of hawks she was hearing in her dream were the sounds of students passing by on their way to classes across the street outside, yelling to each other in the cold morning air. The sun was shining through the slit in the curtain, right onto her face. It was morning. She was alone in bed, since John had risen and was getting dressed in the bathroom.

Her arms refused to move, even though she willed them to. So she slid her feet sluggishly from beneath the warmth and security of her blankets and the free world of dreams. They hit the cold floor with a physical pain. This always awakened her. She groped for her slippers under the bed, trying to gather all her mental and moral wits about her so she could face another day.

The pancake batter was lumpy and refused to be smooth.

Camille grumbled at it as she leaned over the hot stove to get the coffee pot started. Again she thumped at the bowl of batter and began pouring it onto a smoking griddle. Syrup, butter, plates, forks, milk, all were taken from various cupboards and put on the table. John came in, sat down at the table and began to eat as Camille stood and cooked. Hot cakes bubbled and turned, again and again. Finally, the griddle turned off, she sat and bolted down four heavy cakes, adding their weight to her already heavy body. But no one could see it under her terrycloth housecoat.

In the mornings, John did not even like her, much less love her. His words were critical and angry. He hit her with cynical laughter. It always hurt, but she did not know how to stop it. It was not like the two times he had actually hit her with his hand. Both times Camille had made him pay for it with long silences. Now he only hit her with words, but she did not know how to make this stop.

Finally he left for work. The day stretched out long and empty before her. Long and empty, except for painting.

She gazed out of the sliding glass doors, wishing she were floating in some little boat in the middle of the sea, alone.

Standing in the sun with a cup of coffee, the morning sun warming her, a gentle breeze floating around her ankles from the furnace vent under her feet, she lifted her face to the white clouds. She saw a sparrow hopping on the porch, but it flew away when it saw her. Did she look that bad? She checked the red flowers in the hanging pot above the door. She stroked their petals. She could touch a flower and it would not reel from her touch like John did. She could pet her cat without the cat resenting it. The cat leaned against her feet in the sun, also looking outside. He loved her.

A dirty table faced her when she turned around; empty dishes, an empty, dirty floor; a silent, empty house, an empty life. Where else could she go? Maybe to New York? Her work would take her there.

Local art shows were boring. She had always wanted to show her art works in bigger places, ultimately showing them in New York, the Mecca of the art world. She knew her art work was good, but was it good enough?

That night, despairing of her empty life, she silently cried and paced the floor of her studio late into the night. John couldn't sleep, knowing she was crying, and finally forced her to tell him her complaints about this small town and how intensely bored and dissatisfied she was. No one here knew or cared about art, no one appreciated her work as she wanted them to, and there were no challenges.

"What do you want to do about it, then?" he asked her finally. He desperately wanted to sleep.

"I want to show my paintings in New York." She said. She meant "eventually." She had a lot of dreams, but all of them led up to this big one: to have a show in New York.

"So GO to New York! Show your work. Go ahead, go to New York, SHOW your paintings in New York," he yelled. Camille stared at him. It seemed too simple when he said it, but he had said it, and in so saying, not only gave her permission, but had given her a mandate. So she went to bed, but lay awake until early morning, excitedly planning how to do it.

YOU'RE ONLY YOUNG TWICE

The moon hung behind white quilted clouds, dimly lighting up the cold winter night. Her feet, in cushioned tennis shoes and heavy socks, pounded on the blacktop. She could hear her breath and see it come out in puffs from her mouth. Striding evenly, she ran. And as she ran, she thought obsessively of New York and what awaited her there.

The first time Camille went to New York, it was to an exhibition where one of her paintings, chosen from a dozen slides which she sent, was shown alongside other women artists' paintings at Lincoln Center. She had joined this women artists' group long distance, having seen an ad in an art newsletter.

But once in New York, she felt like an amateur showing her work with other amateurs. Much of their work was of doubtful quality. It seemed the other women in the group were all wealthy weekend painters. She did not feel she belonged. The women dressed too nicely and acted too snobbish. Her painting of a sinister man in black shadows was quite different from their gilt-framed still lives and flowers.

But one of those women artists became a friend during the show. Grace Mason was a little younger than she, but was much like her. They had almost the same outlook on life, since they both had come from the South. She and Grace sat together all of one long day, taking their turn guarding the show, and became fast friends. Whereas Camille was short, dark-haired, fair-skinned and married, Grace was also tiny, had long, blond hair, blue eyes and petite features, but was single. Grace invited her and she went with her to see a group exhibition in SoHo that had one of her paintings in it. Grace lived in New York.

Camille decided to go back to New York a second time to seek a solo exhibition any way she could get one. As soon as she arrived in New York she was totally involved in the business of being an artist, showing slides of her paintings to galleries. In New York she felt different, carrying a black portfolio and showing her work to stern gallery directors. Through her friend and fellow artist Grace, she met other artists in galleries and at openings. She was accepted as a serious artist, as one of them. This surprised and delighted her. It was difficult for them to imagine her as the wife of a professor in Texas, so she stopped telling them she was and even forgot it herself for awhile. For the time being, she became a full-fledged artist, walking around New York City carrying her big, black leather case full of slides and samples of her work, along with her resume.

By the end of two weeks, she had managed to book two shows in private galleries.

Before leaving Texas, she had taken advantage of her position as a faculty wife to talk to the art professors at the University, asking for their advice.

When she returned and they found out about her success in New York, a couple of them mentioned she should try to teach art at the University. But she would need to earn a Master of Fine Arts degree first.

It was an exciting thought; to teach would not only be a compromise situation, it would be a situation that would save her and her marriage. With a Master's degree she could practice her art and stay in Billington with John, teaching art at the University, while he taught Philosophy. She talked to him about it. He remained silent, as usual, whenever she talked to him, but he did not say anything to discourage her. After awhile, she decided to go ahead and do it and began applying to graduate schools.

Camille returned to New York for a third time the following spring, to have a one-person show in a private gallery. This time she looked at New York City quite differently. It might be her future home, where she could soon be living and working, if she was accepted in a graduate program. As soon as she arrived, she and Grace had lunch and she told Grace in excited tones about her plans to go back to school. Grace agreed that she should try to get a Master's degree in art. She had earned an undergraduate degree from Pratt, coming from Atlanta right after high school to do so. Now, three years after graduation, Grace was earning her own way as a moderately successful, professional visual artist, living off the income from her work.

Camille had shipped twenty-three paintings from Texas, to

arrive before she did, to put up her one-woman show at Goethe House on Fifth Avenue, across from the Metropolitan Museum.

For this show, Camille had painstakingly painted a series of detailed male nudes. When they saw them, the proper Goethe House staff gulped and smiled politely. Camille spent two hundred dollars on champagne and sent invitations to all the friends she had made in New York. Only Grace and ten of her friends attended the opening, along with thirty supporters of Goethe House, so Camille had two and a half crates of champagne left over. The following day, she agreed to let the staff cover the largest male nude over the table in the hall with a white cloth for a German Women's Club Tea in the gallery. She would not object to the censorship. Camille told a shocked Grace that she felt grateful to them for showing her work at all.

Camille spent most of her trip walking around the city, portfolio in hand, looking at private galleries and showing her slides to whoever would look at them.

Camille knocked at a thick glass door, finding it locked. In the back of the gallery she could clearly see three people sitting at a table. They looked up and saw her standing there outside the glass door, portfolio in hand, but did not even acknowledge her presence or get up to open the door. "There are some strange and rude people in this city," she said to herself.

Walking in New York City was an experience in itself. Everything was exciting and new. Down the block from the gallery the sidewalk had a detour for construction work going on, at a building site. Bright orange ribbons lined the area to keep pedestrians away from the workmen who labored only a few feet away, wearing dusty overalls and sweaty headbands under their yellow hard hats. One tall "hard-hat" leaned over the ribbon as she passed, so close to her he could have touched her. He put up his hand to tip his helmet up and whispered, "It's a lovely day, isn't it?" She laughed aloud at the polite ordinariness of this remark and saw his companions turn to look at him. As she walked on, Camille heard them shouting at him, asking what he had said, and smiled.

Here, Camille had the feeling she must look different than she did in Texas, because people acted so differently toward her. She felt a strange power here, and did not understand it. Here she felt beautiful. Men told her she was gorgeous; women spoke to her politely or looked at her enviously. When she smiled people were kind. Both men and women catered to her. She was always the first one on the bus, because bus drivers inevitably stopped directly in front of her in a crowd. She was the first one through the door, because a man would open it for her. She discovered she would be chosen over others when a row of faces presented themselves at a counter. It happened so often she felt guilty and told herself she would try not to notice or to use this power deliberately.

On the third day, Camille had an appointment with Hal Ward at Ward Gallery in SoHo. She had met him the first time she came to New York. She remembered the first time she saw him, standing with one elbow propped on the counter that separated the office from the gallery. He was tall and rough-edged, an old hippie with a beard and long, dark hair sprinkled with gray that floated around a smiling face. He took an immediate liking to Camille's work and they discussed it in depth on the spot. He told her he wanted to show her work in his gallery. Camille was sure this was a dream. She had wanted her work to be in a gallery. She needed a permanent place in New York to exhibit her work.

During her appointment with Hal that afternoon, he was the same, cool man she remembered and, as his return letter had indicated, he talked about showing her work. She felt her ego swell with pride and anticipated working longer and harder at her art.

This was the third time the plane had flown back to Texas and circled over Dallas, and this time, painfully, Camille felt her new-found confidence draining away. She realized she did not enjoy her return. Her new friends in New York were urging her to move there permanently, but she had balked at that. She couldn't give up John and her life in Billington. After all, he was generously supporting her and allowing her to go away at times, to exercise her own free will.

However, when she had asked him to consider moving closer to New York, or to at least allow her to travel back and forth regularly to New York, as a career artist, he said he did not want that.

"Definitely not" he said. "Even though I consider myself a supporter of women's rights, I hate New York and everything in or near it, and it would cost too much and interfere with your taking care of the house, if you did a lot of traveling back and forth." He pointed out his mother was a model of the liberated woman, who had gotten a teaching degree and taught school for many years, yet even she stayed at home to take care of his dad.

This pronouncement fell as something like a death blow on Camille's dreams, though she couldn't tell what had died, since staying in Billington wasn't a death sentence. She realized he expected her to do the same things she had always done. He quickly told her he loved her and was worried about her, which was why he didn't want her to work in New York. But she had been wondering for a long time if he did love her any more. It was obvious he did not enjoy her company. Did this mean he simply wanted her to care for him all his life?

One lonely evening, when John, in a rare mood, went to sit on the front porch and play the guitar, she remembered how she used to sing with him when they were courting. How wonderful that he was relaxing! So she went out to sit down beside him. He was singing, and she began to join in, singing the harmony to "Unchained Melody" as she had long ago. But when she started to sing, he stopped playing and singing, stood up and, without a word, walked away with the guitar. It hurt to think about it now, how she felt rebuffed and bowed her head, trying not to cry, trying to understand the sudden silence.

John did not recognize her when she walked through the gate in the terminal. He was looking at everyone but her as she pressed toward him in the crowd. When she was standing right in front of him and he finally recognized her, he gave her a quick peck on the cheek and began to tell her all the things she needed to tend to at home, since she had been gone so long. She felt the City and its excitement fading away. All the adventures, troubles and hard work in New York disappeared, giving way to normal life in Billington, Texas.

In New York, she had felt she was more than just a wife, but seeing that John saw her only as a wife hit hard. Hearing John's words, she surprised herself by hearing her own familiar, raised, defensive voice, unused for two weeks, coming out of her mouth. Grudgingly, she found her mind slipping back into the familiar, deadening housekeeping role, requiring small, tedious, decision-making.

Back in her house, Camille dawdled over getting ready for bed. She knew John was waiting for her in the bedroom. A horrible, numb feeling, as if she were an apple with the core cut out of it, was in the center of her, even though she knew she loved to make love. For years she had missed making passionate love, as John and she once had. She remembered how she had enjoyed it, because one of the men she had met this time had been so attractive she had even started imagining what it would be like to have sex with him even though he was Grace's boyfriend. Sex was a thirst that would not be quenched.

She took a long time drawing her bath. Her husband called to her from the dark room, "Come on to bed, Camille. Don't bother to take a bath." She wished she could take time to feel fresh and clean and sexy, to relax in a hot tub and enjoy preparing for it, but John liked his sex quick and dirty. She left the bathtub filled with steaming water and went into the bedroom instead. This wouldn't take long.

He was already naked and so was Camille. He hated for her to wear anything. She saw his hand reach up out of the covers to turn the lamp off as she came in. "The better not to see me," she thought. She crawled under the cold sheets. John moved closer to her, reaching for her crotch. She was cold. The house and the bedroom and the bed were cold. She knew she was still tense from the trip and could not respond very well when she was chilled like this. His hand, too, was like ice, but she willed herself to participate slowly, becoming more sensuous, recalling how New York had turned her into a desirable woman. Men's eyes had told her she was attractive. Now she felt it and returned the love they held out to her, feeling John's heavy body on top of hers, prematurely pushing himself into her.

When John finished his effort, he threw himself over onto his side of the bed with a big, happy groan. Camille knew he would go to sleep now, totally spent and at a distance from her.

"Please," Camille said very quietly into the long silence of the dark bedroom, still feeling incomplete and wanting more. "Please," she breathed even more silently, speaking to him in her mind, begging him to love her. But he had told her many times that men liked to sleep after love-making, while sex woke women up. Men could only do it once a night, he said. His breathing became heavy and regular as he slept. He was happy and satisfied. She would not disturb him again, as he did not like her to touch him when he slept. He got angry when he was awakened after making love. So it was over.

Camille tried, but she could not go to sleep. Now she was sexually aroused. She went back into the bathroom. The water was still hot, so she took a long, hot bath and wrapped her warm robe around her in the silence of the night. The house was dark and she restlessly roamed about in it, trying to feel at home again. She wandered into her studio. Even in the semi-darkness, the sight of the easel, the palette on the table, with brushes standing in pots and the smell of used tubes of paint made her feel better, more comfortable. With the street light from outside shining on them, the used tubes of oil paint appeared to be so many little dried turds and the palettes puddles of dried mud. But by daylight they held the colorful makings of masterpieces. She moved her hand over their dried, rumpled hardness and picked a sable brush to softly sweep over her cheek, as was her habit.

In the dark of the familiar studio, she stood and stared without seeing, out the window. Her New York exhibition had been a disappointment. All her exhibitions had been disappointments, even when she sold paintings. No exhibit would ever be good enough. She would never get recognition or sell enough paintings, even if she sold all of them. She had to make more and better ones. She would show them she was the best artist alive. She had no doubt of it herself.

Camille had another show to prepare now and that was a chilling thought. Hal's gallery, now representing her, was starting her off with a one-person show in the SoHo gallery in November. She and Hal had set the date yesterday. Having never been represented by a New York gallery, she was unsure about how to go about it.

The exhibition was eleven months away. If she was accepted at a New York art school, she might be living in New York then, working on her graduate degree. Before October, whether she was accepted or not, she had to prepare paintings for the show she had scheduled in September at Purdue University, which would then be shipped to SoHo for Hal's show in November.

She turned on the desk lamp and, still standing, opened her sketch book. She picked up a pencil and began to look through the sketches. Soon she was seated under the light, making quick sketches for paintings she would work on during the next few months.

THE HOUSE OF NEVER

"I came upon the scene at the corner. It was dark and all I could see were two women standing, sobbing frantically and holding onto each other as they looked around for a friendly face. Their eyes were filled with tears and their mouths were open, though no sound came from them. Their faces were red and distorted with weeping. I looked beyond them at the huge bulk behind them, which was a car body with the insides torn out. The chrome was twisted like a heap of ribbons and the roof was ripped off, as if it had been opened with a ragged can opener. Water bled from the smashed-in front. The inside seats had stuffing pouring out of them through gashes, spilling onto the street. And hanging, upside down, out the broken driver's window, I saw John, my husband! His face was white, but recognizable under his hair, hair shining black with blood. His open eyes were rolled upward, staring at the ground, his arms were flung over his head, reaching almost to the ground, and his heavy, white body spilled out of the window. Everything was shiny with the blood which dripped down over his face. Red sprinkled the large, pale stomach pouring through the driver's window, while his legs remained inside.

The two women were pointing at him now, horrified. They ran to me and began to sob and press their faces into me. I struggled against their grasp, horrified and shocked at the whole scene, trying to free myself from their wet, clinging fingers, and to move. Everything was burning. I thought the car had caught on fire, but when I looked around, the red, flashing lights were coming from a patrol car just driving up.

I frowned and closed my eyes against the bright lights and the fiery scene, struggling to free myself from the cold, wet arms binding me to the spot. I had to get free and I could not. The lights were getting brighter and redder."

When she was finally able to open her eyes, Camille saw sunlight was shining on her through the window, and she could feel its heat. She struggled in the sweat-soaked sheet which, in tossing and turning, she had wrapped around herself. Suddenly she stopped struggling, realizing John lay sleeping peacefully next to her. Shocked he was alive, she remembered his face, flickering in dreams, and was afraid for him, afraid he was dead. His breath came lightly, and though his arms were flung over his head as if in fright, he was certainly undisturbed by death. His face was beautiful in sleep; his eyes, with thin, parchment-colored lids, were closed, the black lashes moving a little. But fear for him still hung heavily over her.

Camille lay still, gazing at the ceiling, feeling her heart pounding. It was only five o'clock. It would be another hour before she could move. She wondered how she could do it. She was hot, wrapped up in a sticky sheet. It would be impossible to go back to sleep. Her mind was filled up with the vivid images left from the dream that had seemed so real. She could not get the sight of John's dead face out of her mind. Whenever she closed her eyes it was there again, in all of its loud, red brightness; the shiny, twisted metal, the women crying, the sight of John's ripped and bleeding body and his still, white face as he hung through the broken car window upside down.

It was so real it was frightening. She could not imagine that it had not happened. It was so vivid she feared it would happen. She must remind John to drive safely when he left to go to the University today; he should walk instead of driving. She could not close her eyes because when she did the dream came back, so she lay still and watched the slit of light move slowly across the bedroom as the sun rose.

Camille lay still until six o'clock, growing calmer and going over the details of her forthcoming temporary move to New York in her head; something that really was happening. She was nervous about where she would live. Thinking about it and planning it calmed her, and pleasant feelings began to fill her mind. Finally, the alarm began to buzz and she climbed out of the sheet, already wide awake.

Camille had begun to run at night down the streets of her quiet town. At first she felt discouraged, since she could only run a half block, and had to walk the rest of the way. But each day she ran further, until she could run a mile. She went to a shoe store and bought her first pair of real running shoes, expensive ones, paying more than she had ever paid for a pair of shoes in her life. She told herself they would last several years.

Finally, she was able to run a mile easily and then she began to run two miles. She was finding that at night, on the invisible blacktop, she felt alive. The black road floated under her feet. She followed the moon through the leaves, followed the streetlights down avenues of tall black trees. Her breath and the pounding of her feet were all she felt through her body. Eventually, exhaustion drove every thought from her mind, disappearing in the calming energy she poured into her nightly run. She melted in the sweat dripping from her forehead, dripping from her elbows and pouring down her stomach. Finally, her face red and her clothes soaking with sweat, she would see the house lights ahead in the dark.

She flopped down in a chair to watch TV a minute with John, who only glanced at her balefully, but continued to sit silently, watching Johnny Carson as he drank a beer and munched on chips. Then she would rise to bathe and go to bed. John would acknowledge her presence by complaining about how intent she was on running. It disturbed him, all this activity. But she did not intend to stop. She looked forward to her daily run and the way she felt so tired and yet exhilarated afterward. After taking her bath she would fall asleep immediately from pure exhaustion, to sleep soundly for a few hours. But only for a few hours, for she awoke early every morning, dreaming vivid dreams.

"I am going to graduate school! And I have a show in New York!" It had been three months since the letter had come, but her emotions were growing as the time got closer. She felt like celebrating, and she had told John why they should go out on Friday night and have a blast. After all, he was her husband and he should share some of the happiness she felt. He should feel as happy as she. She wished sometimes that they could return to the times when they went on dates, when he would take her to a dark parking spot on a hillside overlooking town for some heavy petting, as he had before they married, and then make passionate love to her.

It was really incredible the way Camille seemed to infuriate him tonight. While it had taken him only a half-hour to shower and change, she had taken forever to put on a new dress. He paced the floor and watched storm clouds gather outside in the dark sky. It was going to be a bad night, since it had already begun to sprinkle. The traffic would be terrible and they would have to walk in the rain. He anticipated frustration. When she was finally ready, he hurried out the door, leaving her to lock it behind them. It was not going to be fun.

His new black shoes slid in the fresh mud as he hurried down the hillside toward the car and he tipped precariously, getting mud all over the side of one of his shoes. He managed to recover and continued on down the dark slope toward their car. Camille hurried along behind him silently, since he was irritated to the point of anger. She always made him feel this way whenever they had to go out. He hated these occasional evenings; having to haul Camille around to places he didn't want to go. She had suggested, no demanded, that they go out to dinner and the movies. He suggested they skip the meal and only go to the campus movie, but she insisted she didn't want to make a meal at home, that she wanted to eat in a restaurant. He made these evenings out as seldom as possible, as they were difficult. What was the point? Eating out and the price of the movie was expensive and never worth what they cost.

She had suggested three restaurants in town where she would like to eat, but said she could not make up her mind and for him to decide for her. He had decided that a fast meal at Hooray's would take less time than any restaurant. They served roast beef sandwiches, which he liked. The sauce they used was good and he hadn't had french-fries for a long time. He would surprise her.

Perhaps he should not have married. He got more enjoyment out of reading and writing than human relationships, but one needed a wife for one's career, and it was a fact that his marriage created a positive image with his superiors at the University, who actually liked Camille.

Besides, he loved her cakes. He liked to have a home-baked dessert, like a cake or pie or something sweet, every night. She was a pretty good cook. That was one reason they didn't eat out. It was not much fun to dress up and go out to eat something that didn't taste as good as Camille's cooking. It was a real waste of time and money, spending time that he could have used writing on his chapter and a waste of the money he had worked to earn.

But it seemed more difficult to be married within the last few years. When they first married she had been so sweet and anxious to please. Now she often acted like she was displeased with everything, including him, though she never said it. She didn't have to work outside the home, but she was still dissatisfied. He did not like to think about all this, so he simply threw himself into his work so that she could have whatever she needed. Perhaps she was turning into a dried-up, bitter witch like those he saw his colleagues with. Why? Was a crazy wife a product of age, or menopause, or what? It was nothing he could control, he knew. He had done everything he could to make life easier for her. She had a life of leisure and it was beyond him why she did not enjoy it.

As far as sex went, he gave it to her every week. Lots of wives couldn't claim that at their age; he knew this from overhearing things other men his age said. He had been faithful. The duties of marriage were important to him as was keeping everything as it should be. He stuck to his guns, no matter what happened. He had promised to be faithful to her and he was going to do it, no matter what. There were many beautiful girls on campus and any of them would lie down for an "A," but he had never looked at them. He could keep away from temptation. It never entered his mind. Philosophical studies kept his mind off the temptation and rescued him from questionable circumstances. At home temptations were never a question and everything was secure and routine.

Only lately had his judgment been questioned. Camille's dissatisfaction and latest binges had intruded upon his peace. Was his marriage in trouble? Perhaps Camille was leaving him. He couldn't imagine why, but the thought began to grow. Talking about how they felt was never done, since the one time when he had said too much and determined never to let her know how he felt again. So all he knew was their marriage was secure as far as he was concerned.

Camille had never disagreed with him or made him worry about her faithfulness. There was no opportunity to be unfaithful in this town. He would have known about it. Other people would have let him know.

And even if she went to New York, she was around artists there and everyone knew that men artists were gay. There was no problem with her associating with artists, as far as he was concerned. Besides, the only person she talked to in New York was a woman. He had answered the phone when she called.

But Camille's going to graduate school was beginning to get on his nerves. Like tonight; she had said it was a "celebration" because she was going. What was to celebrate? She was just trying to annoy him. It was hard to get into a program and the odds that any graduate program would accept her had been small. Why had any graduate school accepted her?

Disappointed in the "restaurant" John has chosen, but understanding that they were late, Camille squeezed into the rotating orange, plastic chair beside the white Formica table, while John stood over her. He told her to watch that the ketchup spilled on the next chair did not get on her white dress. The new dress, which she had liked in the store, now seemed to be cut much too low and was certainly too dressy for Hooray's. But they had managed to get a table by the window looking out at the darkening sky and the cars going by on the bypass, in spite of the crowd. She sat in the little chair and saved the table while John went to the counter and stood in line. He ordered two roast beefs to stay, with fries and tall teas. After he paid the bill, he looked at his watch, pleased with how little time it had taken so far. He returned, holding two plastic trays heaped with paper bags, tall paper cups full of iced tea with plastic caps and a straw sticking up from each of them, a pile of white paper napkins and another pile of little packages of extra barbecue sauce and mustard.

"We can't be late," he reminded Camille as he squeezed into his chair on the other side. "This is a popular film with the students. We won't even get seats unless we get there thirty minutes before it starts."

Having eaten, they began their drive back to campus. They were in the big, luxury car his mother had given them last year. It was only three years old and still ran beautifully. Every other year, when John's mother got a new car, she "sold" her old one to John for a dollar. Financially, it helped them a lot, and they had never had to shop for cars. John was grateful, but Camille was a little annoyed that they had to depend on his mother to choose and buy their cars.

It was beginning to rain. John cursed when the cars in front of them slowed down because of a few drops. Now they would be late. He mumbled to Camille it was because she had taken so much time to get dressed and that had gotten them started late. His anger was rising. Everything he said told her that she was the reason he was enduring this torture.

"Oh, no!" Camille said, as if she had just remembered something. She had her lipstick poised halfway to her mouth. "I forgot to put on panties; I was in such a hurry."

She glanced at John's face. She had recently read a book on how to arouse the sexual fantasies of husbands, trying to find something that would stimulate the sexual side of their marriage. The forgotten panties were one of the ways suggested. This was the least bizarre suggestion of them all. Somehow meeting John at the door wrapped in Saran-Wrap was not her style. But when she glanced at him, John was still silently cursing the idiot driver of the car in front of him. He laid on the horn and honked for all he was worth. He suddenly put the brakes on, and their heads jerked forward.

"God damn it! Now he's actually stopped!"

He had said a swear word. He must be angry. His face turned red as he turned to look at her, then recalling her last remark. In his tight, closed lips and furious eyes she read only contempt for her stupidity, as if dealing with the lower mentality in the rest of the world was not enough, his wife couldn't even remember to get completely dressed. How embarrassing.

Camille bowed her head, and tears came unbidden to her eyes, mortified at her ploy and embarrassed for John, as well. She told herself she would never try any more suggestions from a book to arouse her husband—the author had obviously never met anyone as insensate as he. The slow trip continued in tense silence. John parked the car on the hillside where they were far from the theater, and Camille, in a rain-soaked white dress and heels, ran along behind John's heavy, wet shape in the rain, trying to stay under the umbrella John held, up the slippery hill, to the Student Union Building, where the campus movie was beginning at that very moment.

Driving home, John verbally tore the movie apart, criticizing in minute and accurate detail, the directing, the dialogue, the acting and the plot, especially the rationale behind the plot. Camille began to wonder how in the world she could have enjoyed it, since John was obviously right. She tried to change the subject, saying she was going to church in the morning. John sometimes went. But he said he didn't understand why she went to church; it was futile to worship a god that man had made up.

"I feel like I am doing something good when I go," she mumbled lamely, searching her mind for the reasons she had decided to attend.

A long silence followed.

Camille's thoughts returned to Hooray's when she glanced in the mirror at home that night. A young man had been sitting at the table behind John, who had smiled at her. She blushed and looked down. He was handsome and young, a college student. His lips were full and sensuous in a square-jawed, classic face. He could not have been more than twenty; why would he look at her? When she looked again, he was eating, but he caught her glance and smiled again.

Things like this had been happening to her recently, and she could not understand why. After all, she was a housewife in her thirties. She had never been attractive. She had always been plump and mousy, overweight as a teenager and throughout her twenties. Now she was losing weight because of her running. John had complained that she was too skinny; he resented her running every day. Her looks did not please him. He had tried to lose weight several times, but could not. He might be called overweight, though no one would say it.

Perhaps her new dress drew too much attention? She hesitated before taking it off and looked at herself from the front and back. She had bought some new clothes to wear in New York. After all, John was tenured and had gotten a raise every year. She argued she could feel justified in buying clothes now, since she had not bought any clothes for ten years. Most of her clothes were so worn they had to be thrown away—the dresses and suits her mother had made her when she went off to college fourteen years ago. She needed new clothes for going to school in New York. So she had several reasons to buy herself some new clothes.

Undressing, while the rain poured down outside, she saw her body naked in the full length mirror, and realized she no longer had lumps of fat on her hips, and her stomach was flat. She did not see a chubby, mousy woman any more.

She did not believe it. She turned her back to the mirror and the image disappeared. Once again she was the fat and shapeless slob her husband despised.

Loud rustling and bumping sounds came from all over the kitchen; Camille was putting up groceries, holding three grocery bags, one dripping steak blood and orange juice that had to go into the refrigerator immediately. The Indian summer sunlight slanted in, casting a golden light over her hasty dance to get the bags and bags of newly-bought food put up before it melted or got limp, before supper time. Moving in and out of the slanting light, her shadow hurried across the flowered wallpaper, across the wooden door of the pantry with its wooden surface worn smooth, across the white ceramic handle that fell off sometimes. She reached for the refrigerator door and felt the cold flowing over her feet when it opened. It smelled of ripe tomatoes, dried sour milk spilled in the bottom and an open can of pineapple.

Once the groceries were put up, she put a record on the stereo while the casserole baked, an old record she hadn't played for awhile. In the quiet that followed the beginning of a piano piece, she sat down for a moment to listen and felt the music stirring through her, erasing her tension. It flowed over her, seeping in slowly. The thin sliver of a note, drawn out like a silver thread, whistled off into the universe when she closed her eyes. Then a rushing sound of violins–thousands of them–tumbling over each other in a waterfall of notes, hurrying down, into and rising up into harmonies and falling and floating and dying when the silver thread became a beam of light, a laser ray cutting through them and overpowering them all with its light.

She felt like dancing, so she arose and twirled around and around the room, her feet moving of their own accord, spinning and taking her around the big dining table. She raised her arms and turned slowly, while the room spun around her, disappearing, as if there was only music and the notes beating, turning her harder and harder, hitting her, thudding and rocking and pounding in her. She danced, her hands out, curving up in time to the music, flinging her arms up with triumph, and then down with the ending. She felt the music and her body followed the feelings.

The next song was a waltz and she three-stepped around the dining room, smiling, her arms holding an invisible partner. The dog came in to watch her curiously. The song ended and the next one began, a slow ballad about a little girl dying. John walked through the room on his way to the den. His disapproving presence stopped her for a second, then, full of memories, she flung herself into his arms and began, over his protestations, to dance with him until he was caught up in it too. Then when a slow song came on, slowly and sadly, he put his arms around her and they slow-danced.

Weaving small circles slowly, their bodies moving together till they were looking over each other's shoulders and feeling only each other's body and seeing the walls go past.

"The last time I saw her, lying still and cold . . . ." The singer sang.

Tears came to Camille's eyes. This might be the last time she would dance with him, and the growing certainty was sad. She was going away soon.

They danced their last dance. She had no desire to cling to him, to kiss him or press herself against him. It was the old times, the old thoughts of him in his youth that she missed. It was the early days of their knowing each other, when he was courting her, and the few times they had danced. It was the hopes she held on to for ten years that would never be fulfilled. It was the goals she thought they had, the losing of them one by one, here and there. No children. No moving to a bigger city, no moving from this house, no career for her. No vacations, no holidays together in a romantic place. The constant work and no play. It was the pain that he unknowingly inflicted upon her each day with his habitual criticism and she upon him with her inability to please him, and their losing each other in the importance of separate things in their lives. Their never spending time together, never sharing a song or a kind word between them. Especially painful, the time he was playing the guitar on the front porch, when she joined him and he got up and walked away.

Some of the memories were hurtful, but they were sweet at this moment because they were almost over.

She was unwillingly saying good-bye. Saying good-bye to the good memories they shared. Like the first year, when in the early mornings they made love, and she sang to him as rain fell outside the window of their tiny apartment.

Or the ache of memories of the many nights she cried silently in their bed, so as not to disturb him and arouse his wrath. And before that, the nights he was angry because she was not satisfied with the sex and miles stretched between them. Miles of white sheets. Miles that she could never cross. Miles too cold and forbidding. The probable and intolerable anger that awaited her on the other side of those white miles–the dangerous journey she never again tried to take.

It was the promise she thought he had made to her, that he would be there, somewhere, sometime for her. She had waited for him. She knew he had to be in there, somewhere, warm and soft and loving. She knew he would fulfill his promise some day. He would need her and bring her the broken gift of himself. She was so sure that one day they would be lovers again, that one day he would love her as much as she loved him, that she waited. But he never came. And now she realized she had waited too long, since she had never dared to do anything to bring him back. Waited too long, so long that her love for him had died. It had shriveled up and starved to death, waiting.

As they danced, she thought of the man in her arms, the stranger whose body she held against hers and she silently told him, when he asked why she was crying, that it was just the sad song that was making her cry, just the autumn sun shining in her eyes, the summer ending in the bare trees. It was her time of month. It was her time of year. It was her time of life. It was her turn to live.

She wanted to live. She wanted the chance to weep with happiness again, to make love till she turned someone's heart inside out. She wanted to dance all night until her soul melted in little puddles on the morning streets.

She wanted to tell him "It's not you I'm crying for, my old long-gone, hoped-for lover and friend that I am saying good-bye to. It's not you pulling so strongly on my emotions tonight. It's the lack of you. It's because somewhere I lost you."

The record ended and in the empty quiet that followed, she moved away from John in tears. John asked again if something was wrong. She said no and he quickly went into his den.

The next day she began to pack. She would take only necessities with her. Warm clothes, her art materials, some of the old pots and dishes, the plastic plates and the worn linens. She confirmed her plane ticket that she had bought a week ago. She had originally planned to leave two weeks early in order to find a place to live, but John insisted she not leave until the week before school started and she agreed, praying she would be able to find an inexpensive apartment in that short a time. She had been told it was difficult to find a place to live in New York. Occupancy in the City was 95% and people fought over available apartments.

FANCY FREE

She was flying away. She had been delivered to the airport as the sun sank behind the hills by her silent husband, checked her bags, perfunctorily kissed him good-bye at the gate and boarded the plane for New York.

She felt utterly delighted to be free; but under the delight, something else hung dark and heavy and exciting. Even the coming darkness as she departed was part of the adventure. This time she was flying into the night for more than a couple of weeks. She was going to be a student again. She was going to be young again. She was going to be a career girl—the one she had never been. She would be Brenda Starr and Mary Cassatt rolled into one. She would pretend to be that most exciting of modern heroines, the Single Woman. She was flying away to live in the big City alone.

She would be able to sit in an outdoor cafe or in a dark corner of O.G.'s and lick lemon ice off a spoon, or drink a hot cider and not have to worry about explaining an expenditure or why she was getting home late to an upset husband.

Surrounding the image was glamour and danger. She could roam the streets without the sudden shot to the heart the housewife feels when it is 5 o'clock and she realizes it is time to go home to fix dinner for her family. She would have time to burn. She could eat at 7:00 or 8:00 or even 9:00 at night. The idea was both dreadful and absolutely thrilling.

She had already sampled these small pleasures on her past trips to New York, but now she was going to live in New York for good.

Was it "for good?"

At the faculty club potluck dinner, one of the wives had asked her, "Are you ever coming back from New York, Camille?" All the women knew she was going away to graduate school and every woman's head at the table turned toward her to hear her answer, while the men kept on talking.

"I don't know," she said, frowning and drawing it out as if it had just occurred to her, then she smiled a wicked smile and they laughed in relief. Now the memory of her own words came back to her in their truthfulness. Of course she was coming back, she told herself. She had been reassuring John over and over the past few days that she would be coming back.

She had promised him, but she had not promised herself.

"I wish you could pack me in your suitcase," she heard Jackie Reilly say wistfully. She laughed because Jackie meant it so much that the possibility became real. She looked out the window at the black earth beneath, and watched her small town disappearing until it was a tiny dot in the blinking vastness of night below her. All the schizophrenia of being the good little daughter and wife and some other person at the same time were represented by this dot of a town. Her husband, with his recent pronouncements about duty and faithfulness and suddenly postulated ideas of what marriage was, over the past week. Her town and her husband, with his gray face and his gray ideas and his interminable writing were disappearing forever beneath her wings.

She had brought all her women friends with her in her suitcase tonight and was taking them away. They were all with her in the darkness, their faces still turned up looking up at her as they did that night at the faculty dinner, believing in her, trusting her to do it for them, because they could not do it themselves.

She had tried flying away with them in their afternoon cocktails at the country club that became morning cocktails to get them off the ground earlier in the day. Flying with their prescription drugs designed to help them quell anxieties about dying. Back there on the ground, the drugs were designed to lift their spirits, courtesy of their doctor, till the health of their mind was in danger. "An idle mind is the devil's playground," her mother used to say.

Some had tried to flee Billington through death, the most recent one hanging herself from the beams in her garage. One had flown from the top of the gymnasium into the empty campus swimming pool. Others had escaped by dying from diseases, such as breast cancer, which had claimed three of her friends. Then Camille found some lumps and thought she had it. When it turned out she did not, she resolved to never let death catch her here in Billington.

Now she was flying out of Billington. She had died there and was ascending into heaven. She had already died there a thousand times as an unnoticed helper at innumerable dinners, a faculty wife who stood pale in the shadow of her husband. And before she had been an ignored wife she had been a dutiful daughter. Now her past was dying from those deaths. Perhaps she was mad.

She was flying through the cool, harvest night, marveling that above the plane the bleary stars already flustered like moths and the South still burned on the horizon below her, sending her away into tomorrow.

She was growing into the sky, rising like a young sapling turning silver in the wind, stretching tall. Her time to bear fruit had begun. She was a bird flying home. She was a pilgrim sojourning, seeking her mission and purpose in the big city under orange lights, far away.

She did not remember having been so far away ever, ever having seen her home from so far, from above, like God, without touching earth as she flew. It was so distant from her. So far she almost longed for it again already.

She tried not to think of the home she was leaving, where she had nurtured roses, or of her little dog. All she knew was that she had to leave. It was a matter of life or death. She was fleeing for her life, for her sanity.

She could not think of John. For the past week he had been angry, withdrawn and silent, speaking only when spoken to, except for occasional sudden pronouncements about duty and faithfulness. He was not acting normal. He had left her completely and Camille, earlier angry and baffled at his coldness and seeming lack of love and care toward her, now felt only dead anger toward him. Knowing him as she did, she might have expected it, but the reality was hard to accept.

Some time ago she had begun to notice older couples. Some of them seemed happy together, actually talking to each other, listening to each other and smiling at each other at odd moments. Some even held hands. She tried to picture John and herself as an old couple. But somehow no image of John and her growing old together rose in the space she allowed for that vision. So she tried to imagine John as an endearing older man. She could see him with white hair or no hair, as he was already losing it, and a hoary beard. But his face refused to look any way but cold and gray and unemotional and his eyes would not meet hers, but insisted in looking another direction, no matter how she tried to make him see her. She struggled to bring his true older face up, but all she got was an eerie feeling of coldness and distance.

She could not explain it. He was her husband and said he loved her. She should be able to think of him lovingly and fondly, to think of them of growing older together. But all she got was a disturbing phantasm. This uneasy exercise felt so uncomfortable that she wanted to abandon it. She did not want to think of John being old any longer. Yet she had to. This was the face she had promised to love and obey until death did them part. This was the face she was expected to wipe the last tears from, yet she could not imagine touching the face she would see on the death bed. He had never liked her to touch him.

She imagined what she would do when he died. He feared he would die young, as his father had. Yet his youth had come and gone and he was still healthy, unlike his father, who had smoked and died from lung disease. Possibly John would die some other way. What would she do as a widow? She knew the answer immediately. She would remarry. There were probably other men out there. Not many single men lived in Billington, but occasionally one showed up as a new professor, or passed through on speaking engagements.

She might live alone if he died. She had never lived all by herself. She would move away, she thought, and start life anew, alone, sadly mourning her dead husband.

Sometimes, on those dark mornings in Billington, the days she awoke early, she cried softly, missing her not-yet-dead husband. Some mornings she had lain absolutely still in the bed she shared with him, frozen by an unnamed danger lurking in the dark, which threatening to kill him. It was so real that she would shiver with fear as she awoke. She dreaded the feeling of hate lurking in the darkness of their bedroom so much that she would cover her face until it became light.

During the day she felt guilty for those thoughts in the early morning. A sense of betrayal lingered over her, lurked in her mind, and placed its heavy foot on her spirit so she could not eat or rest well. She ran away from it with unusual energy. When they ate supper, even though John was there, she felt lonely, as if he was already gone.

She had become afraid of him, fearing he might come back home one day and harm her, sensing her thoughts of his death. She walked around quietly when he was at home. Her appetite waned. Food tasted too salty, too oily or too sweet. She could only manage one taste of her soup before it sickened her; she thinned her coffee down. Her stomach turned at the sight of rich foods and she could not eat them. She drank tea and read books during mealtimes, rather than eating. The excitement of going to New York intruded upon everything, combined with the fear that something might stop her from going. But as the time of her departure grew near, the nightmares and waking to things lurking in the night became less frequent. She was impatient to go, to rid herself of the heavy weight of dread she felt around John; to be able to finally relax, to feel no anxiety. She knew it would not happen until she left.

During the day she painted in her studio. She painted images of beautiful landscapes, ruptured and steaming with earthquakes and catastrophes. Faces peered from dark windows and figures ran in the shadows. The day passed quickly when she was engrossed in her work. The canvases were methodically finished, one by one, allowed to dry and then stacked into a pile that would be shipped first to Indianapolis for the show at Purdue, then to New York in October for the one-person show in SoHo. As the final month passed, she became so excited that she could think of only two things, going to New York and finishing her paintings. The days crawled by, yet they weren't long enough.

When the paintings were finally finished, packed and shipped to Indiana, she tried to move the date of her departure up, but John said one week would be enough time to find an apartment. He reminded her she would not be able to move into a place right away if she found it too far in advance. So she ordered her plane ticket, paying for it with part of the inheritance from her grandparents. The ticket said August 29. She decided she would call her friend, Grace, to let her know she would be coming to New York and maybe she would help her.

She felt bad about leaving John with no one to take care of the house in her absence, so she interviewed and hired a housekeeper to come in once a week to clean and cook. John told her he would not need her more than that. She told John she loved him and would come back at Christmas, and she would make sure he would be all right in her absence.

One week before she left she felt she had everything ready. All that remained was packing her bags and asking John for an allowance to live on in New York. She had put off the financial question. Her stomach tensed at the idea of discussing money with him. She sensed his resistance to her plans. In all the months since she had known she was going, he had not once asked her how they would pay for it, or asked her about the merits of the school, its location or the classes she would take at Pratt or even asked how her paintings were coming along for her Indiana exhibition. It was strange that he had said nothing at all, as if nothing at all was happening.

Thus everything went along as if nothing out of the ordinary was to occur, at least as far as their daily routine was concerned. Their conversations concerned only what he wanted for supper and what the day's plans were. He was more silent than usual. It bothered Camille, but that was the way John was. He talked only about superficial things and hid his real feelings, unless he got angry and then it all came out.

Camille had figured out as well as she could what her expenses would be in New York. She had her grandparents' inheritance for the big expenses, like tuition, books, supplies and rent. She had worked up the rest of her anticipated expenses into a kind of presentation, paring them down to the smallest possible amounts, nervous about the surprisingly large totals she had come up with for food, transportation to and from school, laundry, phone, miscellaneous small expenses, school books and art supplies. She arrived at a figure that did not seem exorbitant: $200.00 per month. If she was frugal she would be able to make her grandparents' inheritance last for two years of schooling, long enough to get the M.F.A. degree, if everything went well. But she needed $200.00 a month for daily living from John's income.

She had begun taking graduate courses at the last university he attended, but had to quit the program when they moved to Billington, Texas. She was just taking up her studies again, she would remind him.

She also reminded herself how much money he made now. He was a tenured, full professor at the University, with several published books which were selling, some as textbooks, so, in spite of the frugal way they lived, he made a fair amount of money. The $200 she needed would be a small percentage of his monthly income. She reminded herself how, through her careful record-keeping, prompt payment of bills, and her making small loans from the bank which were paid back because she did not spend them, they had built up credit to find and buy the house they now lived in, which had only a small monthly mortgage to pay. Surely, he would grant her the $200 a month so she could get a Master's degree. He knew the value of a degree.

But asking for $200 was a fiasco. It only brought out the bad news he had been keeping from her for all these months – that he would not support her. Now she had to do everything on her own.

And here she was finally, one week later, and the lights of the Jersey Coast glowed dimly through the scratched window of a DC-7 approaching New York. The sight of the distant coast made Camille realize how far she was from earth, anticipating how far she was from the moment of landing and how far she was from what she was going to experience. She was drawing closer to it all the time, anticipating a silent welcome from the masses of New Yorkers who waited below, their faces watching her in the thousands of tiny lights below. In what appeared to be slow motion, the plane drew nearer and nearer to the airport. The lights on the runways grew larger and suddenly they came up to her level; there was water under the plane. They landed with a thump on land, bounced and came to a stop after a long run down the tarmac.

When Camille stepped out of the front door of the terminal into the New York air, the cold wind hit her and took away her breath. She noted that this was the first thing that had happened to her physically in this place. The change in climate jolted her awake. In the crowd pushing out of the terminal, she was only one of many new arrivals, distinguished by her bobbed, dark hair, dark eyes and slim figure, dressed in a cardigan sweater and jersey skirt.

The New York air was dry and hard, and her huge bags weighed heavy now. Her fingers were chilled, stretched and threatening to fall off by the time she got to the taxi stand with the bags. Besides her two large bags, she carried a shoulder bag on her left shoulder and a camera bag on her right, all of them much too heavy. But hopefully she would only have to carry them this one last time. New York was her new home and soon she would be in her own place. She was alone, but somehow she did not feel alone. She was excited and eager to begin a new life. She was going to take a taxi to Grace's new apartment and would see her new home in the morning.

Grace greeted Camille with a smiling face. Even though it was late, the two of them talked excitedly about all the things that had happened over the past months in the world of art, and about Grace's new art shows. Camille was glad she had met Grace on her first trip to New York. Grace was also from the South, but since she lived in the North, knew she could flaunt her independence in audacious, rather than hidden, cunning ways, as she would have had to do in the South. Small and petite, with long blond hair and an angel's face, Grace had the remnants of a Georgia accent, but had left false charm behind in Atlanta. She was stylish, wavy-haired and had not forgotten her Southern lessons, even though there was a dearth of outstanding role models among Southern women.

But Grace was a role model for Camille, who was happy to find a fellow Southerner living among the foreigners in the North. Grace was ambitious and strong-willed, a woman determined to make a living from her art. She made a living selling her etchings in several galleries and taught part-time in two colleges in the boroughs around New York City.

Just before she was to fly to New York, Camille had called Grace and told her she had been accepted to Pratt Institute, told her about her confrontation with John and how she didn't know what was going to happen when she came to New York, since she didn't have a place to live. After Grace listened to her, she said maybe she could help, that she would think about it and call her back. The next day Grace called Camille in the evening to tell her.

"I've been living on a little houseboat in the 79th Street Marina, but I won't be using it during the winter months, since it is so cold on the river in the winter. I've rented an apartment nearby, on the upper West side. Would you like to live in my houseboat this winter for two hundred dollars a month?"

Camille was happy, but expressed shock at how expensive it was. Grace told her how high rents actually were in Manhattan, that they often ran into the thousands of dollars for a small space. So after Grace talked to her some more, she realized $200 would be only a fraction of the cost of other apartments. Besides, she would be living right on the water and would have a beautiful view of the Jersey shore. The only problem, Grace warned her, was that it got very cold on the river in the winter. Having grown up in Texas, Camille had rarely been on a boat, but the idea of living on one appealed to her immediately. After talking it over with Grace, she accepted Grace's offer and could rest assured that she had a place to live, even before she arrived.

The next day, when she told John she had found a place to live, he looked at her in silence. She could not tell if he was sad or angry. He did not express happiness for her good fortune, as she hoped he would. He had not spoken to her at all since the night of their argument about finances. As the momentary silence continued, Camille tried not to think of the anger she felt; he was not going to keep her from going and realizing her dreams. From the course of events, her going seemed meant to happen.

The morning sky was milky white as Camille and Grace walked to the edge of the stone parapet on the hilltop and looked out over the Hudson River. Below them was the 79th Street Marina, spread out like a small town, made up of white boats, neatly lined up along weathered docks. Grace pointed out that the docks were lettered from right to left, A to E.

"And there, on D-dock, is my boat, the Jezebel," said Grace proudly, pointing off to the left. "Close to this end." Camille looked at the neat blue and white houseboat with great curiosity. It had windows all around and chairs sitting on a deck on top. It looked like a toy from here, one of the many small boats that bobbed and undulated with the morning current. But it was to be her new home for the next few months and she loved it at first sight.

On the nearest end of D-dock was a huge, white yacht. Across from it was another houseboat, where a man was busily hammering on his deck. Off A-dock were some big houseboats that looked like two-story contemporary homes, floating out on the water. There were yachts, sailboats and houseboats, cabin cruisers, skiffs and one enormous ship berthed at the far end of C-dock. Grace said it belonged to the Talmadge-Ford family and that it sailed to the Caribbean every winter.

On top most of the boats were brightly colored plants, lawn chairs and umbrellas for shade. The boats, mostly white, with their masts, lines, folded sails under blue sail-covers, were shining crisp and clean in the early September morning sun. In the calm water, shifting patterns reflected every boat upside down and the sky splattered its blue image on the ripples of the Hudson river.

"Let's go see it!" Camille ran down the steps toward the water, feeling for the first time in a long time, a thrill and excitement about her future. She could not believe how lucky she was to have fallen into this. Every smell, sight and sound was refreshing to her soul. She stopped and waited, then practically danced along beside Grace, chattering excitedly, squeezing her arm once or twice to emphasize how excited she was. Grace smiled and handed her some keys. Camille opened the gate in the tall, chain-link fence built between the walkway and the river to keep passers-by out of the boat basin. Inside, they walked down a ramp onto the dock that led to D-dock and the Jezebel.

The Jezebel was dwarfed by the big, white yacht docked next to it, sharing the finger-slip between them. It tipped slightly as the two women stepped aboard and then gently rocked back and forth, a new sensation to Camille. At the front end of her new home, the deck widened under an overhanging shelter and in back it became a porch with double doors opening to the inside.

Camille used one of the keys to open the door. The Jezebel appeared bigger inside than it looked outside. Inside was dark and smelled of damp wood, with all the shades drawn, but it looked darling all the same. Grace went around opening shades, and soon the interior was sunlit. There were white walls and touches of pink in the decorations. The front end had a bedroom up a couple of steps, with an office, and storage in a small room below it. In the center there was an open kitchen, the "galley," with a bar and a bathroom beside it. At the back end of the boat was a large room that was a sitting room with couches on both sides, and double doors opening onto the back deck.

"I love it!" exclaimed Camille.

"I'll show you the top deck." said Grace, and they went out the back doors and up an outside ladder. The shiny white deck above had two deck chairs, a little table fastened to a wall and a high captain's swivel chair in front of a big steering wheel.

"You mean you can actually sail this thing?" Camille asked.

"Sail? No. But if someone knows how to navigate, you could use the motor to take it out into the river, in an emergency. Hopefully that will not be necessary. This boat sits right here, if you don't mind, where it won't sink, in shallow water." Grace was already climbing back down the ladder. "Come on down when you're ready. I have to tell you how to run the bilge pumps and show you the other pumps, in case it leaks."

Camille stood for a moment, holding the skipper's wheel and looking out over the river, feeling the gentle wind and smelling the sea, keenly aware she was going to be living on the water. The boat rocked back and forth and the whole world swayed gently.

"I left the telephone," said Grace, inside. "You'll want to change the name on the bill." Camille looked over the kitchen and bath. She had everything but a table to eat on. It was going to be her own little house. A big bed practically covered the entire bedroom upstairs in the front of the boat, and the mattress was comfortable. She found her boxes piled in the corner of the bedroom, having been brought there by Grace as they arrived by UPS, one by one, from Texas. Camille had been sending them daily over the past two weeks. She thanked Grace profusely for all her help.

Grace accepted her thanks and started telling Camille how she was glad to turn the boat over to her, that she needed to get away from living here. She was about to explain why, when the boat suddenly tipped sideways and a shadow fell across them from the doorway. A big man had stepped on board and now entered the cabin with a friendly "Hello! I saw you over here, ladies, and I came to pay my respects."

Camille recognized him. When they had first met, Camille had not thought of him as handsome. It was true he was tall, well-proportioned, with broad shoulders and tan face. His nose was as straight as a Roman's, in a long, lean face. He had a square jaw and deep-set eyes, hidden under heavy brows. He looked very Italian.

The first overpowering impression she had of him was of being in the presence of a predatory animal. He moved slowly and deliberately, as a cat might, or a dancer on stage. He spoke with a deliberately gentle voice, too mild for such a big man, and gazed at Camille with shadowy eyes, in veiled surprise, remembering her, too.

He was Grace's ex-boyfriend, the photographer. What a coincidence! Grace had told her all about him one day while they sat in the gallery together. His father had been a well-known sculptor in his day. Vince had inherited his father's artistic talent as well as the family's little-used yacht here in the marina.

But Camille noticed that Grace winced when she saw him, and hesitated before she spoke.

"Hullo, Vince." she said, her cute little mouth twisting into a tense half-smile. Vince leaned against the door frame, smiling and taking in the two women standing before him.

"So you're my new neighbor?" he asked, looking at Camille with obvious admiration.

"Camille," said Grace reluctantly, "you remember Vincent Minotti?"

"Good morning." said Camille, warmly, to let him know she remembered him.

"Good morning, Camille. And good morning to you, too, Grace," he now turned his eyes fully on Grace, as if he had been deliberately keeping from looking at her, had been waiting to see and greet her, and he came on into the room, filling it with his tall presence. He stepped to Grace's side and took her under his arm smoothly, familiarly, putting his hand around her and pulling her arm around his waist in one movement. There they stood together, facing Camille.

REARRANGING REALITY

"The earth shook beneath my feet. I could hear the gasping and crackling of a giant earthquake pounding in my ears. I threw out my hands to balance myself. The earth moved and opened beneath me as I fell into the dark hole that appeared under my feet. A feeling of pure terror engulfed me. I was swallowed up by the earth, blinding me with darkness, yet deafening me with loud noises -- squealing, a thunder like a strong wind, as if I was in a giant throat, moving, sucking me down, down. By now the earth had cracked apart entirely and was falling apart in pieces, the separate pieces floating away from me in space. The light was becoming larger than the dark, the huge pieces moving slowly away in space, leaving me floating with the light of the sun all around me. Flowing gently in its warmth, I was as if in the arms of a mother, the terror of the dark minutes before forgotten, gently floating toward the sun; the heat growing stronger, the sounds of the still-exploding earth becoming fainter and fainter as the pieces drifted farther away."

Camille lay clutching the bedclothes, feeling the boat heaving beneath her, recalling her vivid dream. The houseboat had been rocked by a giant swell from a passing ship. Eventually the motion ceased and she drifted in and out of sleep, delicious sleep, guilty sleep, until morning. She lay flat on her back on the big, soft bed in the boat, and looked around at the light streaming through the old, pink-flowered curtains, the soft-colored, water-stained wood panels on the ceiling, and the empty, white walls with nails sticking out of them for hanging pictures. She felt hunger, but remembered there was no reason to get up early today.

She closed her eyes, intending to sleep some more when she heard someone step onto her deck with a thud and the boat rocked. Then there was a loud knock on the door. Camille jumped up and went to the door in her nightclothes, thinking it was Grace. But when she looked through the crack in the curtain, she saw Vince's big eye peering back at her.

"I've brought you something," Vince's voice came through the door. Camille pulled an old sweater on over the worn flannel nightgown and opened the door a little.

"To decorate your boat." He filled the space, dressed in a clean, cream denim jacket and jeans. He looked like a poster from the old movies where the good guys wore white. But his skin was tan and his hair black and shining in curls, like the bad guys' in movies. Camille's eyes opened wide when she saw what he had brought – a bouquet of purple violets. His eyes were shining, too.
"Violets for remembrance. I want you to remember me whenever you look at them." He said, then suddenly seemed abashed as he reached them toward her.

Camille took them from him carefully. No one had ever given her flowers, though she did not say it. She was caught off guard at this unexpected, romantic gesture, and could think of nothing to say. She buried her nose in them, inhaling a velvety odor.

"Come on inside." she said. "Have you had breakfast yet?"

The corner grocery store had a different smell than the supermarket in Billington. It was not cold, brightly lit and did not smell of floor cleaner and air conditioning, but was crowded and dark and warm with odors of Italian spices, fruits and onions. A man in the back was cutting slices of provolone for a crowd of customers in front of a glass counter.

Vince grabbed a small, rickety grocery cart and began pushing it down the narrow aisle of worn, dark floorboards. He had said "Come on, we need groceries," and made Camille walk with him up the hill to the local store. So, here she was, on her first day of living in New York, listening to Vince discuss the merits of two brands of smoked oysters in a market on the upper West side.

"Neither of them is as good as fresh oysters. We'll go down the street to the fish market for oysters." said Vince. Camille watched in amusement as Vince strolled around the store, looking over the crowded shelves with an expert eye, picking out the best products for a menu he had in mind. Her husband, to Camille's knowledge, had never entered a grocery store in his life, except to buy batteries from the check-out counter for his pencil sharpener. She was beginning to see there were differences in men. Some men cooked. She saw there were other men shopping in this store and Vince seemed at home here.

Everything was old. The tops of the shelves were low and had dusty toilet paper and cereal stacked on them. The vegetables in the bins were not fresh. The bananas looked like they were a week old and the carrots sagged. They had passed a fresh fruit and vegetable stand on the corner and Vince said they would shop for vegetables there.

Vince debated whether to buy rice vinegar or not. "It's too expensive, but I'll get it anyway." He held up a bulbous bottle with clear, white liquid and put it in the little cart with the package of fresh-ground espresso coffee, two bottles of sauces, cereal, sesame oil, tofu, paper towels, flour, and freshly baked bread sticking out of a paper bag.

Shopping was a serious process. Vince discussed every decision with Camille, standing huddled with her, one arm draped across her shoulder and the other holding the product, or he asked how she cooked this or that. They stopped at the deli counter in the back and Vince asked for green olives. The man in a white smock scooped them out of a big tub into a white plastic container and marked the price on the top with a black marker. Camille held the container. Somehow these olives seemed more precious than the ones she bought in cans. They probably tasted better, too.

Approaching the meat counter, a serious discussion was initiated over what kind of meat to buy. Vince preferred seafood, but said "serious meat" was probably more appropriate for the meal he was going to cook, if it was fresh and of good quality. Camille did not ask why he was asking her about everything. He seemed to assume she was going to participate in this meal he was preparing, but she did not want to appear too presumptuous, as he had not invited her. She was prepared to pay for half if she was going to eat it. But Vince was adding staples now and buying enough food for several meals. She probably couldn't afford all this.

They finally reached the check-out counter. A young male clerk rang up each item while Vince watched him carefully and commented on each price. Camille waited nervously, hoping the total would not be too much, because she had only a limited amount of money with her. But when the total was run up, Vince reached in his pocket and paid the lordly sum with cash. Camille pulled all the money she had out of her pocket and held it out to Vince. He took it and looked up into the air, as if he were calculating, pulled a couple of dollars from the stack and handed everything else back to her.

"But half is much more than that," she said.

"Don't worry. I'll let you wash dishes or something," he said, winking. He smiled at the clerk, who knew him by name. "I got some extra things for myself, you know." he said as they exited the store with their paper bags full of groceries. Vince carried three of the bags and gave the lightest one to Camille.

On their way to the fish market Vince told her about the stores they passed and the histories of the clerks. Camille was acutely aware of Vince's huge, handsome manliness beside her, of his graceful way of moving, his good looks, nice clothes and the appearance they must make together. It seemed she had a friend and she felt unreasonably happy. Maybe this was a fleeting thing, but it was nice to know someone who could help her find her way around the neighborhood, knew about good food, knew how to cook, and had store-owner friends. The day was beautiful.

Camille slept late in the morning again. She had been in New York five days. She was sleeping late because she and Vince had gone to a disco the night before to dance. At 2:00 a.m. she realized she was not used to staying up late and had begged to go home. He relented, but kept on saying "Oh, there's 'so-and-so'; I have to talk to them," and dragging her over to meet them, so they had stayed later.

She had borrowed a flapper-type mini-dress from Grace to wear, since she had nothing appropriate to wear to a disco. Grace had asked her how she was doing and seemed only slightly curious about her going out to dance with Vince. Camille wondered how long it had been since they had broken up. They acted very cool toward each other, so she assumed it had been a long time. The dress she borrowed from Grace was white and when Vince came over to her boat to pick her up, he gave her a pink bow to wear in her hair. At first Camille had objected, but he insisted on tying it around her head, over her dark, bobbed hair and let one part of it droop over one of her eyes. She had to keep pushing it up when it fell down, but he said it looked cute.

The Mudd Club was easy to spot when they turned Vince's Jeep down an empty street in a seemingly deserted part of town. Far down the block, people were crowding the sidewalk in front of the door. When Vince parked in front and they both got out, the bouncers opened the rope barring the entrance and allowed Vince and Camille to pass through the crowd and go in. Camille wondered why Vince was so important, but did not ask. Inside, the music was deafening, the room extremely crowded and they served only beer – no sodas. Camille was not used to drinking, but she took the bottle Vince handed her and held it because it seemed to be the right thing to do. She had rarely drunk liquor. Recently John had begun to make wine in the cellar as a hobby. Until then both of them had been "tee-totalers", except for tasting wine at an occasional faculty function.

All of Vince's friends seemed younger than she and punk, but they were nice to her. Some of the girls did not talk; they stood looking at her with their violet hair hanging down in their eyes, chewing their gum, sizing her up, so to speak. But Vince would laugh and hug them and they would smile at him and relax and then were nice to Camille, making urbane remarks in their rough New Jersey or Brooklyn accents.

In the Mudd Club, Camille hardly recognized herself or her world. Here everything was different, nothing was like anything she had ever seen. It was as if she had stepped off of Earth and onto a different planet. The continuous noise of music and people yelling at each other over it deafened her for awhile, and the heat and hundreds of bodies pressing close together all night created the sensation of not needing to stand on one's feet, but to depend on others to hold her up. There was no need to even think or talk about anything coherent with the people speaking nonsense around her. It was a symbiotic experience, as if everyone in the room was one large, breathing body.

Vince asked her to dance and they jammed into the middle of the crowded dance floor. She found she loved dancing. Somehow the music reverberating through her body set her into motion. She wanted to dance every dance and the music did not stop, so she kept on. So did Vince. His style was different than hers. He kept his feet in one small area and did not move around much. He jiggled to the music, but moved like he was doing one of the new dances. He threw his head back and closed his eyes sometimes. But most of the time he watched the other dancers or Camille dancing in front of him, moving her feet as well as her body and spinning around, dancing however she felt. The music was so loud it began to deafen her and after awhile she found she was soaked with sweat.

Everyone dressed however they wanted; some people looked as if they had just walked in off the street in tennis shoes and sports clothes, others dressed like they had arrived from the '20's. Some wore contemporary styles; some dressed in black and chains, others wore skimpy clothes or funny combinations, with hair cuts in crazy styles. Camille did not feel strange any more about what she wore; she felt she could look as different as she wanted and still fit in. Her worry about how she looked disappeared. She felt safe with Vince and the hundred other people who pounded the dance floor alongside her and seemed very much at home here.

Vince wore all black and smelled wonderful. He had shiny metal things on his jacket, but otherwise was dressed simply. He acted like he wanted to draw attention to himself, though he was already the object of many girls' glances. He took them all in, but was careful to pay the most attention to Camille. Whatever she wanted he ran and got. He was sensitive to every little change in her expression and asked her if she was thirsty or felt okay or happy or whatever. When she said she was tired for the second time, they finally started to leave, though it seemed a lot of his friends were arriving, other young men and women all in black, pushing their way in through the crowd in the doorway. They hailed Vince and he went over to them and hugged them, but did not linger long.

Only six hours later, Camille lay in bed, groggily thinking of the night before, floating in the tired confusion between waking and sleeping. She heard thumping outside her window and rolled over to peer between the curtains. Vince was out on the deck of his boat, wearing only a pair of cut-off jeans, tying some ropes to the side of his boat. Some cylindrical white foam cushions were dangling from the ropes and he adjusted the length of each rope so the cushions were at the right height to be between the pilings and the boat when the boat hit them. His yacht was huge and sparkling white. Camille watched him, unobserved, for awhile, admiring his black, curly hair and tan body shining in the sun as he worked. Every move was smooth, as if rehearsed; his muscles rippled under tan skin. His legs were the most perfect legs she had ever seen, though she had admired few men's legs. Mixed with admiration was pride that he liked her, and she smiled to herself.

Today Grace was going to take Camille to do some errands. She would take her to her bank to open an account. So she slowly got up, dressed and ate, put on a T-shirt and shorts and wandered out onto the back deck of her boat to sit in the sun with a cup of coffee. Vince was not seen, since he was now working on the other side of his boat. She sat on the edge of the white deck, her legs dangling off the back for awhile, her coffee sitting beside her, feeling cozy and comfortable in the sun. For the first time in many years she had no pressures at all on her to do anything she did not want to do. She felt supremely happy and free. She would register for classes in two days, but until then there was absolutely nothing she had to do. After that she would have to work hard at being a student.

She closed her eyes and lay back on the deck, feeling the sun soaking into her. She did not open her eyes, but could hear Vince far away, working on his boat somewhere out of sight. She heard water swishing, washing against the side of her boat. She heard someone hammering in the distance. She could hear gulls crying overhead and birds singing in the park that ran alongside the river. She heard an occasional motor boat and the far-away hum of the City, beyond the trees of Riverside Park.

Vince had been wonderful to her. What was not to like in him? She needed someone like him and always had. He knew all about New York, having lived here all his life, and seemed willing to help her out with whatever she needed, to tell her about everything she needed to know. She was learning fast under his tutelage. She had never had a man to depend upon this way.

He was also handsome and romantic and she knew he liked her. She could tell he was dying to make love to her. She knew it because he was so slow and tender with her, sensitive to her every little movement. That was something he did not have to say. She smiled and stretched. She was basking as much in the sun as in the knowledge that Vince was attracted to her.

At noon she met Grace up at her apartment. She watched Grace talk with a new knowledge and curiosity. Grace had been Vince's girlfriend at one time, but she still remained a good friend to her and to Vince, it seemed. As she watched Grace talk, she realized she really liked her and that probably Grace liked her, too. This seemed strange now, and might possibly change their relationship, since she was doing things with Vince now and Grace was not. She saw she and Grace were similar in many ways. Maybe Vince was attracted to her because she was like Grace. But she was different from Grace, too.

She wondered why Grace had given Vince up, and by the intensity of Grace's sometimes puzzled gaze, she knew Grace must be wondering about her, too. Though Camille was dying to ask her questions about Vince which had come to mind, Grace always changed the subject, and avoided talking about Vince whenever she tried to bring the subject up. Grace was obviously nervous when it came to talking about Vince, since she wanted to talk about anything other than Vince.

Grace and Camille walked to the bank up on Broadway and Camille opened her account. Grace also took Camille to the subway stop and told her what trains to take to get to Pratt Institute. Once school started, she would be traveling by subway to her classes every day. It was the cheapest and the fastest way to get there. They also walked down Broadway to the dry cleaner's and to the Laundromat on the street leading to the boat basin.

"How do you like the boat?" Grace asked as they walked back toward her apartment.

"Fine," she said, though thoughts of Vince predominated when she thought about the boat and the questions she had about it. How could she ask Grace things if she could not talk about Vince? "I love it. It is very relaxing for right now, but I know I'll be busy enough soon with school and won't really be able to enjoy it much, once it starts."

"True," said Grace, and continued talking about other things. Grace seemed confident and carefree, yet there was something she was not saying. Camille was not sure she wanted to hear it. Perhaps it was best if she asked her about Vince directly.

"How long has it been since you and Vince broke up?" she asked.

"Oh, not very long," Grace said, "but it was time for it to happen. I'm happy to be on my own now, living away from him." She spoke a little too brightly.

"Are you dating anyone?" Camille asked timidly, hoping she was.

"I don't have any one person in mind, but I certainly want to."

What could she have meant by that? Camille wondered. Did that mean she was still seeing Vince?

"Would you still go out with Vince, if he asked you?" There. It was out. She had asked the most important question.

"Absolutely not. We're finished. That's for sure." She responded adamantly. Camille felt relieved. Vince was free. She did not need to ask any more questions. She didn't even think about whether she was free or not. Vince was all she thought about these days.

The next night, Camille found herself sitting on the top deck of Vince's boat, dressed in a loose linen blouse gathered tight at her waist with a gold belt and a pair of new slacks, watching a gorgeous sunset with bright red colors splaying into the mist hanging on the horizon. Earlier, while showering, she had decided to wear nothing under her blouse, so she was feeling very sexy.

Rastus, Vince's dog, lay at her feet. The three of them, Camille, Vince and Rastus, had spent the whole day together, running in the park in the morning, talking while Vince scrubbed the deck of his boat and she fixed a lunch. He was still below, showering and dressing while oysters baked.

Vince appeared after awhile, smelling good and looking clean and handsome. He drew a chair up to the built-in couch where she sat facing the brilliant red sky and sat down with a big sigh as he leaned back in it. She looked at him. He was looking at her out the side of his eyes. She could see the sky in them. She expected him to say something, but he did not. Instead, he got up and went below again, returning with the stuffed oysters he had baked. He brought them up the stairs on a white plate, flanked by two crystal glasses on a silver tray, served with sprigs of parsley. They had bought the moist, gray mollusks at the fish market during the afternoon and while she was on her boat dressing he had transformed them into crispy white globules covered with buttered, toasted crumbs, lying in their original pearly shells. In his other hand he carried a chilled bottle of wine. He pushed the bottle down into an ice bucket beside his chair.

"Just a little something I dug up in the wine cellar," he said modestly. "A fine old Cabernet Sauvignon."

"Vince!" Camille exclaimed. She knew whatever wine that was, it must be expensive and taste good. Camille felt happy. She could not have ever, in her entire lifetime, imagined being in this situation. Her life in Texas seemed impossibly far away, as if it had never existed. She looked around her now at the marina with its shining white boats, the broad river reflecting the fading red of the sky and felt the warm breezes blowing on her. Another thing that was real and could not be ignored was the man beside her, with whom she had spent most of the past week. Here in New York, she had become another person, unrecognizable, in an overwhelming, glamorous, new world that had no connection with the frumpy housewife who lived in Billington, Texas. She was truly out of her element. It was frightening, sometimes, but right now everything seemed too good to feel anything akin to regret.

Thoughts of John paled and disappeared in the presence of someone who contrasted in every way with him. Vince admired her beauty and intelligence openly, never said anything cruel to her, and showered her with gifts, food and attention. His good looks sometimes made her feel self-conscious, for she did not feel she had done anything to deserve being the object of attention of someone so young and handsome. He was seven years younger than she, yet whenever she felt awkward, he would look at her and tell her how beautiful she was. She had almost come to believe it.

During the past week he had coaxed her into revealing everything about her life. That is, everything but how she felt about him. He had not asked and she was glad, for she was confused about that. Then he had given her his opinion of what she was going through, speaking in a frank, man-to-man tone. He seemed to have gone through a bitter separation from Grace, as well and could relate to her pain in breaking up. She could feel his pain in the attitude he assumed when he spoke about it, which he rarely did. He never actually said Grace's name, out of deference to their friendship. Once or twice, though very seldom, he had talked about affairs he had before he met Grace, as well as a couple he had gotten into toward the end of their seven-year, live-in relationship. The way he spoke, he appeared to know all about love.

"We'll go out to dinner later, if you want," he said, taking her wrist and encircling it with his thumb and forefinger, as if to marvel at how small it was.

"You make me feel protective toward you." He explained, gazing at her wrist in his grasp and suddenly serious. He looked away. "Now, let's relax and have a little drink." He reluctantly turned her loose and poured the wine. He handed her one of the glasses and turned to the panel of dials beside him to flick a switch which turned on some soft music.

Camille leaned back on the couch with her glass, sipping it slowly and beginning to feel relaxed again. His touch had thrilled her and made her body come to attention, but she reminded herself not to take it to heart. It was good to be able to not worry about anything, to slow down. She heard the words of a song playing on the stereo ". . . You put me high upon a pedestal, so high I could almost see eternity." How appropriate.

She took the stuffed oyster he offered her and leaned forward to share them with him from the plate.

"Our song." he said. "The situation you're in right now. We'll always remember this when we hear that song." He raised his glass, ". . . a toast to our song."

Camille laughed in delight and clinked her glass on his. Vince always knew what to say. Her troubles seemed prosaic, her situation tame in comparison with some of the dangerous situations and fiery affairs he had been in. She felt comfortable and safe in his company. He was sure of himself in every way, and always acted confident and calm.

The sun had gone down by now, leaving a purple light glowing over the New Jersey skyline. A huge ship was coming up-river from the ocean, a gray tanker painted purple by the sky. She watched a tiny gray cloud ascend like a balloon from the horizon, as if the sun had exploded upon touching the earth. Music was playing, floating quietly in her head, like the little lonely cloud. She turned her eyes to the wine glass and saw the purple sky floating there, too.

"Everything seems sad this evening." said Vince, finally. Camille looked up at him, but his face was still. Was he unhappy? Was there anything she could do? Was he was mourning for Grace, for others? She felt sorry for him, her friend. He had made her feel better, but he must be suffering inside.

"What is it, Vince?" she heard her own voice, speaking slowly. She felt she was floating above the deck and her voice was coming from somewhere else.

"You've come a long way to be with me here. All by yourself – your own little self. You have no one to help you. And I don't have anyone, either." Her heart was touched by this little speech, which was finally candid about their relationship. She wanted to reach out and touch him, but she could not make her hand move. She willed it to, but her body seemed paralyzed. The wine was going to her head.

She felt sad that she could do nothing to help him; she could not even reach out to him. Vince looked up suddenly and gazed directly into her eyes. As he did, her heart jumped softly, as if something important was going to happen. She felt a little fear, but knew there was no reason to fear, for whatever he said or did, Vince would make all right.

"Fate brought us together," he said at last. He moved to the couch beside her and put his arm around her, pulling her close to him. She felt his warm body and put her head on his shoulder, feeling the fear receding or being pushed aside, as she gazed at the dull purple light in the distance, feeling it shining on her. She felt excitement and comfort. She did not want to move. She wanted to stay like this forever. She felt Vince move only slightly as he looked down at her and then laid his head on the top of hers.

After a while, Vince took the empty wine glass out of Camille's hand and slowly put it down on the deck with his. She did not object as he took her hand and began to stand.

"Let's go downstairs," he said. "It's getting cool. I'll bring the oysters. Do you want some more wine?"

She felt herself floating off the couch and toward the stairs, her hand in his. She stopped, suddenly, remembering to retrieve her glass from the deck.

Vince led her down into the boat and into his bedroom, which she had seen only briefly before. It held only a big, furry white rug, his bed and a single spotlight. Vince put the oysters down on the floor, in the center of the white rug and sat down, slowly pulling Camille down to sit beside him. Camille felt detached, as if she could see everything that was happening from the outside. She saw the boat rolling gently, rocking her against Vince. She saw herself looking into Vince's eyes, which were closer to hers than they had ever been. Up close his eyes were not so dark. They were pure brown with little gold flecks in the brown. She described them to him. She told him his face was tan and smooth, his chin was strong and masculine.

"Tell me more," he murmured and she did.

"Your body is strong! Your muscles feel hard under your shirt." She was stroking his arm serenely, self-conscious only about what she was saying.

"Tell me what you think of love, the kind with a capital `L'," he said. "Do you think Love is forever, or is it something that is different, felt differently every time?"

Camille sat back and thought hard. She picked up the last oyster on the plate.

"Do you want this?" she asked him, scooping out the delicate meat with a little fork and offering it to him.

"No, and you're avoiding my question," he said. Camille's heart was beating hard, she noted. It was true that she was avoiding the question. She had to think about it.

"Definitely felt differently every time," she said finally, after thoughtfully eating the oyster. "At least that has been my experience. What do you think? You've had a lot more experience than me."

"Ah, but that's the mystery," he said quietly. His hand was barely touching her, moving up and down her leg like a whisper. She felt her skin prickling and had to take a deep breath. "Even though, according to you, I'm supposed to have experienced love many times, I feel it is completely new with you, as if I had never felt it before."

"Really?" It was a statement rather than a question that Camille heard herself speak, and she looked down and spoke softly, thoughtfully. "I think sometimes maybe I've never felt it, and never will," now she was whispering, "sometimes." It was something she had decided while she was still in Texas.

"Why? Don't you like to make love?" he asked her. His left arm was behind her on the floor and his right hand moved serenely over her leg and arm, gently smoothing them, moving up and down. She felt as if she was swooning away. She wanted to lie down on the soft rug, but knew she should not. Yet his touch felt so good. She found words coming out of her mouth.

"I think I would like to make love to you," she said. Perhaps she should not have said that. It was actually a hypothetical statement, but it sounded more like a proposition. Maybe she was bolder than she had thought, because when she thought about making love to Vince she knew it would be good and right and wonderful.

His hand began to travel up her arm to the base of her neck, where he bent his head and breathed warm air onto her skin. He lifted her hair at the back of her neck and lightly kissed her there. She turned her head and tried to retract her statement, explaining, "I think about that sometimes."

"I think of it, too, with you," he was whispering in her ear and she shivered. His hand was moving over her body now, touching her ever so lightly everywhere, on her breasts, her stomach, the insides of her calves. She could feel his body trembling beside her, but she could not move. "I dream of making love to you," he whispered. "I've thought of it for months. Ever since the day I met you."

She leaned back against his arm, her head going back onto his shoulder. He had thought of her for months. All she had to do was let go and her worries would be over. Vince made her feel good. She had ever experienced anything like this feeling. It felt so good, his touching her.

His hand was unbuttoning her blouse, fumbling with buttons. She reached up, not knowing whether to stop him or to do it herself. But his hand stopped hers.

"Come with me," he said, lifting her to her feet. They went to the bed together. Camille stood at the side of the bed, wondering what she should do and decided to do nothing while Vince unbuttoned her blouse in the light, using both hands now. He was slowly kissing her bare body as he slowly undid each button, gradually kneeling as he went down, a kiss for each button he undid. Camille felt faint and had to sit down, and when she did she watched, as if in a dream, him slip her slacks and panties off, both at the same time, exclaiming when he saw her with no panties on.

She lay back on the bed and closed her eyes. Vince was gazing at her body without daring to breathe. She looked at him standing there and reached up an arm for him to join her. He began to undress and she watched him through half-closed eyes. He was beautiful all over. The dark hairs on his chest glowed in the light at the edge of his silhouette. His cock was long and stiff, jutting toward her as he bent one knee to climb onto the bed with her. It was happening, she realized. He was going to make love to her.

As he moved over her and his shadow darkened her body in the light of the spotlight, she knew nothing would stop him now. She felt a twinge of doubt. He stopped, feeling her fear, gently took her face between his hands and kissed her lips ever so softly. Then he whispered, looking into her eyes.

"I love you."

"I love you, too." She spoke inaudibly. The statement as soon as she spoke it, became true and made everything all right. Her heart melted inside her so she could barely speak the words. But he saw her lips move and kissed them again, his face reflecting joy.

Purple light from outside suddenly flooded the room. Everything looked smooth. When Vince's full, cool, naked body touched hers, she was immediately sober. No longer was she outside of her body. She felt his skin, sleek and silky, as she put her arm around him and held him against her. His dark hair was fine and soft and perfumed when her other hand touched the back of his neck. An overpowering feeling of gratefulness and warmth arose in her when he pulled back and slid his arm under her, sliding his other hand over her skin, going around her to hold her and pull her close to him. It felt so right and good. It felt like what she had longed for all of her life. What she had dreamed of was finally happening.

That night she slept with her head on his shoulder. She awoke, wondering if her head was too heavy on him, but when she started to move, he pulled her back. Later, in the dark, she felt him sit up and pull the covers over her, tucking them around her so she would not be cold.

THE DIARY

September 4

    What am I doing?

    I look at myself as if I was sitting in the air above myself and I see me in the situation I'm in. I see myself sitting on a tall bar stool, looking across Vince's living room, looking out the windows, looking far away over yonder, far across the black river to the lights of the Jersey shore, which are little bright dots in the dark distance and I wonder: what am I doing here? Below me I see Vince and a couple of his buddies sitting on the black couch and two white deck chairs. Smoke fills the room. It smells like my fall bonfire of maple leaves, but sweet. The smoke rises from the people below me. I am not smoking. No one has even offered one to me. Vince is talking to E.L. and E.L. is talking to him. They both talk at the same time. It is funny, like they are a comedy team. I laugh, but no one notices. Maybe I am affected by the smoke in the room and am giddy, too. I see myself sitting there on the bar stool, looking good in bell-bottom jeans and black boots and the visiting men are kidding with me a little because they don't know me. Maybe they came to see Vince's new girl.

    Vince loves to smoke and smokes a lot. He knows all about pot. He explained it all to me, about the buds and the sensimilla and what strains are best. He has a magazine about it. Other people come over and they sit around on his boat and smoke with him and talk until all hours of the night. I am curious because it is something different from what I was used to in Texas. I wasn't even aware there was such a thing as pot, I thought it was made up in the newspapers when there was a good story about it.

    I am writing a diary, since strange things are happening to me here in New York. I need to write them down. I don't have anyone to tell, and I want to tell someone about what is happening. I wouldn't dare tell my mother. I can't talk to John. When he calls I just feel like hanging up. I think I'm finished with him, but I am afraid to tell him. I am afraid of him. I don't ever want to see him again. I wish I could just disappear from Texas.

    I don't understand what is going on, and if I record it, maybe some day I can look back and know what was going on. But right now, while I'm in the middle of it, I look around me and see only new things; things I never knew were there, though of course they've been there all the time. I just didn't know about them. But now I'm learning a lot fast.

I strain to come up with any explanation of what I'm going through, to make sense of all this, but when people talk, I hear only the words that speak to my need, my need to understand what all this is about. Whatever I read is nothing unless it speaks only to my specific situation. And everything speaks to my situation, I am so anxious to know what is happening to me, to know where I'm going.

One thing Hal had said was, "As people grow older, they revert to their true nature, no matter what kind of warping they received as a child." That was the opposite of what her mother used to say: "Train up a child in the way he should grow and when he is old he will not depart from it." She did not know which was true. She certainly was trained as a child, but it seems as if she was reverting back to some other nature now. She was not doing what she was trained to do as a child. She was not doing what they had told her all her life should be done. She had no guideposts, was going on blind instinct. Maybe her true nature was coming out.

Two weeks had gone by since she had come to New York to begin a new life. She had started school. On Tuesday, Vince drove her over to Brooklyn in his Jeep and helped her register with all the other new students, talking all the time about what he had done when he went there. He told her about how he met Grace, who had been a fellow student. How, when they were students, they lived together while they attended Pratt, then they moved to the marina in Manhattan together when they graduated.

Camille enjoyed that day, since Vince had taken her to Brooklyn in his Jeep. She knew she would have felt much different if she had gone alone. She was able to feel more familiar with the school, since Vince knew it so well. She would always know it as his alma mater first.

That night she heard a popular song on the radio while she was taking a bath and getting ready to go spend the night with Vince. It was called "Torn Between Two Lovers." She believed she, too, could love two men at the same time. However, now, after only one week of being with Vince, she felt Vince winning.

What she really wanted to do was sleep all the time. She couldn't get enough of it. She went to Vince's every night. They made love and then fell asleep. At least Camille did. Vince sat up and smoked a cigarette for awhile and then snuggled down with her. He held her all night. For the first time in her life, she truly felt peaceful and content, as if she was a little baby in loving arms. But she was sleepy all the time, since she stayed awake late with Vince and got up early every morning to go on the subway to Brooklyn. She didn't have nightmares any more, though she knew she still dreamed. She couldn't remember her dreams, but they were good ones because she always awoke with a good feeling.

She had too much to do: School every day, Vince every night. They ate and slept together and were with each other every moment when she was not in school and called each other from time to time during the day, when they were not together.

September 9

I know Vince loves me. I guess I don't love John, or if I did love him, I don't any more. When I think about John and me from this far away, I can see the situation a little clearer than I could when I was in it. For instance, last summer I wondered why I felt pain when John took me to see the little heart he had carved on a tree at his mother's house while he was courting me. It reminded me of the day I agreed to marry him and how at the time it had seemed romantic. But when I looked at that little carved heart last summer, the sight of it created a terrible pain and I wanted to get away from it as fast as possible. I didn't know why I felt that way. Even now, I feel a pain when I think of that little heart, still there on the tree, and I don't really know why, though I'm beginning to understand. It means a lot of my dreams did not come true. The heart said "John loves Camille," but he never showed me he did after that.

What I think is love has nothing to do with words. Words are a means of saying what you are feeling right now. But love has to be acted out, year after year. It can't be spoken. Words can hurt, though, if they are words of love spoken to someone who doesn't want to hear them, like now, when I hear them from John. I know they are not true and I don't want to hear them.

Unspoken love can be so strong and real that it can heal, even if the person never says "I love you." If they act like they do, you know it. When I think of how Vince loves me, I don't think of what he says, because he says all kinds of things. He says whatever comes into his head at the moment. I know he loves me because of what he has done. Not only the love-making, but the consideration he shows me, the little gifts he gives me, the things he does for me. He gives me so much. He gives me everything he has and would give me more if he could. And I give him whatever I have, which isn't much right now. But I can cook and clean and make love to him. I want to give him everything, to lose myself in him, but I stop a little short because I'm afraid I'll swamp him with love and gifts. "To know when to stop" is one of the sayings in the book of the Lao Tzu, which is the book Vince is reading to me. He is a Tai Chi expert and can defeat more than one opponent by himself.

The second night she spent with Vince was not like the first, when she didn't intend to stay. It was deliberate. She had a good talk with herself in the mirror. In the mirror she saw someone she didn't recognize. She looked like someone else. Her face was a different face. It was thinner and smoother, not strained from worry. Her eyes were big and glowing, and her hair looked different. Fairly short and dark, it was thick and smooth now. Her cheeks were pink with excitement; she actually glowed. She looked like a child, but here she was, a thirty-one-year-old woman in love with a 24-year-old boy. She looked in the mirror and wondered if she should wash her make-up off before she got in bed. It was something which had never occurred to her before, though she had been married ten years. She always washed her face before going to bed. John couldn't see her in the dark. But Vince cared about how she looked. The better she looked, the more he liked her. If she washed her face she might look plain. She had to sleep, though, and make-up would come off on the pillow. So she decided to wash off the parts that would rub off on the pillow and made up her eyes a little. When she looked in the mirror again, she didn't look any different. Her cheeks and lips were naturally pink from excitement.

During the past week, they had spent every possible moment

together. They stayed on Vince's boat at night and on the weekend they slept in, though they didn't actually sleep much when they did this. They slept, made love and slept again. On weekends they went to the discos at night. This was fun. They danced all night and drove home when it was getting light. Vince even wanted to go out on a school nights. Camille went, but fell asleep during classes the next day. She saw the sun coming up Wednesday morning as they went home and knew she had to go to class that day. But she loved dancing and making love to Vince. What was hard was getting up after a few hours and going to class.

That same day, on Wednesday, they went together to SoHo to visit Hal at the gallery. Hal had been an old friend of Vince's. They gave Hal a shock, showing up together. Hal had not seen Vince for a long time, while Vince had been living with Grace in the Village. Hal also knew Camille was married. But he acted cool and did not make a big deal about the two of them being together and seemed glad to see Camille, anyway. He did not ask questions about their relationship, but Camille could tell he was curious. She did not say anything because she was embarrassed. Hal asked Vince about Grace, since she still showed with Ward gallery.

Camille's show was hanging at the Purdue gallery in Indianapolis at the moment. It would be showing there for a month. Then it would come to New York for her one-person show at Ward Gallery. While she talked with Hal about the arrangements, Vince hung around downstairs, talking to Ann, the assistant. He had attended school with her, too. It was a small world.

Then Vince and Camille walked around SoHo, telling each other their memories of places they knew. Vince pointed out the gallery where they first met. Camille remembered it well, but let him tell the story. He told her how he was at the gallery with Grace, taking pictures of her work the day Camille came in to see her. Camille tripped over a big sculpture and he caught her as she fell. He held her longer than he needed. She remembered how he said he was glad he was the one who rescued her, because then he could hold her. He told her he liked her the minute he saw her. Camille realized that must have been just before he broke up with Grace.

September 16

Grace, Vince and I went to the movies last night. I don't know why Grace went. Vince sat between us. During the movies I looked over and, even though it was dark, I saw Vince was holding hands with Grace. I was shocked. I don't know to think now. My world is rocked! I can't even think about it without panicking. I thought they had broken up!

Camille and Vince decided to go to bed with full pajamas on and to go to sleep without making love. It was a good deep sleep for both of them. But in the morning they could not help making love all over again in the early morning sun. Camille lay in peace afterward.

"I think I could beat you up if I wanted to," said Camille.

"What?" Vince roused a little from the white sheet he had thrown over himself. His dark hair was in curls on the pillow and his eyes fluttered open, blue as the sea. Camille smiled a little and repeated her statement.

"I don't know, but I think I'm probably as strong as you. You couldn't really make me do anything I wouldn't want to do, physically–or at or at least I could escape, right?"

"Well, let's see." he said thoughtfully. Vince slowly turned over, rolling his lean, heavy body easily onto her naked body and she started wrestling to get away. After struggling against him, with Vince hardly moving, he deliberately let her get her way; then, smiling a little, he easily pinned her down when he decided he had had enough.

It scared Camille to realize he was stronger than she thought. His movements were deceptive. He was gentle because he wanted to be gentle, but his arms were bigger and more muscular than hers and all he had to do was lay one finger against her arm, as he showed her, and she could not move it. He was not even trying. She began wrestling with him for fun, both of them laughing the whole time. It was exciting and sexy, but as she struggled, Camille realized that all the things grown-ups told young girls were not true–a man could easily have his way with a woman, even if she did not want him to.

Suddenly Vince turned over and sat up, dumping Camille off of him.

"My gosh, what time is it? Ten o'clock! I've got to call Mike about the Soborne Show shoot. I was supposed to call him at 9:00." He groaned, picked up the phone and dialed Mike's number while Camille sucked her finger and watched him, amused. He was so serious and different when he was working, compared to how he had been acting a moment before.

"Mike!" he said. Camille leaned over to lick his ear, since he had turned his back on her. He barely felt it and brushed his ear with his free hand, trying to concentrate on what Mike was saying, but now he turned and watched Camille out of the corner of his eye. He reached for a pad and pencil that lay beside the phone and began to write. When he leaned over, Camille began to kiss him all over, beginning at the base of his spine and working up. He started to smile, in spite of himself. He was talking and writing down what Mike was saying.

"What was the address again?" he said. "Oh, yeah. I shot something over there a couple of years ago. Do you have Norman's number, by the way?" And he wrote it down on the pad, said his good-byes and hung up.

Camille got up, put on a robe and strolled out to the galley to fix coffee.

"Today we work." she said. "I'm going to paint all day." The big back room in Camille's boat had become her art studio. She had no furniture, so it worked well for that purpose.

September 20

Vince's and my love is wonderful. He feels my feelings and even thinks like I do. It is really miraculous we found each other.

I am a little worried. Vince is late getting back from New Jersey, where he went today to visit his parents. I shouldn't worry. I will learn to trust him, perhaps. I am learning. But then I think of Grace and jealousy starts to creep in.

Why should I be jealous of Grace? She broke up with Vince and she said she did not want to go with him any more. She is my friend. Why should she lie to me? I guess I am beginning to be afraid of losing him. And of course I am afraid he will go back to Grace, if she lets him. Suddenly, I am afraid both of them are tricking me and have been together during the times he was not with me. Like today,

*he left in his car for New Jersey with his dog, and Grace is gone, too.
I called her house and she isn't home. I have to trust her, though.
Why would she go back to Vince? She seems to hate him so much. I
have to trust her. I'll try to call her again now.*

I just called Grace. She was home.

*I went up to Grace's apartment to talk with her about school.
She seemed happy to talk, but she didn't talk about Vince at all. I just
got back. I hear Vince returning.*

Camille had let herself into Vince's boat and began to make
supper. Supper prepared, she put it on a low burner and picked up her
books to study. She had tried to read, but she was nervous and
worried. Grace had no idea where Vince was. She had returned to the
boat about 8:00, but it was after 10:00 when he came in, making
excuses, acting a little strange and apologetic. He acted as if he did
not want her to be mad. They ate the supper, slightly burned, while
Camille assured him she had not been mad, only worried about him.

After eating, Vince sat down on the couch and picked up the
phone and dialed Grace's number. She heard him asking her if she
would come down to the marina garage to help him bring the big TV
down to the boat from the Jeep. When he hung up Camille asked him
what was going on.

"Oh, I brought my old TV from my room at home. Grace
took the one we used to have. I need some help to get it to the boat –
it's very big."

"I'll help you. You don't need to drag Grace out of her
apartment this late at night."

"No, that's all right. She said she would help. Besides, she's
already left."

"Why didn't you ask me?" asked Camille. Vince didn't
answer or look at her. He was already putting on his jacket. "I'll help
you," she said again.

"No. You stay here," he said, and went out the door.

Camille began to clean up the dishes. The window over the
sink faced out toward the park and from the tall boat she had a clear
view of the entrance to the boat basin and the door to the garage in
the hillside. Her mind was churning with suspicions. After a long
time she saw Grace and Vince coming out of the garage with the

huge TV on a rolling dolly. Camille put her shoes and jacket on and walked down the dock to open the gate and help them bring it down the ramp. Surely they needed extra help on the tricky slope down to the boat.

But she felt like an intruder when she got to the gate. They had already opened it and were talking to each other intensely. When they saw her, they fell silent. The sudden and terrible knowledge that she did not belong there with them, fell on her. It was the first time she had felt like an outsider. Grace was her friend and Vince her lover, but they had something she could never participate in, between them personally. They had lived together for seven years and she would never be able to wipe that out of their minds, no matter how much Vince loved her or she loved him. She had no idea what their relationship had been like. Had it been stormy, or loving, or cool? Why had they finally broken up? Something seriously wrong must have destroyed a seven-year-long intimate relationship.

"Why didn't you wait on the boat? You didn't need to get dressed and come out, I told you." Vince was peeved. "You'll get in the way." But they could not get the TV through the gate while it still sat on the dolly. Camille stood watching them struggle for a while, trying to lift the heavy TV while keeping the gate open. She stepped forward to hold the gate while they lifted it over the barrier, then she pulled the dolly along behind them as the two of them carried it down the ramp, and slipped it under the TV when they lowered it to the dock. In silence they pulled the TV down the dock, onto the finger-slip beside Vince's boat and lifted it into Vince's boat. All three helped hook it up in Vince's bedroom and turned it on to make sure it worked. Camille hung around in the background. She felt out of place.

Grace and Vince were talking again, ignoring Camille, and Camille, realizing they had been having a serious discussion when she interrupted, said nothing. She was aware of unspoken things hanging between Grace and Vince that could not be said in front of her. Soon Grace left, pulling her dolly, and Vince sat down in cold silence to watch TV for the remainder of the evening.

September 23

I think strange things these days. Again, it is like I am looking at myself. Almost like I come out of my body and am floating high over a distant scene playing out on the earth below. I see me, acting like a student during the day, going back and forth to school on the train, going to classes, studying in the library, saying the right things in class, writing term papers, reading books and painting pictures when I have a chance, in my boat-studio. On the subway I see I am just one of the commuters. It is a long commute. Everything is a long distance from everything else. When I am in Brooklyn at school, I am a long way away from Vince in Manhattan. In New York, I am a long way from Texas and from John. I am really not the person John thinks I am, but not in the way he would think. I never was what John thought I was. He thought I was a child-housewife. In Texas I am the little housewife. Here in New York, I am someone that doesn't even want to know what a housewife is. I moved to New York, away from Texas and John. Grace moved away from Vince, too, only not very far, and I don't think he wanted her to do that, either.

In the night, I am someone else completely. I am Vince's lover. I feel his cool body under the sheets of the big white bed. You would think we would get tired of holding and caressing each other, but we don't. He is there all the time. He seems to lean down and take over my life at will. I can't think of anything but making love. Thinking of it is good for me because it makes me relax, and I think of nothing else. I don't do busy work any more to keep my mind off of my life. We spend long hours sitting in front of the TV or sleeping or making love. Vince doesn't have much to do, so he sometimes sits and makes me sit still with him, as if in meditation. He doesn't want me to read or do busy work, or to move. It is something I am not used to doing – being still. It forces me to relax. He needs me to be with him. He needs me. He must need love very badly, but then, so do I. We're very lucky to have found each other.

It was a beautiful night. Camille and Vince lay close together wrapped in a blanket on the deck, looking at the lights of the Jersey shore across a sparkling river. Camille was talking to Vince seriously about her financial problems and other things. It was late and they had been talking for an hour, even though she knew she had to get up early in the morning.

70

"You know, I really shouldn't be living with you. I am still married," she said, "even though John isn't really supporting me any longer."

"He's sending you money."

"I don't call $100 a month supporting me," she said.

"It isn't the usual thing," he said, "You being married, that is, and living with me at the same time, but you don't seem worried about it."

"I know. I don't have any feelings about it at all. What bothers me is just that: I don't feel guilty." She fell silent. Vince smirked a little.

"Why feel guilty, unless you have to? Why not enjoy yourself? That's what life is all about."

"But I'm supposed to feel guilty. Yet, why should I? From everything I've been taught, I can see what I'm doing is wrong. But my feelings say what I'm doing is right, that I couldn't do anything else under the circumstances."

Camille realized, even as she spoke, Vince had nothing to lose in this relationship, so why shouldn't he take advantage of it and draw it out as long as he could? On the other hand, she might have a lot to lose, though she could not possibly think what it would be and did not care if she lost any of it, anyway. She honestly did not feel married. She had everything she needed right here. She felt really free, for some reason. She felt like a single woman having an affair with a single man who had just been dumped by his girlfriend.

"I would be better off financially if I were divorced. As long as I am married to a man who makes over a thousand dollars a month, I can't get any financial aid from the school, and he makes much more than a thousand a month." Camille had been to see the financial aid counselor that day and had been denied an application. "But if I get a divorce I will lose all the security I've worked hard for over the years, the credit I established in John's name to borrow money with, and John's medical insurance."

"Are you thinking about getting a divorce?" Vince asked, beginning to pull his shoes off, leaning down from the deck bench to do it.

"Yes, now I am." she admitted for the first time, surprising herself. "I guess I might as well, since I'm not acting like I'm married anyway." She settled herself into the curve of Vince's body.

"Why? Why divorce John? He'll support you and give you a home for the rest of your life. He seems to let you do whatever you want." Vince put his arm around her and pulled her back against him. He began kissing her on the side of the neck.

"But he doesn't. I want to be free to do what I want. Really free. Free to do whatever I want with you." she turned her head and kissed his ear. "Besides, John is very hard to get along with. I can't imagine growing old with him. He'll only get worse."

"And I'm not hard to get along with?" Vince lay back against the deck and pulled her down with him. "I'm terrible to get along with. Just ask Grace. Haven't you ever asked her about me?"

"Yes." Camille turned her head so she could see his face a little, so close to his. Beyond him a huge ship with all its lights on in the black night moved slowly up-river. Soon they would feel the wake rocking them.

"And what did she say?"

"She didn't want to talk about it." He looked at her for awhile and then bent his head to kiss her neck again.

September 26

My first few graduate classes were scary, until I realized I would be able to handle them easily, simply by doing the work the teachers ask me to do. I haven't been in school for a long time, and when I took those two audit courses at John's graduate school, I didn't have much work to do. But if I concentrate on getting the assignments in, I think I can pass them easily. Now that I am into them, I find them so interesting I am putting extra effort in on some of them. They are so fascinating!. In my Art and Literature class, I am doing extra reading and research in the library for the paper due next week. In Painting, I have to decide what kind of painting I am supposed to do, and do some drawings to show my professor. They will give me a graduate studio when one becomes available, supposedly next month.

Most of the people in my classes are younger than I am, but there are a few my age and some older.

My "New Forms" class is interesting; I have never had a

class like this one. We sit on tall stools in an empty room and for each class a couple of students are supposed to have prepared a work of art like nothing anyone has ever seen before. The art must not be made of any conventional art material, nor be from any art period, including the present, so the wilder one's imagination, the better. Today, when my turn came, I didn't have anything prepared and could think of nothing. Then I saw a large, elaborate, old frame, abandoned in one of the halls and picked it up on the way to class. In our classroom, which is used for a sculpture studio when we're not there, there was a lot of marble dust left on the floor. There was a clear set of bare footprints through this white dust on the dark gray concrete. I put the frame around two footprints in the center of the room and swept the marble dust up everywhere else. That was my work of art.

The students actually make the class what it is. The teacher speaks little, but if necessary, informs us as to the history of whatever medium and style is used. The students arrived, settled in, then discussed the work presented by me and two other students for the entire class period. We had an intense critique session of each piece placed before us. One person tacked strings of varying lengths all over one wall. Another melted plastic. For my critique, everyone laughed, and didn't seem to take it seriously. The teacher pointed out, however, that it was a spontaneous performance piece. Last week John Cody painted codes on a strip of wood. John Cody dominates the class; he is the professor's favorite.

There are several quiet, but serious young women, a few young men who vary in age and race, and an older man, the friend of a tall, red-headed man named Howard Caine. These two are friendly to me. The older man is probably twenty years older than me, is from France, has white hair, a white beard, and a heavy French accent. He is very interesting. Howard wears unique, expensive clothes and has a red beard. He acts very distinguished, but he reminds me of John, since John wears a beard, so I am somewhat put off by any attention he pays me.

Howard Caine found a seat next to Camille on the subway coming home from Brooklyn. He and a woman named Nancy rode the same subway Camille did going back to Manhattan every day, and they had begun to sit with each other and talk during the long trip. Howard told Camille about his family, which now consisted only of his aging father. Howard was nice and Camille encouraged him to talk. He was ostentatiously intelligent, but good-natured. He said he had already started his own design agency, and described it as being successful.

They had to shout to each other over the noise, sitting on the narrow, gray, metal bench in the crowded subway car. The red hair of Howard's beard bounced up and down and shone different colors in the garish light. Nancy sat on the other side of him, craning around him in order to see Camille's lips move, pressed against his big tweed jacket with leather patches on the elbows. Howard had his head turned toward Camille. Camille was flattered he was talking to her, instead of Nancy, in spite of herself. And he was eager to talk. He stood, reluctantly, when the train reached his stop, still talking, and Nancy had to drag him off before the doors closed.

Camille was exhausted, not having slept much the night before. Not sleeping was becoming a habit. She could hardly keep her eyes open in class and slept whenever she could, even if it was for fifteen minutes between classes. She felt she had to study after school, but when she got back to the boat one day, Vince said he wanted to drive over to Fritz and Sally's house in Brooklyn. There they sat for four hours in the big, old, smoke-filled parlor of a dilapidated Victorian mansion.

Fritz and Sally were artists, and old friends of Vince's. They had bought a house being sold for taxes near the waterfront and were fixing it up. It had once been beautiful, filled with little hallways opening onto enormous rooms, staircases that took one down into a windowed lower floor with a terrace out back or wound upward for three stories, to where a student lived. Fritz and Sally lived on the lower two floors. They seemed to have lived there forever, since it was full of odd junk. Heavy, velvet curtains draped and framed the tall windows and ornate clocks, interspersed with children's crayon drawings hung on the walls.

Sally was a big, blond woman, and Camille immediately took a liking to her. Camille followed her around, talking with her and playing with their two little boys, while Fritz and Vince talked in the living room. Downstairs, Camille found that Sally had opened a small florist shop on the lower floor, with an entrance under the stoop. But

Sally had not done much business and the shop had turned into a hobby room as well, with various kinds of projects lying unfinished in piles. There Sally sat down in a rocking chair, waving for Camille to sit too, in the midst of the confusion. Camille said no, she would stand and Sally started telling her how she was tired and disgusted.

"It's no good living with a junky," she said, and elaborated for awhile. Her husband smoked pot and did little else. She talked on and on about her problems. Camille could say nothing. This was something she had no experience with. Eventually, Sally asked if Camille wanted something to drink.

They wound their slow way up into the kitchen, and Sally laughed, embarrassed, when Camille finally asked her what a "junkie" was

"Well, a junkie is an addict. You keep having to support them. It's really hard when you have kids."

Camille was hungry, not having eaten before coming with Vince to their house. She was sometimes weak, which was something new for her, as she had been healthy all her life. Perhaps it was because she was so thin now. Tonight she had developed a terrific headache from hunger.

Sally said she was going to walk down the street to visit some people who were moving out and Camille went with her, rather than sitting and waiting for Vince. These neighbors had a lot of things they were leaving behind that Sally wanted to look through to see if there was anything she needed. They had a table they were throwing out and when she asked about it, Sally told Camille she could have it for her boat. Camille was thrilled and they decided to take it back to the house and coax Vince into putting it in the back of the Jeep to take home. In her boat she was eating off the kitchen cabinet. Vince had given her a little desk and chair, which were the only other pieces of actual furniture she had in the boat, besides the built-in bed and drawers where she kept her clothes. They walked back to the house, pulling the table behind them.

Weak and hungry, Camille fell asleep in the car going back over the bridge. At breakfast she had felt sick, so she had made thin cream of wheat, put honey and milk in it, and drank it as she dressed. She possessed only 35 cents to buy food with that day. So she had bought a hard-boiled egg at the student snack bar and ate a tomato brought from home for lunch. She had eaten nothing for supper. She often felt weak this way and now she worried she might be sick.

When they got back, about 9:00 p.m., she cooked in Vince's boat while Vince brought the table from the Jeep and put it on her boat. She took two Alka-Seltzers while pushing Vince away. He was already attacking her for sex, even before supper. After she ate, she felt a little better and wished she could go to bed. But she had studying to do and knew she probably would not get any sleep before midnight. Vince was watching TV and cleaning his camera equipment. He had had a good week, but he rarely started work before 10:00 each morning, so he could sleep late.

DAWN

October 2

> *It is ending, I'm afraid. I haven't written for the past few days because everything has been so intense. We were close. Maybe too close. Finally, we are seeing what the other really is like. The first magic is wearing off and problems about commitment are beginning to surface. Vince accused me of trying to manipulate him and sometimes he gets angry suddenly, like tonight when I saw his dirty clothes still lying on the floor after several days and I asked "don't you think you might put them away?" He yelled that I was trying to tell him how to think and act.*
>
> *I am beginning to feel like a visitor or a hired hand in his home, being only tolerated. Last night I cooked and cleaned and then we sat, stiffly watching TV in separate chairs, tense and silent, while he smoked. I got bored, but when I got up to leave and go to my boat, he suddenly didn't want me to go and made all kinds of excuses to make me stay with him.*
>
> *He is territorial, in spite of letting me stay with him. He won't let me touch anything that is his except the dishes and the furniture. The other night he gave me my own shelves in one of the cabinets to put my clothes in, and hung my housecoat up in the closet, but he also scolded me for the way I turned the knob on the TV (too fast) and didn't let me touch anything, even to cook or clean, for the rest of the evening.*
>
> *I don't really have anyone I can talk to about this. I thought maybe I could talk to Grace. But if I do, I'm afraid Vince will find out I am talking about him behind his back, since he talks a lot with Grace now. But I need to talk to someone.*
>
> *Vince is also openly attracted to other women. I have gotten so used to it I don't even feel angry at him any more when he talks about them. Tonight he even said some day I might decide to go out with other men.*
>
> *"Well, I wouldn't do anything with them that would make you mad," I said, immediately thinking of Howard, who has invited me to have dinner with him. I might have dinner with him, but I am certainly not attracted to Howard sexually.*

"Bull!" he said. He thought I was lying. When I told him I wasn't, he didn't like that either. He didn't like the idea of me being faithful to only him because it means he has to be faithful, too. I told him he was free, that he could go out with those other girls that were so attractive. It was hard to tell him, but I meant it. He knows it would hurt me if he did and I wouldn't like it. If I am faithful and he isn't, it isn't fair to me.

Once he deliberately said he lives alone on his boat. I guess he meant to say he wasn't really living with me, in spite of the fact that I have slept with him for a month.

I don't belong on his boat. I should be in my own place. But then he neglected to take any of the groceries we bought into my boat the last time we shopped, so I have to eat at his place all the time, now. I don't even have an excuse to leave any more. Making me eat with him and having my clothes at his place seems a rather calculated attempt to make me live with him, in spite of what he says.

Now does he want me to go away, feeling like I am telling him how to live and think? I think he intends for me to go back to my own place eventually. And maybe I feel like it would be the best thing to do, too.

They had been arguing.

"You're being ridiculous! We <u>do not</u> think of the same thing at the same time. And we're <u>not</u> interested in the same things!" Vince was sitting with his arms crossed, his feet pulled up on the couch, withdrawn and smoking. Camille sat in a deck chair which he had positioned between him and the TV, which was emitting a low, uneven noise.

"That is true," admitted Camille, uneasily. "I'm not really being honest with myself, I guess. Some of the things you like I don't like." Vince visibly relaxed.

"And yet when you like them, I like them, too." She was thinking how, when she went with him wherever he was going, she enjoyed it, too. "But perhaps I should think more about what I enjoy and do those things. You want me to and maybe it is the right to do. After all, I am on my own for the first time in my life and now is a good time to find out what I like. But what will you do if I'm not with you?" When she glanced at him, she thought maybe she had said the wrong thing. He looked angry and withdrawn again. Was she subconsciously being manipulative, as he had hinted? After he had accused her of this, she noticed manipulation was something he did, too.

"Do you want a cup of coffee?" he asked.

"Yes," she replied and waited for him to get up and get it, but he did not move. She knew he wanted a cup of coffee, so she asked "Do you want a cup? Let me get it." and she got up to go to the galley.

"Would you be upset if I didn't sleep with you sometimes?" she paused briefly before him. Sometimes she really wanted to go and sleep in her own little bed on her own boat.

"What do you think?" he answered, still sulky and hurt. She bent over to kiss him briefly before going into the galley.

In the kitchen area she watched the back of his handsome head. He had lately had his hair cut short and it was evenly curly all over his head. His black jacket and leather boots set off what was left of his summer tan. She appreciated and was proud of his good looks. She knew together they made a striking couple. People looked at them when they went places together. Sometimes they ate out, but recently they had only been cooking dinners at home. He was a gourmet cook and shopped in the best delis for ingredients, planning everything well ahead of time. His meals were delicious and Camille was an appreciative dinner guest, learning lots of things she had not learned, even in all her years of cooking meals for John, who was a fussy eater.

Once, when he realized that he was cooking all the time, Vince said she had to cook for him for a week. He acted childish sometimes, with emotional, petulant outbursts and sudden verbal attacks on her and things she did. Yet sometimes, like when he was working with his photography, he acted calm and mature. There were many things she admired about him. She had to remember them when he was acting badly.

Tonight she felt rejected. She did not remember rejecting Vince in any way, but perhaps she had. She had unwillingly begun to think of him as younger than she, less experienced in getting along in a relationship and making it last. She still felt like trying to make it work, giving it a chance to work out. To this attitude, he said she was acting superior, was "always right" and did not express her true feelings to him. Maybe he was right. She needed to be more honest with him and admit mistakes when she made them.

Later that night, she went back over to her boat to work, but then returned to his and they made love. He tried some new things with her. He was an expert in lovemaking, and had quite an imagination.

"How many girls have you made love to?" she asked as they relaxed afterward. He sat and thought, looking at her wickedly.

"I can't remember. How many men have you made love to?"

"One, then you."

"No!" He did not believe her.

"Yes. Just my husband. I was tempted, but never had an affair with anyone else. I was a virgin on my wedding night, believe it or not."

"Probably the only bride that really deserved to wear white in the history of our nation." he said, but he acted like he wasn't sure whether to believe her or not.

She thought, "He has never met anyone from the Bible Belt."

A DOG'S LIFE

Vince walked in front of her down the dock. His tall body turned white, then black as he passed under the lights in the black night. Rastus jogged alongside him, so indistinct in color as to not be seen, except when under the lights. The only sound was the long, jingling dog chain and keys. The calves of Vince's legs flashed white, then rolled under him into darkness, his feet silent in white tennis shoes. His head turned back toward her occasionally to be sure she was following him.

He opened the gate and Camille walked up beside him and stood, her hands in big coat pockets, head up, shaking back her self-cut, page-boy haircut, so its blackness shone under the light. She allowed a sliver of her body to be seen in the opening of her coat. He looked down at her, measuring her with a tiny, intense smile that turned his face into something beautiful. In the overhead light, his eyes were black brush strokes above his cheekbones.

He had actually asked her to go with him to walk the dog. He had never let her go before. Some nights he met Grace in the park and walked with her. Camille had glimpsed them together. She felt the cold wind blow up her coat as they turned and walked up the paved walkway by the river. The park reached up into the blackness beneath the trees on one side, while on the other boats bobbed their lights silently on the black water, glowing cheerily in the night. There was a distant sound of music and faint talking, the constant noise of the city. It was much colder these days. Camille pulled her coat around her so she would not feel the cold. At last she was going to walk the dog.

The park lights were stark white as they went up the hill, and cast their bodies in silver. The white sheen made everything look colder. The wind blew from across the river. The bare walkway was silent, except for a distant jogger. The dog pulled Vince along, then stopped and sniffed at a tree. Pieces of paper danced in the wind and rested against the fence. They walked all the way to 71st Street and back. There the gray stones of the apartment buildings raised a barrier against the cold, but were cold themselves. The windows of the buildings were black; iron bars and heavy curtains hid any inside light.

They were shut out, exposed to the raw elements of nature, but they were together. Vince was walking fast now. He did not talk much. Camille chattered about her classes, recounting a discussion she had with one of her classmates, but Vince changed the subject. What he had to say required no answers and Camille was silenced. He did not want to hear about school. That was the way he shut her off and she did not mind. She did not mind being subject to him in some ways. She knew she would be with him forever. She felt eternity with Vince, when she thought about it. He had saved her.

The long walkway back along the river was dark, but had a few obstacles, a broken piece of concrete, a rivulet of water, a downed branch from a tree; and finally they arrived at the gate, grateful and cold. A lot of fumbling with the keys and pushing on the heavy gate let them onto the lighted dock and down the ramp to their boat.

Vince opened the door to his warm boat and suddenly Camille was tired. The lights came on and Vince carefully hung the dog's chain in its place, then his coat, then he went into the galley to put on the coffee pot. It was his routine. Camille slowly walked up the unlit steps to the bed, debating whether to lie down or not. She stopped at the edge of it and looked at the pattern the bedspread made. The pattern blurred as she gazed.

"Come here, little pet. Where do you think you're going? Come back down here and get some coffee," she heard Vince saying from below. She slowly floated back to him, running her hands along her ribs, feeling the leanness of her stomach and hips, sore from running, where her bones protruded sharply. She was "bone tired," she thought.

Vince removed her coat carefully and hung it beside his, then stood against the cabinet and leaned her against him, enveloping her in his arms. She leaned lightly and abstractedly against him, gazing into space, feeling his body like a wool blanket wrapped around her, taking in the rare feeling of his care surrounding her.

"Some day you'll be far away. You'll call me from Kansas City and say 'Vince, I need you," he said, "and I'll hop on a jet and be there that night. I'll always be here and I'll always be ready to come to you."

She pondered that. It was not exactly what she had imagined, but it was a nice thought. She felt better, but alien still. Far away.

"Where are you, little pet? Are you falling sleep on me? Why don't we smoke a little and watch TV?"

"I think I'll go home and go to bed." The words came from someplace deep inside her and she meant them. She was tired and tired of dealing with him. She needed peace and quiet for a change. But Vince was hurt by her words. He pulled away.

"I thought you wanted to stay with me," he said coldly. She realized he wanted her to stay. She smiled wanly at him, trying to warm up to him in spite of her tiredness and went into the bathroom to get ready for bed.

All of his feelings were so strong, so intense; his rage sometimes diverted to her. If it ever got too strong, she hoped she could turn it aside, because he needed her as much as she needed him.

It was a beautiful fall Saturday, cool and sunny. It had been raining in the city for awhile and now everyone was out walking in the clear air. Camille walked down the empty street named Wall, looking at the cold, finely finished bare concrete walls, and ornately decorated columns and porticos. She turned into a doorway and rang the bell. A face appeared in the dark glass and the door opened, a heavy glass door with a dark copper handle and stainless steel frame. The plump face smiled and Penny gave Camille a hug. It was cold inside, and they walked to a stairwell. Penny had a flashlight and they walked up five dark flights of stairs to the fifth floor of the empty office building.

Penny and her husband lived in a crowded room on Wall Street, in what had been an office. Since it had never been intended to be an apartment, she and her young husband had no water and had to go down the hall to use the public bathroom. The room was half filled with lumber, projectors, and a big bed of handmade birch. There was also handmade plywood living room furniture and baby furniture. Their strapping 20-pound, six-month-old baby boy was cute and round-faced, like Penny. The lunch Penny served was hearty, if inexpensive and she seemed happy to see Camille, as she recalled meeting her once at her mother's house back in Texas. But as Penny rambled on, she admitted that she had violent thoughts and felt violent feelings since coming to live in New York.

Lunch turned out to be rather depressing to Camille. They were so poor. Penny's husband was a carpenter, but had no union card and no job. A radical who refused to pay taxes, he was constantly avoiding any kind of authority, such as landlords or police. The cute little, law-abiding country girl from Billington had turned into a different person from the one Camille had known in Texas. Camille had promised Penny's mother she would visit her. Her daughter had moved to New York from Billington two years ago, marrying the young carpenter, who took her away to Manhattan. Her mother had not seen her since, and now they had a baby. She was worried and had only occasionally been able to talk to Penny on the phone.

Vince was feeling better than he had all week. For days he had hardly touched Camille and had avoided her if she came close enough to touch him. Today he was joking around with her, even acting loving toward her in the evening. During supper he only got upset a couple of times. She cooked supper according to his explicit directions. They had mussels, broiled bluefish, marinated cucumbers with bean sprouts, and baked acorn squash with honey and butter. Camille was learning how to cook under his tutelage.

A month had gone by and Camille felt like everything was going well. Vince seemed to have relaxed. Her schoolwork was coming along. She had heard her show was doing well in Indianapolis and Hal, at the gallery, already had invitations printed for her opening. Camille realized her expectations of Vince had lowered somewhat and now they joked and kidded each other about things that had caused trauma during the early weeks. They kept telling each other the other was free, and yet they knew that, should the other do anything that would belie their love, it would hurt. So they were careful not to do anything. They were learning to trust each other.

Camille looked forward to the nights when she could lie in his arms, safe and loved. She felt contentment and security there. She had never felt as secure and as loved as she did now with Vince. He loved her well. And she acted loving toward him, feeling rushes of tenderness and caring for him. He was gentle and good when they made love and she responded with passion. With him she felt wide ranges of sensations that could only be compared to the spectrum of the rainbow. She could see the colors in her mind when Vince made love to her. She had never in her life experienced anything remotely like it.

They lay curled in each other's arms at night, after having loved hard and long. She pressed her cheek against his chest to hear his heart beating while he lay, spent and peaceful against her at last.

"Your dear heart," she said softly. "I hear it beating. I want it to beat forever. I don't want it to ever stop. It is so precious to me." She lay still and listened to it. She heard Vince sigh deeply and realized he was crying.

"Is something wrong?" she asked.

"No one has ever said anything like that to me before," he said and a single tear slid down his cheek. He never cried.

Vince took Grace and Camille to the Brooklyn Museum to see a show he said Grace wanted to see, so Camille had the opportunity to watch Grace and Vince together. They acted like truly good friends. They kidded and played together like little kids, pushing and tickling each other. Camille envied them. She had never had anyone to play with, least of all her husband. She was learning how to be playful with Vince and loved it.

But Vince also had a habit she did not like – that of openly observing and admiring other women out loud. Perhaps, because he was an artist and a photographer, she told herself, he appreciated their beauty. But he made comments about the specific things he liked about them – their body, their hair, the way they walked. Each time it happened, Camille compared herself with them, which was hard to do, since she still had a terrible inner image of herself.

But the fact was, living with Vince had changed the way she looked. She had become conscious of her sexuality. She dressed in clothes that would impress Vince and as a result, other men noticed her, too. Once, Vince openly admired Grace's beauty when Grace complained that she had gained weight. To Camille's surprise and irritation, he told Grace he liked those little "love handles" on her hips. Camille looked herself over in the long mirror and saw her hips and buttocks had completely disappeared. She was straight and thin, with no extra fat at all on her body. For a change, she was smaller than Grace.

After visiting the museum, they dropped Grace off at her apartment and drove down to meet Hal at the gallery. They went upstairs to his office and had a glass of champagne before going out to eat at a nearby Japanese restaurant. Camille enjoyed the experience. The restaurant was interesting, the food delicious and she felt comfortable kidding around with both men. Vince laughed a lot and Hal encouraged him to do more with his photography in a fine arts sense. Hal must like Vince, Camille noted, in spite of the feeling of disapproval she felt from him about their present situation. Vince acted attentive to Camille, letting Hal know she was living with him. Hal acted cool and silent about it, for someone as curious and shocked as he must be. He talked about Camille's opening next month. He asked for her list of people to whom he should send invitations.

Hal acted like the affair was normal and asked them to help him plan a party at the gallery in a couple of weeks. He told them he would put Vince in charge of cooking, since Vince was such a good cook.

Camille came away with an even better impression of Hal than she used to have, and found she enjoyed Japanese food. She had shared a dish with Hal and they all kidded the Japanese waiter. Vince praised the waiter on the Sea Nabe and he discussed how it was made.

The weather had turned cold and was almost down to 30 degrees on the seemingly long drive home. They sat on the couch together, once back in the boat, to warm up before Vince went out to walk the dog. He didn't call Grace to accompany him. When he got back, they cuddled in bed to keep warm.

IVORY TOWER

John was beginning to realize Camille was gone. Maybe for good. She did not want to talk to him whenever he called her on the phone and he knew she had left feeling angry. At first he thought she would not go. Then, when she left anyway, he felt sure she would come back immediately, once she got to New York and found out how expensive it was and that it was a terrible place to live. But she had found a place to live even before she left.

She evidently didn't need him, though he needed her. She was his wife and he needed a wife in his life. He resented her going off at this time of his life. Her place was at his side, especially during these years, while his career was just beginning. He needed her to keep a cozy home and to be a family to him, as his Mother had done while he attended school. It was difficult for a single man to gain respect. He had to admit it was necessary to have a wife for entertaining fellow scholars at the University and to accompany him to faculty events. No, not absolutely necessary, but it did give one a certain credibility, a prestige, an image a single man would not have had.

It would be especially hard to face his cohorts as a man whose wife had left him. The possibility of this last had begun to weigh on his mind with all of the burdens of humiliation it would bring him. He was a decent, faithful, hard-working man who had never even looked at another woman. Camille had absolutely no reason to leave him. He had been the perfect husband.

Whenever he reached this point in his thought process, John would make himself stop and think of something else. He had let the housekeeper go the first week. He did not need someone else to come in and do Camille's dirty work. He could do it himself. He ate out and had even begun to cook a little in the kitchen, a place he had rarely entered. It saved money and took his mind off other problems. There was even a possibility that he might come to enjoy it.

His second book had been published and the publishers had been in constant touch with him concerning its sales progress. If they got it into educational libraries alone or accepted as a textbook, it would sell well over 30,000. But so far progress had been slow.

He needed for this book to be a success. He was in line to receive the honor as the top teacher in his college and this not only entailed good teaching, but having been published, as well.

His classes were demanding. He had one problem student, a young man a bit smarter and more vocal than the rest of the students in his Philosophy 2 class, who challenged him and was difficult to put down. The youth of today were irrepressible. He admired them, but it created a problem in his classes. When he had been this youth's age he, too, had been outspoken, but he had not been disrespectful, no matter how much he felt the professor to be in the wrong. The young man's overly-confident attitude bothered him, but more than that, his knowledge in certain areas sometimes seemed superior, or at least equal to his own, although in other areas it fell far below his. The problem of how to grade him concerned him. He hated to give him a high grade, but, even on essay tests he had shown himself to be superior to other students.

Another matter of concern was his Teaching Aide, Kim. She had come to him from the College of Education and requested permission to intern as his assistant. He was impressed with her credentials – good grades and a willing attitude toward work, as demonstrated in the jobs she had held in the past. She could definitely be used to do research for the book he was working on now. So he took her on.

But she had not done well in her writing. Though she had done the research, her ability to put into words what she derived from it was dismal. She was not a philosophy major and often simply recited theory. He got much more out of asking her about the topic and found she could express herself well verbally, in discussions. Therefore, of necessity, he had spent many hours in his office with her, and their relationship was becoming more relaxed, not as cool and detached as it was at the beginning of the year. He found himself thinking that, as well as being a comfortable professor/aide relationship, they were also becoming friends.

He knew he was a good-looking man, being, in his thirties, a bit older than his oldest student, so this relationship could not ever be more than a friendship. He was married, and could not afford any gossip – it would ruin his reputation in the conservative university atmosphere. Besides, he prided himself on being a faithful husband, as he had been brought up strictly, in a religious atmosphere. All the philosophies and religions he had studied said anything else but monogamy doomed the participant.

One of the things that concerned him about the relationship, besides how much time Kim took away from his writing, was her ready availability. She was always there to spend time with him whenever he called on her. She never overtly flirted with him, but then she would not dare to be flirtatious, under the circumstances. Unless he propositioned her, any advances on her part would appear ridiculous, and would certainly damage her grades and career as a student if she made unwanted advances on him. Of course, he thought, chuckling to himself, if he had welcomed her advances, it would have helped her. After all, she must realize most professors would be tempted by her nubile beauty. She was young and fresh. She dressed, at times, provocatively and, though she tried to hide them under long skirts and slacks and blowzy shirts, she had big, round breasts and gorgeous long legs. Her face was creamy in complexion and she never wore makeup. It was unnecessary, with her dark lashes and big, blue eyes, to enhance what she naturally came by.

Sometimes, when they were close together, going over her atrocious notes in writing, he could see her full, pink lips close to his and the thought of kissing them come into his mind, to be quickly pushed away.

His friend and fellow, Ancient History professor, Albert Carmichael, derided him for not taking advantage of the situation and "sticking it to her," as he so crassly put it. But then, Albert had become crass. His wife was diagnosed with clinical depression, their doctor put her on Valium and now she floated around the house without passions of any kind. Albert, thus deprived of meaningful connubial companionship, sought it in the young women he happened to be teaching.

Albert was not particularly good-looking, certainly not as handsome as he himself was, thought John, but it surprised him how many young women Albert had seduced (or claimed they had seduced him) over the course of the last year and a half.

Not only was Albert enjoying himself, but he seemed to take pride in these adventures and recounted them to John in full detail.

John was at first shocked and disgusted with the obviously downward-sliding morals of a friend whose wife was ill, but then he realized Albert was actually fixated in a younger stage than he and forgave him. After that, he could listen to Albert's daily episodes with an attitude of condescension. After all, one reason he was interested was it was happening in an office like his, down the hall, while in his own office nothing of the sort ever came to pass, not even in his fantasies.

So, when Kim came into his life, and office, and Albert popped in after Kim had left one day and began deriding him about her, John immediately set Albert straight. It was not and never would be his intention to take advantage of the situation, to violate his sacred vows and do as Albert suggested. For Albert was actually suggesting he disrobe this woman, a woman 13 years his junior, and see if her breasts were actually as big as they appeared, or if it was true what Albert said: "no woman who actually possesses breasts as big as that could possess a brain too."

Every day Albert had something to tease him about. Perhaps he was jealous. Every day John smiled, because, even if Camille had left him, even if he had good reason to, he would never violate his wedding vows. Even if Camille's silence meant that she had decided to divorce him, he still had the backbone to resist the temptation Kim represented. He hoped Camille was acting likewise. It hurt to think she might be unfaithful to him after all he had done for her.

FIDEL

October 13

     Yesterday was my birthday. John sent me a card, but all he wrote in it was "Happy Birthday, hope it is good for you. John." On the way home from school I bought flowers. When I got home, Vince led me by the hand into his boat and showed me a big aquarium he had bought me as a present, complete with pump, plants and everything but fish. Last week when we went walking in the Village we stopped by a pet shop and I saw a fish I wanted. It was a huge, white goldfish with a long, flowing tail.

     I was thrilled with the aquarium. I wanted to go right then and get the fish, but Vince reminded me the pet shop had closed for the day, since it was after 5:00. We took the aquarium to my boat and filled it with water. We lay on the bed and gazed at the flowers and the aquarium happily until we both slept.

     Later, John called me and wished me a happy birthday. It was hard to talk to him. He told me he had broken his toe on Monday and walking was hard for him. He sounded angry and frustrated at me for not being there to take care of him. I don't know why I suddenly feel so cold toward him. I tried to figure it out this morning, as I walked up the hill to the subway. I don't have any feelings at all for him. I don't feel good or bad, or even think of him, and I don't miss him. It's unnatural. You would think that, considering the good girl I've always been, I would feel guilty for the things I'm doing. But what I'm doing doesn't feel wrong or right; it only feels necessary.

     Maybe I expected too much from him. I don't know. I remember the times when I would get so frustrated with his ignoring me. I would get so mad at him after a few months that I would just have to tell him. Then he would sing a little song, "How to handle a woman -- is to love her, love her, love her," and would proceed to have sex with me. I would be so embarrassed and not wanting to shame him, would forget why I was mad.

     Last night he wouldn't let me even start telling him about not having enough money and the difficulties of going to school, a subject which he certainly has experience with. He said I should come home and reminded me of my "duty." Does he really expect me to come back to him because he says that? He refuses to think about moving here. He doesn't even want to visit. He just wants me to come back to Billington.

I told him I can't see living in Billington, Texas for the rest of my life, and that is what would happen if I went back. When we married, he told me we would probably move away from Texas after he got his degrees. He knew I wanted to leave Texas and that's the reason he said it. But now I know he could not live so far away from his mother.

When I think about it, I don't believe John loves me, and maybe he never has. He only needs me. Only occasionally during the years we were married has he told me he loved me, and then only as a knee-jerk reaction when I told him first. Last night when he called, he said, as he hung up, "I love you a lot," in the same tone someone would say "See-ya."

If he was trying to tell me he loves me now, it is too late, and it was inappropriate, considering we had just had a terrible, emotional discussion of what would happen if I stayed in New York for the duration of my degree, coming home only during the summers.

I can't remember any present John has given me for a birthday or for anything else. Surely he has given me a birthday present sometime during the last ten years.

Before I left for school today, Vince gave me another birthday present, a silver compact, with a beautiful card. Secretly, in my boat, I am painting him a little painting, a kind of collage, showing all the things we have done together during the past month.

When Camille entered the gate after school the next day the tide was so low she practically ran down the steep ramp with boards nailed across it for footholds. At high tide the slope had been mild, but at low tide, the dock sank, too. The boards on the wooden docks were so weathered that when walked on, they clacked in their nail-holes. She went slowly by the resident sculptor, who was always out on the dock chipping away at logs he was carving into abstract sculptures.

She passed a group of people standing on the dock by a small sailboat whose owner was having a party. They were tall, good-looking, well dressed people, greeting each other loudly and effusively, outwardly proud to have been invited to a boat basin party. They carried bottles in tall sacks to their host, anticipating drinking till early morning, when they would either have to grope their way back to land in the dark, or stumble to their host's couch to pass out.

This seemed to happen every weekend. Camille had no idea what these healthy-looking young people did during the day, but they were always there, drinking and talking loudly on the weekends. She came to her dock and looked up to see Grace emerging from Vince's boat. Grace saw Camille walking toward her and avoided her eyes, obviously embarrassed to have been caught there. Camille stopped to speak, but Grace passed her, as if she was in a hurry and only murmured, "Hello, how is everything?"

Camille said "fine," but by then Grace was already far away. Why was Grace avoiding her? What was happening? She remembered having seen Grace coming out of the boat basin the day before at the same time, but seeing her here again was strange. Did she come every day?

She used Vince's key to enter his boat, feeling upset and curious. But she immediately saw Vince was more upset than she was, pacing up and down at the far end.

"I can't stand it!" he shouted when he saw her. Camille stopped, not knowing whether to stay or turn around and leave.

"Come in! Sit down," he demanded angrily, as if he had been waiting to confront her with a misdeed. Putting her own questions aside for the moment, Camille dropped her books by the door and went to sit in one of the deck chairs facing the windows. Vince had been in a good mood when she left in the morning. But it looked like he had been drinking coffee and smoking constantly since she left, from the litter on the coffee table.

"I can't stand her! She drives me up the wall! What are you staring at? Why don't you do something – go get a cup of coffee or something!" He had not touched her, but the tone of his voice made her feel as if she had been slapped. He was practically shaking, he was so mad. Camille found she had tensed up, anticipating something bad.

All she could think was if Grace was so terrible, why did he continue to see her every day? Camille went to the kitchen and poured herself a glass of apple juice. When she came back into the room, she was feeling a little calmer, but her stomach was churning. Vince was seated in his normal spot on the couch, his head back, smoking a cigarette. The smoke rose around him like a screen and drifted through the room. Camille sat down in the chair opposite him. He wore a sweat-wrinkled Hawaiian shirt, open almost to the waist, showing his chest. The light came in from behind him, low and strong, creating dark shadows on one side of his face and a white pallor on the other, through the haze of smoke. Tendons on his neck stood out and cast long lines from his jaw to his collarbone. She wished could get up, get a paper and pencil and draw him, but she knew if she moved he would jump up and ask where she was going.

"So why do you see her?" Camille asked meekly, after a long silence.

"She's so good," he moaned. "She forgives me for everything I did to her." By now Camille could imagine how he might have treated her. And Grace still liked Vince, she realized, or she would never have returned to his boat, ever.

They finally assigned her a painting studio at the Institute. Camille met her painting professor, Mr. Gutstadt, in the morning for her first private session. The side of the room assigned to her was empty and bare, except for a big easel, a work stand and a stool. The other half of the room was full, overflowing with another student's work stacked in piles and hung all over the walls, a workbench and easels crowding the floor, and well-used painting materials scattered about.

Mr. Gutstadt arrived a few minutes after 10:00. He was a big man with a striking, square German face. A long scar ran vertically downward, from his eye to his chin. He looked around her bare space, his small glasses reflecting the emptiness there in the gray room.

"Camille," he finally said, with a heavy German accent. "Make zis room into a home. Put sketches on ze walls, get an easy chair. Zis will be your home. I want zis to look lived and worked in next week ven I return. You vant to feel comfortable heerin. You vill be spending a lot of time heerin."

When he left, Camille felt her frustrations multiplying. She had barely enough money to buy food and her teacher was telling her to buy an easy chair. She had enough money for paint and supplies, but not much else. She also had to buy some expensive books for her classes. Oil paint was $7.00 a tube. How could she afford an easy chair?

She gathered up her coat and purse and dismally set out for the book store. It was a bleak and dreary day in Brooklyn. The sun shone thinly on the dusty leaves of the trees, the concrete sidewalks and apartment buildings. Beat-up metal trash cans overflowed on the curbs. She guessed it was garbage day from all the garbage cans and piles of junk on the sidewalk. Ahead of her, in the middle of the sidewalk, was an enormous pile of trash left by someone moving out of an apartment. And there, in the middle of the old pans and broken dishes in boxes, sat an easy chair.

Camille approached the chair suspiciously. It was probably in too bad a state to keep. But it was covered with a fairly new, flowered chair cover. She moved closer to examine the chair better. The original upholstery under the cover was blue satin and the frame was very well made. It was not wet, smelly or flea-ridden, as far as she could tell. She looked around at the empty street. No one else seemed to be claiming it. It was a perfectly good wing-backed easy chair, unbroken, with all of its legs intact.

Camille decided to claim it. But getting it back to the studio would be a problem. It had to be taken now or someone else would get it. It was a long way back to the graduate arts building. She tried to lift the chair out of the garbage pile. With a bit of maneuvering, tipping it this way and that, she pulled it off, and tried to lift it. It was not impossible to lift, if she put some effort into it, but it was so heavy she could only carry it a few feet. She had to put it down and struggle to find a better handhold, since it was slipping out of her fingers. She managed to pick it up and carry it a little further. What would people think, seeing her carrying an old easy chair along the street? But there was no one around. The air was chilly and her fingers started to get numb. If she put on her mittens, she would not be able to get a good grip on the thick, rounded arms. So she carried it a little further, put it down, panted for a minute while rubbing her hands together, then carried it a few more feet.

She continued doing this over and over, struggling down the sidewalk, avoiding garbage piles, ignoring traffic or passers-by, making her way back toward her building, putting the chair down and then carrying it a little more. When she rested, she acted like she was just happening to stand beside it, hoping no one would notice there was an easy chair there.

As she approached the corner where her building was, right across the street, a moving van pulled up beside her and a man leaned out of the high window.

"You need some help?" he asked. "I'll be glad to carry that chair somewhere for you on my truck – it's too big for you to carry."

"No thank you," she said gratefully. "I'm just going across the street." The man looked back along the long sidewalk she had manipulated, smiled, shook his head and waved good-bye to her. She carried the chair across the street and into the building, acting like it weighed nothing while she was in the busy hallway with the other students. She managed to carry it straight down the main hall, past the chairman's office without stopping and put it down heavily at the bottom of the stairs. There she finally sat down in it and rested. Now all she had to do was take it up the stairs. She jumped up again, afraid her muscles would get sore if she let them rest too long.

Getting the chair up the stairs was the hardest part. The chair was large and kept on wanting to tip back on top of her. The base legs rocked back and forth unevenly on the steps. She took it step by step to the second floor, where her studio was, and pushed it into the room. She pulled it over to her corner by the window, turned it at an angle so the sunlight would shine on it, and stood back for a moment to admire it.

It looked homey and comfortable. Just what Dr. Gutstadt had ordered. Tonight she would make sketches for the paintings she planned to do. She would tack them to the walls, and along with the art materials she planned to buy, her room would look and feel like a painting studio.

Camille met Vince in the Village at 4:00, near the pet store. They walked around the dark aisles of the little store and found the tank where goldfish were — little glints of silver and gold blobs shining in the dim light of their tank. The warm smell of animals and animal food filled the air. Camille looked at goldfish while Vince wandered around looking at tropical fish. She found the special fish she had seen last week, a white, plump-bodied fish with pop-eyes. His tail was a pure white film, drooping in a veil behind him. He was the most beautiful goldfish she had ever seen, large and healthy. The salesman said he cost $10.00. Camille thought that was far too much, but Vince said it was fine and pulled out his wallet. First, though, he wanted to show her some tropical fish; but even after seeing them and hearing Vince extol them, Camille knew the big, white goldfish was the one she wanted. The attendant netted him and put his plastic bag into a paper sack for her to carry.

Back on her boat, alone in the silence of her room, she placed the plastic bag in the water which she had been preparing for her white goldfish for the past couple of days. He swam around in the bag while the water temperature adjusted. He was beautiful. "I think I'll name you Fidel," Camille said.

A sea-gull circled outside the window as the sun came up. Camille could see the gray feathers and the details on his beak and feet. He seemed to be searching for a warm place to sit. He circled over and over, never alighting. The light was pink while the water, the trees and everything else was silver; everything but the boats, which were pink in the light. It was cool. Fidel was now swimming around, happily freed from the plastic bag he had floated in all night, exploring his new home. Vince had also bought a little ceramic house to sit on the sand at the bottom of the tank. The bubbler created currents in the water, drawing out Fidel's filmy white tail. Camille had come back to her boat early in the morning to see how he was.

She was spending more and more time on her boat. It was peaceful, compared to Vince's, where she never knew when he might explode.

Camille, Grace, Vince and an artist friend from the Village, Jane, were eating dinner in a café on Broadway. Jane was a strange-looking woman with short, red hair. She and Grace recited a story about a couple they knew who had been given a shower upon the occasion of their moving in together. Everyone had given them gifts, as if they were getting married.

"Are you two engaged or something?" asked Jane of Vince and Camille, who sat across from her. She had been obviously watching them with her bright green eyes, and watching Vince openly treating Camille as an intimate. Vince sat close to Camille at the table, across from the two women, sitting almost behind her as if trying to ward off their challenge. Hearing this, Camille hid her left hand, which still bore her wedding ring, under the table. Grace has been talking to Jane, thought Camille.

"Of course they're not," said Grace after a long, awkward pause. "Or at least they're not telling if they are." Both Camille and Vince remained still and silent, avoiding the question.

"I know what. . . Why don't we buy a wedding cake and eat it?" suggested Jane. From the moment she met her, Camille knew Jane was unorthodox. But teamed with Grace, the two of them seemed intent on creating trouble with their wild scenarios. "We could build an extra room on top of Vince's boat as a wedding present, for a studio for Camille."

"Or they can use both boats—one as a nursery. They could string a clothesline between the two!" suggested Grace.

This was going a bit too far for Camille, who was becoming so uncomfortable she felt like getting up and leaving. Vince had not denied they were engaged, so she did not know what he thought. She felt frozen and uncomfortable, sitting and thinking how impossible this one-sided conversation was, until the meal was finally over

After dinner they followed Jane through the Village to E.L.'s apartment. E.L. greeted Camille with a warm kiss and hug, as if she were an old friend, though she had met him only once at Vince's. From their conversation, she realized Jane had once lived with E.L. for several years. He had an eight-year-old daughter living with him named Gretchen. Thin and sandy-haired E.L. was an unremarkable-looking man, though charming. He must be wealthy, thought Camille, from the looks of his apartment. He continually gazed at Camille the whole evening, which made her uneasy, worrying that Vince might not like it, if he noticed. Little Gretchen put on some disco tapes and demonstrated how to do some of the new free-style dances. Camille joined her and danced with her, for awhile playing like she was a happy and innocent child, too

Camille handed in the first page of her assignment, an analysis of her creative abilities. Her Humanities professor liked the direction it was taking and asked her to continue. She reread it proudly on the train back home, wondering what she could add.

"When I was a girl I thought I knew everything. I could see every side of every object without even seeing it. Experience, of course, helped me "see" the other side of it. Once I had seen something, I knew what it looked like and from then on I could reproduce it, in my mind or on paper.

I also could see many colors in everything I saw. I still can. In a gray sky I see purples, browns, yellows, reds. I think other people don't see these colors because they do not look hard enough. If you point the colors out to them, they see them, sometimes. In a green tree you do not really see all green. There is a reason why the Korean language doesn't have a word for the color green. Trees are actually blue and yellow and brown. Horses in a field are blue and red and purple. Mountains from a distance are made of many grays and purples and yellows with a pale mixture of other colors."

YOYO

"She keeps you on a string."

"What do you mean?" Vince was sitting, staring glumly at the TV screen. He was upset with Grace again and the situation was making Camille upset enough to speak her mind.

"Whenever she calls you, you run to her, or you call her back and she pops over. You know, you're like a yo-yo – on a string." She spoke sarcastically, but the truth seemed to pour out of her mouth unstopped by reason.

"You know I'm your boyfriend, not hers." he said, still staring at the TV. But she could tell what she had said bothered him.

He had admitted he had taken Grace with him to New Jersey to visit his parents. Camille remembered she had gone to SoHo with Alice, to look at galleries and got back at 6:00. Vince's boat was still empty when she got back, so she went to her boat and waited, feeling like she wanted to be in her own place and not Vince's, for a change. She had stood by Fidel's tank as the time passed, and looked out the window, thought too much and was too nervous to eat dinner.

She suspected he had taken Grace with him to visit his parents, and now she knew he had. Perhaps he did it every Sunday.

"Why did you take her?"

"My parents are fond of her."

"Why don't you want them to meet me?"

"It would be too confusing to try to explain you to them. All we do is let the dogs run in the back yard. The dogs enjoy it so much." Camille pictured Grace's big, white sheep dog and Rastus leaping and racing in a green back yard. Once both those dogs and Vince and Grace had lived here in this boat. It was hard to imagine the turmoil. But Vince was talking again.

"Besides, I don't want you to witness the terrible scenes that take place every Sunday while I'm there."

Grace had once said Vince and his parents had a bad relationship, fighting all the time. And from what Vince said, his mother questioned him constantly, nagging and goading him unmercifully until he shouted back at her, accusing both his parents of interfering in his life, at which point both parents would fall as silent as dead martyrs.

She had stared out the window all evening and watched the door to the garage where Vince would emerge.

It grew dark as she waited. The rain began, a blowing, freezing rain, through which she could barely see the lights along the walkway. The wind seeped through the window she looked through, in a cold draft. She felt warm tears running down her face.

At last she could make out his form in the doorway and her heart leaped. But behind Vince were Grace and her dog. The sight of Grace there with him confirmed all her suspicions and she turned away from the window, having seen it.

She gazed around her empty boat. The radio was on because it was too still and quiet without it. She thought "I should eat," but she felt sick. She stood still and waited until she heard his footsteps on the finger slip and heard him entering his boat.

He did not call, but her agony was so great that after a few minutes she dialed his number.

"Hello." she said.

"I don't want to talk to you for two hours," he said.

"I was going to fix supper," she said. "Aren't you hungry?"

"I guess so," he said. "I'll see you later."

Camille looked through her cupboards for some food, found a few things and started to prepare them, but she realized Vince had all her utensils and most of the food on his boat. She took the few things she had and went to his boat, going directly into the galley with hardly a glance toward the living room where Vince sat. Vince did not acknowledge her presence. In the kitchen she started cutting up a ham to cook with the potatoes she had brought over. She heard him pick up the phone and dial.

"Grace," she heard him saying, "We're going to eat supper. You hungry?" She stopped cutting the ham and listened in bitter disbelief. With her heart sinking, she was even more shocked to realize Grace had accepted his invitation. She felt like taking her things and going back to her boat without another word. But she found herself remaining, and decided she would confront him later on.

October 21

Last night I was going to tell him I could not stand his attitude about wanting Grace while he had me around, but I lost my nerve. I knew he wouldn't talk about it. He said it wasn't any of my business when I finally asked him if he was still going after Grace. He refused to answer any of the questions I asked him. So I tried to tell him how I was feeling. When I was only part-way through, he interrupted and started telling me little things I did that annoyed him, things which had nothing to do with what I was saying. I was shocked at the things he picked out. Evidently, I have some annoying habits and don't do some of the things he wants me to do, which bothers him, such as not cleaning up the kitchen after I cook. He also said I never carry out the garbage, although he has never told me I should. I protested, accusing him of not talking to me about anything important. "I'm talking to you now, aren't I?" "Well, yes." I said, admitting to myself that words were coming out of his mouth. He continued, "I wouldn't even talk to you if I didn't feel deeply about you." That's as close as he was going to come to saying he loved me that night.

I recalled that, day before yesterday, I had called Vince from school in a panic, suddenly feeling alone and afraid he did not love me any more, afraid that he was gone from my life again, leaving me alone. When he answered the phone I felt comforted just hearing his voice, talking normally and cheerfully. He knew what was wrong and he told me he loved me then.

Vince picked Camille up after morning classes in his car and they drove to the Brooklyn Museum. They looked at new exhibits and some of the drawings in the basement. Vince explained some of the history and techniques used in the drawings, and with Vince's commentary, Camille found she was enjoying the museum tremendously. Afterward, they drove to Fritz and Sally's. The two women drank tea in the kitchen while the men smoked in the living room. Then Fritz took Vince out back. Vince told Camille to come along. Fritz was going to show them his garden.

The tall, weedy, overgrown garden of corn stalks was located in a tiny plot behind the house, surrounded by a high wooden fence which protected it from other old homes and yards all grown up with weeds. They passed the garden and went into Fritz' garage, a big, old, wooden structure that took up most of the back yard. When they entered the high-raftered building, Camille looked up and saw weeds hanging head-down from every beam, like tobacco. Vince looked up too, and began to practically jump up and down, laughing and slapping Fritz on the back. Fritz, a heavy-set man with a bushy beard, said he had grown it for himself so he could smoke as much as he wanted, whenever he wanted. There was a lot, enough to last him a long time, he said. Vince said he had an idea. He had enough to have a big party. He wanted to plan it right away. Then he had another idea – they could sell it. Vince took some of the weeds down and examined them closely. He rolled the heads in his fingers, showing Camille how oily they were.

"That means it's very good stuff." he said, his voice breaking because he was so excited, and slapped Fritz on the back again. Fritz grinned an embarrassed grin, showing crooked teeth through a sandy beard. He began to tell Vince how he had grown it among the corn stalks, scared all the time it would be discovered, but no-one had noticed.

After awhile, Camille left the two men in the garage, talking through a haze of smoke, and went back inside to talk to Sally. Pot was interesting, but after awhile it was boring, if that was all you talked about. When Vince came back in the house, he found Camille falling asleep in a chair in the living room.

"Let's go home and eat. I'm hungry." he said.

Back on the boat, Camille cooked steak, green beans and a sweet potato pie for dessert.

"Are you happier now than you were this morning?" Vince asked after he ate.

"I am."

"I guess I've been in a bad mood the last couple of days," he said. He had ignored her since their horrible discussion of Grace and her own annoying habits. He had not even made love to her, even though they had slept together.

Camille felt so tired she could hardly eat. She felt heartened that he was talking to her kindly, even speaking apologetically.

"Yes, I feel happier," she admitted. Vince went into the living room to sit on the couch and watch TV. After awhile he seemed to be falling asleep. She decided she would go to her boat and take a bath in privacy. As she started out the door, Vince roused from sleep and almost jumped off the couch when he saw she was leaving.

"You're trying to keep me awake," he said grumpily.

"Eat your dessert." she said, turning around. "I'm going to go get ready for bed." She saw he had gotten up and was moving around, silent and annoyed. She left without another word. Sometimes he frightened her.

When she got back, after bathing, Vince sat with her at the bar in the galley and they had espresso and pie. But when he started preparing to walk the dog, Camille got up, too. She needed to go back to her boat to remove her contact lenses. She also felt she should sleep on her own boat tonight. It seemed right. From the way he had been acting lately, Vince would not care. She had not slept on her own boat for a month. But before she put on her sweater to leave, Vince left with the dog, saying that he would be right back. It was almost 1:00 A.M.

Camille heard Vince lock the door behind him. She thought that was strange. He usually did not lock the door. She tried to open the door, but it would not open. He had locked her in from the outside! She tried the knob again, unable to believe he had actually locked her in. She shook the handle and tried turning all the locks. He had an outside lock on the door for added safety and had locked it! Perhaps it was done accidentally, but he had locked her in.

She heard Vince on the other side of the door. He had heard her rattling the locks and had returned.

"What's wrong?" she heard him ask in a distant voice.

A little fear arose in her.

"I just want to take my contacts off."

"Okay." he said and slowly unlocked the door.

She returned to his boat before he did, though he had walked the dog quickly and was gone only a few minutes. He glanced at her with obvious relief and locked the door behind him with all four locks. He turned around and looked at her with a look she did not recall seeing since the first day she met him. His eyes could have swallowed her. They never wavered; they stayed fixed on her, even though he walked steadily toward her. She felt her heart skip a beat and took a deep breath to calm herself, stepping backward. He looked so confident, admiring her, the way she looked, and sure of what he was doing. Without removing his coat, he took her by the hand and led her up the little stairs to the bedroom.

"Lie down on the bed." he said. She was still dressed, but she did as he told her, reassured at least by the fact that he wanted her to be with him. He took off his down jacket and she wondered what he was going to do. He walked over and flipped a switch. The big spotlight suddenly shone on the bed, and everything else was dark. Still dressed, he lay down beside her. Camille lay very still, trying to breathe quietly. He rolled next to her and put his arm over her, pulling her to him so that they were lying close together. She should have been able to relax in his arms, but with the spotlight on her, she could not. She felt as if she were on stage and was a little self-conscious.

"Take your clothes off," he whispered, still holding her close to him. Her heart jumped. But she sat up and began to unbutton her sweater with her free hand, feeling his eyes on her. She slowly took off the rest of her clothes, a long shirt and jeans, shoes and socks. Sitting with her back to him, completely naked, she turned her head and looked at Vince lying there, fully clothed, watching her hungrily, his dark eyes running over her body. Suddenly he was sitting up behind her on his knees, his mouth kissing her back, his arms wrapped around her, one hand on her breasts, pulling her back, one hand groping at her fur, which by now was wet with fear and excitement. She gasped and moaned, struggling to free herself from his hands, which were moving forcefully all over her body.

He rolled on top of her now, so that she lay face down on the bed. His hands moved roughly up and down her back so hard that he was pulling the skin. He picked her up and turned her over like a rag doll, moving his hands up her sides, to her waist, over her breasts, to her neck. With both hands on either side of her face, he held himself over her. He looked her full in the face and then his mouth came down on hers, open mouth on open mouth. She watched him with eyes open wide, pupils dilated with many pleasurable emotions. But then her eyes closed involuntarily as she felt his rough linen shirt on her breasts and stomach and his hard cock bulging in his jeans on her legs, and she could not move. He reached down and unzipped his jeans, pulled them open and forced himself between her legs. At that moment she would have screamed if his mouth had not been on hers, with his hand holding her face against his.

He made hard, rapid motions, pushing himself into her, waiting only long enough for her to open to him. But once in, he slowed down and began the slow, delicate movements that meant to her he was coming. She was vaguely aware of his breath in her ear, panting. He moved more rapidly and strongly and she felt herself responding to the rhythm, until he was slapping the hollow valley with his hips. Finally, in a burst of energy, he gave the last effort and fell on her, exhausted. She relaxed too, beneath him, her body still moving involuntarily, having been drawn to climax along with him.

With him lying fully on her, her body was liquid, a silver river with the weight of him borne on the surface. Her hands moved around him gently, to his trembling back under the linen shirt, pulling it up and lightly touching the silky skin beneath it, running her fingertips up and down the sides of his body, down to his buttocks, smooth and firm, up over the kidneys near the small of his back, so they quivered under her fingertips. He lay very still and heavy, trembling slightly, dead to all but the touch of her hands. She was still stirred by the emotions his strength had brought out in her, by his having made love to her.

"Now do you believe I love you?" he whispered in a hoarse voice.

Camille was in shock at Vince's revelation to her.

She had stayed up with him until 2:00 a.m., as he developed the prints from the show he had photographed. He usually did not let her take part in anything having to do with his job, so she had felt privileged he would let her share this ritual he performed only at night.

There had been stiffness between them lately. He had withdrawn after his show of emotion that night. He had not even kissed her for two days, apologizing and saying he had a cold. Today he had lain in bed all day. But tonight he was talking openly to her, after the silence and depression of the previous days.

He taped a piece of transparent red plastic over the TV screen and turned it on. He must have had a lot to think about, she thought. He had just told her that he had been thinking a lot and had decided to invite Grace to join his family at their family condominium in Miami for Christmas and she had said she was going. Before Camille could say anything in response, he added "Perhaps I shouldn't have done it, since it will be a waste of time. I still want Grace and she doesn't want me."

Then he asked her what she thought about their relationship – his and Grace's.

"It looks pretty hopeless," she said in an expressionless voice, looking at her feet, shocked over the fact that he had asked Grace to spend Christmas with him and everything else it implied. But, when she thought about his side of the situation, it was true she was going back to Billington to be with her husband at Christmas.

"Hopeless, huh?" he said, despair obvious in his voice.

They developed his prints, running clear water over the wet papers floating like clouds in the silver tray. Vince checked the temperature of the water with a thermometer. He prepared everything precisely before beginning each part of the process. Preparation had already taken an hour. The red, transparent film over the TV screen allowed them to watch TV while they waited for the timed exposures. The sound was turned down low. They stood watching the red TV, rather than each other, as they talked.

You know," he said, as if to himself, "I believe Grace thinks I love you more than her. She holds back when I try to get close to her. She asked me the other day why I didn't treat her this nice all the time we were living together."

Camille was silent, stunned by his saying these things aloud and what these things meant.

"It's a shame she didn't want children," he continued, as if Camille was a wall or a chair, with no feelings, "her career meant too much to her. Did you know she never wants to have children?"

"Do you think she'll ever marry?" she asked him.

"I think so. She's the marrying type. But if she marries, she still wouldn't have babies. I want my wife to have babies. Little rug rats are nice, running around the house." He fell silent, watching the little red people on the talk show as they moved their little red mouths and motioned with their little red hands on the TV screen. The timer went off and Vince and Camille moved together into the bathroom, where the pictures were ready to be pulled out of the chemicals.

"I wonder how I would feel if she went out with other men," he said. Camille was surprised at this. She had presumed Grace was already going out with other men. She was very attractive. Men seemed to like her. She was almost certain Grace was seeing other men, but she didn't say anything. Vince's reaction would not be good. Besides, she knew nothing for certain. Grace had never mentioned that she liked anyone else, but Camille determined to ask her the next time she saw her.

She changed the subject. "Do you think I should get a divorce?"

"I think so," Vince said thoughtlessly, leaning over the tanks where the white paper was turning into intricate black and white patterns, not even looking up. She wondered why he thought so, but she did not ask.

"It would be good to be free," she said, finally.

"Do you think you'll ever marry again?" he asked, without moving.

"I don't know." There were so many things she had never considered and this was one of them. She had avoided making a decision, avoided thinking of all the things it would mean if she were divorced. If she did divorce, there were decisions that would have to be made quickly.

"What do you mean, you don't know?"

"It's hard to think of remarrying when I am still married. I mean, I can't even imagine marrying again right now. Marriage is still a state of mind for me. Since I've been married for ten years, it is hard to imagine not being married. I've spent a third of my life in this state and one hundred percent of my grown-up life. Just not being married would be a shock."

The prints were emerging crisp, shiny and black. When she leaned over to look at them she accidentally touched Vince's arm and he pulled it away. She felt hurt by this and drew back slowly, feeling a surge of sadness.

They continued the printing process, hung the prints up to dry on a line and put the finished prints on the dryer, laying each one carefully across the plate. Camille's mind was whirling and she could hardly pay attention to what she was doing. She could not believe he had asked Grace to go with him to Florida for Christmas vacation. And Grace had accepted! She was stunned by the implications for herself. She wondered if he really had done this and decided he had.

He had said it so openly and unemotionally and he honestly seemed to want her opinion on what he should do.

But after all, she was going to Texas and would be with John. This fact must hurt Vince. He never mentioned the fact that she was married. And it was almost as if he had been married to Grace, though she had not thought of it that way, not really knowing how long they had lived together or when they had broken up. The must have broken up just as she entered the picture – something she was beginning to realize now. They had not been just boyfriend and girlfriend, they had belonged to each other for years. Just where she belonged in this picture was suddenly unclear. Still, here she was, definitely in the picture, with the feelings which Vince had aroused in her, loving him and grateful to him for helping her when she needed someone so badly. She would not be able to get over those feelings very easily. She felt herself right in the middle of them now.

"I love you," she said, resignedly, "and I want you to be happy." But she realized even as she spoke that she wanted him to be happier with her than with Grace.

Vince took more prints out of the water and hung them carefully, one by one, with tiny clips on one corner, on the string in a neat row, so that they would drip into the sink.

"I've been rotten to Grace," he said.

He was still thinking about Grace! You've been rotten to me, too, Camille thought. She began to feel tired. She had not slept during the day as he had.

"I think you have been extraordinarily nice to her, from what I have seen," she said coldly. She had been outraged at how nice he had been sometimes.

"You think I should ignore her completely? Is that the answer?" he asked, missing the point altogether. He finally turned the white light over the sink on and it was blinding.

"No, that wouldn't be very nice," she admitted, trying to be honest. She also did not believe it was a real possibility.

"It's 2:00 a.m. She's coming over to walk the dogs," he said, looking at his watch. "Why don't you get the leash and walk Rastus with her for me. I'm feeling pretty bad." He finished putting the last picture up and began pulling prints off the drier. They heard Grace at the door.

"You really want me to go?" she asked, incredulous. This was a switch.

"Sure, you know what to do."

Grace was obviously surprised to see Camille with Rastus on a leash when she opened the door. Vince never let anyone else walk his dog. But she waited politely, standing in the light just outside the door in her white coat and red boots, while Camille put on her coat. She had a polite little smile on her face, but Camille saw her eyes searching the interior of the boat for Vince.

"You're not coming, Vince?" Grace called out, leaning around Camille to look for him, after giving Camille a suspicious glance.

"No." they heard. Grace leaned farther into the room until she finally was able to see him in the bathroom, still working on the prints. He did not even look up to notice how Grace's long, golden hair fell out from under her white fur hat in a beautiful, golden waterfall.

Grace acted her usual self, once they were away from the boats and walking along the river. It was Camille who did not feel as comfortable with her as she usually did, thinking of the conversation she had just had with Vince. There were so many questions she wanted to ask, but could not. They walked their dogs, mostly in silence, speaking of shallow things.

"How did she act?" Vince asked her when she let herself back in.

"Just normal," she said.

"She doesn't give a shit," he replied.

October 26

Today they walked their dogs together morning and night. They don't seem to be breaking up to me.

I don't know how long I can take this. If he loves her, he should break up with me. If he loves me he should give her up. If I pressure him he might decide to give her up, but would always blame me for it. If they are breaking up anyway, which it seems they are doing, since they always fight when they're together, it is taking a long time. I wish I wasn't right in the middle of them.

Most of the time I work in my studio in Brooklyn. I am

painting a nude looking out a window. It is totally from my head. I modeled for it myself, actually. The nude is standing in a beautiful room, trailing a white, satin housecoat, like mine. I haven't decided what she is looking at out the window. My professor comes around in the mornings to see what I am doing and to discuss my work with me. He doesn't ask me to change anything, which is strange, because I am used to professors wanting me to paint like them. He only asks me if I know what I'm doing and when I tell him what I'm doing, he just listens and nods. I didn't know graduate school could be so wonderful. That is the difference between it and undergraduate school, I guess. I have painted for years at home since undergraduate school and have developed my techniques already and suppose I don't need coaching in that area any more.

I share the studio with another woman painter, Karen. We both have a key. Most of the time Karen isn't there. She's preparing for her final exhibition, so I paint in privacy most of the time. Sometimes I sleep in my easy chair for 15 minutes between classes. But it is chilly in the studio. It is warm if I leave my coat on.

Karen's large, finished paintings stood in a neat row against the wall across the room from where Camille was painting. The huge masses of color rubbed or stroked on the enormous canvasses seemed chaotic to Camille, who painted smaller, more orderly, realistic work. She did not look at Karen's paintings very much. She walked back and forth across the spattered, splintered floor in and out of the sunshine, which shone in through the two tall windows. She wore a heavy sweater and jacket, and over that two painting smocks in order to stay warm. Though there was a radiator in one corner that was so hot they could not touch it, the room was cold. The single-paned windows did not close tightly and let the cold air seep in. She and Karen had stuffed old paint rags in the cracks. There was only the sound of Camille's paintbrush scratching on the canvas and thin classical music from her tiny, battery-run transistor radio. Sometimes she could hear someone practicing a horn from the rehearsal rooms in the basement, but sometimes it was quiet for so long she could feel panic rising in her. She would look out the window at an occasional person walking down the sidewalk to reassure herself that she was not the only person left on earth.

Now she scratched around in the bottom of her purse for a dime and hurried down the wide, wooden stairs to the basement and down the long concrete tunnel-hall to the other end of the building, to the lobby of the Music Department, where the telephone booths were. The wooden booths were scarred deeply with names and caricatures she had come to know. She stared at them as the phone rang far away in Manhattan, ringing while she stared at "Harvey" with the extraordinarily large nose, ringing while she read "Giselle -- 375-5382" and suddenly his voice was right there in the booth with her.

"Hullo?"

"Vince!" she said in relief. She had been on the verge of tears, which would flow if he did not answer. But now he was there and his words, or just his voice was soothing the panic, pushing down the desperation and the completely overpowering sense of being alone in this alien world. She had him right there with her for a few minutes while they talked. He was close to her when she closed her eyes. He gave her something to feel good about. He heard her voice and heard her struggling to stay calm and said things that made her laugh and feel comforted.

"Little Pet!" he said affectionately and gently. "Where are you? Why aren't you here with me right now? You know what I would do? I would tickle your little toe till you couldn't stand it any more. I would blow in your ear. I would strip you naked, like a banana and swallow you whole."

"Vince." She was caught up in the game. "You know it's against the law to say such things over the phone. It's illegal to even think the things I am thinking over the phone."

"So be bad. Tell me, what things?"

"What I would do to you. . ."

"Tell me. Tell me what you would do to me, Pet. Say it out loud. Come on," he groaned.

She ducked her head and looked around and whispered things he wanted to hear. She had to use her imagination, but even then she hesitated. She was not used to saying such things out loud. She was not used to imagining such things; she had never had to do it before in her life.

Between the whispering and the laughter, all the panic left her and she went back to her studio smiling to herself, remembering the things he had said and the loving tone of voice he used, having been given another lease on time.

Sometimes he was cold or mean to her for a little while, but the good things he said and did made up for those times, and those were the things she liked to remember. She thought of the nights they spent in each others' arms, or just touching while they slept. Though she had never been taught how to make love, and had never done these things with her husband, it seemed so natural. She had never dreamed of having a lover so attentive and versatile. She was happy with Vince as a lover. This was the first time in her life her physical love for a man had been matched with like fervor. When she loved Vince, he loved her back, usually.

But the pace of living as a student during the day and staying up with Vince at night was getting to her. She was up till midnight almost every night with Vince, who slept during the day, then got up early to jog, dress and get to class on time. She had to spend a lot of energy getting to classes, listening to lectures, painting, doing homework before and after classes and walking to and from the subway in all kinds of weather. It was a relief to let herself into her empty studio at school after her first class, cold though it might be, sit where the sun was beginning to spill a thin line of light across the floor, and know she could rest in her easy chair before going on with the day. She would rest awhile, gazing at her painting until she saw something in it she needed to work on, an arm, the way the light fell on the face, or the color of the hair. Then she would get up, unconsciously gathering her materials and begin painting without realizing she was doing so.

Camille lay naked on the big, white bed, looking down her body. Vince lay beside her, covered only by the sheet, watching TV. The single light cast sharp shadows across her pale skin. She was so thin the bones created mountains and valleys up to the region of her abdomen, which lay soft and flat, pulsating like the sea. One knob rose and fell on the waves and she felt of it. It was hard. Was it a tumor? Was she going to die?

"Vince!" she said, "I have a lump on my stomach!"

"That's not your stomach, silly, that's your intestines." He placed his warm hand on top of hers on the knob, which was subsiding. "You're all right. There's nothing in the world wrong with you. You're completely healthy." She felt immensely better.

The TV was an island of sound and color in the far reaches of darkness beyond the light. Faces and bodies bounced in a rock and roll rhythm on the late night musical. "Deevo," they said, "Deevo." Camille liked them. Their faces were painted up dramatically and they leered and grimaced as if they were making fun of the music they played. It was a subtle farce. She wondered if anyone else got it.

She looked back down at her body and wished she were not quite so thin in some places and so fat in others. Her breasts were too small and she still had fat legs, in spite of the fact she wore one size smaller jeans than Grace, who seemed tiny to her. She had always thought of Grace as small and delicate compared to her. They both had the same small head, square jaw, high cheek bones, crisply modeled lips, large eyes and small noses. But Grace's hair was long and blond and Camille's dark and short. Camille decided to ask Grace if she would like to go to dinner on Sunday while Vince was in New Jersey with his parents.

Vince was propped up on a pillow, smoking, his left hand methodically going from his mouth to the ashtray beside him and back, his eyes fixed on the screen. His right hand remained on Camille's stomach, undisturbed.

Camille felt good toward him at the moment, with this unconscious connection between them. She turned toward him, closing her eyes, to sleep. He looked down at her, reached for the remote control and the room became silent and dark, except for the outside light. He scooted down and they lay together, barely touching, barely moving, aware of every motion. He began to touch her all over, very lightly, as if he was molding her body with the palm of his hand. She lay still, conscious only of his touch, yearning for him, but so tired. He turned his head, eyes closed and kissed her lightly, very lightly, as if she was porcelain and might break.

October 28

This morning when I got up, I had the familiar sad, heavy feeling that comes upon me when I think about the day ahead. The long subway ride, the going from class to class, the effort to participate, the talking to other students between classes, the way I am always exhausted, which makes my eyes close involuntarily and my head nod, even during lectures that are exciting. Maybe today I would have a chance to sleep some in the studio.

I tried to dress without disturbing Vince, making thin cream of wheat for breakfast and taking my vitamin. I wore a sweater, jeans and rubber boots, since it was supposed to rain. I put on my raincoat and unlocked the front door. That woke Vince up. He came to the door to kiss me and tell he me loved me and to have a good day.

He stood in the open door smoking, as I jumped off the boat and walked down the dock. I called back to him, "you have a good day, too." He was supposed to photograph a model today.

When I got back home it had begun to rain. The river looked dark, spotted and turbulent. Vince apologized for acting depressed lately. I told him that was okay and reminded him I had been depressed last week. "That was because I was so bad to you then." It surprised me he said that. He is trying to change. He asked me if his talking about other girls bothered me. I told him it got on my nerves sometimes, but I admire beautiful people, too, as an artist. I just don't tell him every time, if it is a man. I told him what bothered me was when he paid more attention to Grace than to me when we were all together. He said it was because he didn't see her as much, but he promised to pay equal attention to me next time.

So where do we go from here? Equal attention? I must be too deeply involved with Vince. I can say I want him to be free, but if he goes somewhere with Grace, I hurt the whole time they're together. I imagine him making passes at her or even sleeping with her. I watched them out the window tonight when they walked the dogs along the river. They stopped and talked intently at the far end of the walk, then Vince walked away to look out over the river. They stood at a distance from each other for awhile. Then Grace went over to him, they talked for a little while and walked back to the entrance to the boat basin together. What were they talking about?

I pray to God he was telling her not to expect so much from him any more. But he might not have said anything at all and he might just be saying the same things he usually says to her. I couldn't tell. Only time will tell. Maybe he will tell me what he said to her.

And what should I do? Should I tell him to forget me and try to get her back? It is possible they could get back together again. But they have hurt each other a lot and have deep wounds and angry feelings. Perhaps they are not compatible, but, as Vince once said, they have worked out a lot of things over a long period of time. I'm becoming more aware of how long they were together. They have a lot of mutual friends and we meet them sometimes. The friends ask Vince where Grace is, not realizing she has moved out to her own apartment now and I am living with him.

Vince calls himself my boyfriend. He occasionally teases me, saying "Stop dropping crumbs on your boyfriend." He calls me his "Honey" and "Sweetie" and "Pet." I ask him "Am I okay? Do you think you will keep me?" He answers "I think I'll keep you." Sometimes we look up at each other to see the other looking at us as if we wonder where they had come from. It's as if I had discovered some stranger in my bed and ask myself how I managed to find him at a time when I needed someone so much. It is always a miracle to me that I am with him.

THE TRUST ACCOUNT

November 5

I have to tell someone or I'll go crazy, or get an ulcer, or starve to death from worry. So I'll tell you, my diary. I do not know why it bothers me so much, knowing Vince is caught between me and Grace. I know it is me he loves.

I can't eat when I'm under tension like this. The situation is getting to me. All week Vince was ill with some kind of cold. I think it's because he smokes. Finally, he got to feeling better and began to talk to me, but he is still cold and angry. I don't know what to do. I think I'll go talk to Hal. He is the only one I know who I can talk to who knows us both and is not involved.

"I wanted to talk to you before," said Camille, wishing she had talked to him long before now.

"It probably wouldn't have done any good to talk about it before now," said Hal, grabbing her arm to help her step over a big puddle on the darkening streets of SoHo. "I don't suppose. I know about your state of affairs."

"Is that a pun?" Camille laughed a little ironically, then explained. "You know Vince and Grace broke up." She looked at his kindly face, hoping he would understand what she would say. He nodded. "Then, when I came to live in New York, I lived in Grace's boat and Vince kind of took care of me and I am living with him now."

"You're actually living with him? I thought you just lived in the boat next to his." Hal was surprised and it did not feel like a very good surprise to Camille. But why should he be surprised?

They were walking to a restaurant several blocks from the gallery. Renee and Ann were walking behind them and Camille could not help but notice that Renee was listening intently. An old member of the gallery, she had known everyone for years.

"I do have the boat next to his, but I haven't slept there for almost two months."

"Really," said Hal, politely surprised again. Camille spoke in a lower voice.

"I know, it's a shock to me, too." She paused, wondering how to tell him about all the massive changes in her life, but decided she did not need to. Hal was more observant than he appeared. "Anyway," she said, "Now I feel like I'm caught right in the middle, between Vince and Grace. He sees her all the time."

"That's what I call a pickle," Hal remarked.

"No, that is what I call a rat," said Renee vehemently from behind in her nasal tone. Camille ignored her, but Renee persisted in stating her opinion. "You know that Vince is a rat, don't you? I don't know how Grace stayed with him as long as she did. . . ."

Hal interrupted her in a calmer tone. "It is true Vince kind-of took advantage of the situation and now he's not sticking by you," he said. Camille wondered how much he had heard from Vince's point of view, since she knew Vince and Hal were friends and sometimes Vince came to talk to Hal at the gallery.

"I don't know what to tell you," said Hal. "I'm really good at giving advice, but really bad at taking it myself. All I can say is to figure out what you want. Your goals are most important right now. You want to be happy." Camille glanced at Hal's thoughtful, bearded face and thought about the two years she had known him and the changes he had gone through himself in those two years. Hal's live-in girlfriend had left him, but he had cleaned up the gallery, improved the office, made everything run shipshape and started getting out more, making sales. But she knew he still drank a lot. He was struggling in his own life. She realized from his point of view, her position must seem pretty clear. From that viewpoint, she saw she must look pretty stupid to have been taken in by Vince, and yet Hal must understand how entrenched she was in this whole situation. Seeing it this way, she thought she knew what she should do, but doing it was a different matter altogether.

Right now, emotionally, she was terribly afraid Vince might not love her. It was what she had gradually felt happening in John for many years, his waning love for her, and now it was threatening to happen with Vince, only more quickly. She did not want Vince to reject her, she needed love so much.

"Let me tell you one thing," said Hal. "I've observed relationships come and go, and mostly go. But one thing I've noticed: you have to be damned straight with each other. You don't be straight, right from the beginning, the very first things you say, and the whole thing falls apart."

"Of course," responded Camille.

"Not 'of course'. . . . Because you really don't understand." Hal came right back at her. "When I mean straight I mean damned straight. You can't mess up in the beginning. A lot of people take that to mean that you have to put on a good show, be polite, do them favors, all that. But I don't mean that at all. I'm not sure what I mean, but I'll try to put it into words. I mean, like, you have to be honest. Tell the girl how old you are, or in your case, the boy. Don't mess around and say something else, because they will see you lied eventually. I mean, like if you have attitudes toward things, or have things you won't do or don't intend to do, like commit, tell them, because when they find out what your attitudes really are, the jig's up.

"If you are straight with them from the beginning, you will get the benefit of the doubt and everything will be all right. That is, if they agree with you in any way."

"The benefit of the doubt?" asked Camille.

"Yeah, I see it like this," breathed Hal, raising his voice and waving his hands around, "The benefit of the doubt is what credibility you give whoever you meet and like, the more attractive they are to you, the more credibility you give them. It's like you're giving them their own full bank account. You believe everything they say. In the beginning, if they say they're as rich as Croesus, and the same age as you, you believe them. Then, after a little while, you find out they are or they aren't. But if they continue to be trustworthy and everything else they say proves to be true, then their account remains pretty full. But if you find out that something they said isn't true, maybe just one little thing, doubt creeps in and some of the trust is taken away, something more than the little thing they lied about. Some of the trust you have in them is gone and so then their account may be more like half empty, rather than half full. This can happen fast.

"The benefit of the doubt, for this person you don't want to be disappointed in, continues, even after you find out they've lied once about one little thing. It goes on until you discover another lie and another lie and it's like they're making a deduction from their trust account and then another deduction. Eventually, if this continues, the benefit of the doubt disappears and you are left with only doubt, and they have a credit of zero in their imaginary trust account. Then you don't trust anything they say. That's when your relationship is bankrupt. That's when you can't continue in the relationship unless you are sick in the head.

"The relationship breaks up, because in order to have a good relationship you have to have a full bank account – you have to trust the person you're with. If you can't trust them, there is no way to continue because there is no trust. You see? It seems like after three months any false image you clothed them with falls off and the real person is revealed. Or the false face the liar has put up can't be kept up any longer, though I guess some people still continue in these relationships for years, if one of them is blind, or if there is a good enough reason."

Camille was silent, not fully able to comprehend, but knowing that Hal had said something profound. Maybe she would know what he meant after she had known Vince for three months, because already she could see that Vince had faults. She could trust him, but she knew he had some other faults besides lying she would have to deal with if she was to go on living with him.

She was late getting home after the dinner in Chinatown, which Hal paid for. By the time she got home, she had determined she would sleep on her own boat. Vince's boat appeared empty, except for the dog. That was good. She put her things down and went over to Vince's boat. It was dark, so she turned on the lights and hurriedly began to put food into grocery bags. She had bought half the food when they shopped last, so she took only half of what she found. She had no food at all on her boat. Her sister from Seattle was coming to visit her this month, so she had to have some food for her.

She took her pillow, and put her clothes and some other things that were hers in the pillowcase. She put it and the pillow by the door with the sacks of food. She was just getting ready to carry them across to her boat when there was a knock on the door. Nervously, she put everything behind the door and opened it. It was Grace, arriving with her dog to go walking.

"Where's Vince?" she asked.

"I don't know," said Camille, and suddenly decided to let Grace in on what was happening. "Come on in out of the cold." She was almost glad Grace had shown up.

Grace stepped into the boat and Camille felt like she could talk to her again, now she had made the decision. But Grace acted like she was in a hurry and did not want to talk.

Camille did not have a chance to say anything because Vince arrived just then. He seemed thrilled that both of them were there, waiting for him. He did not notice the sacks behind the door. Camille stood in front of them and left the door open until he turned his back. He went to the galley and started to make coffee, telling them both to sit in front of him at the bar. Then he got ready to leave to walk the dogs with Grace. It seemed to take forever. Camille opened the door for them before he could see anything and Vince did not notice anything different. As soon as they left, Camille carried the sack of food, her pillow and clothes over to her boat.

She actually felt relief, undressing and going to bed in the quiet of her own boat. She was very much aware of the silence and played music on the radio to fill the emptiness until she could sleep. She had not heard Vince return, but if he did, he did not call her or come over, so she figured he had realized what she had done and did not object. She fell asleep in peace.

The silence did not last. She had just fallen asleep when music started playing outside. The boat across the dock was having a party. She tried to sleep again. The music was not loud at first, but it grew louder and louder as time went by. She closed her eyes and covered her ears with a pillow. The pounding of the bass shook the wall by her head. Noises of people arriving at the party came through the windows and the loud greetings from the drunken hosts sounded as if they were in her room each time she started drifting off. They must have put a speaker out on the deck so people could dance on top the boat.

Camille peeked out the window and saw people going in and out of the boat, groups standing out on the dock with glasses, laughing and talking. One couple was leaning against her own boat's railing. A few people were on top the party boat, swaying back and forth to the music and more people were arriving. She lay back on her bed in the dark, her eyes open. She was now wide awake. She got up and put cotton in her ears. But the pounding came through the walls and the happy screams of arriving and partying guests came through the cotton. It was so loud it was impossible to ignore.

"Why am I being tortured tonight, of all nights?" she asked herself. A ringing noise was added to the other noises. She began to realize that it was her telephone ringing. She leaped out of bed to answer it, pulling the cotton out of one ear. It was so late. Who would be calling now, unless it was an emergency?

"Hello?" It was Vince.

"I heard the noise when I got back," he said.

"And my bed is right in the front of the boat where the party-is," she moaned. "I can't sleep with all that going on."

"You shouldn't sleep next to a window, except in the summertime," he said.

"What a loud party! I thought it would quit after awhile, but it seems to be getting louder," she complained. "Can they really get away with this in the boat basin? They even have their stereo speakers outside."

"I'm sure it's hot inside the boat with all those people, so everyone goes outside. Everyone has parties in the boat basin. Just wait until it gets warm in the summer. Why don't you come over here to sleep?" He had not said anything about the stuff she had taken and he must have seen her things were gone when he returned.

"It's a lot quieter" he said softly.

"I just wanted to sleep in my own boat for once," she said. "But the odds are against me."

"Bring your little pillow and come back over. I'll leave the door unlocked. Just come on in. I'm in bed."

So much for Camille's attempt at spending her first night alone in two months. How different it was with John, her husband. She was not afraid to be around John during the day, but hated to lie beside him at night.

With Vince, it was the opposite. She was nervous about being around him in the daytime, unless they were out in public. During the day, when they were alone together she felt his uneasy feelings rising, his ambiguity, guilt and anger. Sometimes he would not let her touch him. He jumped away if she came close and moved so their paths would not cross in the room. If he was depressed, he would not speak, or spoke rudely to her, as if she were stupid. He would pick out insignificant things to criticize her about. He accused her of pressuring him all the time for things she wanted, though she was careful not to say anything that might sound like asking. He said he could tell she wanted it, even if she did not say so. Sometimes, when they had plans to go out, he would sit and the time would pass and they would not go, but if she asked him if they were going, he would get mad and say she was nagging him. He rarely took her places any more, and when he did, he did it grudgingly, as if it was a special favor to her. He was so difficult to be around that she looked forward to the times he was not there during the day.

However, if she called him on the phone, he was a different person, loving and soothing her loneliness. He was like that at night, when he was affectionate and childlike, pampering her and making love to her as if to make up for his daytime tantrums.

CONNIVING

At 5:30 on a chilly October afternoon, Vince was sitting out on the deck in what was left of the sunlight, working on his camera. He came inside because it was chilly, and saw Camille sketching the sun over the river and the boats with colored pencils. He must have liked what he saw, because he sat down on the couch and talked with her a little, and then became lost in thought. The hard, pale sun was sinking directly in front of them in a hazy sky, as solid as a silver Nickel, imparting no warmth. The silence pulled the two of them into separate worlds, as they watched the light seeping into the darkness within, their eyes wandering beyond a wall of rising mist, as if a veil was being drawn between them and the black posts of the pier, whose dark outline bent and reflected in the water. The veil of imagination drew over the line of white boats, their afts fading away in the low cloud, lined up neatly with masts jutting straight up in the still water, blue sails, rolled and covered, lines connecting boats to masts, lines connecting the boats to anchors, moist and dripping into the silvery mirrored surface.

The tide was low. Vince said sometimes dead bodies floated down-river and came to rest between the boats like small crafts docked overnight on some journey, bloated and white against the muddy bottom.

Though there were no fish to be seen, fishermen stood on the furthest point of the walk along the river, leaning over the fence with lines cast far out, floating, waiting to snag any fish that passed by. The fishermen, Segal statues leaning on the railing, hats over their noses, were only pale silhouettes in grey mist. Below them, silver water revealed the moist black bottoms of the pilings making up the breakwater as it rose and sank.

The sky lay like a pale pink baby on its mother's breast, heavy with sleep. It was so still that even sound was dead, birds seemed caught up in the stillness too, sitting silent and motionless on the wires. Drops of water seemed suspended in air. The sun, a warm red disk by now, slid further and further down through the fading sky which turned from gray to red at the horizon. Once touching, it took only a short time for the sun to sink behind the black line of the horizon and with its disappearance came a quick darkness. Camille could draw no longer, the light had changed too fast. The mist had come up and darkness engulfed them. She turned on the light.

At 7:00, after eating, Camille got up and went to her boat to dress for a party in SoHo. Vince did not want to go. It was at Alice's and he did not like Alice much.

In her own boat now, Camille was almost dressed when the phone rang. It was Philip, a friend from school, calling. He was someone who realized they had gone to the same undergraduate school and had immediately claimed her as a sister. He spoke only in exclamations, with a lot of energy and good will toward her. He said he wanted to "touch bases" with her and that they would have to get together some time. Camille mentioned her sister was coming to visit her soon, that she was younger, but Philip might also have met her at college. He said he was anxious to meet her. Camille said she would be sure to let him know when she arrived and hung up, feeling better somehow. She had a friend. She left to go to the party alone.

The party was in Alice's loft in SoHo. Alice had invited so many people that the party overflowed into the hall. There were all the famous and undiscovered musicians, writers, critics and visual and performing artists that Alice and her drummer husband knew. There were artist friends of Alice, professional friends of Alice's sister, and there were musician friends of Alice's husband. Camille was glad to be her friend, once she arrived. The celebration concerned the successful closing of her exhibition and Alice was exuberant.

She exclaimed when she saw Camille and began dragging her around and introducing her to people, taking her from one bunch of people to another. Everyone smiled and seemed very friendly, striking up conversations with Camille. They were curious as to who Camille was and what she did. Camille realized, after a while, some of them might be valuable people to know and was less reluctant to talk, in spite of feeling a little shy. She was in the kitchen, pouring herself some seltzer water when another woman came in, looking for "something non-alcoholic." They started talking and Camille discovered that the woman was a professor at the school where Vince had gone. She asked her if she remembered Vince and the sure enough, the woman remembered him very well and had been impressed with his work. That left Camille feeling a little better about Vince.

She left the party early and went back to the boat. Vince was watching TV. Camille sat down beside him for awhile, but he did not want to talk, ignoring her and grunting in reply to any direct questions. So Camille got up to fix him a snack. She told him about the party, but he said nothing and Camille regretted she had left the party early.

As they ate, Vince started acting strangely.

"What are you thinking?" he asked, when she had been silent for awhile. "You have a conniving look on your face."

"A conniving look?" She said, trying to put a more pleasant look on her face. Perhaps she looked unhappy and bored. But changing the look on her face did not make him any happier. Her false smile only made him mad. He got up and stood in the center of the room. The boat was rocking slightly from a wake and the lights threw strange shadows on him. He seemed to be staring at her as if she were some intruder who had suddenly appeared. Camille stood up, uncertain as to what to do. "I'm sorry," she said.

"You're trying to manipulate me," he said, "saying you're sorry, using your feminine wiles to control me. I know you, Camille. I've caught onto your tricks now. You're no better than any other girl, though you pretend you are. You are very convincing until someone knows you. You're just like all the others. All you want to do is control some poor schmuck of a man, get what you can get out of him and get out." His voice was becoming louder and more abrasive. Camille heard her voice rising, too.

"What?" she said. "If I'm doing that, I didn't know it. I didn't know you felt that way about me." She was taken aback with his accusation. "All I want, Vince, is to be with you and be happy and to make you happy." She tried to assure him she was not trying to fool him in any way, as perhaps other women had. But he shouted back at her.

"I'm tired of living out your fantasies! Sick and tired of it! I'm sick and tired of you. You've got a defeatist attitude."

Camille had stood still during his tirade, but when he said that, something he had obviously not thought about and something which did not make any sense to her, she was insulted. She went up into the bedroom, got her coat and pillow and started to leave.

"I guess I am defeated," she muttered. "I've had enough, and I am giving up."

"That's right," he was shouting at her as she went to the door, "Go ahead and leave. I think we ought to split up."

Camille then did something she never thought she would do, something she had never done before in her life. She turned around and shouted at him.

"I am not defeated! I'm fed up with you. You say one thing and then do something else. I can't trust you to do anything you say any more. You don't even like me and I don't like you either. You're certainly not going to defeat me. I'm leaving!" She stood staring at him, her face red and challenging, her coat half on, clutching her purse and pillow, in front of the door.

To her surprise, his mood immediately changed. It was such a transformation that all thoughts of saying anything more disappeared. Vince's body slumped, his eyes went to the floor as if he were about to cry.

"I like you, Camille," he said in a low, loving tone of voice. "I love you. Please don't leave. I want you to stay." He walked toward her slowly, his hands out toward her. Camille stood frozen, unbelieving.

Vince wrapped his arms around her stiff and distrusting body. He hung his head down onto her shoulder.

"Please. Please." he murmured. Camille could not tell if he was crying or laughing. But whatever his mood, he really wanted her to stay. She felt the stiffness leaving her body.

"Come on," he murmured gently, pulling the pillow out of her hand, where it dragged on the floor, "Put your little pillow back on the bed where it belongs. Hang your little coat back up on its hanger." Slowly he took them from her and put them back where they had been, now speaking softly and reminding her of the promises she had made to him, to love him always. Camille watched him doing this, unbelieving at first, but feeling the familiar feelings of love coming back into her, replacing the anger she had felt only minutes before. She was still shaking over what had happened, but a sad smile came unwilling to her lips when he turned and looked at her in silence for a long time.

Camille awoke early, feeling his hand moving over her arm. They had not made love, but in the cold, dawn light he was awake and stroking her body as she slept.

CASH CROP

When Camille left for school, Vince told her he would see her at 6:00 for supper. She was cheerful and seemed to have forgotten about the night before. Vince went to the garage, got in his Jeep and drove to Brooklyn. Before Camille had left that morning, he had felt sure she would suspect something. But he was going to have to devote himself to another side of his life from now on. He needed to make a lot of money and this was the only way to do it.

Vince drove straight to Fritz' house. Fritz had already begun loading the pot into the back of his own van, which was parked inside the big garage. The big bundles of weed were dry and cracking off. Vince, seeing this, began ranting.

"Hey, Man, you need to wrap them up first. What do you think you're doing? Take them back out – let's do this right. What if someone stopped us and looked in the back? Besides, you're dropping half of it on the ground."

Fritz moved fast for a man of his size, and between them the two men removed the weed already in the van, putting each bundle into a garbage bag, wrapping it with twine before they did. Then they took down what was left hanging from the rafters and wrapped them. They had to stop and go to the deli for garbage bags and beer about halfway through the morning.

"We're going to make a lot of money, huh?" asked Fritz.

"You bet. My friend, Chino, he knows the right people. You can trust him."

"I've put a lot of work into these, you know," warned Fritz. He had put three bundles aside for his own personal consumption, but Vince had convinced him to give up the rest for cash. He would be able to buy as much Hawaiian Gold as he needed over the winter with the money. After they loaded the van, the two men went into the house to rest and eat. They could hear Sally in the basement with the youngest boy, still not old enough to go to school. She was singing and working away on her flowers, stopping occasionally to speak to the child. After awhile the little boy climbed up the stairs into the living room. Peeking around the corner into the kitchen, he saw his father eating a sandwich. Vince sat in the big chair in the roomy kitchen, looking into the living room furnished with broken antiques and worn oriental rugs through the large door and saw him. The child ran past him to Fritz, demanding something to eat.

"Sally," called Fritz, "get on up here and get something for the baby, for Chrissake!"

Sally came upstairs, taking in Vince and Fritz eating with a pleased look on his face.

"Hi, Vince. What's up?" She was questioning Fritz, more than Vince. It was early in the day for Vince to be visiting.

"We're cutting a deal," explained Fritz, looking a little uneasy.

"Yeah?"

"You see, Vince has a friend."

"Yeah?" Sally stood in the door, her hands on her big hips, hoping to goodness what he was going to say was not what she thought.

"You and me, Baby. We're going to make a lot of money."

"You and me, Baby? I hope so, but I hope we're making this money working at a legal job."

"No way. You know me," joked Fritz, glancing at Vince for support. Vince had no patience for this kind of repartee. First he turned his chair around, then he stood.

"It's about time we headed out, Fritz," he said coldly.

"Yahoo, get along, little Dogies," returned Sally, just as coldly. "What, you taking the herd down to Mexico or something?"

"Or something," said Fritz lamely, as he went out the back door slowly. Vince was going by him on his way out to the garage. He wanted nothing to do with Sally. She reminded him too much of his mother.

"Where are you going?" demanded Sally, as she saw Fritz getting away from her. She feared his going to jail almost as much as his getting stoned. He was no good to her either way. She went toward the back door as Fritz backed out and turned to the bright November sun, following Vince's broad back.

"Stop!" she said, suddenly at the door too, "I can't let you do this! Fritz!" She made a grab at his shoulder.

Just then the baby brushed by her skirt, trying to go out the door. She reached down and grabbed the child's arm. Picking him up, she held the struggling child to her chest.

"Look, Fritz." She demanded.

Fritz turned around to see his crying baby and wife standing in the doorway.

"If you go and do this, this is the last time you'll see us."

"Oh, Sally. You're always saying that," said Fritz, half disgusted and half scared. Vince was waiting for him in the garage, watching him from the darkness. He had to go.

Camille sat stony-faced on the long subway ride to Brooklyn, got off in a daze, waited at the transfer platform, arriving at the school in an hour. She went to her classes like a robot and found herself sitting in her easy chair in the afternoon wondering what in the world she was doing. She made herself get up to go to her New Forms class, but she kept on wondering what she was doing and tears kept coming to her eyes. She felt like she was going to cry right there in class. She could not pay attention to what was going on. She got up and went to the teacher, told him she was sick and left. She walked back to her studio in the chilly sunshine, paying attention to nothing around her and barely got into the studio before she started crying. She threw herself into the chair and sobbed for the better part of an hour. During the next two hours she sat and wrote a letter to John on notebook paper. It was a purging experience and she cried as she wrote.

Dear John:

"I left you feeling angry and despairing. Although I am still numb, I am beginning to feel again. It is very painful."
Camille

Camille got home at 4:00 and waited two hours. During the two hours she felt an aching horror. Vince was not home and she did not know where he was or what was wrong. Why did she need him so much? She just wanted him there. Nothing else. Just to know he was there. She watched the clock. Six-o'clock came and went and he still had not returned. He said he was going to have his car repaired in New Jersey, at some garage near his parents' house. She knew he had asked Grace to come to New Jersey to pick him up in the afternoon and suspicions began to rise in her. She watched the parking garage

131

door, where Grace still parked her car. About 7:00 she saw Grace came out of the garage and walk up the hill to her apartment in the semi-darkness. But Vince was nowhere to be seen. Camille gave her time to get home, then called her.

"Oh, God, I forgot!" Grace squealed. "I have to go get him right now."

"Can I go with you? I've never been to New Jersey."

"Of course. Meet you at my car in five minutes."

It was beautiful, driving along the river at night. Camille had never seen the waterfront from the highway, which ran high on a bluff along the river, with the lights of New Jersey on the other side. Grace and she suddenly seemed able to talk about their relationships with Vince. It was a sparse conversation, but Camille felt better talking about it. Grace, at one point, said she wished she had found someone to talk to at the same point in her relationship with him.

"I don't want you to feel like I am butting into your affairs," she said. "That's why I haven't talked to you much." After that, Camille felt better about talking to her.

"At first," said Camille, "I was upset when he got into one of his moods, but I didn't have anyone to talk to."

"Well, you can talk to me, you know." They drove in silence for a while, watching the lights on the Washington bridge, shining like a draped necklace across the black velvet river.

"I think I pamper him. He plays on my guilt feelings."

"He doesn't play on mine," declared Camille. "I don't think I have any. I've really thought about it and I really can't feel any guilt. I think I should, but I don't. Yet, why am I always the one to say 'I'm sorry', as if I was the one at fault, even if I'm not?"

"That sounds familiar," admitted Grace.

By the time they arrived at the agreed-upon garage in New Jersey, Camille was feeling much better, even though there was a nervous weight hanging around the edge of her thoughts. They saw Vince standing outside the garage, smiling. He waved at the men he had been talking to and got into Grace's tiny car. On the way home the conversation was light and frivolous. Vince seemed happy to see the two women, especially Camille. They sat all crushed together in the front seat of Grace's little car. Vince put his hand on Camille's knee and smiled at her whenever she looked at him.

PATRICIA

It was a special day and Camille awoke early. Vince held her close for a few minutes before she got up, not wanting to let her go. It was 5:30 a.m. and Camille dressed and went to the airport to meet Patricia, who was coming to visit for a week. Patricia had timed her visit to be there before the opening of Camille's New York exhibition. The paintings she had done in Texas were due in from their Indianapolis viewing at Purdue, on Monday and should be ready to hang in Ward Gallery that day.

Patricia had continued to live in the South since graduating from college with a business degree, working for banks in Dallas and, eventually in smaller towns. She seemed to move all the time. She had quit her last job and was in the process of looking for another. Patricia was also a talented folk singer, but never appeared to have enough money or ambition to get out there and push herself.

When Camille met her at the airport, she seemed even bigger and blonder than the last time Camille had seen her, over two years ago. Patricia's baby face had turned a little harder and drier, as had her attitude. But underneath, she was still the same baby sister Camille knew. It was good to see her again. Memories of singing songs together, of spending nights talking about boyfriends in high school, when their parents thought they were sleeping, of camping trips later on when Camille was home from college for the summer, all these came back to her the moment she saw her. She gave Patricia a big hug. Patricia smiled, dropped her two huge blue bags and hugged her tightly, sniffing back some tears. Then she began complaining about the long trip and the airplane ride. After getting into the city, they went into a coffee shop for breakfast, each one carrying a suitcase.

"Well, tell me: What's this about your having a boyfriend?" said Patricia, turning to her bluntly, once they were seated. Camille had not expected her to sound quite so challenging. She had confided in her a little, in the two letters she had written since arriving in New York, mentioning that she was living with Vince.

She had painted a glowing picture of Vince to Pat. Pat had

133

enjoyed numerous affairs, but had never married. Camille had not expected her to disapprove. After all, it was her first affair, and Pat had lived a wild, carefree life. Surely, she would understand and approve.

"You'll meet him," Camille almost blushed as she told Pat about him. "I'm staying with him, so you'll have my boat to yourself. You'll be right next door." She knew Pat would think Vince was handsome and would like him. Patricia had never really liked John, and John had never approved of Patricia. So, somehow Camille thought Patricia and Vince would certainly like each other, since Vince was so different from John.

They met. They did not like each other.

Camille was surprised and realized Vince saw Patricia as a defensive and possessive woman, threatening to alienate them. He was afraid Camille would abandon him during the week she was supposed to stay; and that she would dominate Camille's time. And Patricia saw Vince as some kind of intruder, a villain taking advantage of her at a weak moment, seeing much evidence of this in the radical change in Camille's life-style. As soon as Patricia and Vince met, they looked each other over suspiciously and proceeded to be at odds with each other. "Perhaps they are too much alike," thought Camille.

Camille showed Patricia around the city the first day, to see the sights. She told Patricia about her new life, what she was doing, and about her financial difficulties. They went to Central Park and walked down Fifth Avenue, had afternoon tea at the Ritz Carlton and bought roasted chestnuts from the vendors. Because they were together, they had a good time. But when Camille told Patricia that the paintings she was supposed to hang in her show had not arrived yet, that they were supposed to have arrived a week before, Patricia began to worry aloud.

"What if they don't arrive? What will you do?" she asked.

Camille assured her everything would go smoothly. The truckers had promised her they would be delivered on Monday.

"Two times I called the gallery they were shipped from, and both times the director assured me they were shipped last week. The second time he said he was calling the trucking company to track them and make sure they knew where they were. They had not pinpointed them exactly, but he said not to worry. Actually, my whole exhibit is in a truck somewhere. If it doesn't arrive, I won't have a show. I can't imagine they won't arrive on Monday." But even as Camille spoke, she became nervous. This was something she had not let herself think about, but now she had to. She thought she would ask Vince what to do. Then an idea formed in her mind. But it was so drastic that only in an emergency would she would try something so drastic. Vince would know how to help her do it.

On their walks around town, Camille saw that Patricia was a country girl at heart and was nervous to be in the city. Patricia was not used to homeless people begging, or the rudeness of the clerks in the stores. She was uneasy in the subways, thinking that because no-one would look her in the eye they were all trying to hide something.

The two women walked to the Empire State Building, wrapping their coats tightly around them in the wind. The sign outside said it was too windy to go to the top. Patricia was visibly disappointed, but admitted she had been a little nervous about going up, since she was afraid of heights.

Finally, over a cup of coffee in the coffee shop they found on the first floor of the Empire State Building, Patricia took a long look at Camille and asked, "Are you happy?"

"Yes," said Camille, "But there seems to be a cloud hanging over my head all the time. No, not a cloud. It's more like a cement block. I keep on waiting for it to drop and crush me. Or it's like there is some kind of wall around me, blocking me off from the world. I can't explain it."

Patricia answered, "I know. Sometimes I wonder what happened to that good, innocent, free feeling I had when I was a little girl. I remember feeling happy and innocent as a child, but I never feel that way any more. Why?" Patricia spread her large hands out before her and looked at her manicured fingernails. She was thinking it was hard to play the guitar when she had to dress like a banker. "Do you think you can be happy without money? You've always had someone to take care of you. John and now you have Vince. What would happen to you if you didn't have any money? Would you be happy then?"

"I don't have any money. But if there was no man around, I don't know if I would be happier or sadder. I really don't want to depend on a man to earn money for me. Besides, even if he does, that isn't what would make me happy – the money."

"Right now, all I want is someone to love me." Just the same, Camille was beginning to wonder what would happen to her without John. Financial insecurity was something she knew nothing about. But this admission, said out loud, sounded less than admirable and Camille felt as if she had lost a battle. Patricia was gazing into the distance, into the mirror behind the soda counter, and seemed not to have heard.

Camille took pictures of Patricia standing in front of the Statue of Liberty and Patricia took pictures of Camille on the ferry. As they were returning over the water, it grew dark. There were not many people on the ferry on the way back to Manhattan and they got a good view of the skyline with the twin buildings of the World Trade Center towering over the other buildings, their silver shafts shining against the sky, growing even taller as they drew near. Patricia took pictures of the silver lights of the city in the gloom. Camille gazed at the skyline. Unable to see the boat basin up the Hudson River, she wondered if Vince had returned home. She was strangely anxious to see him and felt more than usually anxious.

November 12

Patricia says I see Grace as a threat because she might take Vince away. It is a dynamic triangle, she says. She thinks that's why I get so nervous whenever we're apart, or when he seems to push me away. She thinks I ought to see a psychiatrist. She can't understand why I didn't leave him when he said he had invited Grace to spend Christmas with him and Grace accepted. Except I am not sure that Grace did. She has never mentioned it. I doubt she has.

A Monday morning phone call determined the paintings were located somewhere in Pennsylvania and would not arrive in time for the opening of the show. As a matter of fact, they would not arrive for at least two weeks. So Camille put her plan into action. She took oil paint, thinner and 30 large pieces of heavy print paper up to the top of her boat. She had thought it all out when it appeared her paintings might be delayed.

On the roof, Camille poured the thinner onto an old window

pane she had found that was slightly smaller than her big pieces of paper. She took a palette knife and smeared green, blue and gold oil paint from the tubes of oil paint into the thinner, spreading the colors over the glass and into abstract designs. The oil paint cracked and flowed in the thinner. She laid a piece of print paper on the wet glass and, when she pulled if off, had the image she had created in reverse. Then she poured more thinner onto the glass and began again.

In this way, she turned out thirty loose, abstract monotypes, working solidly all morning on the top of her boat. It was a beautiful day and most of the prints turned out very well. Camille nodded to herself, thinking it might be a good show after all. The paint thinner made the paint dry in flakes that adhered permanently to the paper, leaving washes of pastel and gold soaking the background. The colors were subtle and natural, cracked or flowing, lying on the cool or warm backgrounds.

Vince had joined in executing the plan enthusiastically, saying he knew where to get acrylic and framing, so in the afternoon, after choosing the prints she liked from the ones she had made, Camille measured them and made a list, with the size of frame, matte board and clear acrylic she would need for each of them. Vince called the stores and ordered the mattes and acrylic cut to size. Ready-made frames were ordered overnight on a rush basis. The next day, Tuesday, Vince, Patricia and Camille went with Vince in his Jeep to each store where they had ordered materials. Creating an emergency show was a big process. They had only one more day left, as the opening was set for Thursday evening.

Tuesday evening, after running around all day, Vince and Patricia had supper with Camille on her boat and then went to Vince's big boat to relax. Camille had a hard time convincing Patricia to join them, saying she did not have to smoke pot if Vince invited her. Camille told her he probably would not ask, but he did and Patricia said no. In spite of that, Patricia seemed to feel a little better toward Vince, seeing as how he was in the process of rescuing her sister from having no show, helping her plan the exhibit, knowing where to go to get supplies and skillfully running them around town in his car to pick them up. Patricia had remained in the double-parked car while Vince and Camille ran in and carried out supplies. Camille wrote checks on the account that held her inheritance. It was going to be very expensive, this opening.

Vince told Camille he was sorry, but he had work to do Wednesday night and could not help her put the frames together and hang the show. Camille felt distressed at this, not really believing him, but Vince had already done so much, having delivered the prints and materials in his car to the gallery. Then Camille remembered Philip, a friend at Pratt, who had wanted to get together with her and Patricia. So she called him and invited him to help.

On Wednesday at noon, Philip met them at the gallery, where they were going to frame and hang the show. There were four of them putting the frames together with the monotype prints in them, all Wednesday afternoon, since Renee, who worked for the gallery, had heard about what they were doing and came to help them, too.

Philip and Patricia hit it off immediately, laughing and telling jokes they remembered about Texas Aggies. Fortunately, Philip, young as he was, was expert at framing. He was also an artist and had hung lots of shows. They formed an assembly line on the floor, one putting the print on the mat board, one finding the same size acrylic and putting it all in the proper frame, which had been assembled. by someone else.

Finally, all they had to do was hang the show. But it still took three hours to hang twenty-four prints. They spent a lot of time deciding what colors went together and at what level to hang them.

When the show was finally hung, it looked professional and impressive, with blues, greens and gold glowing on the stark white walls under spotlights. Hal dropped by late in the evening to see how they were doing, with a couple of other people from the gallery. They told him what they had been through, having to create Camille's one-person show in three days, and he expressed his admiration. He said he was sure the show he saw on the walls now would be successful. Finally, Camille made a list of titles for the secretary to type for labels and price lists, and they finished at midnight.

Camille locked the gallery doors behind her as she, Patricia and Philip stepped out onto Prince Street. With their hands in their pockets and their shoulders hunched against the cold, they walked along, going to a sushi bar down the street to get something to eat. The night was clear and cold, an auspicious beginning for the exhibit, which was to open in 20 hours.

In the glow of the streetlamps, the three Texans swished through the leaves from young trees planted in the sidewalks, as if it was hill country. Camille felt exhilarated. Her paintings would not arrive for a couple of weeks, but she still had a show up for everyone to see. She slipped one arm through Philip's, feeling grateful to him for helping. He was the same height she was and immediately turned his face toward her with a glow in his eyes. He put his hand over hers and said confidentially that he liked her prints and knew everyone else would too. She smiled back into his black eyes, feeling embarrassed for a moment.

"I'm treating," said Camille as they entered the tiny restaurant. But no-one was hungry, so they shared a plate of sushi, hot tea and Sake. They were truly exhausted. Sitting at the sushi bar, they watched the little boats float by until their eyes blurred, still talking about the details of the show and reminding each other when they should arrive. Then they parted with tired smiles.

Early the next morning, Camille was up and running, as she did every morning. The fog drifted in from the river and over the track. She ran through the wisps and into the sun at their edges. Huge silver timbers from fallen piers lay in the black water near the shore at angles, creating an early morning abstract, ripples surrounding them at exact distances as they moved slowly in the tide. More timbers of the same gray hue, broken, with metal straps still around them, stood erect, or leaned out of the water. They formed another abstract pattern against the bright light beyond. It was cold and damp by the river. The air from the river smelled like mud, but the breeze blew above it fresh and clear. With fresh New Jersey air going in and out of her lungs on this special day, Camille ran the track ten times, then back through the park running along the river to the boat basin. She felt the heat of her body rising, turning into sweat, the sweat cooling her skin with the chill wind she made with her running.

By the time she got back to the boat, the sun had begun to burn off any remaining wisps of fog and turned the sky into a bright white. Vince was awake and in the galley, humming already, making coffee. He had pulled a pair of old jeans over his nakedness.

"I wanted to run with you," he said in a disappointed voice, pouring himself a cup and walking toward where she was hanging up her jacket, with a multitude of questions. "But I couldn't get up. I have to walk Rastus now. Going to take a shower? You're sweaty. You really ran, didn't you? Boy, you got up early. Excited?"

The day had begun. Camille was going to classes, but would leave school early and go by the gallery to make sure the titles of the artwork were hung before she came home to change into evening clothes.

OPENING

The gallery was crowded and loud with talk and laughter by the time Vince arrived. Camille was standing near the door, and greeted him with a little kiss. She was greeting everyone who came in. Hal stood near her, checking out the prospects, talking with special friends and generally being his best, charming self. Camille looked up just in time to see Vince glance back at the door and see Fritz come in. She ran up to Fritz, happily greeted him and asked him where Sally was.

"She left," he said shortly, without expression.

"What?" said Camille, not understanding. She wondered if he meant she had come and had already gone home. But by the time she was ready to frame her question, Fritz had disappeared into the crowd.

Howard was right behind Fritz, with Nancy and some of the other students from Pratt. Meanwhile, Vince, putting on a strange, tension-filled face, had grabbed Fritz's arm to lead him away and missed seeing Howard holding his arms out to Camille by the door, smiling broadly through his red beard, and pulling her to him to give her a big kiss.

Camille laughed nervously at Howard's grand manner, but complimented him on his beautiful red jacket and the expensive shirt he had worn. He preened before her, knowing he looked good, then turned his attention to the prints around them. "What have we got here?" he asked, looking surprised, and insisted Camille accompany him around the room.

When there was a lull in visitors, Camille was able to sit with Patricia at the desk with Renee answering questions about the prints. Camille talked with a couple of people who were interested in buying a monotype, but was interrupted by a tap on her shoulder. When she turned around, she saw her old friend, Charlene, who had driven in from Connecticut, where she lived with her husband and two little daughters.

After turning the clients over to Renee for the final pitch and sale, she kissed Charlene on both cheeks and squatted down to greet her girls and give them a hug. She looked into Charlene's face and held her hand.

"My best friend."

"Since high school." Charlene chimed in. Her face lighted with a little smile that said how proud she was of her family and of Camille. It made Camille remember how Charlene looked when they first met and how much they had changed. But she was interrupted again.

"I just love the green one. How much did you say it was?" Camille turned to see a woman who had been inquiring about prices earlier. She turned back to Charlene.

"I'll visit with you in a few moments. Look around and have something to drink while I talk with this nice lady." Charlene nodded and happily herded her family away, exclaiming over the colors.

Before they left, both E.L. and Howard were sufficiently impressed to buy a print each, and soon the interior designer working with Renee bought two large ones that matched. Another sale was in the works with Renee and Ann was putting little red dots on the walls beside the ones that sold. Vince came up to Camille with a glass of wine and a napkin with a slice of bread topped with a piece of brie cheese. Camille gave him a grateful smile and he stood and watched her while she drank the wine and took a bite of bread, as if he alone was responsible for her health and well-being. Then he went to stand with Grace against the wall to stay out of the way and keep an eye on her. He was wearing blue denim jeans, a white turtleneck sweater and a camera, which he used occasionally, but he was far from inconspicuous, being the tallest, best built, most handsome man in the room. His plain clothes did not hide that fact easily.

Charlene met Camille again at the front door, where she was saying good-bye to one of her women friends.

"These are different from your usual paintings, Camille," Charlene said, as she ate a piece of toasted French bread with brie. "But I really like them. They're so. . ." she searched for the right word. "So fresh?"

At one time Charlene was also going to be an artist. The girls had met in high school art class. Charlene had become a school teacher. When Camille married, Charlene was her maid of honor, but Charlene did not get married for a long time, as she enjoyed living a fairly libertine life. At that time in their lives, Camille envied Charlene her freedom, while she seemed to be only as a slave to her husband, working in an office to pay for his schooling and being a housewife. Then Charlene married a boyfriend and immediately became a very conservative mother, quitting work to do so.

The two women observed each other as they stood in the fading light from the open door and eating. Charlene's hair was still thick and black, though a couple of white hairs had now appeared.

"Who is he?" asked Charlene, out of the blue. Camille looked up, trying to decode her look, but Charlene was only smiling her tiny, tight smile while she ate. She nodded in Vince's direction to indicate who she was talking about.

"Who?" Camille asked innocently, but she choked on her bread. Charlene was either very observant or she had taken the opportunity to gossip with Patricia. Camille had not mentioned Vince in the brief letters she had written since her arrival in New York. She knew Charlene would not understand how she, the resigned and trustworthy housewife for a decade, could take a lover. It would have been too difficult to explain.

"You know who," Charlene said. "The stud leaning against the wall between 'Thunder Road' and 'Green Mansions'." Camille had made up the names of the prints in a hurry last night.

She noticed how Charlene's red coat caught the light and reflected red onto her chin, so much so she looked as if she were bleeding when she turned her head. Her skin is aging, Camille thought. It looks dry, as if it is crumbling around the edges, even though lines had not yet appeared. Even under intense scrutiny, Charlene was still beautiful, as the structure of her face was classic.

Camille was plotting how not to reply to Charlene's prods. But Charlene was too wise to outwit and she gave in.

"Charlene, you vixen, you noticed." Camille took the liberty of hugging her, hoping she could understand. She saw Charlene's dark eyes suddenly grow warm, remembering how close they had been as young girls together. Charlene was the first person for whom Camille had felt real love, the love of a girlfriend for another true girlfriend. That love had endured over the years in bits and pieces and whenever she saw her she felt it again. When she looked into Charlene's eyes, as she was doing now, Camille felt as if Charlene was truly her sister, more of a sister than her own flesh and blood sister. Charlene knew her and was closer to her than any sister would ever be.

"You know he's special to me?" Camille spoke softly. She saw worry lines suddenly appear on Charlene's forehead.

"He's my friend; his name is Vince." Camille spoke reassuringly.

"You haven't slept with him, have you?" Charlene asked, leaning forward to whisper this.

"Why, why would you ask?" asked Camille, surprised. "He's been all the way across the room from me all evening."

"Well, bless your poor little heart. Shame on you." Speaking like this, lapsing back into her Texas accent, Charlene did not seem so cross, just annoyed and worried. "Remember, dear, you're married. You have to be careful. Don't flaunt it."

Charlene had been her heroine all the years she had lived as a free and single career woman. The affairs she carried on had fueled Camille's imagination, even though she had been living an austere housewife's life at the time. Married life had changed Charlene.

"Remember the last time I visited you? When I came to New York last year?" asked Camille. "When you actually advised me to have an affair?"

"I only meant. . . I only meant it hypothetically," finishedCharlene lamely. "You were so curious to know what it was like, to make love to any other man besides your husband. I thought a little fling might help you see it was not such a big thing. Most men are terrible lovers and I thought it would discourage you, I guess." Camille started to remark that Vince was a fantastic lover and it had done just the opposite, but thought better about saying so.

After the opening, Hal invited everyone over to his loft. Grace, Vince and Camille walked there with Patricia, who had brought her guitar, as she planned to entertain, and Arturo and Philip joined them, meeting Vince for the first time. A big feast was laid out on the table. Music was playing on the stereo. Some of Hal's friends, who were new to Camille, were there, including the most famous artist in the Ward Gallery stable, Paul Frank. A local Asian artist, a young potter named Steven Gem, had brought a friend with him named Paco.

Paco immediately began cuddling up to Camille, leaning close to her, paying her compliments and crooning things which were everyday conversation if they were love words. He was extremely attractive, in spite of this flirtatious manner, having dark, curly hair, a handsome masculine face with heavy black eyebrows over beautiful, soulful eyes, and a good body. He wore a neat, blue shirt and smelled strongly of cologne. He asked Camille if she spoke Spanish and when she said she was from Texas and spoke a little, barraged her with words she could not understand. She searched the room for Vince and saw him sitting close to Grace and talking with Renee.

Most of the evening Vince had been acting very happy, talking with everyone, favoring neither Grace nor Camille. Camille began to believe he was acting much more mature lately. He was not being possessive of her, or ignoring her. But as the evening wore on, he began to hang around her more, talking with her, pulling on her sleeve when he stood by her, putting his arm around her, playing with the necklace she wore, unconsciously brushing back her hair from her eyes so he could see her face better. It was unmistakable–he was saying she belonged to him.

Paco, who had been overly friendly earlier, was getting the message and began to pay more attention to Grace than Camille. He sat down by Grace, leaned close and touched her arm. Camille had enjoyed his attention, and in spite of herself, felt a little annoyed at Vince for scaring him away. She wondered how Vince would feel now, seeing Paco go after Grace.

Hal brought out his camera and took photos of everyone. In one of them Vince was hugging Camille. In the next Vince, Grace and Camille were all together with Grace perched on Vince's knee and Camille on the chair next to him with his arm around her. Hal asked for titles of each picture as he took them and Grace shouted "Before and After" for this one. Everyone who knew them laughed, including Vince and Camille.

They danced to loud music and ate roast chicken. Patricia brought out her guitar and sat in a corner, warming up. Camille noticed her beauty in such a natural pose, as she hung over her guitar with long hair falling down over it, in the lamplit corner. She had not heard Patricia play in a very long time and her whole demeanor when she played was such a contrast to her business-like banker personality.

Paul Frank approached Camille and asked her to dance a slow dance. Camille thought he would be a serious, quiet person, but he turned out to be one of those people who love to dance and danced perfectly with her, as if they had danced together many times. Camille found herself enjoying him more than she realized she would and danced three dances with him.

Patricia then sang some folk songs and told jokes from her old coffee house routine. At one point she stepped up on top of Hal's enormous TV to sing. "Now I've sung on TV in New York," she announced as she stepped down. Everyone applauded. It had been a successful night, with Camille having sold seven paintings, and her friends celebrating her show opening.

At midnight, with only a few people left, Hal suggested that everyone to go with him to a punk-rock club uptown, the Rocker Room, owned by a friend of his. Vince objected. "I don't want to use my beans up on a cheap kid place," he stated loudly. Camille turned her head away, feeling embarrassed and disappointed. Renee took her hand and pulled her aside.

"Please make him come with us," she begged Camille, "We need another car and he's got enough money. You're the only one he listens to. I know him. He wants to wreck it for everyone else. He knows everyone is depending on him and he won't do it. He gets attention that way. He's a spoiled brat." Camille saw everyone crowding around Vince, begging him to take them uptown in his Jeep.

"Come on, Vince," she said in a cool voice. He started giving in then. Renee pleaded with him as well, until he agreed to go. Hal drove half the group to the Rocker Room, leading the way; Vince drove the rest in his car. Paco crushed in beside Grace in the back seat of Vince's Jeep and put his arm around her. Patricia, Renee and Camille sat in the front seat with Vince. When they arrived, Camille realized they were in a bad section of the city. The doors, walls and windows of the club were painted black. The bouncer, a big man, stopped them at the door.

"Five dollars each," he demanded.

"We're friends of the owner," said Patricia and shoved her

way past him. Vince was aghast a Patricia's audacity and nudged Camille angrily, telling her to make her sister cool it. But the bouncer obediently stepped back and let all of them pass. Vince caught up with Patricia halfway down a dark hall lined with teenagers in acrylic boots.

"That was really dumb," he said loud enough for Camille to hear. "You don't treat bouncers like that."

"What do you want me to do? Curtsy?" Patricia asked him. "I'm not afraid of him."

"Well, you should be," said Vince. They had come to the door of the main room and had spotted Hal, who was already seated at a long table against a wall. He had saved them some chairs. Everyone found places to sit. Vince sat across the table from Grace and Camille. Paco sat beside Grace. Camille noticed Vince glaring at Paco, and began to think Vince was really there because Grace had come, and not because she had asked him. From that moment on, she could hardly concentrate on the music of the band or notice anything going on in the noisy, smoky room, a room so crowded she could not see the band. She was only aware of the tension in Vince.

Paco, meanwhile, was constantly whispering in Grace's ear, kissing her hand, gazing into her eyes, telling her jokes and dancing with her whenever she let him. She had not resisted at all, but was drinking steadily and laughing too much when she talked. She seemed oblivious to Vince and his explosive attitude.

Camille had a sinking, sad feeling inside her. Vince remained completely silent during eternity they sat there, glaring at Grace and Paco. Camille tried to draw him into conversation, but he refused to talk. He finally asked her to dance and bought her a drink. They had not been to a disco together for a long time and Camille felt happy when he finally asked her to dance with him.

They sat down for another set by the band, but she was bored and her attention was straying. She could hear little, but the voices four young men talking behind her were loud and clear.

"Where do you find girls around here?" said one, with a New Jersey accent.

"It depends on what kind of girl you want," replied the younger. Both looked like teenagers to Camille. "If you want to find rich, uptown girls, you go to places on the upper East Side. If you want to find arty types, you go to the Village or SoHo. If you want to find hot rockers, you come here." Camille looked around. The club was dirty and filled with raucous youth. The band was playing and singing a loud, heavy-metal piece and everyone crammed up to see the singer, standing on the tables to see better. It was certainly a place for a certain type of young people to meet.

At 1:30 a.m. Vince, Patricia and Camille decided to leave. Everyone else wanted to stay. Grace said she wanted to stay and Paco said he would take her home in a taxi. Vince was displeased with this arrangement and pulled Grace aside to speak with her. Grace looked like a little rag doll with his big hand holding her upper arm up, she was so drunk. In the crush of people, Camille could not see or hear what Vince was saying to her. He came back to Patricia and her hurriedly, saying "let's go," with a grim expression on his face. Grace was already back sitting with Paco, leaning against him, with Paco's arm was around her. When she looked back, Paco looked up and grinned confidently.

When Camille came out of the club, she was glad Grace had stayed behind. It made a statement about her relationship with Vince.

At the boat basin, Patricia went to sleep on Camille's boat, as usual, and Camille went to Vince's and got ready for bed. When she emerged from the bathroom, she saw Vince still had his coat on.

"Aren't you coming to bed?" she asked. He did not speak. He just lay down on the bed, still refusing to speak. After awhile he said he was just going to rest awhile before walking the dog. She saw him close his eyes.

Camille lay down beside him under the covers and fell asleep, but slept uneasily, knowing Vince was still dressed. At 3:00 the phone rang loudly, startling and waking them both. Camille immediately knew it was Grace, and knew why Vince had not undressed. Vince took the phone into the living room and talked in an undertone, so she unable to hear what he said. When he hung up, he came back to the bed and sat down.

"Grace needs a drink," he said. "Do you mind if I take her some of the rum you bought?"

"No," she had to say, puzzled. Grace was already drunk, she knew. Something was happening. Her mind was racing. She had no idea of what to do now, how to keep him with her.

She watched Vince to go the galley, take the bottle of rum from the cabinet and put the leash on the dog. At the last minute he turned and asked her if she wanted to go with him. She knew he did not want her.

"I trust you," she said, wishing she did.

"I'll be back soon," he said quietly and closed the door softly behind him.

Now Camille could not sleep. She got up and ate some ice cream and read a magazine, then she lay down again. The time went by slowly. "They're lying on Grace's bed," she thought. "He's giving her the rum very slowly in a small glass. She has passed out. He is undressing her. She is crying." The image was strong in her mind and she had to get up and walk to the window and look up toward the city, where Grace's apartment was. She could see nothing but the dark night through the trees. "Their dogs are curled up together on the floor, asleep. Vince is making love to Grace. He deliberately is not calling me. She stops him whenever he thinks about me. She is drunk and can't stop him when he kisses her. All she can do is cry about what Paco tried to do to her."

It was 4:30 when light began to show in the eastern sky. Camille lay down on the bed and the tears ran slowly out of her eyes. She tossed in agony. "Why? Why? What should she do? Why am I here? I should get up and leave and when he comes back I won't be here and he will know why. I should have left him earlier. I will go over and sleep on my boat."

She picked up her pillow and walked toward the door. Then she remembered Patricia was there. She would have to explain to Patricia and Patricia would say "I told you so." She paced back and forth in front of the door. Everything was silent outside. She cried loudly as she paced, her pillow wet and crumpled in her folded arms. She should leave him for good. She walked to the phone. Why didn't he call? She squatted down and dialed Grace's number in the dark that was just growing light inside the bedroom. No one answered.

The phone rang and rang and rang. She let it ring a couple more times and hung up, even more worried. "They are asleep, or are whispering to each other to ignore the call. They know it is me." But the telephone, still in her hand, suddenly rang, making her jump backward. It was Vince. "Pet?" he said. "Grace told me not to answer.

She was afraid it was Paco." He sounded very much awake.

"Why didn't you come back?" she asked in a weak voice, in spite of herself, but feeling her anger melting at the sound of his reassuring tone of voice.

"Just go back to bed and sleep," he said gently. "I'm going to walk the dogs now and I'll come back to the boat soon."

So she crawled back into the big, cold, empty bed, all rumpled in the morning light, lay down and tried to cry some more, but could not. It was cold and she could not get warm. She kept on listening to the slightest noise. At last she drowsed. At 5:30 Vince opened the door. She was lying stiffly now, angry at last. He stood near the bed in the shadows. The dog came pattering up behind him, seeking its spot to sleep by the bed.

"Are you mad?" he asked.

"Yes."

He walked around the room, remarking on how cold it was.

"What did you do at Grace's?" she asked, finally.

"What do you think I did?"

"Whatever Grace wanted you to do," she said angrily, not knowing what that might be, but sure he would do it, whatever it was.

"You're right," he answered. They were both silent with thousands of unspoken words flowing unspoken between them.

Vince undressed silently, took a shower and brushed his teeth. At last he got into bed with Camille, lay close to her and caressed her until her stiff body relaxed and she curled in grudging acceptance of him. She found him making love to her and then fell asleep, exhausted both physically and emotionally.

Camille awoke, feeling sleepy but comforted, to the sound of the telephone. Vince handed it over to her. It was Patricia, who told her she was leaving to go visit a friend upstate New York, something she had planned to do today. She said she was leaving now and would eat breakfast on the walk up to the station. Camille wished her a good trip and fell asleep again for a short while. She had to get up and go to school today.

THE TOKEN

Camille felt exhausted. She got to the top of the hill and went down the stairs into the subway. Reaching into her purse to find a dollar token, she could find nothing but two quarters. Her hand groped desperately around in the little purse to see if there were any more coins. She thought of how she must have lost today's token yesterday, hurrying for the train, or perhaps she had used them all up. She was going to go to the bank today for more money, but she had nothing now and the bank did not open until 10 o'clock. She needed money to get to Brooklyn somehow. She did not want to go all the way back down the hill to the boat, though she might have to, to ask Vince for two quarters.

She considered asking a stranger, so she could purchase a dollar token with four quarters, but she would have to beg for them. How humiliating. She would be like the beggars who constantly hit her up for coins in the streets or subways. She had stopped before the turnstile to search her purse and had remained there, blocking the people trying to hurry in. Now she felt tears coming to her eyes as the train arrived. How could she have come to this low point? She turned and faced the crowd, saying out loud, "Can anyone help me? I need two more quarters to get in."

A young woman coming up behind her asked her if she had a problem and she explained she did not have a token, or enough money. The woman, without hesitation, handed her a token and said "You can give it back to me the next time you see me," and went through the turnstile. Camille, stunned, thanked her profusely and passed through to get on the train.

She saw the woman again on the platform and smiled at her. The woman smiled back as if they shared a secret. Then the train stopped and they got on separate cars. Camille never saw this kind woman again, though she looked for her for days afterward.

Once seated on the A-train, Camille began to relax. Then she started wondering if the people near her had heard her begging. She imagined that they were looking at her, wondering what a fairly well-dressed, middle-class married woman in her thirties was doing asking people for money. The humiliation of it sank in and tears came to her eyes.

If she had enough money, she would not be in this situation, with only 50 cents to her name. John had done it to her, only giving her a hundred a month to live on. One hundred dollars a month was not even enough to buy tokens to take her to class, and eat, and wash clothes with.

She looked down at her wedding ring. She was married to a man who had plenty of money, yet she was forced her to go around without any. She was down to a few pennies most of the time, humiliated when others bought cokes and she could not even find 50¢ to buy one for herself, or, in this situation, to be forced to ask other people, strangers, for money to get by. She depended on Vince for food when she could not afford to buy it herself. John was doing this deliberately to bring her to her knees. Or he was not even thinking of her at all, a deliberate thoughtlessness on his part, which was not surprising. He did not want to bother about her, and so he did not. It appeared to Camille that this was the way it had always been with him. He just wanted her to leave him alone.

She tried to blink away the tears of self-pity, berating herself "to not feel sorry for yourself." But there were too many tears. She blotted her eyes with a wadded tissue she found in the bottom of her purse before they started to stream down her cheeks.

Yet she would not have things any other way than how they were now, when she thought about it. She wanted to be here in New York, going to school. If John did not want to help her, she would just have to do what she was doing all by herself. She would get by. She would finish her degree as fast as she could and get a job. Maybe she could get a job even before graduating. She had survived so far. She felt the resolve rise in her, partly because of her anger at John. She was determined not to let him beat her down.

"I can do it. I really have no doubt I will survive, that I will come out of this all right. But doing it is so hard. It is harder than I imagined it would be. John thought I would find it too hard and I would come crawling back with my tail between my legs. But it feels so good to be free of him, to not have to think of him, to have to care for him with his thankless reliance upon my dedication and holding me to my "duty", to not have to worry that he will impose himself upon me every day. I can endure anything if it means I can live my own life."

And that was what it all boiled down to, endurance. She could endure almost anything for the sake of being free to make her own decisions.

"He was over there fucking her, you know," she said. Camille could feel Patricia's eyes boring into her as she said it. "How could Patricia be so mean?" she thought. She knows it hurts me to hear someone say that and say it so crudely. My own sister.

"I don't even think about sex any more," Patricia explained. "It does you in, in the end. Men are rotten at heart You let them fuck you and then they think they can get anything out of you and they take advantage of you somehow or other. They think they can walk all over you as long as they give you a good fuck afterward. It makes me not even want sex any more."

"How can she live without it?" wondered Camille, when she thought about Patricia's words later on. "I can't."

November 15

This is painful for me to even write about, but I have to tell you, diary. I thought I could talk to Grace, but since last night, I don't trust her any more. Good things happen, but it seems to be the bad things I end up telling you. Vince is both good and bad for me. I really should tell you both the good and the bad.

Perhaps I should tell you his bad qualities first, because then when we break up, as we must do eventually, I can go back and read them and not feel so bad.

For instance, this morning when I got up to leave after a sleepless night, he asked me where I would live when I get back from the Christmas holidays. It was not a good time to ask me that question. Maybe this is his way of saying he does not want me to live with him any more or even to live in Grace's boat. Maybe Grace wants to move back into her boat after Christmas. He doesn't talk to me directly, he just asks me loaded questions.

He is also very erratic. I don't know when I come home from work whether he will be ranting and raving, or gentle and quiet and good to me. I think this is called intimidation, this inconsistent behavior. It certainly makes me nervous. He might even be violent, but he has never touched me in a forceful way. I don't think he would ever hit me. If he did, he could kill me easily.

I don't know where he goes during the daytime and I feel jealous. He may be seeing other women, or Grace.

I am jealous of Grace, especially. I don't know what she wants, and maybe he doesn't either, but he is willing to give it to her, whatever it is.

I must tell you his good qualities, too, to balance the picture out. I can't just paint him black.

He knows everything about New York, and I know nothing. He told me about his childhood, growing up in Little Italy, then moving to New Jersey. His father is wealthy and a well-known philanthropist, from what he says. But he doesn't talk much about him. He grew up on the streets of Jersey City. He belonged to a gang and has a tattoo on his right hand where you'll see it if you shake hands with him. Every once in awhile strange-looking (to me, because I'm not used to them, I guess) men stop by and see him. They are quiet and wear suits, but they are young, like he is. They must be people from his family or his past.

He knows every part of the city, from the Battery to the top of Harlem. He says he goes into Harlem at night sometimes and sees awful things. I don't know why anyone would want to go there. I would be afraid. But that is just him., In spite of the fact that he does not really like to leave his boat, he goes into dangerous places without fear. He seems unafraid and double-parks anywhere without getting tickets. He knows where you can buy anything for the best price, no matter what it is. He helped me get a new futon for my bed, a little desk, and the table from Fritz and Sally's neighborhood. He says if you have a need, make a hole the shape and size of the thing you need will fall into it. It seems to be true.

He is also a romantic. He gives me little gifts every once in awhile. He gave me the silver compact and some other little jewelry-type things, to hang around my neck. He gave me a tiny, fine etching of a couple making love that he made. He has good taste. He seems to love me. That is his best trait. In spite of what he says and does sometimes, at other times he is very caring. I only have to call him or come to him with my need for love and he fills it.

TRYING AGAIN

"So, Patricia's gone?" asked Vince. They were standing in his boat's galley, holding cups of coffee Vince had just made, looking through the salon windows at the sunset. On the wall was a calendar Jane had given him. Camille was painfully aware of that calendar. It filled the wall next to the bathroom with numerals so large they could be seen from a distance. The sunset slanted in the windows, as it had every afternoon since she had arrived, but it was coming earlier and earlier every day. Eternity suddenly did not stretch very far. The slant of the sun foretold less light and less heat.

"I think I'll go out tonight," ventured Camille.

"Go out where?" said Vince.

"I might go to a friend's house, or something," she said. She had to start weaning herself from Vince, getting away from him sometimes. The day would come when he would not want to see her at all. She had to start moving away from him on her own.

Vince turned to rinse out his cup. His black hair shone under the light in the gathering dusk, the bulk of his arms under the ironed white cotton shirt floated steadily and faintly fragrant near her face as he worked, washing out a few dishes. She was aware of the rough texture of the cloth, thick, even threads not quite white, with blue shadows.

"You going to let someone pick you up?" He asked lightly. She searched for some jealousy in the question, but could not find it. She did not understand.

"What?"

"Haven't you ever been picked up?" he asked.

"Picked up? No."

"You know, at a party or something."

"You mean, literally picked up?"

"You've never been literally picked up, I bet." He laughed, looking at her puzzled face. "What, never been picked up? My Pet never has been picked up?" He swooped over her and, taking the coffee cup out of her hands, lifted her off her feet and up into the air.

"He's going to drop me. I'm too heavy to be picked up." she

thought. But there she was, high above the ground in his arms, as high as he was and he was holding her as lightly as he might hold a tiny baby, with her legs draped over one of his arms and her arms wrapped tightly around his neck in fright, her eyes closed. She felt higher than she had ever been before. The sensation took her back to her childhood, to days she had long forgotten.

"Let me down!" she demanded, pressing her face against his neck in fear, but laughing at the wonderful sensation. Then he began to walk with her, carrying her over the bare fields of a January day on her father's birthday, when she rode screaming on his back and he plunged like a bronco in the down a hill. Beyond and before that, in the smooth flowing of his walk to the soft cloth and heat of her mother's breast. Back, back into the innocent happiness of trust, she let her head rest on his shoulder. Forever he carried her up, into the sun, into the shade of his cave, where he lowered her down like a cloud into his soft bed. Falling in slow motion back into a pillow, he fell slowly over her, resting the full weight of his body on hers, covering her with himself in the early dusk, engulfing her, his arms lifting her arms from around his neck, his legs lying on hers, his face on hers, lips on lips, tongue moving on hers, his body on her body.

Everything was heavy, dark and warm beneath him and she moved her body under him, closely, feeling his body tense and ripple until it curved into hers. He was holding her arms and his free hand was running down her to the places that curved and had valleys to sink into, to speed over, to return to and touch again.

November 17

It's amazing how much less confused I am since Patricia was here. She showed me how things looked from another viewpoint. I hadn't had anyone to bounce things off of for a long time and we talked every moment we were together.

We talked a lot about my life. She had sensed things were wrong with me from my letters and she came to see what was going on. She was unhappy about what she found. She did not like it that I stayed with Vince rather than with her at night. I'm sorry I didn't, but I needed to stay close to Vince, afraid I would lose him if I did not, I guess.

She always assumed John had been good for me. She was

afraid that now I was acting impulsively and would regret it later. She attributed my actions to a midlife crisis, but since she won't reach my age for six years, she was sure she would never act as I do when she gets this old. She was almost judgmental, but because she was afraid for me. I tried to dispel her fears for me, but I have to take some of her criticism seriously and I did two things she asked me to do.

First, when John called, I tried to tell him how I felt about him. She said I hadn't been honest with him. Actually, I've hardly talked to him. I'm afraid to. I've always been afraid to.

He seems to be calling me more. I liked it more when he left me alone, like he did when I first came to New York. Talking to him is painful. I don't even want to answer the phone any more, thinking it will be him. I don't want to consider him part of my life or think about him at all. I can't think of anything to say and try to get off the phone as soon as I can.

So the next time he called, I told him I felt that way and it was because I was feeling very angry at him—very angry. He seemed bewildered at that. I couldn't tell him why I felt angry, I only knew I felt a lot of pain when I heard his voice and I told him this, too.

Secondly, on Patricia's advice, I told Vince how I felt about him and Grace. I admitted to him that I was jealous of Grace. Patricia said my jealousy was obvious to her. I guess in admitting it to Vince I admitted it to myself as well. At first he acted mad, but then, over the next day or so, he seemed to sober up and tried hard to please me. At least it was good for one day.

Then, yesterday morning he deliberately told me he was going with Grace to walk the dogs. I expressed surprise that he was going to meet her.

"I don't have to take that shit," he said, slamming the door behind him. But when he came back he was more subdued and acted nice to me again. Still, I felt hurt.

Last night he could have met her to walk the dogs, but he didn't. Now he only calls her when I'm not in the boat, rather than calling her right in front of me. Or, if he does talk to her in front of me, he mentions me to her and says "we" in reference to us, yet he says he still only thinks of me as a girlfriend, nothing more.

He had grilled steaks outside, though it was cold, and Vince and Camille were eating them with mashed potatoes inside.

"Philip has invited me to a party at his house, near Pratt. It's on Friday," said Camille.

"I might go with you, if you invite me. I remember those school parties. All-nighters. They were great," said Vince, his mouth full of steak.

"You're invited," Camille was happy Vince wanted to do something with her.

"Maybe I'll go."

When Friday evening came, Vince was smoking and listening to music, his head back on the couch.

"You going to the party with me?" Camille said lightly, coming into the room.

She saw his eyes open. He looked haggard all of a sudden, his hair had gone uncut for awhile and he was unwashed, his face angry and sullen. Loud rock and roll music pounded around him.

"You're pressuring me again," he said. "You want me to take you places, to get into things I don't want to get into. People go to parties to get laid or drunk and I don't want to do either of those things tonight."

"Okay. But I'm going. I don't know how I'll get there and back at night—I guess by subway, as usual."

"At night? You can't take the subway to Brooklyn at night. Don't be stupid."

"I'm going," said Camille and went to her boat to dress. She had bathed and was drying off when the phone rang.

"When are you leaving?"

"In a half hour."

"I'll pick you up in the Jeep, Peep." He laughed. Now he sounded happy.

Walking up the dark street from the parking place, they found the address. The house was old and set back in the yard, brooding among other elegant homes built around the turn of the century in the neighborhood surrounding the art institute. Now students lived there. The windows were all lighted, music was pouring out and a single ornate lamp over the door lit up those who arrived.

Philip answered the door. He was happy to see Camille, but not so happy to see the large bulk of Vince in the darkness behind her. Camille introduced them and Philip pointed the way to the kitchen, where the drinks and food were. Camille and Vince got beers out of the refrigerator. Vince had brought a bottle of wine. The party was being given by the students who lived in the house, five of them, all of whom had invited all of their friends. It was crowded and rowdy. The dining room had become a dance hall with a stereo. Every room was dimly lit and in every corner people stood or sat around with drinks and talked.

Lots of them looked familiar to Camille. They were fellow students and faculty members. As they made their way through the crowd, Camille introduced Vince to people she knew. He recognized a couple from the opening of her show. Philip found them again and started up a conversation with Vince. Camille left them standing with their beer cans in front of the fireplace and went looking for friends. Vince, in his huge, loose, superior way, towered over the shorter, bearded, more compactly-built Philip, who seemed intent on out-machoeing him. She went to the kitchen and had a laugh with Gladys over finding a refrigerator that held only beer. She saw another girlfriend in the living room and sat down with the women to gossip.

Vince came and stood in the doorway and started talking with Janet, a nice girl from Camille's drawing class. He was making a good impression on her, Camille observed. He could be handsome and charming when he wanted to. But as she looked at him through the smoke, all she could see now was insecurity in the way he glanced at her occasionally and a bit of hostility as he looked at her out of the corner of his eye.

"When he looks at me, he sees all the women who have hurt him, probably beginning with his mother," she thought. Camille still wanted to be the one who did not hurt him, in spite of his expecting her to do so. She wanted to be the one to make him realize he could love and trust someone forever.

Her friends were all glad to see her. She chatted with some she rarely had a chance to talk to at school. She danced with Vince and two other men who asked her and really enjoyed dancing.

Vince talked to the blond Janet, whenever he could, mostly

while Camille was dancing with Philip. Philip acted sad and sweet toward her, and she could tell he liked her. He stayed and talked with her awhile, telling her he was looking for a girl to marry and saying he didn't mind if she was older than he. Camille sensed he meant her, but she just listened, nodding, pretending it was about someone else. Perhaps he was thinking of someone else. At least she could be a friend to talk to.

Vince was driving home through Manhattan, at last. Camille was tired and ready to fall into bed as soon as they got to the boat. But before they got there, he pulled the Jeep up in front of a delicatessen on a corner and went in to buy "Boros." That woke Camille up a little, as she looked around her in the dark city, waiting for him to get back.

He climbed in, the pack of cigarettes in his hand, and sat back to open them, stripping the cellophane off.

"You know Janet very well?" he asked.

"Well, yes, I know her, kind-of." Camille said. She hoped he did not want to have a long discussion while they sat in the car in the middle of the night on a dark street corner.

"Why don't you invite her over to your boat some evening?" he said, "Just say you want her to see your boat or something."

"Why?" Camille felt uncomfortable about this line of talk. Vince leaned forward, the unlighted cigarette in his lips, turned the key and revved the motor hard. Still they did not move.

"So I can see her. You can tell I want to fuck her, can't you? Couldn't you tell?" He jammed his foot down on the gas pedal and put it into gear so they jolted out of the parking place. He drove fast through the quiet streets. Fortunately there were no other cars, as he swerved around corners and raced up the empty streets. Camille turned her head away from him and watched out the side window. She wished she was somewhere else. He was acting crazy. He was probably drunk. The buildings were zipping by her. She would have been safer on the subway.

"Okay. Just get me her number," he said. Camille clenched the door so hard her hand was hurting. She held onto the seat belt with the other as they raced. He might be angry, but now she was angry, too. She would not argue with him, since he was obviously trying to fight.

"You'll do it, right?" He glanced at her with a long, serious face, then glared ahead. His profile was the kind you might draw if you were drawing a gangster, his eyes half closed, dark hair, aquiline nose and cigarette dangling from his mouth. He honked. Another car was ahead of them now, going much too slow for him, and he was very drunk.

"Sure, I'll do it." said Camille, resolving to never speak to Janet again.

Vince was stoned, as well as drunk, when he fell into bed without taking his clothes off. Camille looked at him passed out on the rumpled bed and saw a stranger. She was not part of him. She had more in common with the friends she had partied with that evening than with this unconscious man. She realized, seeing him this way that she was really on her own and would be happier without him.

GRACE PRINTS

November 20

It is all very confusing. John now seems to be trying to intrude on my life here. He called and talked to me a long time tonight. He got the letter I sent him, explaining how I felt, written after Patricia left. It disturbed him. I listened to him, in spite of a constant, overwhelming urge to hang up. I didn't want to talk to him, no matter what I said in the letter. When I hung up I thought it was sad that now he wanted to talk to me and I finally didn't want to talk to him at all, after all those years of silence from him whenever I wanted to talk about us. It's too late to talk about anything now.

He told me he loved me and, out of habit I said I loved him too. So he asked me if I would sleep with him when I came home. I had not even thought about that and, to my horror, found myself saying "of course." It must be a habit of mine, to do whatever he wants me to do. I tried to change the subject and told him I had a cold.

"I don't care." he said. I tried to tell him about my exhibition and how it had gone so well. I didn't have a chance to tell him about the opening or that it was a success, but was telling him I had to create a show in three days because the paintings meant for the show didn't arrive, when he interrupted, saying he didn't want to hear anything about New York. I was completely silenced. I felt like slamming down the receiver right then and forgetting him forever. Why does he always make me feel so worthless? So we can talk about absolutely nothing but him and his hurt feelings? I couldn't think of anything else to say after that, so we said good-bye.

I was tense around the opening of my exhibition, but now I don't feel so nervous. The fact that the monotypes sold well at first made me feel secure and proud. It showed me that I can be independent in the city. However, Vince has, in some ways, forced me to become dependent on him.

Grace had come over to use Vince's darkroom to print some of her negatives. The three of them closed every door and put the red transparent film over the TV while Grace began the development process. At first it was fun. Camille fixed coffee and popcorn to eat while they worked. But during the waiting periods Vince was all over Grace "like a dog in heat." That was the only way Camille could describe his actions. He was touching her whenever and wherever he could and began to roughhouse with her, wanting to wrestle, and strangely enough, Grace did not seem to discourage him.

"If only you would let me pay you for using your darkroom," she said, looking up at him with her big eyes and smiling a little, winsome smile. "You know there's not another one available in the city. You won't accept money?"

"You can let me sleep with you," said Vince. Both of them glanced at Camille as soon as he said it. Camille turned away. She wanted to leave, but she could not because they were in a darkroom and opening the door would mean ruining the prints. So she went to stand by the door and as soon as the lights came back on, she left.

The interior of her boat was cold and dark, but after she turned on the heat, the lights and the radio, she felt much better. She stuck her hand in the aquarium and paddled it around. Fidel was always happy to see her, nuzzling the side of the tank when he saw her. She drew water in the tub, pulled the telephone into the bathroom and took her clothes off. Somehow, hot water relieved some of the mental pain when she slid into it with a book to read. She put the book on the side of the tub, and eased into the steaming hot water, distracting her mind with the intense heat at each level as she slowly sank. Finally she lay submerged entirely, up to her nose. She looked down the length of the tub, trying to keep so still that no part of her body would float and disturb the absolutely flat surface of the water. She closed her eyes, but red thoughts ricocheted through her mind and surfaced, in spite of the peace and quiet, telling her he did not love her any more. If he really loved her he would not hurt her. And she hurt. She hurt and felt so confused.

The telephone rang, shattering the stillness. The noise made her jump. The surface of the water was shattered as she reached out and put the receiver to her wet ear. It was Vince. Loud music was playing in the background.

"Why did you leave?" He was annoyed.

"I didn't want to be around you and Grace."

"Don't you ever leave like that again, without saying good-bye." He sounded mad.

"I did say good-bye, you just didn't hear me, you were so intent on Grace."

"Oh." There was silence. Camille waited. "I'm sorry if I said something you didn't like," he said. "Grace is gone. Please come back." He was sincerely sorry. He really did not realize what he had done.

He could change so suddenly, it amazed her.

LOCKUP

"I have a friend named Joe. I always go after his wife at parties. Every party when we are all there. Joe doesn't mind."

"I would mind."

"You wouldn't be there." Camille realized what he said was true. She would not be at a party like that. She was from another world. Seeing herself from his viewpoint was like seeing herself as she might see a different person, a little, naive girl from the sticks that had wandered into his world.

Where had she been all her life? Had she been encased in a shell? Was she a victim of amnesia? She felt she was waking up from a deep sleep, arising and looking around at the real world for the first time, looking for something familiar and, not finding it, wondering where she was. Was she dreaming a vivid dream, or was the first part of her life a dream and this reality? Right now, the latter seemed true.

"What I am doing in New York, on some strange man's yacht in the Hudson River, in my bathrobe, cooking supper for a man several years younger than I? Tonight I will sleep with this strange man and early tomorrow morning I will emerge from the boat and go to a school located far away in a remote town called Brooklyn, traveling there from this island, under the ground, even under a river, traveling by a network of tunnels with trains in it, called subways, until I emerge on another island," she thought. How strange and unreal it seemed, because she could not see the city and the river as she traveled under them in the tunnels.

But she could not close her eyes and sink back into that deep sleep. She did not want to. Besides, she could not escape this life that easily any more. The new patterns and rhythms of her life were becoming her reality. She had gotten used to acting the way she had been acting the last couple of months. She had gone along on a path and could not suddenly be back at the beginning of it again—the beginning was 'way back there, in the darkness behind her. Even if the path was going the wrong way now, she could not get off of it. There was Vince she had to worry about now. He obviously depended on her being there, but he had behavior and addiction problems. He couldn't sleep without her, and she depended on him being there for her even more. Her life was enmeshed, to a great degree, with his. Either they would learn how to co-exist or burst apart. They had become mutually dependant. She had gotten herself into a mess.

"I'm starving."

"I'll have the noodles done in a minute." Camille watched the steak cooking in the oven grill while she strained noodles, adding butter, milk and cheese to them.

"I'm going to watch TV," said Vince, getting up. He had been writing something on a piece of paper at the bar. "Can you put on some coffee?" He strolled off to find the remote control.

"He was right to wonder if we could get along, when we first met." thought Camille when she looked to see what he had been writing. It was a list of the things he had bought for her recently, with what they cost. If she offered her hand to Vince, he wanted to take her whole arm. She really could not give him gifts any more. Either he acted like she owed it to him or told her she was using it to try to get something else out of him. Now he was keeping an account of everything he gave her?

They watched TV while they ate. Afterwards, Vince complained about his tooth hurting and lay on the couch while he watched. Camille could stay awake no longer and said she was going to bed. She went into the bathroom, brushed her teeth, took off her robe and got into the bed. Vince turned off the TV in the living room but did not move from the couch. He reached up to switch off the lamp over him and all was dark.

"Why are you on the couch?" called Camille in the darkness.

"Why do you want to know?" he returned.

"I do not want to keep you out of your own bed," she said. "If you don't want to sleep with me, I'll go sleep in my own place."

"Yes. Why don't you?" he said.

It was dark and she did not turn on the light. She got up and started dressing. She heard Vince get up. He came up the three steps to the bedroom and turned on the spotlight, blinding her. She kept on dressing and gathered up her pillow. Neither spoke. Vince stood just outside the edge of the spotlight, watching. Camille moved around under the light, as if he were far away, outside her world, in the darkness, rather than just a few feet from her.

"I don't think we should see each other any more," said Vince. Camille looked in his direction. What did he say?

"Not see each other?" she repeated.

"No. . . . Of course we'll run into each other outside, since we live next door to each other. We'll speak, but I don't think we should hang around together and talk. We should make a clean break."

"Break up?" So this was the way it was done? People just decided not to speak to each other?

"I want you to stay out of my life and I'll stay out of yours. I know you watch me through your window."

"I don't," she protested unconvincingly. She realized one evening when she stood against the door, looking through the curtain, tense, without moving, to see who was coming and going from his boat, he had seen her. Now it seemed sneaky and shameful.

"You can't spy on me, either, then," she said to him. He laughed a bitter laugh. She tried to see him, to make out his face in the dark, with his coal-black hair, white teeth shining and eyes glittering as he laughed.

Finally, she just stood there. He was throwing her out. How could she never speak to him again? To only say hello on the dock as they passed? How could he do that? How could he even think of it? It was she, Camille, the one who had slept with him, curling up in his arms for so many nights. They had wept together, made love countless times, cooked together, and eaten together. What he said they had to do was impossible. She could never say anything like that to anyone. How could he say it to her?

Angrily, she grabbed up her pillow and started for the door.

"Since it's still early, why don't you take your toothbrush and food and other things with you?" he said. So she found two paper bags to put things in to take to her boat with her. Somehow the motions of packing were soothing and she did not feel angry doing this. Vince began to act helpful, helping her remember things to put in the bags. He was not as abusive as he had been earlier.

"Well, good-bye, then, Vince," she said finally. She did not look at him as she went out the door with her arms loaded, carrying the bags and her pillow to her boat. She set the bags on the floor inside her boat and began putting things up in cabinets, and in the bathroom. The phone rang just as she finished putting the last item away.

"I need my keys."

"I'll bring them right over." She took the keys to his boat out of her purse and went across the dock into his boat again, remembering she had left her nightgown in his closet. She took it out and walked back to where Vince was standing by the door, holding it open. She stopped and stood in front of him. It was obvious he did not want to talk and she could think of nothing to say. The one thought that came to her mind was that he was hard to put up with, but she did not want to say it so bluntly.

"Everyone is different," she said. "Everyone has their eccentricities. You are just hard to get along with."

"Even if you do stay in Grace's boat when you come back from Christmas, we can't stay together," he said.

"I guess so," she said, but wondered why not. Perhaps he meant because he would have other girls coming over to his boat. "Well, I'm going to Texas for Christmas vacation soon. And who knows what will happen by the time I get back."

"I wonder if you love me," he said quietly. Camille looked into his sad, sullen eyes and did not speak. To say "I love you" was inappropriate and inadequate at this time. Her eyes said so.

"I know you do," he said, finally, his eyes dropping.

Camille left him standing in the open door, keys in hand. She turned back at the door to her boat and told him to be sure and lock his door, since she could not do it. He did not move or say anything, so she went into her boat.

She began to clean up a few things, preparing for bed. The phone rang.

"I'm not going to give in and ask you to live with me," he said.

"What do you mean, give in?" she asked. Had she ever asked him to ask her? "If you love someone, you stay with them. It is that simple. No one is trying to make anyone 'give in'."

"I don't want it to end like this," he said after a moment's silence. "Maybe I don't feel good because of my toothache. Why don't you stay in my boat tonight with me and tomorrow you can stay in yours." He sounded hopeful and happy again, as if his toothache explained everything.

Camille hesitated, feeling the pain of being thrown out of his boat and hurting badly from it. She really did want to stay with him, after all.

"Okay," she said, then wondered if he was playing some kind of game to see if she liked him. If he was playing a game, she did not know the rules and was only blundering along in her naive way. She really did not know what else to do. She was unused to such games.

"My door is still unlocked. Just come over in ten minutes. You don't need to knock."

Thinking of going over to his boat now was almost as exciting as the first time she did it. She waited the ten minutes, then entered his boat through the unlocked door, locking it behind her. She went past the salon and galley, passing the bathroom, where she saw him through the half-closed door, taking a shower. He had not shaved or bathed for two days, or even combed his hair since Philip's party. She stopped.

She could see him naked, emerging from the shower and going to the sink, where he stood, unaware of her. His body was really beautiful; tall, strong and muscular, with smooth olive skin, the image of the Greek and Roman ideal. He had a body the Greek sculptors tried to imitate. But tonight Vince was alive and moving around, glistening with water and sweat.

Camille was aware of his vulnerability when she saw him that way, from behind, with broad shoulders, the smooth, hairless skin of his back, the pale, lean buttocks, his lean calves, the squared-off muscles at the back of his legs, both slightly hairy, tan and long. She spoke.

"I'm here." She said cheerfully. He turned the upper part of his body and glanced at her with a smile behind white shaving cream. "I'm going to get in bed," she said.

She pulled off her pink robe and walked to the bed, aware of him watching her now, and how she must look to him in the silk nightgown as she turned her back.

She climbed into the big bed, feeling comfortable, but tired. He had soft music on the stereo. She felt herself growing warmer with thoughts of how he would soon touch her, and ran her hands down her body, up and over her breasts and nipples, tensed in anticipation. It was hard to wait to see him, see his eyes gaze down at her body and become excited, to look at his body, and to feel him at last. Even waiting for him was intense pleasure.

At last he stepped up into the bedroom, turning off the lights as he came. He smelled clean and fragrant, lifting the covers and letting the cold air enter with him. He lay under the sheets close to her, his body cool and fresh from the shower, pulling the covers up to her neck, then his. Everything was quiet and still. He rolled toward her, putting one long arm over her in the darkness, wrapping himself over her and turning her toward him. They held each other tightly, as if they had not been together for months, as if to heal the hurts that they had just inflicted upon each other. They began to caress each other in many ways. Finally he took her hand and brought it down to his cock. She held it and squeezed it, pressing it against her body. It grew harder and harder in her hand.

For a long time they lay, touching each other. He was anxious to please her that night and slowly did everything he knew she liked. She did things he liked her to do, as much as she was able before he would stop her, groaning.

At last, after all the delays and anticipation, he entered her and they flowed together, their bodies moving in a long, slow rhythm for a long time before he began to move stronger, with focused intensity. The motion was set up in her and she moved with him, then against him until they both came in long, crying gasps, together.

"Why is it that through sex we can love each other and give to each other, while in everyday life we have so much difficulty doing the same thing?" she wondered.

MOVING IN

In the morning he was suspicious and silent again. It was as if he did not want anyone to love him. "Perhaps it is too much for him to deal with – the fact that he loves someone," thought Camille. She went back to her boat and, since it was Saturday, began to fix it up to live in for the first time since she had left it, two weeks after she arrived. She began to build a shelf with some boards she had brought home for that purpose some time ago. But she had no tools to build with, except a hammer and nails. It was an excuse to call Vince, since the silence in her boat was beginning to get to her. She asked him if she could borrow his drill and saw and ran over to get them, said thank you and came right back.

The rest of the morning she built the shelf, looking out of the back windows from time to time at her view, which she enjoyed, at the water and boats, and feeling almost happy. She looked all over her boat and thought of ways she could fix it up. But the lack of money hung over her head like a cloud, stopping all her plans. She had only a radio for entertainment. She listened all day and late into the night to anything that played on it, even talk shows, when they came on. She heard a little old lady talk about how her purse was stolen in a restaurant and how it was returned and how people had been so kind to her and New York was not as bad as people thought it was.

She listened while she worked, eating a little, cleaning up things and building her shelves with the saw and drill, sawdust piling up on the floor.

When the sun began to go down, she looked at her clock-radio and saw it was 4:30. She climbed up to the top of the boat, where she could look over the other boats and see the sunset. Vince's boat, next to hers was dark and silent, rocking on the swells, dwarfing hers somewhat, it was so large. As the sun sank, so did her feelings. It was always a hopeless time of day, empty, with nothing to do but face the coming darkness. It was too early for supper and she was not hungry anyway. Besides, she felt pains in her stomach when she ate and sometimes she felt nauseous, maybe because she hadn't eaten.

She was tired of building shelves. Supper would be all alone tonight. She went down to the telephone, hoping Vince had not gone out. She had not seen him leave. She dialed his number and walked aimlessly around her boat, listening to his phone ring and ring, becoming more nervous, until he answered at last. All day she had thought of things she wanted to tell him.

"I borrowed your drill and saw this morning so I could talk to you, not because I wanted something out of you, like you said when I took them."

"I know," he said.

". . . and last night was good . . . for me," she added.

"I'm sorry about last night," he said.

"I'm sorry, too."

"What are you doing?" he asked, sounding more cheerful. She told him about her shelves and said he should come over to see them when they were finished.

"Will you sleep with me again tonight?" he asked.

"I would like to, if you want me."

"I want you." He groaned. "I was supposed to go over to New Jersey today, to see my dentist about this tooth."

"Why didn't you?" she asked.

"I don't know."

He probably felt bad and wanted to stay home and feel miserable, as he usually did when he felt bad. She also knew he hated to go to the dentist.

She went over at 6:00 to fix supper and spend the night.

December 2

I got John's usual monthly check. He has decided to send me an extra $50.00 per month, making it a total of $150.00.

I am dreading seeing him again. I know he'll pressure me to stay in Texas, and I don't know if I will be able to stand the pressure in the fragile frame of mind I'm in. I feel a lot of stress from the adjustment I made to move to New York and I am just now learning how to accept the city and live in it.

But I am also feeling stronger in some ways. I feel I am just waking up from a long, deep sleep, seeing myself in a new light and I like it! In Texas I didn't like the person I was. Here I feel excited about who I am. I feel like I have had some success in art and that gives me a new image of myself. People buy my paintings and my teachers at Pratt praise my work. In the long run I think I can see some hope ahead. But my personal life is so confusing that working it out takes a lot out of me.

Vince and Camille were finally living and sleeping separately. She saw him when she went running. She called him one morning and he met her when he went to walk his dog. He acted friendly, but cool, which was his usual attitude toward her now.

After she ran, they sat on the bench, but it was too cold to sit long and talk. He invited her to go with him to breakfast, so they got in the Jeep with the dog and drove downtown. He made her wait in the car while he ran into a store for photo supplies, and she smirked and shook her head knowingly, realizing that he needed her to sit there while he was double-parked. Then they went to the Continental Hotel coffee shop for brunch, Camille still in her red running outfit with her hair all blown around. They laughed a lot during breakfast, eating waffles with strawberries and whipped cream on top. Then Vince drove her back to the boat basin.

In the afternoon, Camille knocked on Vince's door. She had a bag of laundry to take to the Laundromat and was going to ask if he wanted her to take his shirts along to the cleaner's. The door opened slowly, a little crack at a time. Through the half-open door she saw him; cigarette in hand and a slow smile spreading over his handsome face. When she looked down she saw he had on a T-shirt and nothing else. He did not speak. He just beckoned with the hand with a cigarette in it, indicating she should come in. He took the bag of laundry from her, his eyes wandering up and down her body. He snuffed out the cigarette, took her hand and wordlessly led her toward the bed.

She stood there, feeling the warmth of his beautiful body before her. There he silently undressed her.

She lay beside him afterward, while he slept. By now, the sun was going down and the light was soft and golden behind the two tall towers she could see on the far side of the river. The dog snored softly on the floor beside the bed. But Camille felt cold and alone. She cuddled against Vince's still body, asking him to hold her.

"Stop moving around so much," he said grumpily in his sleep, and made no move to hold her at all, falling back to sleep immediately. She lay beside him a few minutes more, feeling neglected and used. She closed her eyes and before long fell asleep, thinking that when they awoke he would feel better and would hold her some more. But when she awoke, after fifteen minutes or so, Vince was bustling around the room, getting dressed in a black suit and long black coat. He looked different than she had ever seen him look before.

She got up, made a cup of tea, drank it by herself, as Vince did not want any, and slowly got dressed. Vince sat, completely dressed and ready to go out, on the couch, smoking and waiting for her to leave. Unspoken thoughts and questions hung in the air.

"Vince. . .," she began, and stopped, unsure of herself.

"What do you want?" he said in a childish, mocking voice. She felt intimidated by the tone and fell silent, took her laundry bag by the door and started to leave.

"See you later, Honey," he said.

She could not believe he would be so cold. She turned around and looked at him. He had not moved.

"I love you," she stated.

"I love you, too." His smile seemed a little forced. Was he mocking her?

She left and climbed the hill to the laundry in the growing darkness, feeling worse all the time. At the brightly lighted Laundromat, she put her clothes in the washers and settled down to wait for the process of washing and drying. Every fifteen minutes she felt a terrible urge to use the pay phone that hung at the end of the noisy Laundromat to call him and tell him how unloved she felt. But each time she thought she would, she thought again that perhaps she should not and never did it. She sat and read a magazine and wondered how she could feel so absolutely desolate after having just made love.

THE MUGGING

December 9

 Vince's and my relationship has reached a tense, awkward stage. He won't touch me. If he calls me and I go over to his boat, I have to sit in a chair at a distance from him and not speak. We watch television only. If I move he tells me to sit down and won't answer me if I speak. But, in the silence, I am finding it easier to think. It is even appearing to be funny to me, this situation. Not because he makes jokes or wants me to laugh, but because the situation seems so ironic.

 I am gaining confidence around him, in spite of the fact that he acts so stiffly toward me. I don't care about what he does so much any more. I'm not supersensitive to his every move as I used to be a few days ago. But I am still afraid of him a little and afraid to displease him.

 In between these sessions, I am studying for finals.

 Last night, when I left to go study, he kissed me good night at the door as I left and it was enough. I still want him to touch me and I want to touch him, to comfort him. He seems to be in distress.

 The day before yesterday he said, in the heat of passion I guess, that we were going to have to start living together again some day. I looked at him, disbelieving, and agreed. Perhaps it was just a passing thought, but it was nice. It means he doesn't reject me completely.

 But then later he said we shouldn't eat together any more, that sometimes he just has to be alone, meaning that was the reason we are living apart now. But it made me think. I couldn't live with him if I didn't eat with him. Eating together is important to me. How could we live together and not eat together? Eating meals with him makes me feel better toward him. If we eat together, I feel better about being with him. I don't feel right about sleeping with him right now, and that quick liaison the other day made me feel too much like a prostitute. I realize I really have to care about someone to sleep with them.

 Talking with John last time made me realize I can't be thinking about Vince while I am trying to make connections with John again.

175

I am writing this from my boat late at night. Vince hasn't been back to his boat all night and it is 2:00 a.m.

Camille was having withdrawal symptoms. Her feelings went back and forth from happiness to utter despair, remaining there for long periods of time. She was kind to Vince, doing whatever he wanted, up to the point of sleeping with him, which he asked for less often now. She felt extremely jealous of Grace, thinking Grace must have a lot to do with her separation from Vince. She tried to reestablish relations with Grace anyway, reminding herself that Vince and Grace had been a couple long before she came on the scene and that she had been friends with Grace first, not Vince. She tried to encourage Vince to do more of his photography. He seemed to have abandoned his occupation and was sometimes gone till late at night, probably partying or something, but certainly not doing his photography. He was often depressed, moody and exhausted after these all-nighters, sometimes not speaking to her for a couple of days afterward. She tried to boost his ego by appreciating his real abilities in photography. She still cared about him and wanted to help him.

Vince helped her, occasionally. He took her to the gallery when the show came down and put some of the paintings which had arrived two weeks late in their wooden crates into the Jeep and brought them back to her boat. The gallery kept some to show to collectors. Camille used the well-built crates as tables and shelves on her boat. Meanwhile, the first semester at her school was winding down. She already had finals in a couple of her classes and was completing some paintings for final review by Dr. Gutstadt. She was especially concerned about the painting of the nude at the window for some reason. She bought her tickets to fly to Texas and back for Christmas. Going to Texas was something she did not like to think about, but at least they were round-trip tickets.

On their way to the gallery, Vince took Camille by E.L.'s to visit. They sat around E.L.'s table and talked and shared a smoke. Camille talked with E.L. about psychology, which she had studied in college. He was an expert in the field, it seemed. He lent her a book to read, Rollo May's The Courage to Create. She enjoyed talking with someone about a topic on a somewhat higher plane than food or sex.

Vince had given Camille a fish and said she should bake it, but at her own house. He did not want any. She had cut her thumb earlier, while trimming mat board in preparation for a final review in painting. She lay down on the bed in her boat, placed her throbbing thumb above her head on the pillow and slept, forgetting the fish slowly baking in the oven in butter and garlic salt. She slept 45 minutes, then, smelling the fish cooking, got up and ate it.

It tasted surprisingly good. It seemed like it had been a long time since she had really enjoyed eating. During the day she had eaten very little, scrambled eggs for breakfast with toast and tea, and some yoghurt for lunch. It was now 8:00 at night. Even the fact she was eating alone did not make the fish taste any less delicious, she was so hungry. She decided she should call Patricia and talk to her, but she could not afford to make a long distance call, so she sat down and wrote her a letter.

After writing the letter, Camille began preparing for the next day, setting out the items she was taking to New Forms class for her final demonstration, a clear plastic rod wrapped in a sheet of Mylar. She would send light through the clear plastic, which created color patterns by bending the light.

The telephone rang. She looked at the clock. It was 9:30. Vince asked her if she wanted to come over and watch a good movie coming on TV. So she took the things she was working on and went to his boat. He helped her create the box that held the rod and the light, which acted like a projector, while they watched the movie. At midnight it was finished. Camille felt very tired. She gathered up her things, gave Vince a peck on his proffered cheek and left.

Vince watched her go. He was sorry she did not have a TV. He would have to get one for her.

Camille was lying in Vince's bed, half asleep. Morning light was just coming in the windows. She had awakened when Vince got up to dress. He picked up the telephone and called Grace, asking her to go to New Jersey with him. Camille felt hurt. She had just spent the first night with him in a long time and here he was, calling Grace to spend the day with him.

"Why don't you ever invite me?" she asked, getting up and dressing, with her back to him, wanting to leave. "Why did you invite

Grace? I thought you didn't want to see her any more."

"I don't want to," he said slowly. He searched around for the dog's leash. "We're going to run the dogs at my parents' house."

"Maybe it's a habit." Camille muttered. "What we have here is your basic love/hate relationship. You both want to hurt each other. She's curt and rude to you and you hurt her in other, more subtle ways–doing little things you know will hurt her. Like–you'll probably tell her you slept with me last night."

"Maybe." he said.

"You need to decide. Maybe you haven't really decided what you are going to do," suggested Camille. "I need to decide, too, what I'm going to do. Should I divorce John?" She looked up from buttoning her blouse with a curious look on her face.

"I need to divorce Grace." Vince made the statement resolutely. "That's what I'll do. I'll divorce her. I'll get the papers from my friend, Joe. He's an attorney. He'll play along with it. We never married, but she always talked about it, saying we were really married. We did live together seven years, after all; enough to be a common law marriage. It will be a joke."

"Now what?"

"I've got an idea. Let's mug him!" Grace said. She and Camille were hiding in the bushes watching Vince. They had all gone out on Saturday morning to run and walk the dogs. He stopped for his dog to pee and the two women had continued on down the walk. They had looked at each other with a smile and jumped into the bushes together. "We'll jump on him when he comes by."

"All right."

When Vince walked by, looking ahead to see where the women had gone, they leaped on him from behind and both grabbing him around the neck, tried to drag him down. He staggered and almost fell, but realized what they were doing and, with a grim but happy look, tried to shake them off.

The two dogs jumped around them, leaping and barking excitedly at the noisy game, adding to the noise of the women screaming. Vince bent over frontwards and grabbed them, one under each arm. He tried to throw them over his back as he leaned over.

"You can't mug me. I'll mug you!" he said, lifting each one up in the air in turn, while the other tried to rescue her.

In the heat of playing, they did not feel the cold, but after a minute Vince said he was freezing. He invited the two of them back to his boat to warm up. They gleefully went back down into the boat basin with the dogs trailing after them.

Once in the boat, the two women looked at each other merrily and jumped him again as soon as the door closed behind them, laughing and screaming. Camille tackled his legs this time, while Grace grabbed his arms and tried to pin them behind him. But he stood unmoving, as strong as a rock and the two women could not throw him down. His legs seemed glued to the floor.

"Come on, now. You'll have to do better than that. There are two of you and only one of me." he taunted. He was using the energy of the women against them. Their attacks on him only caused them to fall down, as they seemed to glance off his body. Then he moved. He turned toward the two women and, with Camille clinging helplessly to one of his arms, he lifted Grace up and laid her down on the floor, rolling on top of her as she struggled to get up. Camille tried to rescue her. But with his other arm he grabbed Camille and pulled her down too, still screaming. To hold Camille down, he had to release Grace somewhat and she jumped up and tried to help Camille get up.

It was great fun, though scary for the women, who knew it could turn serious in a second, if Vince wished. He was still bundled up in his puffy ski jacket and the girls were still in winter running clothes and the heat began to get to them. Camille could feel heat pouring out of the opening of his jacket as Vince lay on top of her, pretending to bite her neck. The next moment Grace was down on the rug, laughing, and Camille was jumping up, pulling on Vince and screaming "I'll save you!" with true emotion.

Finally they stopped in mutual exhaustion, and stood panting for awhile. Vince moved into the galley, took his jacket off and offered to make hot chocolate while they cooled down.

Camille said she would go home to shower and come back. When she returned, Grace was still there. Somehow the horseplay had relieved a lot of the tensions the three had felt between them for the past couple of months. Camille found it easier to talk with Grace. The two women talked a lot, sitting, facing each other on twin deck chairs while Vince sat like a peacock on the couch, his dark eyes appreciatively moving between them, watching their legs and the movement of their arms. Grace suggested Camille should come up to her place for supper later in the week and Camille agreed. They were friends again.

After an hour, Grace got up and left. Once she was gone, Vince's mood deteriorated, so Camille decided to leave, too. She said good-bye, but Vince stood in the window, glaring at the gray water out the back of the boat.

He had not been able to sleep last night. Events from his childhood haunted him; he relived the terrors of the streets of New Jersey. It still bothered him that he killed someone when he was a teenager. Occurring over and over in his dreams, he saw the body falling. The gang was fighting with a rival gang on the top of a building. He stabbed a boy and threw him over the edge. When they ran he could not look back. He just remembered the boy falling down.

Sometimes he frightened Grace and now he frightened Camille. He was not the gentle man they thought he was. He had too many dark thoughts inside him. He had done terrible things.

He missed his buddy Chino, who lived in Miami now, but stayed in touch and visited sometimes. He had a good business, running a cigarette boat out beyond the Coast Guard limits and back. Chino still helped his friends and now he was helping Chino, too.

Camille tried to eat supper, extremely aware of being alone in the world. She found it impossible to put the food to her lips. Her stomach felt as if it was coming up into her throat and tears kept coming to her eyes. She made a decision that on Monday she would go to the school clinic and find out what was wrong. Now she could eat.

She consumed the hot dog quickly and washed the one plate she had eaten from, and then looked around the quiet boat. Clouds had begun to cover the sky with a blanket of dark gray, as if it would snow again. Inside herself she felt jangling red threads, as if some of the live nerves had no connection at one end, having been cut at their source, and each one was screaming. She felt like screaming herself, but forced her mind away from the thought, looking for distraction.

Fidel swam slowly in his lighted tank, his long white tail

trailing peacefully behind him. She put her finger up to the glass and he nosed it as if he could feel it through the glass. She put her hand into the water, which was cold. He swam trustingly into it and she cupped it around his slick body and held it gently, without feeling any resistance. He did not struggle, and when she released him he drifted slowly downward for a second, as if he had been asleep.

Camille felt her insides calming, the sensations of tensions resting, leaving as she watched beautiful, calm Fidel swim.

The next morning Vince called her and came over to her boat. He said he wanted her to type something for him on her typewriter. He couldn't type.

"What is this, why are you doing this?" she asked when she saw what he had. He rolled some official divorce subpoena papers into her typewriter and motioned for her to sit down. It was difficult to believe he was going to play such a cruel practical joke on Grace after having, just a few days before, played with her innocently as if he held no grudges. She refused to sit, so he did, and began to type.

"Jane thinks it's a great idea," he said. "We'll all get a good laugh out of it."

"I don't think Grace will laugh. I don't think she will like it at all."

"Look at these papers. Do they look official?"

He sat down at Camille's typewriter and started typing dates and names. It did look official.

"Where did you get them?"

"Joe. It's just an extra one from his office. He's an attorney."

"Oh. Vince, you can't do this," she said.

"Leave me alone. I know what I'm doing and Grace will love it, once she realizes it's a joke."

"Who is going to sign it?" asked Camille, indicating the place for the sheriff's signature, "Not me."

"No." He snatched the papers out and turned them over, putting them in the typewriter again to type the other side. "Jane's coming over now. She said she would sign it and take it and put it under Grace's door this morning. I'm going to take Grace to New Jersey with me today. You don't have to take part in it, if you don't want to. I just wish you would type this damn thing for me. I'm terrible at typing." He was pecking at the typewriter slowly. Camille stood back and waited for him to finish. She had to get ready for school. She did not tell him that she and Grace had planned to have supper together that night.

"Just don't say anything to Grace about this." He stopped and glared at her, meaningfully.

"Vince. This is terrible. But I won't." She had thought of warning Grace, but perhaps she should stay out of it. "You've been planning this a long time, haven't you?"

"For a couple of days. There." He pulled the paper out of the typewriter and looked at it carefully, making last minute corrections with white fluid. He examined it once more and, hearing something outside, went to the door. Jane was there. At Camille's invitation, she came in.

Her short red hair was cut in punk style and she wore a furry black coat, a short dress and tall boots. Her white face looked ghostly in contrast with the dark colors, kohl-blackened eyes and red lips. It made her look old. She glanced around the room.

"You've changed your place a little, haven't you?" She saw the almost empty room held only shelves that Camille had built to work on and her drawing and painting equipment. "I like this; it's more of an artist's studio than a boat."

They soon left and Camille returned to her routine of getting ready for classes. She told herself she would not speak to Vince again that day. She was sure Grace would be in bad shape that night and she wanted no part of it.

She was bathing and getting dressed to go to Grace's when the phone rang. She got up and pulled it into the bathroom with her while she put on makeup.

"Are you feeling okay?" Vince asked. "What are you doing?" He must be curious about why she had not spoken with him during the day, but she did not want to hear about his day with Grace.

"I'm getting ready to go to Grace's. We're having supper."

"Oh." Vince remained silent for awhile. Camille did not offer anything else. "Well, call me when you get back."

"Okay. Bye."

She was anxious, wondering what Grace's reaction to the divorce summons had been. She must have found it by now, having returned from New Jersey in the late afternoon. It was still too early to leave, so she dabbled her hand in Fidel's aquarium. A tensor lamp shown through the side of the glass, sending waves of light rippling along the length of white wall behind it and casting a huge shadow of the fish there. Fidel swam through the ripples, his long tail streaming behind him, with the wall as water, his shadow traveling the length of the room. He was present in spirit while she sketched awhile at her table, hovering over her on the wall she felt a giant Fidel watching her. Looking at the aquarium she could see his tiny, silvery body. He was much more beautiful than his shadow. Pure white, his plump little body glistened with health. His large eyes protruding black above a white, gasping mouth, seeming to watch her with interest from behind the glass. When she moved closer to him, he moved closer to the glass, pressing on it here and there, trying to swim into the sea he saw Camille swimming in, to be with her.

"Fidel." she said aloud, almost frightening herself with her own voice. Then softer, "Here, Fiddy, Fiddy." She put her hand into his sea, feeling the sudden coolness of water, the strange resistance to fast movement as she moved slowly toward Fidel, who waited.

Suddenly the telephone rang. She reached for it and let her other hand drip.

"Hello?" It was Vince again.

"You want to watch Masterpiece Theater with us? I invited Grace to stay here and watch it." Evidently her plans had changed. Camille was disappointed. She had looked forward to going to Grace's that night. Vince was intruding into their lives, changing their plans now.

"I'll be over soon," she said. She realized Grace had not even been home yet and therefore did not know about the summons under her door. Vince had not wanted her to find it just before Camille arrived for supper, so he had made her stay at his boat. She must have been there when he called earlier.

Camille went over to Vince's. She was thinking of how she might warn Grace about what she would find when she went home. But perhaps she would think it was a funny joke, as Vince said she would. It must not be too serious or Vince would not be doing this to her. She knew they had shared many practical jokes, played on each other and on other people.

Grace and Vince were sitting in their usual places, acting as they normally did. The program had begun. It was good and Camille did not have a chance to talk to Grace alone, as Vince remained with them. They did talk about how their plans had changed for the evening, but Grace promised Camille supper another night. She was exhausted from the trip to Jersey.

At 11:00 Grace gathered up her coat and her dog and said she was going home. Vince and Camille sat waiting after she had gone. It seemed like a long time before the phone rang. From the way Vince looked, she had taken the joke badly, thinking he was actually suing her for divorce.

He listened to her talk for a few minutes.

"I always said I wanted a settlement from you when we broke up," he said, trying to sound serious and not to laugh. "According to common law, you are my wife." Camille watched his face. It changed from laughing to being angry. He listened for another minute, and then hung up.

"She hung up on me," he said, puzzled.

"Didn't you tell her it was a joke?" asked Camille.

He looked at her glumly and dialed Grace's number. When she answered he said "It's a joke!" But she hung up on him again. He dialed her number again, but she refused to answer.

Now Vince was feeling upset. He put on his ski jacket and went out, saying he was going up to her apartment to try to talk to her. He told Camille to wait for him here. She waited a half hour and he returned.

When he got back he said she would not answer the door. He unzipped his coat and paced around the room. It was beginning to rain a freezing rain.

"I have to talk to her, so she won't feel so bad," he said, zipping his coat again. He was getting worried. He took his black hat and put it on and went out. Wait here. You can sleep in my bed if you're tired.

When he came back at 12:30, he told her Grace had finally let him in. He had stood out in the wet snow until then, in front of the building, calling her name from below. She talked to him for an hour. He sounded guilty, but not very sorry, thought Camille.

Camille was still lying on his bed, where she had gone to

sleep, exhausted from the hectic day she had spent. He turned off the light and the TV and lay down beside her with his clothes on. She put her arms around him when he rolled over by her. She kept on falling asleep, but stayed with him all night. She felt an allegiance toward him. This "divorce" had been significant for all of them.

THE DATE

Vince was sitting with Camille at the table in her boat while she drank a cup of coffee. He was coming over to be with her more than she went to be with him these days, especially since she had decided to sleep at home.

"I've decided to do things with other people more, Vince. I've been thinking a lot about it and I've decided." Camille made the statement bravely, but glanced at Vince uneasily. "If you hadn't asked, I would not have told you I was going out. I would really like to have supper with you, you know that, but you don't need to act surprised about me going out. You've told me enough times I ought to go out with other people."

Vince was glum.

"You sure get around for someone who has no experience," he said.

"Francis is an old friend. I knew his mother in Texas and when I came here she gave me his number. I've known him a long time. I always call him when I come to New York. He was doing insurance sales and singing in a choir, but now he's an actor. He only takes me out to dinner to catch up on the gossip back home."

Vince took this all in, but didn't respond immediately.

"I don't care if you do sleep with other men," he finally said, nonchalantly.

"Oh yeah?" Camille's voice showed surprise. What he said implied his own attitudes, but he was jumping to conclusions about hers.

"Yeah." Vince smiled, understanding. He stood up and walked over to Camille, clinching her crossed legs between his long ones as he stood over her. Camille put her hand on his firm stomach to hold him away.

"I got a letter from John today," she said.

"Well, hey, I got a letter from Chino. Did you know that it's 80 degrees in Miami?"

"My fish would like that. It's been cold on my boat."

"You'll get used to it, my poor little Pet. You came all the way from Texas to get snowed on. Are you sure you like New York? Don't you want to go home, now that it's getting cold?"

"I like the cold. I hate hot weather. I'll never forget the day John and I got married. It was 104° in the shade. It never got below 90° on our wedding night and John decided we should stay in a motel without air conditioning to save money. That's all he ever cared about, saving money."

"You were poor. He was smart."

"Why are you defending John?"

Vince didn't answer. But she had something to tell Vince. "I have a doctor's appointment tomorrow afternoon. I'm having pains in my stomach.

"You're catching cold."

"In my stomach? My Dad died of stomach cancer, you know, I want it checked out."

"So every time you have a belly ache you have to have it checked out. Maybe you're pregnant."

"That's impossible. I take birth control pills. But what if, by some miracle I was?"

"Miracles happen occasionally, especially if one sex sleeps with the opposite sex enough times."

Camille thought. "I wouldn't mind," she said.

"Vince Jr. . . . I've always wanted a little rug rat running around the house." Vince said, standing and turning his back.

Camille sat up straight in her chair and stretched. Vince had wandered away.

"You wouldn't like it if you had it, with all the crying and a little baby poking into your photographic equipment," she said.

"He could live with you, next door to me." He picked up Camille's telephone and dialed a number.

"Gracie Baby!"

Camille grimaced. Vince might call Grace from his boat, but to do it from hers felt like trespassing. Feeling annoyed, she picked her coffee cup up and walked down the studio toward the back windows facing out on the water. She needed to get dressed to go.

"The reason I called, Grace, was to get the recipe for Babaha Gonoush," she heard him say. He scribbled on a piece of paper for awhile, then hung up after a curt "Thanks."

"Did you see Grace today?" Camille was suspicious.

"We went around the galleries in SoHo."

"Yes? So what happened?" She knew she was going to hear a story when she saw an embarrassed smile.

"Well, in one of the galleries I was talking with this woman."

"What woman?" Camille asked.

"This very gorgeous woman that happened to be there. The trouble was, Grace wanted to leave after awhile and I wanted to finish my conversation with this woman."

"How strange. And then?"

"I really wanted to ask this woman out, but Grace ruined it all by the way she was acting. I should have gone to SoHo alone."

"Yes, you should have," Camille agreed.

Vince ignored her and went on talking.

"I don't know if I can date other women. You and Grace are so near and so available."

Camille couldn't believe what she was hearing. "I feel like throwing what's left of my cold coffee at you," she said.

But Vince went on, as if he was talking to himself. "I want Grace to go out with only me, but I want to be free to go out with other girls." Camille could think of nothing to say. Now she wished he would leave. She had to go.

"Come on, Pet. Let's go to the grocery store and get the ingredients for Babaha Gonoush. I want you to taste the dish of kings. You aren't doing anything tonight, are you?"

"Yes, I <u>am</u>. I'm going out tonight, remember?"

Vince acted hurt. "Oh, yeah. Oh well. We'll do it tomorrow."

Camille finally felt like she should mention something else to Vince, since he had brought it up, "Do you want to know how Grace feels about you?"

"She finally told you how she felt about me?"

"Yes, in a way." She didn't tell him Grace had told her this some time ago. It had been in her mind, though she hadn't felt like telling him before now. He sensed something bad coming. "You didn't ask, so I didn't tell you."

"I'm asking now. What did she say?" She could feel his defenses rising.

"She said she didn't want to go with you any more."

188

"She said that? I don't believe you. You just want to discourage me."

"No, that's not the reason. Really." she added, when she saw his pained look. "I would have told you before now if I had wanted to discourage you. She told me this at least a month ago."

"I know you, Camille, you're a catty one. I suppose she told you that you shouldn't tell me."

"No, actually she didn't."

"Then why didn't you tell me before now? Oh, I know. She was just trying to make you feel good so you wouldn't be jealous of her. Besides, I guess there were a few days last month she didn't want to go with me any more. I can understand why she would say that."

They were both silent for awhile, while Camille felt guilty for telling him. Why had she done it? Maybe she had wanted to hurt him and she had. Or perhaps she had wanted to see if he would be hurt and he was, which meant something else.

"How about you?" he asked, after a minute. "Are you planning to have other guys over here? I plan to have other girls to my place. It wouldn't be fair to you if you didn't have someone over, too. As a matter of fact, it would really turn me on to think of you making love to someone right next door. I could watch through the window. Would it turn you on to watch me make love to some gorgeous chick with big breasts and everything?" He was making motions with his hands and body. Camille turned her head away. He was trying to make her mad.

"I wouldn't watch if you had someone over."

"Ah, come on, Pet. You would too. You can't lie to me." His voice was hard.

"I don't know if it would be sexy or not. What turns me on is doing it with you."

"Well then, why don't we do it now?" He sounded sincere, but he was being outrageous. Camille didn't know what to make of him. She had to stay cool.

"What about my dinner date?"

"Cancel it." He came toward her, as if to embrace her.

"What about all my resolutions?" She was really tempted.

"What about all of mine? Tomorrow we'll keep them."

Camille got up and brushed past him to go in the bathroom. "I have to get dressed to go out tonight now."

"Oh, no you don't," said Vince, grabbing her. "I'm not going to let you go."

"Come on Vince." She shook him loose. She didn't want to kid around with him any longer. "Let me go. I have to get ready. I'll see you tomorrow."

So he left. She hadn't wanted to hurt him, but it seemed like he asked for it.

Camille met Francis at the gate at 7:00, and they walked through the misty upper West Side, looking for a place to eat. Francis was a tall man with a heavy body and a bass voice. Dressed in a black suit and tie with a gray overcoat, he looked as impressive as the opera singer and actor he was. His large, square face was comforting, and she found he was older and more intelligent than he looked. He acted kindly, even fatherly, towards her. He didn't make any advances, even though she told him she no longer felt attached to John, and was planning to ask for a divorce. He simply listened and asked questions about her life. He told her she was a great painter. He had attended all of her New York openings.

They found a good Thai restaurant and ate a delicious dinner.

Francis told her about his emerging career as an actor. Evidently he was doing well, making commercials and auditioning for parts in movies. Camille was in awe of him.

The waitress brought the bill for the dinner, which Francis paid, even though Camille offered to pay half.

"My dear, no!" scoffed Francis. "The lady doesn't pay for dinner. I won't have it. I invited you. You must allow me to act the part of the gentleman." His hand was extended to reach for the bill and closed over her little hand for a second. Camille smiled and he allowed her to withdraw it.

"A real Southern gentleman," she said, gratefully, letting him know how she felt. He was willing to be a friend.

"If you need anything at all, if you need help with anything, just call me." he said sincerely after they had walked back, chatting about the people back home. Camille assured him she would, but knew she would not. How could she bring someone else into her confused life at this point when life was already too complicated?

BABY DOCTOR

Every face wore the same expression. Maybe it was the hour, late afternoon, or maybe it was the fact that the hours would stretch on and on and two hours of waiting in the noisy room created common pain and boredom. Seated in quiet futility in rows of battered blue fiberglass chairs, the faces of the Puerto Riqueños, street people, poor blacks and poor whites reflected the look of encroaching stupor.

After signing her name to a list and waiting two hours, Camille decided to go to the desk to see if her name was still on the list. Shortly after that, her name was called and a husky, bustling nurse showed her into a small, cold room with a cushioned metal table in it.

"Undress, please. Put on this gown and lie down on the examining table," she said. "The doctor will be in to see you soon."

Camille undressed and slipped the flimsy paper gown over her arms, where it hung loosely, like a paper-doll dress. Holding it together in the back, she crawled up on the high table, which had another piece of paper pulled over it, and lay down, her eyes toward the ceiling, feeling the cold of the vinyl cushion cover seeping through two layers of paper into her back. The minutes ticked by. She had been nervous when she came in, but now nervousness had become steady tension.

Her eyes focused on the ceiling made of acoustical tile. It was squares of white-painted pressboard pierced with holes in a random pattern. She tried to make out a pattern in the dots, but no three dots formed a straight line. They did it deliberately, she thought, to annoy. Someone designed the acoustical tile so no one would be able to say it was produced mechanically, even though it was. She determined at last, after examining most of the tiles in the ceiling, that the dots were truly Random in the highest technical sense and turned her attention to other things. The bars that held the tiles in place were also painted white. She saw the bars were made of metal because the paint had chipped off of some of the strips, exposing the aluminum. She looked at her watch. She had been lying there for seven minutes. The table had not warmed up at all. It would be hard to sleep on such a cold, hard bed, even if she was tired.

Fifteen minutes later she was cursing herself for not bringing a magazine in with her to read. The nurse had said the doctor would be in soon, hadn't she? Maybe she had forgotten to put her chart outside the door so the doctor would know she was in here.

She had never seen her chart. Her records had been transferred from her doctor in Billington, Texas. They held all vital information about her body which was possible to derive from tests. Every time the doctor had looked into her ears, eyes, or mouth, listened to her heart or tapped her knees with a hammer was on it, the little notes he wrote down when he asked questions. It had the time she visited for a minor eye infection; the list of all the immunizations she had been given and all past doctors and operations. Anyone who saw it would be able to see if all or parts of her body were healthy or if she was nearing death.

Camille had never seen it, because it was either held in the strong hands of the nurse, or was in a rack outside of the closed room that contained her, or in the hands of the doctor when he entered, propped at an angle so she would not be able to see what he wrote. But she had never been allowed to get near it herself and she knew from past experience that nobody would ever tell her what the true result of each test was. If she asked, they would look at her and say, as if they were afraid of being too honest, "You're fine." She would never know what was written on those mysterious papers.

She was about to go to sleep. Her eyes were closing. But it was too cold and she was too uncomfortable and worried about what the doctor might say. Where was he? She could hear footsteps and voices out in the hall from time to time, and a child crying in the examining room next to hers, but no one came to her door.

"I've been forgotten," she thought. "Eventually the hospital will close and I'll still be lying here on this table. I won't know until the lights go out. I wouldn't have time to get dressed before they lock the doors. I'll be locked in here in the Clinic all night. When Vince comes home he'll call me but I won't answer, so he'll come over and knock on my door, but I won't answer and he will go away, thinking I've gone out with someone else. I could possibly be trapped in here over the weekend, if they don't open the Clinic tomorrow. Grace would wonder why I didn't come to her house, since I told her I was coming to dinner tonight. And Charlene would wonder why I didn't show up at her house in the morning, since I told her I would be coming up to Connecticut to visit her tomorrow."

"I don't know my way around in here. I'll have to grope my way down the hall in the dark. The night watchman will hear me and when he hears someone trying to find their way in the dark, he'll pull his gun. But maybe before he shoots he'll yell `Halt!' and ask me what I'm doing here. I'll tell him they put me in an examining room and forgot me while I was waiting to see my doctor and he'll understand."

Suddenly, the door opened and a very young man came in. He looked like a lost teenager. Camille sat up quickly. He wasn't dressed like a doctor, but Camille saw his name tag on the blue plaid shirt before she could scream. It said he was an M.D. He wore a stethoscope and in his hand he carried her chart, a file folder with papers sticking out of it. He sat down on the little metal rolling stool, opened the file and, like a wondering child, leafed through and peered at it awhile through new horn-rimmed glasses. Then he looked up at Camille.

"And what is the trouble with you today, Ms. . . (he glanced at the chart once more) uh. . . Mrs. Monroe?"

Camille was back in the waiting room. The doctor had examined her, poked her stomach all over until it was sore and asked her a lot of questions. She was waiting for the results of her blood test. He had told her she didn't look as if she had lost 35 pounds in the last six months. She had attributed it to not eating very much, not being able to eat anything with sugar, salt or fat in it, and running every morning.

The waiting room was even more crowded than it had been earlier, if that was possible. There were a lot of families with children in the area where she had been told to sit, in the pediatric area. She watched a tiny Latino boy run up to the soda and juice machine and kick it repeatedly. Then he went back to playing with a tiny mechanical toy which he wound up. It ran underneath the chairs and tables and between people's legs. He crawled after it, through the trash, beneath the seats of people completely unaware of him.

Suddenly her name was called. She was given a slip of paper

and told to go in a room where they would reveal her test results.

"You are healthy. Your blood pressure is fine, your heart, lungs and intestines are in good shape, you're not pregnant, nor do you have stomach cancer. You may have a little ulcer that is bothering you, however. There is nothing serious."

Camille was relieved when she walked out of the clinic. She thought about all her body had been through in the past year. She had started running six months earlier. The changes had been enough to change her looks. A picture taken a year ago would not have been recognizable as the person she was today.

She had been through a lot in the past six months, and not all of it was physical. She knew her mind was confused. Everything anyone said seemed to have special meaning to her, if it in the least concerned the directions one's life should take. She was searching for what she must do with hers. There were lots of big questions she had to decide, and soon.

Grace and Camille sat eating Grace's homemade Chicken Divan in Grace's little dining area and discussed the terrible joke Vince had played on Grace. She told Camille that it would have devastated her parents if they thought the divorce was real – that's what had made her feel so terrible. The two women began to feel the camaraderie that had brought them together in the first place, as Camille told Grace she was thinking about going out with other men. She confided she didn't see how she could keep up the relationship with Vince. He was impossible to live with, though she still liked him. She didn't tell Grace she still loved him. She didn't need to.

Camille told Grace about her visit to the clinic and how they couldn't find anything wrong with her, even though she was losing weight and having stomach pains.

Camille was curious as to whether Grace was possibly dating other men besides Vince and when she complained about Vince and said if she were out of this relationship she would be looking around, she was also fishing for indications of how Grace felt toward Vince.

But Grace remained vague about relationships with other men, and expressed sympathy with Camille's going through the ordeal she was going through with Vince. She said she understood. The two women hugged warmly when Camille left to go home.

GREEN HOUSE

She stared at the dark shapes whizzing by out the window. It was very early Saturday morning and she was on a train speeding along the tracks which had begun under enormous Grand Central Terminal and went North underneath the city of New York. She could hear the loud, soothing sounds of the rails under her, the rhythmical vibrations coming through the brown naugahyde upholstery. Sometimes she saw nothing in the glass but her own reflection looking back. Her eyes were dark and she wore a slight frown. In the window her eye automatically traced the line of her cheek, as if she were drawing it, turned at a three-quarter angle. Beneath the swell of the brow, the lean cheekbone, broken by the pursing mouth, the lower lip sloped gently to a square jaw–a smooth line. Her hair was cut in a black cap, its darkness offsetting her pale skin. Her eyes were so dark they were not discernible in the shadow beneath her brow. It was a face she would have drawn, if she had paper and pencil. She rarely looked at herself in the mirror, and whenever she saw her own reflection, she inspected it with curiosity and always was surprised at her facade. She had no concept of how she looked as a living body walking through her life.

Suddenly they emerged from the tunnel into bright daylight. Beyond the window and her reflection, she now could see walls and buildings, large and abstracted by speed as they rumbled through upper Manhattan, across the river and between the scars of Harlem, black windows on orange walls, brown and peach paint flaking off of brick, the tops of narrow, squared-off brownstones top-heavy with deteriorating overhangs.

Then Camille gazed in awe at whole blocks of tall, burned-out brick buildings with windows gaping empty of glass or interiors, with smoke-stains plumes over each window, insides hollow and black, ruined, looking as if they had been bombed out. Only the bricks were still standing, everything else had been burned by their last inhabitants: the squatters, the homeless, the illegal. But not in one big fire. Buildings that were hollow shells of what they once were had gradually had their wooden insides burned, slowly in hundreds of small fires, one window-sill at a time, as needed to warm thin, blackened arms laced with scars on the hundredth frozen night, on the nights it stormed or that unforgettable, intolerable moonlit night when the temperature went down to -4 degrees. The floor began to come up, board by board, since the snow blew horizontally in through the empty holes that once were windows. Survive tonight or die. The stairs were burned last, starting at the top, driving anything living downward. Camille saw the blackened shells, all that was left, as her train sped by on tracks that rose to ten floors high in this section of the city.

Will Green picked Camille up at the train station and drove her to their house.

Will and Charlene lived in a house built on top of one of the Stamford hills, surrounded by tall, thin trees. It was custom-built to exist without paid utilities, solar heated, solar energized, and they drew water from their own well. It was a tall house, made of wood and stone, with lots of glass on one side, where a greenhouse jutted out beyond a glassed-in porch. They drove up the hill and parked in front of the garage connected to the main house by a passage over the front entrance. The garage had an apartment over it, reached by the passageway.

Charlene came out of the kitchen with an apron on, wiping her hands and smiling. She hugged and kissed Camille. She looked far more relaxed and natural in her home than she had in New York.

Camille was anxious to talk to her about what she should do with her life and Charlene was as eager to talk to Camille alone. But first she fed the children and sent them off with Will to their music lessons.

At last the two women were able to sit quietly over cups of tea on the greenhouse-porch in the morning sun, going over all that had happened in the past few months. It was the first chance Camille had to talk to Charlene since she had come to New York.

"I have to tell you, Camille," said Charlene, speaking right out, "Vince is the sort of man that makes me nervous." Her dark hair bounced down in bangs over her brown eyes. She wore a plaid blouse that picked up the red in her cheeks and lips.

"I can see how he might. . ." said Camille. "You met him under strange circumstances. We didn't want anyone to know we were together and I know he was acting suspiciously." She gazed into the amber liquid of her tea and pushed the large crystals of raw sugar in the bottom back and forth, willing them to make her tea sweet. Charlene was into natural foods and the raw sugar refused to melt.

"I think I ought to tell you what kind of person he is," Charlene spoke sternly, maternally. "He is a playboy, a lothario, a cad. He's the kind of man that just plays around with girls." She spoke the words as if pronouncing some kind of dire judgment on Vince, and Camille laughed.

"You don't need to warn me. I know. But because he is that way, I also feel free to do my own thing. I don't mind if he does play around. We still love each other."

"Love?" said Charlene. She leaned back in her chair and crossed her long, tan legs and arms, looking at Camille as if she had lost her mind and it was up to her to bring her back to her senses.

"So you love him?" she said. "Well, things are further along than I thought."

A lot further than you know, thought Camille, realizing that Charlene didn't know they had been lovers.

"You don't know Vince," said Camille. Or me either any more, she added in her mind. How could she tell her? "Vince has given me things that John never has . . . he cares about how I look, he takes care of me physically. You know, he cooks or brings me a cup of coffee or an aspirin if I feel sick. He is sympathetic when I have worries and he thinks about me all the time, taking care that I get things I need, even when I don't know I need them. He knows what I want and he's always there when I need him.

"But he has forced me to be independent, too. He doesn't like me to cling to him. He respects me more as I become more independent. John expected me to be dependent on him and punished me if I wasn't. Yet the more dependent on him I was, the less he respected me. That's the way people are. You can't respect people who are dependent on you. You despise them a little, if you have power over them. You think of them as inferior, if you are to be responsible for them; you feel like you have to tell them what to do."

Camille paused. Charlene was frowning and biting her dry lips.

"John encouraged you to go out and try to sell your art. You said he told you to come to New York."

"I know. He did push me out to do something with my art. But I think he just wanted me out of his hair. I was so bored and anxious all the time about making my art and having nowhere to sell it, I was beginning to make life miserable for him. I really don't think he expected me to succeed at what I was doing. Actually, I don't think he was thinking of my career at all. I was just in his way. He wanted to write and I was disturbing him more and more with my anxiety. At first I think he expected me to come crawling back to him, fresh from a humiliating experience in New York. At least now I know that he doesn't care one way or another about my art."

"What do you mean?" she asked. "He actually said that?"

"Well, yes, in a very convincing way. When I try to tell him about my show or about my school, he doesn't want to hear about it, or about anything I've done here. He actually interrupts me and says he doesn't want to hear."

"Has he been in touch with you a lot?"

"He calls from time to time. But I . . . we don't talk much. We don't seem to have much to say to each other."

Charlene fell silent, thinking and sipping her tea. She bit into a powdery breakfast roll with her baby teeth. Camille watched her absentmindedly as she thought about what she had just said on one level and taking in the way the sunlight fell diagonally through the bare branches into their glass cocoon onto the ferns and flowers growing behind Charlene on another level. She thought about how the heat was flowing in a circle, the sun heating water on the roof, flowing through pipes into the basement where it heated rocks and the warm air flowed up through the grates into the house.

"You think John feels threatened? He shouldn't mind if you're successful, since he certainly is. He is very successful in his field, you know. Is he really totally unsympathetic?" She gazed with her flat brown eyes into Camille's green ones.

"Well, no." Camille squirmed a little. She didn't really want to talk about John. Everyone seemed to defend him. Even Vince. She would rather talk about Vince. He was easier to understand. "John just doesn't care. He never has been a warm, caring kind of person, you know. You know him. It is no surprise to me that he doesn't want to talk about what I'm doing. He would rather I ask him how <u>he</u> is doing. Then he is happy to talk. Once we start talking about me, he cuts me off. Besides, Vince is a great lover."

Charlene looked at Camille sharply, but Camille couldn't read what her eyes wanted to say. Could it be that she was sympathetic?

"Is that all he is?" Charlene asked. "An intellectual element is important, too, you know."

"I know. It's that Vince is so different from John in every way. Vince is a feeling person, a passionate person. I am learning a lot from him, but not intellectual things. What I'm learning is more about how to live life and about different ways of thinking. Who knows what will happen when I come face to face with John at Christmas-time. Maybe it will be easy for Vince and me to be apart. But maybe I'll miss him."

"Yes, what about Christmas?" interrupted Charlene. "What are you going to tell John?" This was something that Camille didn't want to think about.

"I'm only going to be there a week. John has an important business trip to make right after the holidays."

"Are you going to stay married to John – I mean in the future?"

"I don't know. It would be hard to stay with him in any way now. When I imagine my future, I don't see John in it, except very superficially."

"Superficially? What do you mean, superficially? He is your husband. I can't imagine my husband being superficial in my future. Will is either there, or he is not there. That's how I see it."

Camille realized that Charlene was a little more upset over her situation than she should be. Charlene and Will must be having problems themselves. She wondered if any marriage was perfect.

"I guess John just fades away when I imagine my future. That's all." she explained lamely. "It's hard to imagine having to deal with John from now on – on and on into the distant future. I have to go back for the holidays, but I am dreading it. I'm actually dreading it, Charlene." She spoke with more passion than she meant to, surprising herself. "I don't know if I can sleep with John after all this."

Camille was still talking to Charlene at noon. They had settled into the big white couches in the two-story living room as they listened to classical music and Charlene crocheted. After the tour of the house, she told Charlene the story of how she had met Vince.

"I can't even remember how it was with John, after sleeping with Vince. I find it difficult to imagine of coming face to face with him. As a matter of fact, I can't imagine dealing with him, talking with him or even seeing him – or having anything to do with him in any way. I guess I don't want to face the music."

"What music?"

"Well, he will remind me of my duty to him, of our wedding vows, of our parents' expectations, etcetera, etcetera. I don't want to hear all that. And then, after I listen to him rant and rave and get angry at me, he will want me to go to bed with him." She spoke with a touch of horror in her voice, making Charlene look up from her sewing.

"Of course he'll want to sleep with you. He's missed you. It's been a long time." Charlene said. "How do you think he feels? He has feelings."

"I don't know if he does. That's just it. If he is kind to me, I won't have any reason to resist him. I hope he is. I hope he wins me back, but I don't think he will be kind and sweet and gentle with me. He will lecture me or be cold, stiff and silent, expecting me to understand things he hasn't said, the 'things that should be perfectly clear without their having to be said.'" She paused, feeling pain.

"You know. I don't hate John. I really hope he does want me, that he will tell me he missed me and wants me to love him and that he loves me. I want that, in a way. I want him to tell me that he wants me to be happy and that he'll be supportive of me during this difficult time." She paused again, feeling tears nearing the surface. But then she spoke in a dead voice, knowingly. "But he won't do that."

Charlene didn't reply for awhile.

"You'll have to get into the proper frame of mind if you're going to be with him for a whole week," she finally said. "You have a lot of problems to resolve in your own mind before you see him. It sounds to me like you don't really want to stay with him. But do you actually want to leave him, to divorce him?"

"Divorce!" Whenever she heard the word it sounded so drastic. Why was it always assumed it would be the conclusion, the solution, what people thought had to be a natural ending to her situation?

"You may have to face it, Camille. There will be a lot of things to think about, if it's to be divorce, you know." Charlene did not elaborate and Camille began to wonder what they might be. She had heard there were terrific problems she would have to go through.

"I don't know if I can divorce John. I feel a lot of anger toward him, for some reason. Why do I feel so angry at him, Charlene? He hasn't done anything to me. He has been the perfect husband, faithful and earning a good living, home every night. Maybe it's my fault. I spent years of being more and more what he wanted me to be. I denied what I wanted to be. I did what he thought I should do. I spent a lot of time being afraid of him, afraid he wouldn't love me if I didn't do what he wanted and then being angry because he didn't understand my fear and frustration, because he didn't love me even when I did what he wanted. And Charlene, when I'm angry and afraid and I can't do anything about it, I get very frustrated."

"To tell the truth," said Charlene, after listening to Camille's impassioned speech, "I think it's a wonder you have stayed with him all these years." Camille was surprised to hear this from Charlene and was suddenly grateful to her for supporting her feelings, rather than John's.

Just then Will and the two girls returned for lunch. The women spent the rest of the afternoon playing games with them, fixing supper and eating it and talking together over coffee with Will after dinner. Camille had to leave and catch the train back to New York before it got too late. Will drove her down to the station to catch the 8:05 in the chill dusk. Charlene had made her promise she would come back soon to visit.

The street lights had an aura around them from tiny snow crystals as Camille emerged from the subway in New York. The trip down the hill to the boat basin was slippery. There were only a few cars at this time of night and fewer people out on the streets. She thought over her day in the country. She, Charlene and Will had discussed the fate of the United States during supper. Will took every sign as a portent of disaster. Camille taunted him with her optimism and Charlene listened, concerned at the fervency of their conversation, all the while providing abundant dishes of homemade food. It always seemed strange to see Charlene in this setting, as a contented homemaker, after having grown up with her, both of them acting like liberated, teenaged, tomboys riding horseback through the fields, and then knowing Charlene as a wild, single woman through many of the years she herself was married and living so ascetically herself. Now their roles had switched. She was living the life of a libertine, according to Charlene, and Charlene was acting like a prudish housewife.

She crossed the street and struggled to keep from sliding down the path that took her through the trees to the rotunda. She slipped once on the wide veranda steps as she made her way to the edge of the river and was even more careful from then on. The huge bulk of buildings looming behind the trees and the city beyond were reduced to cutout images behind the cold, pale arches of the rotunda, while the sidewalks and river before her were cold, black and steel-gray. Ice crystals had melted into shining pools inside the circle, but around the walls were the dark shapes of homeless men and women who slept in the shelter of the rotunda, even when it was freezing.

Below her were the boats in the black waters of the Hudson. A shower of ice crystals flowed between her and them, obscuring hard outlines and covering everything under the lights with white frosting. She held her hood over her face as she made her way down the ramp, which acted like a wind tunnel, funneling icy winds directly off the water. Inside the gate, she saw the silhouette of the dock master in his warm, lighted office.

Finally in her boat, she gratefully dropped her heavy bag beside the door, sighed with relief and turned on the heat. When she turned to put her bag away, she saw Vince at the door, through the window. It seemed like a million years since she had seen him. She never knew how she should greet him, as she never knew his mood. She opened the door and noted, for the first time, how haggard he looked; his hair long and stringy in the wind, his body looking thin and his clothes wrinkled. He stood, filling the doorway, hesitant.

"How would you like to go out to dinner tomorrow night?" he asked, his face cracking a meager smile and a pale gleam coming into his eyes as he looked at her. She saw them search out the violets he had given her the first day. They were still in the jelly glass by the telephone, dry, but whole and still purple. "Hal invited us," he explained, slowly moving inside, as Camille held the door open for him.

"Sure," Camille said. "Come on in. How about some hot chocolate? I'm freezing to death." Vince went into her little galley and opened her refrigerator door, leaning down and peering into it.

"You got anything else?" he asked.

"You beggar!" Haven't you eaten today?" she laughed.

"Come here, woman," he said. His face was still hidden behind the white door, but his arm reached out and grabbed her, pulling her over to him, where he held her tight against his side so they could both look into the refrigerator. "Fix me some of that good ol' homemade Texas grub. How about some of that country ham you made last week?"

"You ate it all up." Camille went to the stove and, with her coat and mittens still on, lit it and put hot water on the top. It would be freezing in the boat until the propane heater could heat it up.

"I guess hot chocolate will have to do," he said, sitting down at the table, grabbing her again and pulling her over to him so he could kiss her on the hip and then on the lips.

RUNNING OUT

The next day Vince had decided he didn't want to go to dinner with Hal and his friends, but Camille insisted that he go, shaming him into it. Still, before they left he changed his mind twice, which annoyed her.

When they got to Hal's, they were introduced to a young couple with a six-year-old daughter. They had a drink with Hal in his office and drove to a Ukrainian Restaurant that theyheard had a good reputation. Vince was acting grouchy and stand-offish to Camille, but during dinner he began to relax and act better. The little girl took a liking to him, crawled all over him and played with the silver studs and zippers on his black leather jacket and he enjoyed that.

The food was good; all of them laughed and talked a lot, swapping stories about restaurants. Hal told the couple about the artists in his gallery, especially about Camille and Paul Frank. They said they were interested in Camille's art and Camille realized they were potential clients that Hal wanted her to befriend.

They parted on the sidewalk outside of the restaurant after dinner and Vince drove Camille home. By now, Vince was feeling much better, acting very cozy and chummy with Camille, saying he would miss her during the holidays and asking her to spend the night with him tonight. Camille had learned about his moods and though that his earlier bad spirits had probably more to do with a visit from Grace. Vince was always upset after he saw Grace. So she said she would.

In bed he leaned over her and stroked and kissed her hair while they watched TV together, laying back against the pillows, naked. She leaned against him as he held her and cupped one of her breasts in his hand.

"I'm glad we went tonight after all," he said. Camille felt satisfied and grateful that he was feeling well.

After school these days, Camille was going directly to her boat and staying there. She had homework to do and was working on a painting in the boat studio. Although Vince came over and visited her sometimes, she saw many people coming and going from his boat. She still had a need to see him every day, somehow, but tried not to think of him as her lover. She painted, instead, which took her mind off everything else.

Grace invited Camille to join a group of women artists who were going to have an exhibition of their work in December. So Camille began to call friends to invite them to the opening. She got another letter from John. He admitted to having doubts about what kind of relationship they had and said she could stay in New York part of the year and be with him the rest of the year. However, he said he would never visit New York because he hated the city. He left no room for any decision-making on her part. She assumed this was his attempt to compromise.

"Forgive me for whatever I've done," he wrote at the end of the letter, "and change things back to the way they used to be. I love the girl I married." How could he say that? asked Camille of herself. Things could never be the way they used to be when they married. She was not and could never return to being the girl he had married, which meant he could not love her now.

From his letter, she realized John was actually saying he would not give up anything for her, the town, his job or his routine. As her popularity had grown in New York, she had asked him several times to consider living closer to New York, maybe in one of the small towns outside of the city. "Never!" he had said. The more she grew to love it, the more he seemed to hate New York

A sense of sadness and loneliness pervaded her after reading his letter. She could not bring herself to answer it. What could she say? Nothing was ever going to be the same. She didn't even know why she felt so angry, so she could not say what she was supposed to forgive him for. If she mentioned anything, he would point out that he had been the perfect husband.

She sat with Vince in the living room of his boat, as if she were visiting someone who was sick, because they sat in silence, in an atmosphere almost devoid of communication. They talked very little. Only the noise of an album played while the TV screen showed something else. Vince's dog was on his bed. He was always on the bed these days.

"Geddown!" Vince yelled when he went up the steps and Camille could hear the accommodating thump as the dog jumped down.

"You know Padorewski?" he yelled from the bedroom.

"Yes," she said, recalling the small man with red hair she often saw around the boat basin, rain or sun, in a grey raincoat.

"I saw you talking to him, Camille. Don't ever let him in here. Don't ever talk to him. He's a cop," he said as he came down the stairs.

"A cop?" Camille was surprised. She had never seen any indication that Padorewski was a policeman. "How do you know? He never wears a uniform. He doesn't look like a plain-clothesman."

"His socks," said Vince, now breathing out great clouds of smoke from his position on the couch.

"Socks?" Camille was at a loss. She could not recall Padorewski's socks.

"They're white." Vince's voice was short and impatient with her ignorance. "All cops wear white socks. Regulation issue."

"Oh. Well, all I've ever said to him was 'hello.'" Camille answered defensively, still not convinced. Why should Vince care if she spoke to someone she saw every day?

"It would seem strange if I didn't speak to him, Vince. He seems harmless enough." Camille murmured the last sentence, but got no response from Vince.

When she left, Vince stood, accompanied her to the door and gave her a little hug. She felt better when she remembered that later. It was sad. Things were changing between her and Vince.

She felt the cold wind stinging her face most, until the all-consuming effort of simply breathing distracted her from such minor things as bodily discomfort, noises or the thudding of her feet. She ran fast. Too fast, Bobby said as he passed her with his ten-mile-long legs. She watched his back with the two long strips of sweat soaking through his shirt even on this cold day and thought, "I don't want to be an athlete. I just want to run." Running fast took her away from everything. Her mind lifted with her body, floating above the surface of the track where her legs pounded in an absence of feeling. Occasionally she changed her stride to use other muscles, but found herself running the same way again after awhile. Running was flying and forgetting; forgetting the world of little pains and feeling the beautiful, pure white agony of breathing until it hurt and hurt so good that you wanted to breathe deeper and run faster, so you could fly off the earth.

The aching loneliness she felt on these early morning runs was the same aching loneliness she had felt on the plains of Texas when she would step out of her car after taking a long, aimless drive, to drink in the emptiness around her, knowing no soul existed within hundreds of miles; where she could look at the horizon and see nothing. Nothing. Not even hills; only flat land between her and the thin line where it met the sky. Then, the first thrill of its vastness over, the awe would turn into pain, a longing, inexpressible and unfulfillable -- the longing for a kindred soul, a companion in her isolation.

Here in the city she felt the same ache. But here it was in the early morning as the sun rose and she gazed down the long track, or down the long sidewalk along the river, running on forever, knowing that a million people lay in their beds or looked out their windows or moved about in their apartments along this river within a square mile of her, while all she could see was empty sidewalk, chain link fences, dead lawns and moist dirt paths. Devoid of life, the people had fled.

But they would return. Within the next couple of hours, runners and walkers would fill the sidewalk, people would be going to work, the tennis courts would resound with bouncing balls, thin young women would walk dogs, old men would carry shopping bags back from the grocery store, the sun would stand above the city, and the wind would bring them all the odor of coffee from New Jersey.

She lived to end each day, not looking forward to it, not looking forward to anything, really. Her time was spaced in hours. She no longer felt the weeks flowing from weekend to weekend. Every day was the same. From hour to hour her emotions rose and fell, responding to a chance remark or remembered slight. She plunged from dull hope into gut-wrenching despair nowadays within a matter of minutes, something it used to take her years to do.

She seemed to have no control over her feelings. She felt as helpless as a weightless leaf lifting and plunging on rushing waves, being swept downriver.

Toward the end of her run she began counting the laps, telling herself she only had three more to go, just two more, just one, and then the lovely last lap, knowing she could stop at the end. She knew she shouldn't stop too quickly, so she walked another lap and found herself at the other end of the track before she knew it. She walked back to the boat, breathing hard and deep in the crisp morning air, her body suddenly becoming wet with sweat beneath her jerseys.

Standing in the hot shower, she looked down the shining lumps and ripples of her body where the water flowed over cold, numb surfaces. Her skin resembled a streambed where water swirled over obstacles hidden under a shining, silver-white surface. She felt the heat of the water at last. Her body was no longer numb.

She was aware of her body as she had never been aware of it before. Other people made her become aware. Strangers told her about it on the streets. It was as if she had been invisible until now. Sometimes she wished she were invisible again, not sure she liked the attention.

The Camille she now saw in the mirror was sleek and pale, with smooth black hair, jutting cheekbones and eyes too big for her face. She was lean, strong and moved easily.

Her body was loved, too. And having been loved, her muscles were built with the tensions to which love had subjected them. Her body was made for love.

One of the sayings on her bulletin board read "You only live twice." Her body would not last forever. It would age soon enough, though she intended to wear what was left of it out. If she looked younger than her age now, all the better; she found she liked younger men. She found she liked men of all ages. And they seemed to like her. She had found an undiscovered woman within herself that loved to dance all night and flirt with men.

Her hidden thoughts were becoming conscious in this atmosphere of free expression. Until now they had been like rocks beneath the surface. Now she spoke them aloud, and was coming to accept them. Sometimes she still thought of herself as a dull housewife, heavy and unappealing. And when she felt unsure of herself, of her attractiveness, as she did now, she longed for Vince, who had given her this gift of seeing herself as good-looking and kept on assuring her that she was desirable. He had told her many times how beautiful she was. She still had a crush on him, like a schoolgirl, that seemed mixed with leftover fantasies from her teens, and memories of how as a baby she must have been cuddled and held and cared for. She longed for someone to rock her and say sweet, loving words to her; to love her however he might choose, just so long as he loved her. And another thing she knew was that Vince would love her forever. She was in his blood, as he was in hers. He would always love her in his own way.

Now the shower water mingled with her tears and her thoughts running over and through her, till the water dried her fingers like old logs on the beach before she leaped out, thinking maybe she had missed the ringing of the telephone in its splashing.

She toweled off, her skin turning to goose bumps in the tiny, cold bathroom. She shivered at the rivulets of water running out of her hair down her back. The mirror was clouded when she stood before it, grey smoke fading her face and letting her imagine she was still a young, pink girl behind the steam. It was good to have nothing on her body on a winter day when it was cold outside. Inside, her body was clothed in air and she could move loosely in it until she had to put on a constricting brassiere and slip a nylon teddy over her head, damp curls wetting it so that it stuck to her body.

On the way to school on the subway she read an article in a magazine. The article said that it was foolish for a woman to divorce if she is trying to liberate herself and seek self-fulfillment. She wondered why. What if the husband was hindering those very things, then it would be worthwhile for her to divorce. What if you just don't love your husband any more? The article didn't discuss that.

She knew she had to write to John, to answer his letter. So she sat down to write. But she could not do it. What could she say, except that she would accept his attempts to "think straight" and that she would try to do the same? His letter made it seem like he was making an extreme effort for her. She wished he wouldn't. He made the $100 he sent her monthly sound like a big burden. It put a burden on her mind to hear it. He resented supporting her? Now was she supposed to feel responsible to him for sending her $100? She didn't want to feel responsible to him. She didn't think she could expend any more emotions on him than she already had over the years. She just didn't feel like agonizing any more. She was wary of the guilt he was trying to impose. She was running on empty now. She had given him all the love she had had in her, with nothing coming back in to replenish it. There was no emotion left to expend on him any more.

She felt like giving everything up; everything meant nothing any more. She felt no different now about leaving than when she left Texas. Only now she knew the horror of loneliness and it was worse than she thought. Still, as bad as it was, it was better than living in Texas. If she could only manage not to feel lonely in New York she would be all right. She was getting over Vince and reaching out to others. She was changing herself and the way she was acting and thinking.

The end of the year was coming. She usually made resolutions as goals for the coming year. She would write some resolutions, as usual. She thought about it and, sitting down to write a letter, instead wrote:

1. *I am resolved to act more decently. Like a grown-up. I will act as if I have responsibilities to school, family and myself. That means withdrawing from the life I've been leading with Vince and doing things I NEED to do before the things I WANT to do.*
2. *I am resolved to stay healthy.*
3. *I am resolved to immerse myself in my work and not think about my relationship with Vince. It looks like it is over with, anyway.*
4. *I am resolved to find new friends.*

The last resolution soon became reality. A woman had just moved into the floating home right across the dock with her baby. She was young and beautiful, a model living with an older actor who had sublet the boat. Camille found her standing in front of her boat, searching through her purse for her keys when she came back from classes the next afternoon. Her name was April and she had a darling little baby boy in a stroller. Camille greeted her; they struck up a conversation, introduced themselves and obviously enjoying each other's company, agreed to get together soon.

BLACK WINGS

In the afternoon, April came over to visit with Camille, having put her baby to sleep. It was not a cold day, so April opened a window on her boat and Camille's door was left open a crack so the two women could hear if the baby woke and cried. They drank a cup of tea as rice boiled on the range. Camille was thus able to examine her new neighbor April's petite good looks close up, and decided in some ways they were alike. It made her feel akin to the younger woman. April told Camille how she and Charlie had met. She had grown up and always lived in Tamiment, Pennsylvania and Charlie was an actor who had come to town with a theatrical production on its way to Broadway.

"I went to the play and my single girlfriend invited me to the cast party afterward. There was Charlie, tall, handsome and looking distinguished with white hair, and he was immediately attracted to me. Me, of all people, a little old housewife with a kid, living in a hick town! Even though he was older, he was young in spirit. He found out where I lived and sent me flowers, notes, candy. He called me, took me out whenever I could get a baby-sitter. It was the first time in my life anyone famous had ever noticed me. I could hardly resist it. As a matter of fact I couldn't resist him," she laughed at what must have been a pleasant memory.

"But what about your husband? And your baby?"

"Oh, little Chuck isn't my husband's baby, he's Charlie's baby."

"Oh, I see." said Camille. April had been even more daring than she, she realized.

"Yes, my dear. Charlie and I are living in sin. Ain't it wonderful? Didn't you say you are still married, too?"

"Yes, but it isn't turning out so good for me." Camille glanced towards Vince's boat. "My lover and I don't live together."

"How come? Is something wrong?"

"Oh, not really. I guess things are going along all right. We're living next door to each other."

"That could be all right. That way you have everything; your freedom and your lover."

"I guess. . . . But you do, too. You aren't married to him, but at least you're living with him and not separately."

"Charlie and I are really in love. I couldn't live without him. You're right. I couldn't just live beside him."

"How long have you been together?"

"About six months."

"But how old is little Chuck?"

"Nine months old. Yes, you guessed it. I actually knew Charlie two years before I decided to run away with him."

"But. . ."

"My husband is terrible. If you only knew him!"

"He didn't love you?"

"No way. And look what he's doing to me now! He's not only suing me for divorce, but desertion, adultery and anything else he can think of! I can't afford to divorce him, I would be broke for the rest of my life!"

"Really?"

All this about divorce was new for Camille. Perhaps there was something she should learn. But April proceeded to relate how her conniving husband, with whom she had a son who was now about seven years old, was trying to keep her from obtaining custody of him and was also trying to "pin all the stinking charges he could think of" on her.

"So you have a little boy back home. . . I mean, in Pennsylvania?"

"Yes, he's only seven. I have to get him back. My husband came and picked him up one day after nursery school and took him away and won't let me see him."

"How can he do that?"

"Believe me he can and he did. And, though I've tried everything I know of, I can't find out where he is most of the time and I was only able to see him for five minutes one day, in the company of about five people who were guarding him at his school. My husband had said bad things about me to them and they almost didn't let me see him at all."

"That's terrible. At least you have the baby."

"Yes, little Chuck. My husband knew Chuck wasn't his, so he

didn't want him." Her face was drawn and distressed, remembering her ordeal.

"Sad." Camille commiserated with her, leaning forward to touch her arm. "You know I'm still married, too and trying to decide what to do."

"You have children?"

"No."

"You're lucky. You won't have all this trouble."

"So, you just left your husband and came to New York with Charlie?"

"It sounds romantic, but it isn't. My husband was so shitty after I got pregnant. At first I decided not to tell him the baby was Charlie's, but I got so mad at him one night, I told him and the shit hit the fan. He threw a hissy and beat me up, as usual. Only this time I was pregnant and I decided it wasn't good for the baby. What if I lost it? Charlie had told me to take care of myself. So I ran away. I was about seven months pregnant."

"Charlie was in New York and I was in Pennsylvania. I called him and asked him if I could come live with him. But he couldn't do anything since he was going to have to go shoot a film in Zimbabwe or somewhere, but he sent me some money. So I got myself a little apartment in town, for just me and my son and decided to live by myself.

"My husband couldn't stand it. He came crawling to me, begging me to come back. I couldn't resist him. He is so sweet when he wants to be. He said he would claim the baby as his and everything. Finally I got so low on cash that I had to move back in with him. Besides, I was just about to have Chuck. I had him and stayed with my husband for about three months. After I moved back in, things went back to normal, with him drinking and beating me up and everything. So when Charlie came back to the U.S. he called me and came to see me.

I surprised him with Chuck and he said I had to come to New York with him right away. I knew I had to run away, but I couldn't do it right then because Petey had to finish the school year. But before the end of the year my husband found out what I planned to do. I couldn't help but tell him one day before I left—me and my big mouth—we had this big fight and I said I was leaving him. Next day,

Petey's last day of school, he picked him up early before I came to pick him up. What he did was hide him for awhile. But I had to go ahead and move, 'cause after that fight I couldn't stay with my husband any more. But when I went back to Tamiment I went back to Petey's school and there he was. He told me he missed me. I was so happy to see him I cried.

April had surprised Camille with her story. Camille looked at April's beautiful face, shining before her and imagined her crying. Her eyes were not teary or soft. They were alive, cautious and hard. To think that someone this young, barely twenty, with such a beautiful, soft body and face could have had such a life. She had a little boy in school, carried on an affair, bore an illegitimate child, flaunted the fact before her tough, abusive husband, and had actually fought him. It was hard to imagine. She could not imagine her face, so smooth and beautiful, being scarred and bruised. April must be brave. She had been a bad wife, a bad mother, and had done everything Camille knew you should not do, but she still admired her.

"At least here in New York I can work on my career. There are two thousand modeling agents here!" April's face glowed with enthusiasm. One of her long, graceful hands waved a paper napkin as if it were a filmy scarf.

"I'm sure you'll hit the top," said Camille.

"Thanks," said April, suddenly subdued.

Camille got up and, trying to make cheerful conversation, dished up the rice and served it at the covered card table where they sat. She had made broiled fish, rice and peas. She put a candle in the middle of the table and used her best, which consisted of square, yellow plastic plates, a new set of silverware she had bought at the dime store and some glasses Vince had given her, since he had too many. She used a big piece of drawing paper for the tablecloth, on which she scribbled some daisies for a design at the last moment. April watched her do all this, entertained and placid, as if she was used to being served.

They ate companionably, feeling like they had known each other a long time, swapping stories, finding out their differences and similarities. At 8:00, since it was dark, April went to get her sleeping baby and, seating herself on her chair again, pulled down the low neckline of her black dress, exposing one full, perfect breast and placed the baby against it. Little Chuck suddenly awoke with a scrunched up face. His head turned, mouth searching for the nipple. With this picture of the perfect mother and baby in front of her, Camille saw how Charlie could have adored her at first sight, and even after that–she was incredibly beautiful as a young woman or as the Madonna she appeared to be now, so much so that it obscured her dubious past.

Camille realized something like April's bad experiences could happen to her. John could fight with her, become angry and make it hard for her. If he did, she would just live in New York. She did not really want to go back to Texas. She could not go back to Texas. She felt alienated from it, recalling the hurt she had suffered there. The City was a good place for her. People here were kind most of the time, and much more interesting. People in New York were busy with their own lives and did not have time to worry about her simply because there was nothing else to think about. In a small town one had nothing else to do except become morose about one's prospects. The City was a good place to go when you have problems, she thought. You can suffer by yourself, yet alongside others who have the same problems.

However, Vince was not Charlie. Charlie took some responsibility for April and took care of her and her baby. Vince would be too nervous for a baby. Also, if she got pregnant she did not know what he would actually do. He would probably go back to Grace. She was realizing more and more how close Grace and Vince were, and had become over the years. Just as she was becoming attached to Vince, she was becoming aware of the depth of Grace and Vince's relationship. She was an interloper and it hurt to realize it.

She did not tell April about Grace. Let April remain under the impression Vince and Camille were lovers and their relationship was good. And it is good, Camille told herself. Her misgivings did not change things. He was still her friend.

She stayed up till 2:00 a.m., working on homework after April left, so she was very tired the next day. She told herself she should get more sleep. Vince's schedule of staying up all night had ruined hers. A couple of mornings a week she had to get up early to make a 9:00 a.m. class, or go to the library to study and when she did go to bed she did not sleep very well because she was thinking about so many things.

Finally it was quiet. Camille tossed around in bed, trying to find a comfortable spot. She lay still at last, sleep beginning to fall heavy on her, her eyes closing, the torpor of each second making every wave she heard splashing gently against the dock appear minutes apart. The waves crashed less and less and the sound of people's voices in the distance thrummed against her consciousness. The voices, voices of two men and a woman, grew louder. She hoped they would pass by, as party-goers sometimes did in the night; maybe they would pass by to their respective boats. It was too late for anyone to be arriving.

Then, suddenly, the sound of a small outboard boat motor starting up nearby startled her into wakefulness. The boat must have been parked near her boat, against the side dock. The voices continued, rising over the noise of the motor, shrill and argumentative. Now she was awake, listening to the woman yelling and the man's voice shouting back at her. She heard the motor start to gun and then the woman yelling "let me off!" Immediately, Camille was at her back window, staring out at a small motor boat tied up at the dock behind hers, where a young woman was attempting to climb back out of the boat and onto the dock.

One of the men had her coat clutched in his hand and was pulling her back into the boat. She turned and struggled to wrench her coat away, her breath coming in white puffs in the silky lamplight, as her voice, strident and demanding, shouted curses and commands. The man who held her stood up and reached to grab her arm. She recoiled. A second man sitting in the back of the boat by the motor, did not enter into the fight. They all sounded drunk. The standing man gave a big jerk and the woman fell back into the boat on her side.

"Go!" yelled the standing man to the silent one. But the boat stayed where it was when the woman said "Don't you dare! I want off. I will not be in this boat with you!"

"How are you going to get home?" the man yelled over the sound of the motor.

"I don't know -- I'll walk!"

"Over the bridge? At night?"

Camille noticed a light had come on in Vince's boat. She was certain he too had heard them.

"Get back here!" The standing man's voice changed, as if he was aware they were being watched. But the woman started screaming and struggling again to crawl out of the boat. As the man still held her coat, she slipped out of it and struggled toward the dock, getting one leg out of the boat. He grabbed her again, put his hand over her mouth to silence her screams and wrestled her to the floor of the boat, where it looked like he was hitting her. Camille saw Vince's door open and he was suddenly outside, standing on his deck above the motor boat.

"Let her go." He said loudly enough for all to hear. "The lady wants to be free to go."

"You mind your own business," the man snarled back, obviously drunk, but determined to take the lady with him to Jersey.

"I'll get a taxi from here!" the woman said. Her mouth was uncovered for a second as she took advantage of the diversion that Vince caused. Suddenly she jumped out of the boat, but the man was right after her, up on the dock, grabbing her and pulling her back. This was too much for Vince as he jumped off his boat and came around to the smaller boat in a second, standing between the man and the woman.

"Let her go!" he repeated.

"I told you to mind your own business..." the man said, but hesitated before the unmoving stance that Vince had taken as a barrier between him and the woman. Meanwhile the woman, stopping only a moment to size up the situation, grabbed her coat out of the boat and hurried off down the dock, stumbling in high heels.

"Get out of my way! Come back here!" The man yelled, trying to charge by Vince, but Vince put one arm out and the man literally reeled as he ran into it. He stepped back and took a swing at Vince, but Vince ducked and the man almost fell into the river with the force of his own momentum. This made him very angry and he rushed Vince, who stood as still as a mountain in the center of the dock. At the very moment he reached him, Vince, like a ghost, was not there and the man fell forward on his hands and face. Camille could hear the force of the blow as he hit the dock. His hurt and angry yell brought the second man to his feet, a man as big as Vince, but obviously not as drunk or as rash as the first man.

"I want you two to leave before anything worse happens," said Vince, taking advantage of the moment. The calm way he said those words made both men stop and think.

"Come on, Jeff." The man in the boat said. "Let's go. It's late."

"But what about Jillian? Damn her, she'll be the death of me yet. I've got to go and get her."

"Forget her." The man in the boat said, grabbing the first man by the arm and pulling him back toward the boat. "She'll find a way home. Come on, let's get out of here. Let her go home alone."

Jeff, picking splinters out of his hands, cursed and pressed his forearm against his bleeding nose, and carefully remaining out of Vince's reach, stumbled into the boat and was thrown into a seat by the second man. The boat motor roared and, after casting off the lines, began to move into the middle of the marina and slowly out to the river, becoming lost in the dark.

Vince went back into his dark boat, without speaking. He did not call her and Camille immediately went to sleep without another thought, until the next morning, when she found half the people in the marina seemed to have witnessed what had happened and were talking about it.

Would she ever be loved again? Camille ached for someone to be close to. The thoughts of how close she felt to Vince were still with her. She knew she could experience a close, comforting love but she did not have it any more. She was sad, wondering if anyone would ever love her. Then she told herself, "Of course there will someone some day, there is always a possibility of finding true love."

She was trying to keep the tears from flowing out of her eyes, but she knew she had to think of other subjects, because she was on the subway, jammed into a crowd of people on their way to work, sitting on the bench below the eyes of those standing.

The man sitting pressed next to her glanced at her. He did it surreptitiously, with his black eyes and sweat-moistened dark skin, but she knew he was trying to see her face to see if she was crying. She swallowed her sobs, trembling, and when she closed her eyes, the tears flowed down her cheeks. She wished tears would come through her nose and she could blow them away, but they ran slowly down her cheeks and she dared not wipe at them for fear of drawing attention to them. She could not help their flowing, even though she was in public. They came unwillingly, even though she deliberately thought of other things. Maybe the man felt sorry for her, instead of curious. The large woman above her was looking at her sometimes, trying to decide if she was crazy, and was acting nervous. Two teenaged girls squeezed her on her other side. In the morning rush, everyone was crushed together, a bunch of fruit squashed into a container too small. The huge, flowered woman hung unwillingly over her, handbag dangled in her face; people squeezed by to get out whenever the train stopped.

"Are you okay?" the teenager at her side gently asked her.

Camille nodded, embarrassed. She was sorry she was crying in public. She tried to speak to the two girls, to reassure them, and opened her mouth to do so, but there was a large lump in her throat and nothing came out. The attention of the girls distracted her, though, and she was able to sober up and stop crying. She took a deep breath to relax her throat and spoke.

"I was just feeling bad," she said. "But I'm all right now." Embarrassment suffused her and she turned her face down to a book she held on her lap and tried to read it. Desire Caught By the Tail it said on the cover. She was supposed to read it for class. She read the words, but found them impossible to understand. She felt so many emotions already. It was an emotional story. Images swept through her inner mind, emerging from the darkness into her consciousness and she pulled out her notebook and wrote in it, instead of reading:

> "Black wings on the black floor. Black feelings going, going, going all the way. It comes out. It goes in. It writes, it uprights. It goes in and goes out. It flows All the Way to Texas. All the way back to the sugar-coated crystal-frosted cake, the sweet-dream flowers, white dungeons beneath the grass, all sweet dreams, all sweet flowers of youth, to where all the long-lost sweet bye-and-byes are. Are all gone. And long, cold winters of longing come. Where am I?
> I am in twin towers, in sky-piercing trees, in

gray granite bowers. In dawn-dim canyons built by people, in great hollow screams of brakes, in cold sky-blue whispers of wind. I am on long, whistling trips through black stone oceans, on a platform, on a plane, on a train long and longing to settle, to rest my weary wings in cooler depths, where flowers petal and little leaves green and warm shallows wash."

Writing calmed her. She remembered last night when she had walked into a light pole while walking into the wind with her head down. She had felt stupid when it happened, but now she felt the bruises on her head and shoulder. She could see the bruise on her face in her compact mirror under the tear tracks. She dug around in her purse for a tissue, found a yellow one wadded into a ball and blotted at her eyes, smelling the sweet smell coming from the tissue which had nestled in her purse next to her makeup.

THE PEPPER-POT AND THE LAMP-POST

The school semester would soon be over. She had to think about what she must do. She thought about the parties she had been invited to. She intended to enjoy them. They would help her get her mind off other things. At the next station she got up to press her way out of the door and change trains in lower Manhattan. She changed trains again in Brooklyn to catch the GG. By the time she got to school she was feeling better.

The snow made it hard for the students to walk from the subway this morning. They were slipping and sliding on the slick sidewalks, silent when they bumped into each other in narrow places. She turned to the right, along with the crowd, to go in to the campus, which was now all black and white and gray. The huge iron gates, more ornamental than useful, were swung wide open and the wide walk between them filled with students going in to their first classes.

As she entered the campus, she felt the familiar excitement again of going to graduate school. She was a student here!

Her first class was in the oldest building, up the wide stairway in a cavernous entry hall, echoing with the sounds of students talking, laughing, yelling, and stomping snow off their shoes. Up two flights to the landing, flanked by wide windows, dark wood making crosses against the white of the sky with snow falling.

She glanced outside as she went past the windows, seeing the campus from a different angle, from above. She could see dark paths crisscrossing over the white lawns where students in colored coats moved. She saw the pale, gray, stone structures of the library and administration buildings across the quadrangle, with the bare branches of the trees before them turning into a fuzz of tiny twigs against the white sky.

Then she was short of breath in the upper hall, and saw two male students lounging against the door at the top of the stairs who were smiling and greeting her—Howard and Bob, the tall redhead and the short friendly one. They were her friends now, having gone through a whole semester with her. They teased her as she passed through them and turned back to them, once inside the room, returning their smart remarks with a smirk. They followed her in.

In the classroom there were about twenty stools of all sizes and conditions. On the floor someone had swept up a pile of dust and left it. This room served as the sculpture room on other days. The enormous windows were frosted and reached all the way to the high ceiling. Some of them were open at the top, chains holding them at an angle out from the rest. The heat was intense, even on this cold day, unless windows were open. A couple of students stood near the windows and spoke and moved around at their approach. The teacher still had not arrived.

The teacher would not arrive until the moment class was supposed to start, because he was back in his office at the rear of the room, a big office with one glass wall; an old-fashioned office, where he could see out and observe the students.

Howard and Bob walked with Camille to the stools and sat on either side of her. A couple more friends also pulled their stools up to sit around Camille. She felt as if she were surrounded by friends. She had a warm feeling here at school. She felt as if she were liked here. She and the other students would spend a couple of hours together today, talking about art, and then separate to go to other classes, probably not seeing each other again for a couple of days. But when they returned, it would be as if they had not been apart. When they happened to see each other in other places, on or off campus, in nearby stores and cafes, they felt a camaraderie.

At exactly 9:00 a.m., the teacher came in, followed by Steve and Mark, his favorites. He went to a corner of the room, dragged out a stool, sat on it and began class.

Out in the snow afterward, Camille walked with Bob and Howard back toward the gate. Their bulk did not help keep her warm, but at least she did not notice the cold in their company. Bess trudged along behind them, on her way to the art store across the street, adding comments to the conversation from time to time. They all parted at the corner, but Howard followed Camille across the street and asked her if she would like to have something hot to drink at the coffee shop there. Camille looked down the long, white sidewalk toward the graduate building where her studio was, hesitating because she should go there and paint. But she did not often get treated to a cup of coffee, so she turned to go with him. He was obviously delighted and pushed the door open for her, making her go under his arm to enter. She laughed because he was so tall she could do it easily.

They sat in a red, vinyl booth on one side and watched other students coming and going up and down the aisle beside them, squeezing by because it was so crowded and talking loudly because everyone was talking at once. On the wall over the lunch counter were drawings of the owner, Ed, done in caricature, in charcoal, in pencil on a paper napkin, in ink behind glass, and so forth, dozens of them, all done by art students over the years. Other kinds of drawings were pinned up and a new cartoon was taped to the front of the cash register.

Camille picked at the black linoleum tabletop, tracing the pattern of the imitation marble and talked with Howard, alternately watching him and her hot cocoa steaming. It warmed her face as she waited for it to cool. As Howard's red beard moved, the multi-colored hairs glistened in the bright light coming in at an angle from the window beside them.

Camille looked out the dusty window. Students outside wore blacks, green plaids and red against white snow. They all looked cold. They carried books and big black portfolios as large as themselves, and bags over their shoulders. They wore black hats, boots, mittens. Howard was talking to her, saying something in an annoyed voice. Camille listened to him then, noting he was a little upset with her for not paying more attention to him. Why was it necessary that she pay attention to him? Sometimes men did not make any sense and she barely had enough patience to deal with them when they were in this mood. The things they talked about were scattered and obscure. They seemed to expect her to pay a lot of attention to them, because they had given her a little attention.

Howard was persistent. He wanted to take her out to dinner. He had asked her before. She declined. He said, well why don't I take you out one week and you take me out the next. That way it won't cost either of us too much and we'll go to nice restaurants that way. She looked at him dubiously. She knew she could not afford to take him out at all. But at least she would not owe him a favor for taking her out. She told him it would be okay, but after Christmas. He asked her if she was divorced yet and she said no, not yet, and drank her hot cocoa.

When they got up to leave she felt more depressed than when she went in. But Howard paid for the drinks and at least she felt warmer for the long trek to the graduate building. Howard insisted on kissing her good-bye on the lips as they parted. He did it nonchalantly, as if they were friends, but he always had to kiss her good-bye on the lips, though no-one else did. She left him without looking back.

Her studio was cold, but it was warmer than the outside. She put the painting smock on over her coat at first, until she warmed up. She moved the canvasses around and got out her palette, placing it on top of the table. She squeezed yellow, blue, red, black and white oil paint onto the palette and poured turpentine and linseed oil into the twin cups clipped to the edge of the palette. She gathered a handful of brushes from the drawer and, after adjusting the canvas, was ready to paint. For the next two hours she would be immersed in the process.

She painted on the nude for awhile, standing in front of the easel, thinking about what she would do sometimes, sometimes moving up to the canvas, changing what she had already painted, painting new areas, changing colors a little, adding highlights to painted areas.

After an hour, she stopped and looked out the window to get her mind off painting. This was necessary because she would see it more objectively when she turned and looked at the painting again after having removed her mind momentarily from the painting. An objective perspective was important for her. She knew from experience that the painting would eventually become warped by her internal astigmatism, a physical thing she dealt with, lodged in her own eyes and brain. She would not be able to see the astigmatic warp until she saw the painting afresh the next day – that is, unless she looked away and then back, at times, during the process. She felt akin to El Greco because of this.

She would attend another class after lunch. She brought water from the rest room down the hall in a cup, boiled it with an immersible heater and poured in soup powder. For lunch she sat in her easy chair at last, something she did not allow herself to do until this time of day, and sipped the "split pea" soup, the tea and ate the crackers and apple she had brought with her today. She looked at the large painting her studio-mate, Karen, had painted recently. Karen's show was to go up next week and she had been working on a large painting and framing the smaller ones. Karen seemed a nervous person, rarely speaking to Camille when she came in. She felt superior, supposed Camille, because she was graduating and Camille was just beginning. But at the end of this semester, Camille told herself, I will have completed one fifth of my graduate work.

After lunch, Camille added final touches to her painting for the day, doing some things she had thought of during lunch. Then she cleaned her space up and took her brushes to the rest room to wash them. Back in the studio, she took off her smock, put on some lipstick, a hat and mittens, gathered her books and locked the door behind her.

The first afternoon class was on the main campus, as the morning class had been. After class she had to go to the library and write some more on the paper she was completing for Humanities. She loved the library. The library was old and stood as a testimony to an age when artistry was prized more than efficiency in architecture. The stacks were of ornate iron, the floors of glass blocks. It was an inspiring place to work.

She found a quote she wanted to use sometime, in the D.H. Lawrence essay called *Why the Novel Matters* she was reading. He had written it in 1936. She wrote the word "love" beside it and read the passage again:

> *Me, man alive. I am a very curious assembly of incongruous parts. My yea! of today is oddly different from my yea! of yesterday. My tears of tomorrow will have nothing to do with my tears of a year ago. If the one I love remains unchanged and unchanging, I shall cease to love her. It is only because she changes and startles me into change and defies my inertia, and is herself staggered in her inertia by my changing, that I can continue to love her. If she stayed put, I might as well love the pepper-pot.*
>
> *In all this change, I maintain a certain integrity. But woe betide me if I try to put my finger*

on it. If I say of myself, I am this, I am that! – then, if I stick to it, I turn into a stupid fixed thing like a lamp-post. I shall never know wherein lies my integrity, my individuality, my me. I can never know it. It is useless to talk about my ego. That only means I have made up an idea of myself, and that I am trying to cut myself out to pattern. Which is no good. You can cut your cloth to fit your coat, but you can't clip bits off your living body, to trim it down to your idea.

Camille looked at the big clock on the wall in the library; it was 5:00 p.m. After class and working in the library she was feeling hungry for supper, so she decided to go home. She had to take the train back to the boat basin soon, if she was to get there before dark.

Leaving campus in the cold was difficult to do. It was snowing and then the dreadfully long ride on the subway. She knew she would get cold on the way to the subway stop and then get cold again walking back to the boat basin from the subway stop in Manhattan,. She decided she would stop at the grocery on the way home and get something to eat. She needed tea and sugar and maybe a vegetable. She had about five dollars to her name.

The weather was clearing by the time she got back to the West Side of Manhattan and the fresh snow was beautiful in the afternoon sunshine. It was beginning to melt. When snow melted, it was terrible to walk in because it became slushy. She shopped in the little grocery-deli and, with the added burden of a bag of groceries, picked her slippery way down the hill to the boat basin. It seemed to be warmer in her boat than usual and Camille noticed there was a new propane heater in the window. Grace had gotten the gas man to install it during the day while she was gone and had turned it on for her. That was nice.

She fixed supper and ate. Supper was the hardest time of the day for Camille. It was then that she missed the company of other people the most. She wished she could share her meal with someone. She tried to call Grace, and then April, but no-one was home. So, after she ate and washed dishes she started painting in the little studio at the back of the boat, looking out over the river and watching the changing light on the water, as she always did. The sun had gone down. Usually the sunsets were beautiful, but tonight's was bleak.

It was extremely cold at night now, though sometimes, even when the wind was blowing off the river, she felt warm inside. She worked until it was pitch black, feeling grateful for the heater Grace had installed. She did not think to turn on any lights until the lights from the dock came on. Then she turned on her lights and decided to eat dessert, a cream puff, without tea. She sat at the table and ate it in silence. After awhile she turned on her newest purchase, a black and white TV which she had bought from a couple moving out of a nearby boat. Its distracting noise and light filled the empty air with a racket. She tried to find an old movie, and then went back to work studying for finals.

Vince's boat was dark. By 12:00 midnight, he still had not called. She had not seen him on his boat the entire afternoon and wondered if he was around. He never went to sleep before 2:00 a.m., so Camille knew it would be all right to call him this late. To her surprise, he answered the phone immediately, and in a hushed voice told her to come outside quickly. Camille knew something was wrong by the tone of his voice. She put on her warm coat and boots and quietly locked the door behind her. When she stepped off her deck out into the dark, she realized he was standing on the dock behind her.

"Come with me," he whispered. He walked ahead of her, leading the way up the dock to the gate, out of the boat basin, and up the hill to the upstairs door to the garage. From that door one could look down the narrow metal stairs and out over the entire garage. He stepped just inside the door, onto the metal landing, pulling Camille in behind him, and closed the door, so that they stood in complete darkness. She stood in the corner behind him, wondering what was going on. She was a little frightened by the way he was acting.

"What. . .?" she began.

He motioned to her to be quiet before she could say anything else.

The air on the landing was chilly, damp and still, smelling of urine and moist stone. Camille stood still, letting her eyes adjust to the darkness. She could only see Vince in silhouette beside her, staring intently down over the cars in the cavernous underground garage. He was leaning back rigidly against the door he had closed. He did not move at all.

Camille was about to speak again, impatient to know what was going on, when she saw his hand slowly move, the hand he had held against his knee. In it was a gun. She could make it out now. She froze in her corner, wishing she was somewhere else. Why had he brought her?

"Did you hear shots?" Vince asked in a low voice.

"No." Camille's voice seemed too loud to even her own ears. She sank even further down in her corner behind Vince. The draft moved around her, through the cracks around the door, bringing mixtures of gasoline fumes and oil to her nostrils. She could hear the dull thud of cars passing over the highway above them.

"Some creeps are trying to steal cars, my car," said Vince. Camille looked down through the sparse metal railings separating them from the parking area below. Her eyes had adjusted to the darkness, but she could only see the dark, huddled shapes of parked cars, icily outlined by an indirect light located somewhere high in the dripping roof of the underground garage.

"I think they're gone now," said Vince. "Oh no." His voice sank. "The police are here. Be still!" He stepped back, almost stepping on Camille. She could not move in her corner. They stood that way for a minute, then, unable to stand the suspense, they both stepped forward to look over the edge.

Below, a police car, its lights off, came purring down the entrance ramp. All of a sudden a bright beam from the squad car flashed across the parked cars. Two men dashed from behind one of the cars. Vince stepped forward quickly, raised both hands and fired one shot. Camille startled, stared into the darkness, trying to see what had happened. One of the men ran away from Vince's car. The police car came faster through the garage, shining its beam around and over the cars. Then its red light started flashing and a loud voice boomed out. "Halt!"

They could see both men running. One ran away from the light, his footsteps echoing hollowly in the cavern, ducking behind parked cars as he ran. The other man followed him, but running in a more circuitous route. There were shouts and deafening shots from the police car, echoing like thunder around them. It looked as if both men had escaped through the door in the side of the garage which led to the park. After what seemed like a long time, the police car started again with a roar, speeding around toward where the men had run, its tires squealing noisily at the corners. It wove its way to the other side of the garage, where the door was. There it stopped and turned, finding its way out to the park again, tires squealing as it sped toward and up the exit ramp.

There was silence and blackness again.

"God damn them!" said Vince quietly, leaning out over the railing. He spoke in a low voice, explaining. "I saw them. They were going through the garage, going into every car, working their way toward mine. I called the police twice, but they never came. When they got to my car I shot at them. I wasn't going to let them get away with my stuff. They had the back door open. I think my shot hit the door. They heard it and looked up at me, or at least in my direction. Did you see them? I don't think they knew where the shots came from."

"I didn't know you had a gun," was all Camille could say. She found she was quivering from fear and excitement and her voice came out shakily. "What if you hit someone? Wouldn't you be arrested?"

"They would never know who did it." Vince was standing loosely, rolling the gun over in his hands affectionately. Then he put it in a little bag. "This gun isn't registered."

Camille could feel his excitement, though he acted casual. There was tension and delight coming through. They walked back to the boats at a fast pace. They stepped inside his boat, after he motioned Camille to come in, and Vince paced back and forth, his coat still on, looking out the windows from time to time.

"Did they get anything out of your car?"

"No. I scared them off. But I'm going to go back to close up the car in awhile." He looked out the window toward the garage. "The one guy, he looked right up at me when the bullet went over his head and hit the door frame. That's when he went around to the other side of the car. The other guy was already there and they laid low. Then I went back to call the police again. I wish I had killed one of them, but I don't think I hit them." He paced up and down the room, looking out the window each time he passed.

"Sit down." he commanded in a still nervous voice, when he noticed Camille still standing up. She sat abruptly. "You want some coffee?" He quickly strode to the galley to put on water.

"Sure," said Camille, wondering if she should leave. It was scary being around him and she was tired from working all day. She stayed only a few more minutes, drinking her coffee quickly, then pleaded exhaustion.

PEOPLE FOR LUNCH

Camille met Grace at noon at a restaurant in SoHo. Grace arrived with another friend, Maureen, who was also a one-time girlfriend of Vince's.

Grace introduced Maureen to Camille outside and they all went up three steps into the old building. The bar inside served special coffees and was very crowded. They went past the coffee bar into the back room, where they were seated beneath hanging plants and a skylight with stained glass windows. The colored light shone softly down around them and the tables were small and old. It was neither elegant nor expensive, and seemed more like someone's home. They were at a table in a corner and the three women looked around and commented on the weather. There was an old cast-iron stove nearby that gave off a dull heat. It felt to Camille like she was at home, being a part of a group of women sitting at a table, eating lunch.

She wondered what Grace and Maureen usually talked about when they had lunch. Surely they did not talk about children, or their new car, or how they were decorating their house for the next party or their husband's latest fault, as the women in Billington, Texas did. She did not know Maureen at all, so Camille listened while she and Grace talked. They discussed what various other women they knew were doing and the stage of life they were in now and who everyone was going out with. As they talked about mutual friends, Camille heard them say they admired women who were strong enough to not begin relationships that promised to be degrading, shallow or casual.

"A casual relationship is going nowhere," said Grace. "There's not going to be any depth there. Why start it?" She dipped her spoon into her cream of broccoli soup which had just arrived.

Maureen turned to Camille curiously when she asked what "casual" meant. Maureen was larger than both of the other women, very buxom, with a lot of curly, reddish-blond hair. Camille supposed she might have appeared attractive to Vince at one time. He probably hated her now, as that was his usual pattern. She had never heard him mention her name. Maureen stopped talking and gazed upon Camille with large, black-eyeliner-rimmed eyes. Her hair kept falling into her face, for, though she had pinned it up loosely on top of her head, it kept on escaping from the pins in a very charming manner. She lifted her fork as if it was a wand and waved it around as she talked.

"Honey," she said, "it means the only reason he wants to see you is for sex. Speaking of which. . . ." and she turned her whole body toward Grace again, waiting expectantly for something.

Grace first glanced at Camille for a moment, and then smiled a tiny, embarrassed smile. "I'm seeing someone," she explained, "but," and here she paused and addressed herself to Maureen, "I don't think it's casual. He seems pretty serious. He's over at my place or calls me every day."

"Do you like him?" asked Maureen, giving a little flip to her head, acting as if she was bored and picking at her salad.

"The only problem," Grace spoke again, "is next week he probably won't call at all. He's very 'on and off.'"

"Sounds like he's not sure," commented Maureen.

Grace looked at Camille over her lifted spoon, now filled with soup. "Please don't mention this to Vince," she asked of her. "He wouldn't understand. You know how jealous he gets, unnecessarily so. After all, I'm not living with him any more. Just because he hasn't effected a closure doesn't mean I haven't, and can't date other people." She tipped the side of the spoon into her mouth as the two women watched her face closely for any tics, eyebrow lifts or downward glances, trying to discern her true feelings.

"Effected a closure?" queried Camille. The vocabulary was new to her. She was astounded at the way they talked so casually about relationships.

"You know. He hasn't dealt with our separation – made it a fact in his mind so he can deal with me on another level – the level on which everyone else deals with me." She said it so matter-of-factly that Camille felt the whole world knew the dynamics of this kind of situation except her. It seemed an intriguing idea.

Everyone was thoughtful while they ate for a few minutes. Then Maureen said "Did you hear about Serena's boyfriend? How he broke off with her?"

"No!" said Grace, slowly looking up, trying not to appear too eager.

"Well, he tells her, <u>after</u> they make love one night, 'this is the last time.' He isn't going to see her again. Can you believe it? <u>After</u> they make love . . . to say something like that. Then he got up and left."

"Rude and thoughtless," pronounced Grace loudly, looking at Maureen with disgust written on her face while she chewed. Camille was horrified. The poor woman! To think that anyone could be so heartless was a major shock to her.

"Serena was furious," said Maureen. "She'll never speak to him again. And what do you bet he'll call her again?"

"I don't blame her," said Grace.

Camille was speechless and astounded at the cool, rational way the two women discussed something so terrible. Their analysis of such events was so . . . so cold-hearted and objective. She wished she could act as uninvolved in her own affairs. It was as if they looked at their own and other people's emotions through a microscope, observing cells' movements toward and against each other with detachment, in order to predict what the next squirm would be, dispassionately, as if they were laboratory technicians.

Grace talked for awhile about her new boyfriend, who was into computers. She complained about his lack of resolve in committing himself to a steady relationship with her. But in spite of her complaints she seemed thoroughly impressed by him. Since this was the first she had heard about him, Camille asked her how long she had been seeing him.

"A couple of months." she said. "I haven't dated many people since Vince and I broke up." Camille was surprised she was dating anyone. She had never said a thing that would suggest to Vince or her that she was dating.

After lunch, the three women walked to the Village Gallery where they and others were planning to hold the group exhibition for the Westbeth Women Artists' Group, located in a big building on the West side of the Village. They were the first to arrive at the meeting. The superintendent let them in the empty gallery space with his ring of keys.

The group of women looked around the unlit, echoing rooms with tall ceilings, examined the dirty walls that would need to be painted before they could use them and the layout of the space, trying to decide where everyone would show their work. Camille and Grace decided to share one of the small rooms, since their work would go well together. But the walls were filthy in there, as was the floor. Grace left to go get her prints and Camille asked the superintendent for paint. He led her to the storage room, where she got a brush, a big bucket of white paint and started painting her space.

More women started to arrive and claim their spaces. Some brought paintings to begin hanging. The Village Gallery had hired a young man to paint and mop. He arrived and started to mop floors. At 5:15 Camille looked at her watch. She had finished painting over the dirty spots on the wall of her room. Grace had not returned, so she went to Ward gallery, a few blocks away, to get a couple of her paintings. Grace was there, hanging her work when she got back. Many other paintings were hung in the rest of the gallery, as well. The other women artists stood around in the rooms, deciding where things would look best.

Camille measured and pounded nails into the wall, trying to hang her paintings level. She could hear several of the women arguing in the room next door. They couldn't decide whether an artist named Judy should get the choice spot in the entrance, where her paintings would be the first ones to be seen when people arrived, or whether she should get the spot by the window, where her biggest painting would be seen outside. Judy wanted the spot in front and she and someone named Phyllis almost had a fight over it. They reached a compromise at last, allowing Phyllis to hang one of her small paintings in the window alongside Judy's big one, as she had too many paintings to fit into the entrance area. Judy grudgingly allowed this, even though she had the biggest painting, admitting that she did not have enough paintings to fill the area designated for her. All this was going on while Camille methodically measured and hung her work in the second room.

Camille was thinking of Vince. He had told her he was going over to New Jersey again, to take his car to the garage. He had said he would call from there, would try to reach her at the Village Gallery, but she had not heard from him. She had invited him to eat supper with her and he was supposed to tell her whether he could or not.

She had to go back to her boat to retrieve a painting and bring it back down to the Village Gallery. She had just made it back and was inside her boat when she heard Vince go into his boat. So she called him.

"Vince! I didn't know you had come back," she said. "You said you would call me."

"What about?" he said sullenly. She could tell by the tone of his voice that he was in a bad mood.

"You were going to tell me if you could eat supper with me or not."

"I told you twice last night -- NO!" In actuality, when Camille had talked to him last night he had been doubtful, but had said he would call her and let her know and had made sure to get the telephone number for the Village Gallery from her so he could call and tell her for sure.

Camille hung up, got her painting and went back to the gallery, hung it, talked with Grace about the opening, how the room looked, and began to clean up. It was 10:00 before she got back to the boat basin.

She dumped her tools and hanging items on the floor of her boat and began sorting them out. She had borrowed a portfolio of Vince's to carry the painting in, so after washing up, she took the big portfolio under her arm and stepped outside to return it to him. In the dark she could make out the form of April, out on the deck of her boat, leaning against her door. Camille called to her, and when it was obvious that she had not heard her, went closer. She looked upset, with tears welling out of her huge, black-rimmed eyes.

"Oh, Camille!" she turned to her with relief, "I'm locked out."

"What happened?" Camille asked. April did not have a coat on, and was dressed only in a robe and slippers.

"I walked out of the door and it closed behind me. It's locked. Chuck is asleep inside. I'm glad he's not awake or he would be crying, but I'm freezing. I've tried everything to get back in, but I can't."

Camille tried her own key in the lock, but of course it did not fit. "I'll try a bobby pin," she said, pulling one out of her hair. They tried wiggling it around in the keyhole, but nothing happened. The door was made of metal and had a big, strong lock. Camille suggested she would try the windows, but April already had. They were all double sealed storm windows closed against the cold and locked from inside.

After making a trip around her boat, Camille saw April going over to Vince's boat. She knocked on the door and Camille joined her, a little nervous about what Vince would do, since he had not been in a good mood earlier and was unpredictable with strangers.

Vince took a long time answering the door and when he did, he came outside with a bag full of laundry, as if he was leaving. Camille could tell by the surly look on his face he was not happy to be disturbed. But when he saw April with Camille and they told him the problem, his mood changed. Suddenly he was the chivalrous gentleman. He went back into his boat for a credit card.

"When is Charlie supposed to get back?" Camille asked April. April stood shivering and looking at her boat in despair.

"Not until after midnight. He's in rehearsal. The baby may wake up before then. If he finds I'm not there, he'll cry. that's what I'm worried about."

Vince returned with a credit card and some paper.

"You can slip the credit card in the crack between the door and the frame and it will open," he said, pushing the card into the crack. Nothing happened. He tried the paper, but it bent. He folded the paper and tried again. It bent again. April was becoming more and more nervous. Finally Vince said he would go for Eddie, the dock-master, who could open it with his skeleton key, and he left.

Camille led April, shivering, into her boat and they opened a window so they could hear the baby if he cried. Camille put on a pot of water to make hot coffee for April and started cooking some chicken breasts and rice, as she had not yet eaten.

Soon Vince returned, still carrying his laundry bag. He walked right into Camille's boat without knocking and plopped down in the other chair at the table, across from April. He acted as if he always did this. He said Eddie was coming. Camille served them coffee and checked on the chicken.

When Eddie arrived, he opened April's door with no problem. She checked on the still-sleeping Chuck with obvious relief. At Camille's invitation, she got her key out of her purse and came back to the boat to finish her coffee.

Vince had never talked to April before, other than greeting her on the dock, and he was asking her all kinds of questions, finding out everything about her. Camille knew he was attracted to her; who wouldn't be? She was truly beautiful, with her fine-boned face and skin as smooth as porcelain, her eyes of dark blue, rimmed in thick black lashes and long, lustrous black hair. She even looked beautiful with no makeup and an old jacket on over her robe.

When the chicken was done Camille cut it up and served it with rice and a sauce she had made out of onions, flour and condensed milk, a little cheese, salt and pepper, which was all she could find in her cabinets. They ate it with green salad.

As they ate, Camille realized Vince was playing the same game with April that Grace and he had played with her, recalling things Camille and he had done together, calling on her for details, to show April they were intimate. He was showing April he was part of Camille's life.

The phone rang and Camille answered. It was a woman who had bought some of her paintings, calling from New Jersey, saying she was coming to the opening at the Village Gallery with her boyfriend. Margie invited Camille to go skiing with them on the weekend and to bring Vince, whom she had met at the opening. Camille looked up from the phone and asked Vince if he wanted to go. He said no, he had to pick up his car early on Sunday.

Camille was a little puzzled. It was such a wonderful opportunity, to go skiing, with someone else paying for everything. She thought maybe Vince had never skied. She had never asked him. Or perhaps he did not want to spend the weekend with her. But she did not question him, just gave her regrets to Margie and said she would look for them at the opening this week. Margie said perhaps they could take her and Vince to dinner after the opening and Camille accepted her invitation without consulting Vince.

"Listen," she said to Vince when she returned, "I just thought. . . what about the party we're invited to on Wednesday? You know, the one in the loft in SoHo?"

"I'm not taking anyone," said Vince, sullenly.

"I was looking forward to going," Camille complained. "I was looking forward to seeing an artist's loft. I've only seen a couple." April listened to them tussle over the plans as Camille talked Vince into taking her. Camille felt a little bolder with Vince, since she had an audience.

They heard footsteps on the dock and a handsome, white-haired man poked his head in the partially open door, saw April and smiled.

"What's going on here?" he asked jovially, "a little boat party?" Charlie was immediately likeable, a person who was big, seemingly always happy and kind.

"Come on in." Camille said and began to explain why April was there. Charlie stepped into the boat, red-cheeked from the wind, his thinning white hair blowing out from underneath a knit cap. But he said he could not stay because he was so tired. April rose at his words, suddenly looking a little tired herself, took Charlie's hand and they left, thanking Camille and Vince for their help and promising to come again.

Vince and Camille were left alone. Camille rose and silently began to clean up. Vince finished his coffee and a cigarette in silence and said he had to go walk his dog. When he left, Camille finished washing dishes, tired now from all she had done that day. But she sat down to type the final draft of her term paper, which had to be handed in on Monday. The semester was drawing to a close and there was a lot to finish up.

She was still typing at 3:30 A.M. when Vince called.

"I noticed your light was on," he said, "aren't you going to sleep tonight?"

"I doubt it," she said, "I have to hand in this term paper on Monday and this weekend is the opening of our exhibition, so I'll be too busy to do it tomorrow."

"Well, I'm going to take my shower and go to bed," he said.

Camille wondered, in her tired stupor, if he was offering her an invitation, but decided that, even if he was, she would ignore it. She had seen enough of him for today. After he hung up she decided to stop typing and finish the next day. She was too tired to continue – her eyes kept on closing.

SLEEPING WITH HOWARD

The next day was a busy day for Camille. It was a day that "gave her something to worry about so she wouldn't worry about other things," as Vince would have put it.

Bobby Holliday was running on the track first thing in the morning, when she arrived. He ran with her awhile, giving her pointers. He told her she ran fast for her size, perhaps too fast. On her fifth lap he timed her. It was a quarter mile track and she ran it in one minute, 40 seconds. He came out on the track and joined her as she jogged to cool down, talking as they ran.

"I'm playing at Sweet Basil's in the Village on Wednesday," he said. "Can you come?"

"I certainly will," she said as she puffed along. "I'm going to a party that night and then we'll come by the club to hear you."

"Fine." Bobby smiled down at her from his height.

"I've got a busy day today," said Camille. "I've got to shop and meet some people for lunch and then get ready for an exhibition."

"And I thought all you artists did was seclude yourselves in your studio and paint," said Bobby.

"Yeah, like all you musicians do is hang out and jam," returned Camille. They were slowing as they came down the track to the entrance. "Be sure and save me a place at Sweet Basil's."

"All rah-eet," said Bobby, slapping her hand in a farewell gesture before running off, his tall, black body already showing through the sweat on the yellow T-shirt he wore.

The weekend went fast. The exhibition opening at the Village gallery went well, with lots of friends showing up to mingle with friends of all the other artists and create the bedlam everyone wanted to feel at an opening.

Margie showed up with her boyfriend, Cal, and another couple; the men were both lawyers. Margie wanted to see Vince again, but Vince had not come to the opening. They were standing around together; Margie reminded the men they were taking Camille out to dinner afterward, and that's when Howard sidled up to

Camille, wearing a beautiful red, wool coat. He always dressed fashionably, and, with his height and looks, was always noticeable.

His ears had perked up at the sound of a dinner invitation. Camille suggested Howard could go as her date and everyone seemed to like the idea.

Camille and Howard looked at all the paintings and visited with all their friends before they left. When the group went into the cloak room to get their coats, Cal closed the door behind them and got out a little white paper package, opened it and offered the contents, a white powder, to everyone. Camille asked what it was.

"White Lady. Bliss." He replied. Everyone refused it but Cal himself, who put a tiny bit up his nose. Outside, the six people got into the two BMW's and drove to Tribeca, to an expensive French restaurant where Cal knew the maitre d'.

They were seated at a good table, served bottles of excellent wine and ordered food. Cal, a criminal lawyer, began drinking immediately, and the more he drank, the more aggressive he became. As the dinner progressed he acted more and more like he was the center of attention. He pretended as if they were before the judge and began to pick on Camille loudly, as if she were on the stand. He directed very personal, pointed questions to her. It seemed amazing to Camille that in spite of taking drugs and drinking, he still had his lawyer's wits about him. He addressed Howard and asked him how long he had known Camille and if they were in love or just dating. Howard only answered the first question, saying they had known each other for about three months.

"How old are you?" Cal addressed this question to Camille. Everyone at the table got very quiet at this direct demand.

"Thirty," answered Camille truthfully, after she counted up to be sure. There were sounds of disbelief and Margie said she looked twenty.

"How long were you married?" Cal asked.

"Ten years."

"What did your husband do?"

"He teaches philosophy at a University." Camille began to wonder where this was leading and why Cal was pursuing this line of questioning, being too naive and hassled to realize she did not need to answer.

"How long you been separated?"

"About four months."

"Do you still love him?" At this, everyone at the table began to protest this intrusive examination of Camille.

"Cal!" Louis exclaimed, "Such personal questions! You don't have to answer," said Louis to Camille.

"Just curious." said Cal dismissively, and fell silent. But he continued to watch Camille and she could not imagine why he would ask her such personal questions.

Dinner was served and eaten, along with a lot of jokes and rib-aching laughter. Lawyers can be very funny, thought Camille. It was wonderful, being among witty, educated people. She wondered if she would enjoy living this kind of life so much, if she did it all the time.

As they left the restaurant, Cal still did not appear drunk, although he had consumed almost a bottle of wine. He was talking to Howard rather loudly, trying to convince him to go back to Camille's place for the night. Camille listened, amused.

"Come on, we'll drop you two off at her place."

"Really, Cal," she finally protested herself, "I probably am going straight to bed. I'm not used to drinking and I was up late last night."

"But it's only 11:00! If we did not have to drive all the way back to the Jersey shore tonight we'd be partying until dawn."

"Well, I have to be at school early in the morning."

Howard agreed with Camille, politely, saying. "Just take me by my place on your way."

Camille thought she detected a sense of relief on Howard's part when Cal finally let him go home, rather than having to go all the way back to the boat basin with her.

"Well, you're both coming skiing with us this weekend, aren't you?" asked Cal, peremptorily.

"Oh, yes, please." chimed in Margie. "I'll fix up the guest bedroom for you. I've redecorated it in a dark rose."

"Thank you very much, but I have to sit with the exhibition this weekend," said Camille. She could not imagine spending the whole weekend with Howard, being expected to sleep with him, sharing the guest bathroom with him and so forth.

"Maybe you could arrange for someone to sit for you." said Howard, who had been sitting quietly beside her as they drove through the narrow streets toward his home. Camille looked at him in surprise.

"I'll call you later this week," said Camille to Margie hastily, wishing they had not asked her in front of Howard. She certainly could not bear to spend a whole weekend with Howard, Cal and Margie, though she realized it was very nice of them to ask her.

So she sat in the dark as the car sped along and conversations swirled around her, wondering what Howard would look like without any clothes on. They dropped him off at his apartment building in Little Italy and he kissed Camille good-bye on the lips again. He was very polite, but was he as nice without his elegant clothes? His body was so tall and lanky, it was hard to imagine. Camille shook her head and thought of other things.

They dropped Camille off at the entrance to the boat basin and she walked through the cold wind to her boat, wrapping her flimsy coat around her.

Inside her boat she turned the light and radio on. She needed distraction, since it was so quiet and empty. The hollow feeling she had was worse than any void she had felt. It seemed deathly quiet, and even though she had the radio on; she almost went to turn it on again because the music did not soothe her as it usually did. She stood at the door for a moment and looked out the window at Vince's empty boat. There were no lights on there. He was gone. She changed into her nightgown and brushed her teeth. She got her literature book and crawled into the cold bed, turning on only the bedside lamp. But her eyes closed before she could read one page.

During the next few days Camille sat in the gallery a few hours each day and studied for exams. She went to her last classes and prepared paintings for the end of the semester. Christmas was coming and she dreaded it. There was a holiday spirit in the air, even though there was no snow. People seemed a little more polite. She had come to enjoy New York. The people were interesting. They did not seem different than people anywhere else.

In the town she came from in Texas, were they hard and unfriendly. When she moved there, as a bride of two years, the college professors and wives treated her as if she did not belong. The citizens of the town of Billington seemed hospitable, but it was shallow politeness. If your family had not lived there for generations, you really did not belong. She was much more accepted in her parents' home town, one hundred miles away, since her grandparents had lived there and raised her parents there and everyone knew both families.

Camille's mother called on Wednesday morning, from her new retirement condo in New Mexico, asking if she and John were coming to visit over the Christmas holidays. She wanted to prepare for their visit and she had heard nothing. There was complaint in her voice. Camille made excuses, saying some of John's relatives were coming to their house during the holidays. She did not have the courage to talk to her mother about the things that weighed most heavily on her mind, chief among which was that she planned to divorce John. Her mother would not understand. It would ruin her holidays if she knew. It also seemed such a foreign subject to interject into the conversation; a conversation that took for granted she and John would be married forever. No one in her family had ever divorced and she knew the disapproval of the whole family would come down on her head when the news came out.

THE LITTLE BLACK BOOK

It was almost 3:00 when he saw it by the telephone. It was Kim's address book. He knew it was hers because he had seen her fish it out of her pocketbook and use it. But he had never touched it. It was always out of sight even when she slept, in with her wallet and all of her other personal belongings, in her purse by her bed. But there it was, sitting all by itself, out on the desk beside the telephone. How had it gotten there? He picked it up, surprised at its light weight. It was small and brown, the thin, leather cover frayed and coming off the spine. It was so small it fit in the palm of his hand. It was slightly curled from the constancy of being used or being in her pocketbook. She must have left it by mistake when she came back to the office this morning after spending last night at his house. She had the key to his office in order to access the filing cabinets they kept their research in.

The afternoon sun was shining in on him through the bare branches outside the window, warming his office a little. It shone on the gold edges of the pages. He should put the book back down and not pick it up again, he thought. The possibility of slightly burning the cool quiet of a Saturday afternoon, an afternoon when he could get a lot of work done, was there. But he did not put it down. Kim had gone to the mall on her scooter about an hour ago. He knew she had because they had talked on the phone earlier. She had called him and said she would meet him here to work on the new chapter at 5:00 this afternoon; so she would not be here for quite awhile. He knew her habits by now. He would have plenty of time to look at the book without her coming in on him. He opened the cover and looked at the first page.

Kim Bonney
1193 Ridgewood Highway, #5
Billington, Texas
(817) 687-1275
Car license: lLUC643
Social Security No.: 911-48-8077

He turned to the page where his name would be written, under the M's. There it was, inked in simply with her best printing, JOHN MONROE; below it were his phone numbers, obviously entered since she had started sleeping with him a month ago. He glanced down the page where the names of men she met after him would have been written. There was only one other entry, Mitchell, scribbled quickly, with a prefix number for the next county. His heart jumped. So she had met a Mitchell after she had met him?

"So what?" he said to himself. Kim met lots of men. She had been free and single when she met him, and there was no reason to think she might have changed, at least for awhile, after she started sleeping with him. A folded slip of white paper fell out as he turned the page, a sales receipt. He fetched it back off the carpet where it had fallen, near the desk, and saw it had something written on the back, a name with a phone number, written in someone else's handwriting in bold black ink. It was another man's name.

"My gosh, All she knows are men!" he thought as he turned it over to see where she got it. *The Blue Parakeet* it read, with the usual accounting of numbers below, totaling $24.79 and a date at the bottom: November 16. He realized the date was last week. He had to see a calendar. What day was that?

He turned the slip of paper over to see the name again. "Mike T." it read in rough, hurried schoolboy cursive, "469-1149" and around it were marks in pencil. Doodles, with the lines drawn over and over, enough so that there were grooves pressed in the paper, as if she had sat for a long time talking and doodling around and around the name.

He looked at calendar he kept on his desk. November 16 had been Tuesday. What had happened Tuesday? It was a regular class day and he had a dentist's appointment in the afternoon, had marked it on his calendar. When had she had time to go out to the Blue Parakeet on Tuesday? He did not even know where the Blue Parakeet was, though he had heard talk of it as a local singles' bar.

John pulled the Billington telephone book out from under the desk where it sat with a thin layer of dust on its cover and turned to the yellow pages. Blue Horizon, Blue Jean Co., Blue Moon Diner, Blue Parakeet Bar. There it was: The Blue Parakeet Bar, 1057 Dallas

Drive. It was a bar. And she had spent $24.79 on drinks on Tuesday. His mind was buzzing. It was hard to think. He had to get himself together and think. This man, Mike T., probably was just someone who had pressed himself on her and given her his number. But then she had called it. She had obviously called, or he had called her–and they had talked for a long time. The doodles must have been done while she nervously talked to him. He realized he was shaking. Could he be jealous? He should just put the book back down and forget it.

He folded the sales slip back up and replaced it in the back of the book. He did not remember where it had been. Maybe it had been in the middle. It must have been in the middle because it fell out while he was flipping the pages. He moved it to the middle and put the book back on the desk, trying to remember how it had been placed beside the telephone. He turned his back on it and looked out the window, his mind in shock. He was still shaking. Tuesday, Tuesday. What had happened on Tuesday? He picked up the stack of papers he had lain on the desk and walked back to the window again, automatically shuffling through the papers and trying to read what was written on them.

On Tuesday he had gone to his dentist appointment during the day. He had not been able to work that evening, as they usual did, since he did not feel well. He had not talked to Kim on the phone that evening, after having told her he was going to go to his appointment in the afternoon. But where had she been? He came back from his appointment in the late afternoon and had begun to work, and he assumed she was in classes, but he didn't know what classes she took and assumed they were all over the campus.

He usually spent most of the day teaching, and in between them was in his office, counseling students or writing. Kim usually spent the day going to class and working on her own work or his in the library. On Saturdays she did nothing, sleeping till late and then going to the mall, unless she had tests, and then she spent Saturday studying in the library. Usually the two of them worked in his office on Saturday afternoon, then ate supper at his house. On Sundays she hung out with her girlfriends over brunch and obviously talked about men, as she had related some of the flattering things they had said about him. But her real love was writing the book with him late on Saturday afternoons and every evening after classes. She told him she enjoyed it and had let him know how much she loved it by her actions. She was always there, every evening, to work with him on it, unless there was some good reason not to. For a student, she seemed to have a lot of leisure time, but that was the graduate student's life today, he told himself.

It was hard for John to imagine having leisure time. He had studied and worked hard for years, as a student, making the honors roll in every school he had gone to. Even now, though he enjoyed his job, he hardly had a minute to make a personal phone call during his busy day, or even to take lunch. The idea of sitting around all day with nothing to do would be as foreign to him as living in a prehistoric cave with no books. His house was full of books, but Kim's apartment featured a balcony over a fancy courtyard and a swimming pool. When the weather was nice, Kim lay there in the sun. John had joined her once, when he was becoming involved with her.

He remembered the thrill the first time he saw her long, tan body, stripped down to a tiny, shiny bathing suit, laying as if waiting to be ravished, by the pool. He was expecting to see her beauty, but when he actually walked into the courtyard and saw her and how beautiful she was, compared to the other women around the pool, he could not believe his luck. Her blond hair and piercing blue eyes were the frosting on the cake, because she had a beautiful face and a great body to set them off. She rose and came walking across the concrete toward him, towel in hand, and had him sit on the plastic chair beside her, while he surreptitiously looked her up and down.

She stretched out again on the plastic lounge chair in her newly-bought chartreuse and pink suit, looking like a Playboy Bunny. His admiring stare flattered her, but then he became self-conscious. He knew he was a lot older than she. His hair was thinning and his body was not perfect. He had not exposed it to the sun since he was a kid, so his skin was pale. His face was handsome, but his physique was not what it used to be. His main impression of himself was "fat." He hated it, but there it was. He could not bring himself to lose weight and he usually did not feel very confident around women like Kim.

At one time he had been very handsome and had a good, slim body. That was when he was first going with Camille. John had met

Camille while he was still in undergraduate school. They had been young and had studied together. Some nights they spent together they had not studied. But when they graduated, he realized he did not want to be separated from her and suggested they live together. He received a grant to go to graduate school, which began in the fall. She went to live with her parents for the summer. He found an apartment in Chicago and when he started graduate school he asked her to come to Chicago to be with him. By then he had decided to marry her and, on short notice, they married at the end of the summer in her parent's church.

They had been married ten years. They had not had children because he was waiting for the right time. Camille wanted them, but he refused for the time being, as he could not imagine children running around while he was trying to write. Perhaps after he finished his book.

Kim was the first affair he had since they married, and the first woman he had "courted" since Camille. Although he did not have much experience with women, he found he had a real talent for saying witty things. He found himself saying things which surprised even him. He heard words coming out of his mouth he normally would never have said; funny, insightful things, which Kim found hilarious.

And Kim made him laugh, too. She had a habit of telling dirty jokes and this somehow loosened him up, even though they were jokes he never would have repeated, even to his men friends. Then there came a time when somehow almost everything he said in her presence seemed suggestive. She giggled and blushed at his simplest phrase and after his first embarrassment, he found he loved it.

John had little experience with sex before Camille, outside of some petting with a couple of girls in high school. None of them had been as forward as Kim, none as skilled at making him feel good, none able to flatter him, none saying she loved him so easily, and no-one had ever told him she wanted to be with him forever, maybe even to live with him some day. Kim had told him all these things within the first month they had become involved, before he could hardly dare to hope it might come true. At that point, his thoughts of Camille were almost at the point of wishing she would never come back.

It was a whirlwind romance and John had been swept off his

feet by this beautiful woman. She was so smart and beautiful, so understanding, so discreet, so funny. They laughed a lot, in bed and out. She knew exactly what to say and do in every situation and seemed to need him very much. The only thing that bothered him was he knew that she sometimes drank. One faculty friend in the department mentioned having seen her in a bar. And sometimes when he called her apartment at night she was not there. He knew she drank some, but he had never seen her drunk.

He recalled that first night when they had stayed up, working on the final draft of one of the chapters until the sun was rising and John was actually leaning on Kim, he was so tired. She had brought wine and they had finally imbibed. He had drunk one glass and actually become a little drunk. He said he had to go home, but he had accomplished a lot and he felt wonderful about it. Kim said she should drive him home, since he had drunk liquor. He protested, but she led him to her car and there, in the early morning light, gave him a long, probing kiss that aroused him. She drove him home and took him up to the door and went inside with him. They fell into bed together and it happened.

He had to admit he had fallen into sin in spite of himself. He had felt guilty afterward, but when he confessed to Albert, Albert reminded him that Camille had left him and was probably sleeping around in New York. Besides, every man has an affair every once in awhile. He had been married ten years and he had never cheated on Camille? What a waste! All this was according to Albert. But John needed little excuse to make love to Kim again.

She was sleeping with him regularly within a month of their first night of having sex. John was a little stunned by it all. He had never had another woman in his house besides Camille and was nervous about it. The neighbors seemed to think nothing of his going out at night by himself and never saw her come and go. But in spite of the danger, he would rather she stay over at his house.

When he stayed at her apartment he was put off by the people in the lobby, the array of sports equipment, skis, diving equipment, the tremendous amount of makeup in the bathroom, clothes jammed into her closets and thrown all over her bedroom. He accepted them at first, in his pride of having her. But eventually he could not tolerate the mess and she slept over at his house a couple of times each week, coming over late and leaving early. She would put her scooter on one side of the garage, his small car fit in the other half, and they closed the garage door so the neighbors would not see.

It never entered John's mind that Kim would be unfaithful to him. When he was with her she never talked about other men, and when they occasionally walked down the hall together, she never looked at or spoke to other men unless they spoke to her first. Some of the men students knew her. They smiled and spoke, but she was straight-faced with them and never encouraged them in a sexual way, as she originally had with John. He knew she had gone out with some of the students before she met him. She had told him that and he appreciated her honesty.

When he first told Albert about Kim, Albert seemed amazed and envious that she was actually sleeping with him. Afterward, Albert discreetly asked around and told him she had a reputation. After that Albert acted hostile toward her, which annoyed John, as Albert was his only friend and now he would not be able to talk about Kim with him. He assumed Albert was jealous.

A few days later, Albert again told John she was known to be a flirt and had lots of boyfriends, which John took to be sour grapes on his part. He knew she had gone with one or two other men in the past from things she said, but obviously she had settled on him. She had reassured John that he was her one and only. Not that she had always said it, but he knew it was true from the way she acted.

It would be a shock to him if she was going to bars and picking up men. Now – of all times! He was sleeping with her two nights a week. Why would she need to do that? She did not need other men now. She said their sex was fantastic. She wanted it and he enjoyed it, too. It did not seem to be as exciting for her as it had been in the beginning, but still it was good. He was always ready to satisfy her when she wanted him to, though sometimes he pulled away in the mornings when she would caress him. That may have hurt her feelings, because she always wanted to hold him in the mornings and he did not want to be held right then. Surely she understood he could not feel loving all the time.

She got plenty of sex from him doing it twice a week. She would not need other men for sex. "Why eat hamburger when you can get steak at home?" his dad had always said to his mom when she teased him about all the women he met as a doctor. Yes indeed, Kim was getting steak now. He was good to her. He was well-educated, had a high position at the University, treated her as an equal and did not even look at other women or talk about his wife, even though he was married. Surely she must be feeling lucky to have a good-looking professor to gaze at over the dinner table or find sleeping on the pillow next to her those two mornings. He kept the house spotless and they always ate well at the little diner near the office when they took a break from working.

But some nights she did not even get back to her apartment until late, after she attended evening classes. Studying for tests, she said when he called and asked why she had not been there earlier. Did it happen last Tuesday? He tried to recall.

Last Tuesday he had gone back to his office after the dentist's appointment, which had lasted from 2:00 to 4:00. He had worked about two hours, had felt bad and gone home. She did not call all evening. It was after 6:00 when he got home. The dog was whining at the back door when he came in, Camille's old Peekapoo, Poo, which had been hers for years, had come with her when she moved out of her parents' house. Poo's black-rimmed eyes were wide and his big pink mouth was open, panting when John looked down into the little flat face. He opened the door and let it in. He asked the dog if it was hungry. Camille had loved that dog. It was strange she could just leave it like she did. The same way she had left him, without another thought, without caring about them. The dog's long hair got tangled and dirty staying outside all day and it needed a bath sometimes. He resented that she would leave him with such a burden. He noticed the dog's food dish was empty and so was the water dish, so he fed him and started straightening up the kitchen, still in his suit and tie. No-one had called his machine since he had left that morning. He went to the bedroom and changed his clothes, putting on an old T-shirt and slacks.

He had no plans for the evening, except to eat supper and call Kim to come and work on the book. He expected she would come over to work with him after she got out of classes and changed, probably closer to 7:00. In the beginning she had always shown up at his door right at 6:00, just as he arrived, but now she sometimes worked in the library until 6:30 or 7:00, studying.

He started supper, putting a pot of water on the stove for spaghetti. Since Camille had left he was actually learning to cook and preferred to cook, rather than eating out. He was proud of some of his dishes, and cooked for Kim some nights.

He called Kim's answering machine and left a message that he was expecting her and would see her soon. He tried to sound cheerful.

At 7:00 Kim still had not arrived. He had been half-watching the news and it was over. He decided to start working. Supper was ready and still in pots on the stove. He sat down in the den at the desk to work, called Kim's apartment again, got her answering machine again, but hung up. Then he went back to the dining room to set the table. At 7:20 he called again. Kim still had not come back to her apartment. She was late. He started to nibble on the spaghetti as he stood over the stove, listening to the noise of the TV. Strand by strand he lifted the long white strings and curled them into his mouth from above. They were getting cold and dry. The dog wanted out.

Still nervous, at 8:00 he sat down at his desk and began writing on the new chapter. He threw the cold spaghetti in the trash at 8:30. At 9:00 the phone rang. It was with a sense of relief that he lifted the receiver, knowing it was Kim.

"Hi, Darling. What's happening?" He was happy to hear her voice, but also felt angry at her. Obviously she had not gotten his message.

"I actually made supper for you, but it's cold now. Where are you?"

"I worked late. There was a thesis I couldn't locate. I'll be over as soon as I can, Honey, sorry."

"Why didn't you call earlier?"

"I was in the stacks, with no phone nearby. Honey, what was I supposed to do, pull one out of my pocket?"

She sounded disappointed that she had not been able to come over right after classes. "I'm sorry I snapped at you, Kim." He said.

He could hear the forgiveness in her voice when she said, "That's okay. I'm sorry too. It's just that when I'm in the library, there's no phone and I can't call – I want to, but I can't."

He remembered just then there had been a sudden burst of music in the background and some scuffling and laughter from somewhere, and all was silence again.

"What was that, where are you?" He had asked. He remembered realizing she must not be at home.

"Oh, somebody turned the radio on here in the store. I stopped at the drug store and I'm on a public phone," she said and there was a muffled sound while John could hear her talking to someone, telling them something through the muffle.

"All right," she said, when she came back to him, "I'm starving, though. Maybe I'll grab something."

"Okay," he said, "I've already eaten. When do you think you'll get here?"

"Oh, I don't know. Probably about 10:00, by the time I eat, get home and change and get over there, but we will still have time to get some work done, Honey. "

"Okay. Bye." said John, hanging up after hearing her give him a kiss over the phone. She was so sweet sometimes. Even though she was exasperating, she was worth it.

Had that been Tuesday? Yes. She had arrived very late that night, he remembered. It had taken her long time to get to his house from the drug store. She must have gone to the bar on the way. She arrived at his house about midnight, smelling like medicine.

"I picked up some cough medicine on the way home, Hon," she had said. "I'll put it in the bathroom. I need it for my cough. I took some already." She kissed him and pulled his cold arms around her. He relented and hugged her. They worked a half hour, could not stand being so close to each other, and went to make love in his bed. She fell asleep immediately. John took longer to fall asleep. It still felt odd to see a strange woman in his bed.

The cough medicine was still in the bathroom medicine cabinet. He had seen it when he reached for his razor this morning. A little of it was missing. But now he knew she had gone to the Blue Parakeet and spent $24.79 on drinks. Why had she bought cough medicine? To cover up her alcohol-breath? Had she actually been that deliberate, that devious, to think of doing something like that? And what about Mike, the man who had written his name on the piece of paper? He must have called her since then. He knew she had not been out late any other night this week. And today was Saturday.

On Saturdays, when she went out to meet her girlfriends at

the mall, she was usually gone for hours. She loved the mall. She went to every big department store and each little boutique. He knew for sure, because he had gone with her once. They had wandered around endlessly, looking at all the clothes and jewelry in every store, spending hours on this frivolous search. She kept on talking about how everything would match other clothes, calling him over to look at one thing or another until he was exhausted. She did not buy much after all, but she obviously loved to window shop. He refused to buy any of the things she wanted, as to have purchased them would have been a waste of good money. Shopping seemed to be her favorite hobby. Only that one time did he go shopping with her; she went shopping with women friends from then on. Shopping for clothes did not exactly appeal to him and he wondered, if she was so smart, how she could spend so much time on it, though it was true the new clothes she bought looked good on her.

"My God," John whispered to himself as doubts began to sift into his thoughts. "My God." He felt a little dizzy. Had she been playing him for a fool? He was staring out the office window now with glazed eyes, seeing not the trees with the afternoon sun shining on them, but Kim, laughing and going into the Blue Parakeet last Tuesday. It must have been sometime before 8:00, maybe earlier in the evening that she went to have a few drinks, then called him from the telephone booth, her friends trying to open the door and talk to her while she was talking to him; that's when he had heard the music and voices. He could see Kim's laughing face clearly, her blue eyes, sparkling as she covered the phone and pushed them back out of the booth. He saw the faceless face of some man named Mike, laughing, with his arm around her shoulder all evening.

He could see her perfectly made up face with irresistible blue eyes, looking into the faceless man's face, as he asked her for her phone number. When they handed him the tab she asked for his. Mike did not have any paper, so he would write it on the back of the tab with his pen. John could just hear his hearty, faceless laugh, see his tanned hands with a gold pinky ring writing his name with good schoolboy penmanship and trying to end it with a flourish, Mike <u>T</u>.

"T" for Temptation," he thought

Then he could see Kim calling him the next day, fidgeting in hot remembrance of his body as they talked on and on, her doodling around his name as she talked, saying the things she had said to him. "You know you drive me crazy, don't you?" she had said once to him. "I can't wait until next time." "I want to know all about you. What books did you write? What cologne do you wear? It really turns me on. You are the most handsome man I've ever met." All those things she had said, saying them this time to Mike, whoever he was.

Now it was Saturday and she was late. Where was she? Did she go to the mall as she said? He knew she left at 2:30 because he had talked to her before she left, so where did she go and why was she gone so long? She said she would not be gone long. It was after 6:00 and she was still gone. The winter sun was now sinking behind the brown trees in a thin attempt at a sunset.

Was she with Mike T. right now? When she arrived at his apartment did she offer him her body and go into his dark bedroom where they could tumble and roll on scented pillows in sexual abandon, throwing each piece of clothing on the floor as they removed them from their healthy young bodies, one by one? He could see her face, fervent with love-making, the face he saw as she had mounted him in ecstasy the first time, looking now into Mike's faceless face, now seeking his invisible lips. His Kim.

He could not believe it. His Kim? She was cheating on him. But he was the one that was ridiculous. She was not really his. And he was not hers. What was he thinking of? He was married to Camille. And Kim was just a student aide. But she had said she loved him. That must account for something. She had hinted she might be his forever. She admired him. She adored him. She knew he was the means by which she would become famous, for helping him with his book. He had even offered to co-author a book with her after this one.

It could not possibly be true. She had once said she loved him, although he could not recall her having said so recently. She had been at home every night, telling him over the phone she wanted to hold him so much. And sometimes she did. Once he drove over to her apartment in the middle of the night. He called her every day to see what she was doing and to see if she wanted to eat supper with him before they began working. She had started sleeping with him regularly a month ago.

He could not believe his own mind. What was happening to him? He was in torment and all of this torture came from one tiny piece of paper he had happened to see.

Suddenly, John was acutely aware of everything physical around him. It was cold in his office. It was getting darker and the temperature had dropped. He turned on his desk lamp and reminded himself to turn up the thermostat in the hall. The lights were off in all the offices except his. He felt alone and abandoned by everyone, but refused to give in to any emotion. He walked slowly toward his desk. It seemed an eternity to reach it. He turned on the radio. It was tuned to a station Kim liked. He should sit down and work, writing as he always had done. It was his way of avoiding the world when it was too hard to face. Why couldn't he do it now? It was what he had always done, without thinking of anything else. Without thinking of Camille or their home or anything else. It was his security, his writing. It was his future and his past and had always been his way of assuring himself that all was well.

"Hello, hello. Is it you I'm looking for?" sang a sad voice from the radio. He snapped it off.

The white light on his desk glared on the white papers, the bookcases around the room and the rows of leather-bound volumes that lined them. It was cold and silent in the room, but John's cheeks felt flushed. He felt full of a terrible energy, yet so frozen by his thoughts that he would have jumped out of his skin if the phone had rung.

Against his will, his thoughts were drawn back to the small address book lying on his desk. His eyes fixed on the small brown book lying there beside the phone. He had to see it again. Was the receipt with Tuesday's date really there? Or was it his imagination that had thrown Kim into another world so quickly? How could such a small thing do so much? There had to be a logical explanation. Kim was not out looking for men. She was a brilliant graduate student, devoted to him and his book. He could not let one student disturb his life this much. He was reading too much into one little piece of paper. He must have been mistaken. The date could not have been this week's.

This time, when he picked up the book, he was acutely aware of its soft texture and how worn it was. He opened it again slowly, turning the first pages carefully to see what else she had written in it. The A's had a combination of four men's and four women's names.

The B's included her mother's number and one for her brother. But there were also about three men's names, Bob, with an address in Billington; Ebon Barker, a real estate agent by the looks of the office address and number, and Bill, with just a phone number.

And so it went through the rest of the alphabet, sprinklings of various numbers, some of the women she was in classes with, her doctor, but lots of men's names. Some of the names had little notes after them. John forgave her for some of them because surely she had written most of these before she had met him. "Great Bod!" was written after someone named Barry, "Head" after David. Some had plusses or stars; some were crossed out, but most had no notes. Some of the pages were more worn than others. Mike T's name was not listed in the M's or the T's.

But then, there it was again, in the center of the book, the white piece of paper with Tuesday's date and Mike T's number on the other side. He looked it over again, but it had not changed. It was there in black and white and the doodles were real–pencil lines drawn over and over in little pointed ellipses with hatch marks and circles. He looked at the front of the bill again, the name, the date, the numbers. He handled it carefully, so as not to wrinkle it in any way. Then, almost reluctantly, he folded it again and placed it back in the book under the M's. He looked through the rest of the book and his heart sank as more men's names jumped out at him. He had no idea she knew so many men.

He thought he heard a noise outside the door and jumped. He quickly closed the little book and put it back beside the phone, careful to place everything as it had been, and listened. His heart was thudding in his throat. It sounded like Kim, arriving to work with him. She had not gone to Mike's after all. He listened for a moment and realized it was quiet again. It must have just been someone walking down the hall. Still, his ears were burning and his heart pounded hard from the noise. He walked away from the desk, going to the window again to look out at the pale sunset. It was late. He should go home. He could not believe she was doing this to him.

After all, it's not such a big deal, he told himself. One man's name, one phone call. Maybe she had called him, hoping to see him and nothing had happened. He had not answered. Probably she had not called him with the intention of seeing him, but with some kind of business to do over the phone and that was the end of it. That would explain the doodles over a long phone call.

But why had she kept the paper? She had not put his name in her book. Yet. That was a good sign. There was no address. Maybe she did not know where he lived, even. Surely he had called her or she had only called him once. In all probability she did not call him, but he had called her. But somehow he knew she had called him, since she had doodled on his number. Probably she had called him when she came by his office earlier to get her books. He had trusted her to use his office at will.

He went to the desk again and turned off the lamp. He could not work; he was going home. But there lay the book by the telephone, inside the circle of light the lamp made in the dusk. He had an urge to call the number. Would Mike T. answer? Should he call? What if Kim was there? Would she imagine it was him calling and tell Mike not to answer? What would he say to Mike if he called? What if they were in the middle of lovemaking? Mike would not even answer the phone. His faceless body would be convulsed in orgasms of joy and Kim would be there in the shadows below him, her body writhing in the dark as the phone rang and rang and rang.

Of course she would not be there. If he called the number, Mike would answer and would not know who he was. He could hang up. Yes, Mike would answer. Maybe Kim would be there and he would think she was expecting a call if he asked for her, and Mike would hand the phone to her. What if she was there and she answered the phone? What would he say?

"Hello, Kim. This is John. When are you coming over to the office?" He could say in a cynical, deadly voice. Or "Hello," (she would recognize his voice) "Don't bother ever coming back." Or "You dirty whore. Damn you! Damn you!" then he would slam the receiver down. He tried to think of worse curse words. "Slut" was the only one he could think of, but it sounded outdated and not nearly strong enough.

But of course, in reality, she was not there. If he called, Mike would answer and when he asked for Kim, Mike would say "Who? I don't know anyone named Kim." Then he would know everything was okay and it was all in his mind. He would know there was nothing wrong between them. It was just a number someone had put on the back of her receipt when she left the bar. That's what would actually happen. Or more probable, no-one would be home and the phone would ring and ring. Or an answering machine would come on. At least he would know Mike was a real person and what his voice sounded like. Would it be a deep, sexy voice, or a high, tenor one?

John looked at the clock. It was 6:30. In one tense move, feeling as if he was doing it against his will, he picked up the address book and removed the paper. He should take it home to his bedroom. Somehow his bed was safe. It was a place where he could cry, hide in and cover up and sleep in when he was depressed. It was soft and cozy and warm and he had experienced love there. Even now it was waiting, made up neatly with a clean coverlet. He wished he could sit down on the edge of that bed right now and feel at peace.

He unfolded the white paper and spread it out beside the telephone on an empty space of the smooth, worn oak. He could not wait until he got home. He knew he would dial the number. He should call without thinking any more. He should just do it. It would relieve his mind. It was something he had to do for himself, and for Kim, to prove she was not guilty – that she would never hurt him. She was out shopping at the mall and a stranger named Mike would answer who didn't remember her. But, on the other hand, if she were there he would know what kind of person she was.

He picked up the heavy, black receiver and dialed the numbers slowly. His fingers were shaking, his nerves were so tight. He could hardly see the dial. The phone on the other end rang. The reality of the ring made his stomach tense up. It was a buzzing noise. There was a real telephone ringing somewhere. He could hardly believe it was ringing. It was an actual number. It rang again. There was a sudden noise as the receiver was picked up. It was a shock to hear an actual, ordinary man's voice say politely in his ear, "Hello?"

"Hello," said John in automatic answer, after only a moment's hesitation. He had to sound confident. "Is Kim there?" There it was– the big question, the question that would answer everything.

"Ye-es," the man said slowly after hesitating, wondering something. John could not believe there was a yes. That yes was not possible. He must be mistaken. For a split second he entertained the thought that there was another Kim who lived there.

"Yes," said the ordinary man's voice, a little more confidently, "just a minute." Then a hand went over the receiver, blocking out all noise on the other end. What should he do? Should he hang up? Was that someone else named Kim who lived there going to come to the phone? What should he do? He could not move. He had to hear if it was his Kim's voice.

He could hear two people talking behind the muffle for a second. That would be Mike, asking her who knew she was there, had she told anyone she was coming to his house? And she would be saying no and would be curious to know who it was and they would give each other long, curious looks and then she would take the phone.

"Hello?" a voice said faintly.

It was Kim's voice.

John felt something thud in the bottom of his chest. His hand went down slowly and carefully as he replaced the receiver.

SWEET BASIL

The party was going strong in the other room, where loud music blared. Camille sat with Grace in a window seat overlooking Broome Street in SoHo, Vince sat in a chair facing them. They were in the studio section of an artist's loft and around them sat other people who drank and talked. Vince and Grace began to talk to each other in voices so low Camille could not hear them, which aroused her jealousy. She strained her ears to hear what they were saying, trying to appear not to do so. She heard enough to know they were talking about the other people at the party and the concentric circles of relationships each person spawned. It was not that interesting to Camille, who knew no one there, but the fact that Grace and Vince were trying to keep her out of the conversation made her listen and comment. Finally, Vince remarked that her ears must be better than a bat's, since they could hardly hear themselves talk.

Just then, Camille looked up and saw Arturo come into the room. He spotted her at the same time and came toward her, sitting down beside her, to which Vince evidenced obvious disgust. After acknowledging his presence, Vince ignored Arturo, turning his back to talk with Grace. But Arturo did not notice Vince at all and expressed delight that Camille was there; he was soon voicing the normal clichés, automatically asking how she was, and what she had been doing lately. She had a hard time thinking of something to respond with when she realized Arturo probably knew more than she did about what she had been doing lately – she had been in such a fog as far as school went and he had been there at school and at the opening of the exhibit she was in.

Arturo's tried to engage Vince and Grace in conversation, but he went unheeded so, feeling left alone with Camille, he asked her if she wanted to dance. She said okay and he led the way to the bedroom, where the music was playing. The large room had been turned into a ballroom through the installation of lights covered with red and green film and by shoving the bed against one wall. The music was deafening, making conversation impossible. But Camille did not mind, as she enjoyed dancing and was happy there was someone she knew at the party besides Grace and Vince, who were acting snobbish. She constantly searched faces around the room, looking for familiar ones. Florence, the only other person she knew, stood holding a drink in the doorway, clasping her cousin Herbert from Baltimore by the arm.

Happy to be expressing herself, Camille danced frantically. Arturo was really dancing, as well, his tall frame jangling like a puppet, as he abandoned himself to the music with his head thrown back. During the slow dances, however, it hung forward over her as he clung to her and pulled her against his body. They danced for a long time. From time to time Camille glimpsed Vince and Grace, still talking conspiratorially, though sometimes they got up and went to get drinks.

After an hour Vince got up and, seeing Arturo at the bar resting from all the dancing, joined him, leaving Grace sitting on the window seat by herself. Camille tried to draw Herbert, Florence's cousin from Baltimore, into conversation; but he seemed as if he didn't know anything about what was going on. He was even more naive than she. Giving up on talking, they stood together and watched Arturo and Vince talking and dancing with a couple of pretty young women they had found.

As midnight came, Grace, Florence and Camille found themselves weary, and silently leaning against a long hallway wall, watched strangers leave the party. Herbert had left with a girl he had picked up just before midnight, surprising everyone. Florence remarked Herb had told her the only reason he would come to the party was to pick up a woman.

"Well, he wasn't disappointed, then." Camille said.

"He could have come home with us, at least. Now I'll have to get up in the night and let him in. He doesn't have a key." Florence was mumbling now, drunk, with a toothpick in her mouth. An empty glass with an olive pit in it was held at the ready in her hand. She was too assiduous to put it on the floor, as it was glass.

"Think positive. Maybe he won't come home tonight." said Grace.

"Maybe he won't come back at all." laughed Florence.

"Do you know anyone here?" Camille asked Florence,

curious to know if she was the only one who was new at this kind of thing.

"No. I think the three people I knew left."

"Except for Vince," Camille said.

"And Arturo," said Florence.

"Vince and Arturo," said Camille. She did not feel qualified to make any remarks about either of them, though she felt like it.

"Vince is such a loser." said Grace. She could not resist the topic, obviously. No one picked it up, so she continued. "Even if he makes it with a girl, he'll kick her out in the morning."

"Is that a loser?" Camille asked her, piqued.

"Did I say loser?" Grace seemed confused and Camille realized she was drunk. "Maybe that's what I really meant." Grace thought for awhile. "I don't know what I meant." She stood there thinking, moving this way and that, trying to get comfortable against the wall. "Maybe I meant 'jerk'," she said after awhile.

"I wonder if Arturo would kick someone out in the morning." said Florence, after a silence. They were all thinking about different things. Grace and Camille looked at Florence. She was thinking about Arturo. "He's not a loser. He does real well in business," she said.

"I'm sure he's not a loser." Camille assured her. Florence looked at her, wondering if she should be grateful. Camille looked at Florence's pale blue skin, showing orange on the high parts and dark blue in the cracks around her nose and mouth. Her eyes were so dark in the dim, neon-lighted hallway she could not see them at all. She turned around and looked down the hall momentarily to see if she could see either Arturo or Vince.

"Yes, he's a loser." said Florence sadly, fervently. When Camille turned back to her, she realized Florence had been looking at her or past her for awhile. The hand with the toothpick moved halfway up to her mouth and then fell, as she appeared to lose track of her thoughts. Grace peered around Florence to absently stare at Camille. Her light hair shone silver in the light from behind and her eyes also appeared black holes in her faintly illumined face. Then Camille realized she was looking beyond and behind her, from the frozen stance she was in.

Turning her head around, Camille looked down the long hall

behind her. Framed in the doorway of the brilliant room at the end of the hall stood Vince and a woman almost as tall as he. The woman, graceful and beautiful even after the long night, had hair which hung straight to her waist. Her body, poured into a leotard and tiny skirt, revealed her breasts and thighs as if she wore nothing. She stood leaning slightly backward and Vince stood over her, leaning forward. His face was in profile as he gazed into her face from about two inches away. It was obvious from her body language the woman was charmed by him. They made a striking couple. Both were tall, well-dressed, and beautiful. Camille felt her heart give a sudden thud and felt pain. She did not want to watch, but like Grace she stared transfixed as if they were the audience in a movie theater.

Vince moved toward the girl ever so slightly, as if to kiss her. But she moved her head away, teasing him and saying something. He straightened up and whipped out his lighter to light the cigarette she brought to her lips. He then lit one for himself and they stood together, the smoke rising from their mouths which, even from that distance, appeared to be steam rising from bodies. They were gazing at each other, talking little.

Why does he like her? Camille asked herself. Am I not better than she? I'm not as tall, but I look as good as she does. And I am better for him. Why would he chase her? Why is he wasting his time? Why does he feel lust when he sees big breasts and long legs? He's like a male dog after a bitch in heat whenever he sees a woman. Why does he need others when he has me?

But Vince's hands were moving now, as he began talking rapidly, moving up to her arm in a familiar, slow motion, stroking it. The girl laughed luxuriously. The sound of the laugh came rippling and singing down the hall, though no words could rise over the noise of the music. Vince moved his body closer to hers, allowing people to pass behind him. The people walked toward Camille, Florence and Grace; toward the front door. They blocked the view of Vince and the woman, whose bodies had been touching when last seen; but when the people were gone so were Vince and the girl. More people came to stand in the hall by the front door, laughing and talking and arguing. The noise of voices and music was deafening.

"I'll drive." screamed one man loudly to the rest. But he was hardly noticed.

"I'll be right back." said Grace, pushing past Florence and Camille and going back to the room where Vince had been. "Get ready to go;" she called back as she left, "I'm going to get Vince and Arturo."

At 1:00, over Vince's protests, they were on their way to Sweet Basil's, the jazz club on Seventh Avenue, all crammed together in Arturo's car. Camille realized she had not been in a big, old car since she had left Texas and enjoyed the luxury of Arturo's big Cadillac. Somehow Grace had corralled Arturo and Vince, and had lost the tempting woman they had seen him with. Arturo found a place to park in the crowded street and they walked to the door of the club. It was jammed with people. Lots of people stood on the sidewalk, looking in and listening to the jazz being played loud enough to be audible outside.

Pushing through the crowd, Camille gave her name to the man at the door. Vince kept on repeating that he didn't want to pay a cover charge and therefore did not want to go in.

"How much is the cover charge?" he asked the door man.

"Five dollars apiece."

Vince was in a foul mood and his mouth turned down at the idea. "I'm going home," he announced.

"Vince, Bobby gave my name to them!" Camille said, running to grab his arm as he started back down the sidewalk toward the car. Arturo, Florence and Grace were following him like sheep. "Please, Vince. I want to hear Bobby play," Camille begged. She repeated it again, as she tried to stop his rapid retreat. She could see the faces of the others reflecting doubt she would have her way.

"Camille!" someone suddenly called her name from behind.

"Please, Vince. Stop, for heaven's sake! Someone's calling me!"

"Camille!" They heard her name called again from the entrance to Sweet Basil's and they all stopped and turned around. Bobby Holliday was pushing through the crowd of fans, his body and arms rising above them, waving at Camille. Camille hardly recognized him in his black suit and white shirt. She had only seen him in running clothes at the track.

"Bobby! Hey, Vince, it's Bobby Holliday, coming after us,"

said Arturo. Vince turned and his sullen face reluctantly acknowledged this was so. He knew Bobby Holliday was a well-respected musician in New York, even if he did not like jazz.

Bobby came running up to them.

"Hey, Camille. Hey, where you all goin'?" Bobby was there, warmly hugging her, kissing her on both cheeks, shaking hands with and smiling at everyone. "You came after all! Aren't you going to come in and hear me play?"

Vince was impressed enough to turn back as Bobby explained: "The maitre d' told me Camille's name had been at the door, but she was leaving, so I came out to see what was wrong." He smiled and Camille felt better; she would hear him play now.

Bobby's hand held her elbow tightly all the way through the crowd, leading them inside, to a front table which stood empty, evidently reserved for them. They were all seated, a little quiet and embarrassed at the attention they were receiving. Vince was sullen and silent. He would not look at Camille and glared at Bobby. Camille tried to ignore him and smiled happily.

Bobby went to the front of the stage, where he announced he was going to continue the show and play an extra set because the audience had been so great that night. A big cheer went up from everyone. But when Bobby put the big, gold saxophone to his lips and blew into it, there was a hush, as the sound was sweet and pure. The note flowed in a cool blue tune that moved up and caught a beat as the drum and piano moved into it. Then the whole group was playing the first melody, and continued playing it in its many variations, in improvised singles, one by one. Camille had never heard anything like it. And tonight she felt Bobby was playing just for her.

Bobby joined them for a short time during the break and Camille introduced everyone. Again, Vince tried to speak only to Grace and exclude everyone else, but Grace brushed him off, acting more kindly toward Camille. They reminded Camille of little children with their games.

Arturo was listening to the music and Florence was falling asleep when the waiter brought the check. He gave it to Camille because the table was in her name. But Bobby saw it and came and grabbed it away from her. Vince was impressed at last, falling silent, since he had been complaining about how much all this would cost him.

Finally, back at the boat basin, Grace and Vince went out to walk the dogs together, though it was after 2:30 a.m. Camille went directly to her boat to sleep. She heard them return to Vince's boat and her phone rang.

"Grace is leaving." Vince said. "Why don't you come over?"

"No thanks," she said, "I'm already in bed, asleep." Vince talked on a few minutes, sounding irritated and tired. But she did not want to see any more of him tonight.

The next day she and Vince argued.

"You acted like a snot." He said. "You don't know how to act at parties."

"You didn't pay any attention to me at the party." she said in her defense, irritated.

"Do you always have to have all the attention?" he returned, and continued to attack her verbally, cold words coming out of his handsome mouth, while he sat on the couch. She sat in front of him in the deck chair speechless, while a separate, inner turmoil went on inside her. She had been verbally abused before, by her husband; and now she was finding she had to listen to abuse from Vince. But she was fast becoming intolerant of it. Vince did not argue or criticize as well as John did. He did not have the vocabulary and philosophical background to utterly cut someone to pieces in their own mind. She especially despised someone who did not know what he was talking about trying to tell her she was inferior to him.

She felt sullen and angry when he finished – a feeling she remembered and was familiar with. The anger made her feel like she was coming back to her old self.

That night Camille wrote a letter to Vince.

Dear Vince,

I'm not complaining for any particular reason and I don't want you to feel sorry for me. I just felt unhappy at the party because I invited Grace to go with us, knowing that you would want her to go, even though I knew that her going would mean that I would feel left out. I am on your side. I feel that yours and my relationship is ending naturally. I think you are acting maturely in ending it and want to assure you that you have been good to me. I hope you will be kind to me these last few days before I have to leave. Please don't hurt me now. I will remember that you cared about me and that you played an import role at a crucial time in my life, and I will remember you with love.

Love,
Camille.

In the morning, she slipped the folded sheet under Vince's door.

She stopped by the gallery as usual, to see how the show was going, on the way home after school. Grace was sitting with the show and there was Vince, sitting with her. Taken aback, Camille paused only a moment before going in. When Camille appeared, they both stopped talking and she knew they had been talking about her by the way they looked at each other when she appeared. Then they both acted very polite toward her and seemed to treat her with respect.

Back at the boat basin, Camille slept a little and did some cleaning up. Vince returned and worked on his boat. They both left their doors open, and soon they were going in and out of each other's boats as if it was one big house. When evening fell, Vince asked Camille if she wanted to come over and see the old movie, "The Thing with Two Heads," on TV, so she went. It starred Rosie Greer and was so ridiculous that they both laughed until they could not sit up straight on the couch. When the movie was over, Vince turned off the TV and turned to her. He had his arm around her and pulled her against him.

"So, how are you doing now?" he asked gently.

""I'm doing okay," she answered tensely, thinking he was going to say something serious.

"Saturday is my birthday and I'm going out," he said. "Aren't you going to a party in Brooklyn, or something, that night?"

"Yes." she said, suddenly sad, where she had been so happy a moment before. Her eyes moved away from his as he looked down into her face. Alfred had invited her to a party and she had told Vince she was going with him.

"So, who are you going out with?" she asked Vince.

"None of your business," he said coldly, pulling his arm back and turning away. He sat forward on the couch to light a cigarette so she could not see his face.

"Is it Grace?"

"Why would you want to know?"

"I was thinking of asking her to go with me," said Camille, innocently.

"I don't think she would want to go to a student party, but you could ask her. Maybe she will. I don't know." His back was still toward her.

So he was not going out with Grace on Saturday. But why didn't he tell her? She would have found out eventually. Besides, she knew in the back of her mind and had to accept the fact that Vince would take Grace out all of the time if he could. She did not want him to like her so much, that's all. She had learned something new about herself again.

"Tomorrow night is the Christmas party at Hal's gallery, remember," said Vince. "We promised to bring ham. I'll drive you." He stood up, as if to dismiss her.

"Well, I guess I'll go home now." said Camille.

Vince finally turned around and looked at her, squinting his eyes in the smoke. She went up to him and put her hand on his shoulder. He did not flinch or back away. He just bent his head down and she kissed him on the cheek. He did not move, but stayed as he was, looking at the floor, the thin plume of smoke drifting out the open door as she left.

It was more complicated than she thought. She thought she could just go out and have other men friends. Other than Vince, that is. But it was not that simple.

The Christmas party at the gallery was at 7 o'clock. At that time, Camille, Grace and Vince were on their way, with lots of food in the car. It kept on trying to snow as the three of them drove through the silent streets. By the time they got to the gallery and parked a lot of people had already arrived, a cheery sight as they looked through the big window into the gallery. This time Camille recognized almost everyone there. A lot of my friends, she thought, all gathered in one place.

Paul Frank was there with his tough-guy face and long, dark hair. Camille felt her heart jump when she saw him. She immediately joined the group of people he was talking with, smiling at him as she came up. He smiled back, continuing a description of his new 5,000-square-foot loft with cathedral ceilings. But he seemed more animated when she joined the group and directed most of his comments toward her. He had, she realized, brought two women friends with him. But he was aware of her the whole evening, looking at her from time to time and smiling when she glanced in his direction, which made her nervous. She remembered how he had asked her to dance at the last party, that he was a very good dancer, and was very attentive to her as they danced.

Eventually, he approached her alone with a glass of wine, which he put into her hand and stood near her as she drank it, his hand on the wall by her, essentially blocking them off from the others.

"I wish you were standing under the mistletoe right now," he said in a low voice. Camille almost choked, but he did not move or indicate anything other than friendship, so she just smiled up at his beautiful face, conscious of his intense, dark blue eyes boring through her. She had to look down at her drink again. That he was famous was present in her thoughts, though all she could remember at this close a distance was how they had danced together and how natural it had been. They seemed to be suited to each other in many ways. But he reminded her of John, something which both repelled and attracted her.

"I've been meaning to come by and see your boat," he said, "But I wasn't sure you really wanted me to." He cast a meaningful glance at Vince. She followed his look and saw Vince huddled over the food with Grace, involved in conversation. Hal was standing with them, observing everything, include her. Hal knew what was happening, more than they.

"So, maybe you would like to come over to my place some time." Paul's voice, so near her ear, startled her and brought her mind back. She felt panic rising. What was wrong? Why didn't she feel like accepting his invitation? Paul detected hesitation and said a little more quietly, "Tell you what . . . . I'll come visit you first and then you can decide if you want to come visit me, okay?" He sounded kind, yet confident. It should have been what she wanted to hear. There was a tension, a kind of sadness, low in her mind and in her stomach.

She was more aware of Vince straightening up and looking around for her than she was of Paul. But she turned her head away and spoke to Paul quickly.

"Okay." She looked politely into his eyes and smiled. "Friday?"

Paul seemed surprised, but agreed. So she smiled again, said "call me later," and ducked under his arm.

Camille managed to find a few moments to talk to Michael, whom she admired and considered a true artist. He made exquisite, delicate pots as simply formed and fragile as egg shells. She enjoyed talking with him, because their discussions were always purely artist shop-talk, about techniques and materials, and she could talk without inhibition. It would be wonderful to be able to talk with Paul about artists' techniques, she thought, but they had never done so and somehow she felt they never would. Sexual feelings thundered between them, drowning out any other topic. But Michael, who might also be considered very attractive, was able to talk with her and she with him, enthusiastically and with great fervor about their latest art projects, the shows they were in and what new materials they were using, without so much as a single thought of sex entering in.

Camille was also able to talk with Hal, whom she adored. His ideas were the reason she had come to New York in the first place. They talked about the work presently showing in the gallery; he praised her work and she asked about his family. After awhile she decided to ask Hal what he thought about love. A little hesitantly, she began.

"I know some people say you shouldn't fall in love with someone right away. But what if you want to? What if you need someone in your life? People say that isn't a good enough reason to fall in love and decide you want to spend the rest of your life with someone. My experience of that was a big mistake, when I married someone because I was lonely. I think I found I was lonelier after I got married than I ever was when I was single."

But Hal had only heard the first part of her question and said, "All this stuff about wants and needs is a bunch of hooey. Of course we need someone. We all need someone. We're driven by our needs. Freud said our primary motivation is sex. I think it's love, not sex, that is needed. We need it, and if we don't find enough of it, we go out to find it or a simulation thereof. Some people think they can substitute sex for love. We might get hooked on the simulation, but we still have that need. . . for love."

Camille nodded. The simulation thereof. . . .

Jinn, a Korean potter, who had come with Michael, came

walking up to them, and they dropped the subject of love to discuss his pots.

Paul, Frank and Grace were the best known artists at the party. But the others artists were on their way up the ladder. All were young, enthusiastic artists. Camille was beginning to feel at home in the group.

They ate their fill off the buffet table loaded with food. Vince grabbed her hand, dragged her over to cut the ham and sat beside her while she ate. The music was turned up and people began to dance. Paul came over and asked her to dance. She accepted and danced awhile with him. It was fun and she really enjoyed it.

"You're good at everything you do!" she exclaimed to him as they rested for a moment between songs.

"You don't know everything I do. . . yet." he said, and she blushed.

Towards midnight she found herself standing in a group of people, nibbling leftovers, chatting with Vince and Grace and others. She was surreptitiously watching Paul across the room, preparing to leave with the two beautiful women he had brought. She could tell by his actions that he was telling them to wait a moment. Then he glanced around, looking for her, caught her eye and walked across the almost-empty gallery toward her. The realization he might be coming to speak to her scared her for a moment. She felt flattered, but quenched the feeling as he came up to the group. He might want to say good night to Hal.

"Good-bye, Hal. Thanks for a great party and Merry Christmas." He shook Hal's hand. "Bye, Vince, Paco, Michael, Grace." He spoke to each of them, shaking each hand in turn. They all fell silent in deference to his manners.

"Camille," he said, pausing when he reached her, taking her hand, which she extended to him like everyone else, but pulling her toward him with it and kissing her on the mouth. "I'll call you before Friday, okay?" Camille could only nod, dumbly.

"Good-bye everyone," he said, waving as he walked away. They all said good-bye in unison. Camille, watching him go, felt rather than saw everyone's eyes travel from his back to her.

Her feelings were mixed. When she thought about it later, she realized she really did not like being singled out like that; as if he had chosen her and she had no choice in the matter. She knew she could not start a new relationship with Paul at that point. She told herself when Paul called she would talk with him on the phone and forget about asking him over. He was only fooling around with her and would understand. Yet part of her hoped he was not fooling around.

The next morning Camille felt compelled to call Vince and talk with him, to reassure herself everything was all right. When he did not answer she realized it did not bother her too much that he was not there and she had come a long way since a month ago, when she would have felt panic and started crying when he did not answer.

EATING WITH YOUR FINGERS

Camille had a class meeting in SoHo, at her teacher's loft, at 2:00, but it was still early. She decided to walk around SoHo, so she caught the subway downtown and looked at a few shows before going to her professor's studio on Greene Street.

When she arrived at Son Ho Min's loft on Spring Street, she found some of the other students already there. It was small, compared to the one where the party had been last week, but this was a real artist's loft. Thousands of canvasses and paintings were neatly stored on racks built in layers on every wall. Only the bathroom was a separate room and the bed was a cot in a corner. A hot plate served as a kitchen, next to the bathroom, so he could use the sink. Son Ho Min 's whole life was built around painting. Camille felt she really could respect him for that, though it was hard to imagine living this way. Professor Min proudly showed the students his current paintings and drawings, discussing his work as he did and answering questions about his techniques. It made Camille feel inspired to be more dedicated to her craft.

Camille walked out into cold, empty SoHo streets afterwards. This popular part of town was bare and uninhabited on the side streets. It had begun to snow, but she walked to the corner of 10th and Greenwich Street. This was where the restaurant was that called her gallery and asked if they could display some of her works on their walls. She went inside, took one look at the dark interior and decided against showing her work there. No one would be able to see it.

When she got back to the boat at 6:00, the sun had gone down and she was freezing. She closed herself into her warm boat and slept two hours. When she awoke it was dark. Groggily, she pulled herself up and turned on the light. She was still dressed. She put water on the stove to boil, reached for the phone and called Vince. She was almost surprised when he answered.

"Well, if it ain't Cinderella, home from the ball," he said. "What does it feel like to have met your Prince Charming?"

"Which one?" she asked, taunting him. "You know you're the only Prince Charming at the ball for me."

"Come on, Camille," his voice turned hard. "I know you, and you're dying to go out with that hot cock."

"Don't insult me. You don't know how I feel. I can't help it if every man I meet falls for me." If he could be mean, she could be saucy and maybe he would lighten up.

"It's not a one-way street, you know, kid." Vince still was not amused. "I didn't notice you turning him off."

"Why should I?" Camille paused, then plunged on. "But it's a losing battle. I really can't do it. I would like to go out, but I just can't. It's just too much, what with having other significant relationships just ending. I really can't imagine involving myself in someone else's life right now. I have enough problems to deal with."

"That's a lie." He said after a pause, sounding bitter. Camille was surprised at his hardness.

"No, really," she insisted, sincerely. "That's how I feel." She did not think she could be more honest.

"I thought all you do is make friends." he said. "You like getting involved in other people's lives." He was referring to the fact that, in spite of the short time she had been in New York, she knew almost everyone at the party and had made a point of talking to the ones she did not know.

"It's hard, having to make new friends," she said. "I have to make the effort to make myself interested in other people."

"You're not under any pressure to make new friends," he said immediately. She wondered what he was trying to say. Was he trying to tell her he did not want to be blamed for her having to make other friends? The thought made her mad. He kept on pushing her away.

"I guess you really should go out with other people," he said. "I guess you're right. You're right. I'm wrong."

"That's it!" You want to put pressure on me, don't you?" she shot back.

"What I want," he said in a slow, sarcastic voice she had not heard before, "is for us to not see or speak to each other at all. For us just to say 'hello' when we pass each other on the dock. Starting right now."

Camille was stunned. How had it come to this? He sounded so convincing she could hardly speak. If he had said this to hurt her, she would have started crying, but perhaps he really meant it and in that case she did not know what to do. Perhaps he was right. She was silent, then she spoke very quietly.

"I don't think I could do that. I would miss you too much. But," she said, realizing their separation would become a reality when she left for Texas, "I guess I am going to have to start missing you. . . even before the holidays, which aren't very far away now, since I leave pretty soon."

Vince said nothing to this and was silent. Camille said nothing more, afraid he would just hang up. But he did not. She heard him say in a quiet, indistinct voice, "We'll have enough time to go out to dinner one more time."

Then he said, louder, "Don't choose people to go out with from among my friends. That's as uncouth as eating with your fingers." Camille wondered if he meant any specific friend. Was it Paul he meant?

"You don't even know who I am thinking about going out with, if anyone," she said. "I understand what you're saying, but I think you've got me wrong." Was she protesting too much? There was silence and she added as an afterthought, "I don't even want to know the people you date."

"I don't want to talk any more." He said. But after a moment of stiff silence between them he continued, his voice so brittle it was about to break, "We're not married or living together, you know. Actually, we're 'just seeing each other'. That's all." It sounded final, but she did not know what he meant. At least it was better than "not seeing or speaking to each other" which he had said earlier.

"I still depend on you for some things, you know," she said.

"You're not dependent on me. I haven't let you get that way."

"What about the time you locked me in your boat?" She asked. "You didn't do it just once. I know you did it more than once. You didn't want me to go back to my boat while you were gone. When you like someone, you depend on them. You depend on them to like you. That's the kind of dependency I'm talking about. There are other ways people become dependent, you know." She was afraid to go on, afraid he would say again that he did not want to ever talk to her again. Surely he would not do that.

And yet, when she lay alone in her bed after the conversation, thinking of what he had said, not crying, but feeling surges of strong emotions—of grief, then hope, then anger, then love, going through her, she realized she also felt a strength she had not felt before. She was beginning to accept the fact that she was alone. The greatest pain in separating is learning to be alone, she realized.

She had never physically lived alone. She had lived with her parents, then at a strict religiouis college in a dorm with other girls where her every move was monitored. From there she had married and lived with her husband. In New York she was suddenly alone, stranded on a desert island. Like Robinson Crusoe, making a friend when you're alone is life's greatest joy. Right now, her life's greatest joy and greatest pain was Vince.

WHERE THE WILD GOOSE GOES

Christmas trees were beginning to be sold on the streets. Everything reminded her that it was almost Christmas and she would have to go back to Texas. She would really have to be strong, as she was going back to Texas. She would have to be with John for one terrible week before he left on his business trip and she went to her mother's. In that one week she, they, would have to decide what she would do for the rest of her life. She wanted to return to New York, but she had to go to Texas first. She could not go on living like this, neither single nor married. She felt single. She would have to be single. She did not feel married to John, but she still was, officially. She wished it was all over.

Divorcing John meant giving up security, security in knowing there was someone there and there would be financial security for the rest of her life. She would not have a house there any more, a dog or a garden. She would have to begin a new job, find a new home. Everything from now on would be dependent upon her own self. Every decision would be hers and it would have to be right. There would be no one else to blame if it went wrong. She alone would be responsible. But if she won, it would be to her credit alone. Alone. Did she want to be alone, or stay with someone she did not love? It was a tough decision and she did not want to make it. She would have to face it and make it, nevertheless.

On the advice and insistence of her sister, Camille decided to see a therapist. She looked in the yellow pages because she was afraid and embarrassed to ask acquaintances for recommendations. Then she found out one of the churches she had visited had a counseling service for free. She made an appointment with the Assistant Minister, who said he was a counselor.

Before she went, she sat down and wrote out on paper the pros and cons of the decision she had to make, of whether to get divorced or not.

Rev. Seabottom sat reading the list she had handed him as soon as she got into his office. The office was old and dark, but had large windows with curtains that were wedged open with books on the window sill. She looked at the bare branches of the trees outside the window as she waited for him to finish. Everything in his office looked bleak and dark and smelled damp. Rev. Seabottom's thick body was topped by a head with a thick beard and, although she tried look away as he read, she saw his pudgy hands, folded over a rich-looking vest, fingers tapping nervously. When he finished reading he looked up and asked how he could help. So Camille began to talk. Rev. Seabottom's mouth twisted unconsciously as she recited the story of what she had recently done. She found the words pouring out of her and talked almost continuously for an hour. His only words were to designed to encourage her to continue. He frowned when she mentioned John's unwillingness to help her handle her art whenever she had art exhibits, but otherwise made no indication whatsoever of his thoughts. After forty-five minutes he looked at his watch and nodded at her to silence her.

"Your hour is up," he said.

"Tell me what to do," she pleaded.

"What do you want me to say?" he asked. "It all seems terribly sad." He looked at the door longingly, as if he wished she would leave. Camille had not expected this kind of reaction. Wasn't a therapist supposed to help you make decisions? She had not meant her story to sound sad. She did not feel sad about what had happened, just confused. Wasn't he supposed to be objective and suggest alternatives?

"What part sounds sad?" she asked.

"All of it," he almost sounded accusing. "Your not missing John at all." He stopped speaking and murmured something to himself, as if reprimanding himself for something. Then he began again.

"It sounds as if you have already made up your mind what to do. You have to do what you think is best for you." He began to rise, as if dismissing her.

But Camille was not going to let this happen.

"I haven't made up my mind at all," she protested. "Does it appear that way to you?"

"No, not at all," he said, sinking slowly back into his chair, as if he had been cornered. "One must not fall back into the old roles.

You must start being open and honest with John and let him know your feelings toward him. Tell him where he stands. Then see if your feelings change toward him." He leaned back, his deep leather chair creaking with the enormous weight of his body, while a meek smile on his face made him look as if he wanted her to go away.

Camille sat there, looking at him and wondering if he had heard what she had been telling him for the past hour. She wondered if he had any inkling of what she was going through. Maybe she had not expressed herself well enough, how afraid she was to tell John anything. How telling him where he stood was the last thing possible on earth she could do. She doubted she could even face John, much less tell him where he stood. John did not want to know how she felt toward him, and if he knew he would kill her.

"Wouldn't it hurt John if I told him?" was what she said.

"I feel sorry for John. I would advise you to go back and live with him for awhile before you decide what to do."

"But I don't have much time," she replied, almost panicking at the thought of living with John again. How could she stand it? She was anxious to make Rev. Seabottom understand her predicament. "I'll only be in Texas for a week before he leaves on a trip. He's going during the holidays because it's his break from classes. He couldn't go any other time and as soon as he returns I'm supposed to come back to New York to finish the semester."

"Well," he said, becoming rather agitated; one of his pudgy hands grabbed the other as if he was trying to keep it from shaking a finger at her. "As I said, it looks as if you've already decided. I only had one hour and I'm afraid I must close this session. It would be good for you to join some sort of support group. I have a support group forming in this church that you can become a part of. It might be good for you to know other people who are also divorced. You'll find them to be very supportive and understanding of what you're going through."

Camille looked down when he stopped, feeling chastised and wondering if that was all he had to say, when he added, "You know, of course, that you are already mourning the loss of your husband. It might take years before you can have a close relationship again with anyone else, since you've been hurt so much." His voice sounded so dark and sad when he said this that it almost sounded like he wanted to sob. It was hard for Camille to know if he was feeling sorry for her, for John or for himself.

At first she had suspended judgment on him, until she decided he was unsympathetic to her ordeal and then she felt judgmental toward him. Now, suddenly, he seemed very emotional, as if he was personally involved and she almost felt sorry for him. He must be speaking from personal experience. And why should she join a divorced persons' support group when she was not divorced yet?

As this was the first time she had ever gone to a therapist, she wondered if this was what was supposed to happen. She left feeling more depressed than when she came in. She wanted to be close to someone so much, and yet he had said it would be hard for her. Perhaps he was right. She did feel herself backing off from any close relationships with men and not allowing herself to be close to any man who wanted to be close to her. Perhaps Vince had wanted to be close to her and she had rejected him. Perhaps she should open up more, let someone be close, after all.

It really was true, she thought, as she walked in a daze toward the subway, practically bumping into people in her preoccupation, she did not really want to get emotionally close to anyone, not even Vince any more. That morning before she had left, Vince had called her several times, telling her how he wanted their relationship to be. He wanted it to be distant, with no commitments, yet he wanted to date her and talk when they happened to meet (which they inevitably would, as they lived next door to each other). With each call she had felt more depressed about it and had not protested any of his new rules. It had not been the best way to start her day, and now Rev. Seabottom's advice was very confusing.

NO HOPE CAN HAVE NO FEAR

Vince's boat was dark until early morning. She did not remember what time it was when she woke to see the lights shining from his windows. Was it 4:00 or 5:00 a.m.? She had a hard time falling sleeping again. She was sleeping in her own bed every night, but she could hear every noise outside. She could hear Vince when he came in and when he went out. During his last phone call he had told her he thought they should not talk to each other any more. Yet as he hung up he said he would call her later. Then he left his boat without calling, so she slept very restlessly, tossing around and throwing the bed covers around, expecting a phone call at any hour.

It was 8:00 when she finally got up, having slept soundly for the last four hours. Soon the phone rang. She was pulling on her jogging pants as she reached for the phone, knowing who it was. The light out the window hurt her eyes and she covered them as she talked.

"Hi. Did I wake you?" Vince asked brightly.

"No. I was up, just getting ready to go jog." She was not very happy with him and her voice reflected this.

"Oh! Well! I was getting ready to walk my dog."

"What a coincidence," she returned, sarcastically.

"Grace is going to meet me on the walkway." He fell silent. She wondered why he had called.

"I'm sorry I didn't call again last night."

"That's all right," said Camille. That apology for something small made up for some big omissions he had made, and she could accept it.

"I was exaggerating yesterday." he said, and paused. She waited. "I exaggerated for the sake of emphasis. You know what I mean."

"I know what you mean, and I agree with you completely," she said, very sincerely. He was only momentarily stymied.

"I'll see you outside, then," he sounded hopeful.

"Good-bye," she said. She was thinking her life would be a lot less complicated if she did not have to worry about Vince. Still, it was good to have someone to talk to in the mornings and he was good for that this morning, since he seemed so cheerful. Usually he was grumpy in the mornings. But sometimes he was good on the phone, joking, making word games and feeling happy.

Camille was surprised she felt so good, physically, after the rough night she had passed. She saw Grace and Vince standing on the walkway and approached them with a smile. They all talked easily, but the tension from the past few days was still with them. She finally ran on, with Rastus at her heels, leaping up on her. She sped up, trying to outrun the dog. But Rastus cut across the track and intercepted her on the far side when she came around. The day was chilly, but beautiful and clear. It felt good to run. When she finished, she ran up to Vince.

"Your tits show when you wear that sweatshirt," said Vince, disapprovingly. She paid no attention to him and concentrated on petting the dog.

It was Wednesday night. Camille realized she had not prayed lately. She used to pray every night, but lately it had not even occurred to her to pray. The Bible says God forgives you and gives you support, even when the world around you may be crashing down around you, they said. She was trying very hard to believe this, but could not feel God anywhere. She was sitting in the bathroom, the most isolated room in the boat, feeling terrible. She had tried to pray, but could not. There did not seem to be anyone there to pray to. It was like calling a telephone number and hearing it ring and ring and ring when it is so necessary for the person on the other end be there.

The pain she felt in her stomach was physical, not mental. The mental pain was turning into a physical one because the mental pain was too much to bear and the suffering was so all-encompassing it included her physical body. She could not remember hurting so much in her entire life, even when she had gotten a big splinter in her foot as a child and almost passed out from the pain when her father removed it. She wished she felt only the pain as she had felt then. At least it had been a physical pain and was curable and short-lived.

The therapist had said she was mourning over the loss of her husband already. But when she thought about it, she realized she had long since mourned the death of her marriage in small spurts and had come through it. The pain she felt now went far beyond physical and seemed like it would never end. She must remember to never put herself in this position again for the rest of her life – a position where she could get hurt this badly.

She sat on the closed toilet seat, her head alternately down on her knees or stretched back in an effort to relieve the strain. She knew the Bible and the book <u>The Rise and Fall of the Roman Empire</u> were on the commode lid behind her. She had been trying to read them over the last month and somehow the <u>Rise and Fall</u> was winning. Right now she could not bring herself to touch either of them. Nothing could help or distract her any longer. She could not even cry. She could only groan over the pain in her stomach and the agony in her head.

"Why am I hurting? I don't want to hurt any more. No more. Please. No more. I must keep away from everyone, including John and Vince. I need to get away from them. How can they hurt me so much?"

She rose and nervously walked back and forth in the tiny room, lit only with one bulb above the sink. Her breath was coming in short bursts and her arm crossed tightly across her chest as she talked out loud, trying to formulate thoughts into something coherent.

"On one hand, I can't talk to John and he's the one I should talk to. Everyone says I should talk to him. But he won't let me talk. Everything I say is threatening to him or something. He turns it back on me to violate our trust with. He doesn't want me to talk to him. I don't think I will ever be able to tell him I want a divorce. He'll hurt me if I tell him. I am afraid of him, but I have to face him and tell him. I don't want to go home. I would rather die than face him."

She stopped at the bathroom mirror and unconsciously looked in it. She noticed her hair hanging around her thin face in wet strands and pushed it back. Her eyes, in their dark sockets, were red-streaked and puffy. She looked deeply into her own eyes. She saw someone else and felt sorry for this person. She should do something for this pitiful girl. She tried to imagine killing her, this distressed person she saw in the mirror, but this person was a stranger, someone she had never seen before and she realized she could never kill this strange and distraught woman she was looking at.

So she had to go face John. She had no other choice. Maybe

he will kill me, she thought. But I don't want to die. I have so much to look forward to, if only I can get away from him. What if he kills me? He might kill me. He will kill me with one angry blow when I tell him; kill me right on the spot. That's what I'm afraid of. I can see his arm striking out at me as it has in the past; quickly, before I can defend myself, hurting after the first shock of the blow is realized.

Or he might hurt me later, striking verbally at my inner soul, which he knows so well from having lived with me for so long. He knows how to pierce my heart and blow out the little flame that burns there. He has done it before. I was dead once. Now I'm beginning to feel painfully alive and he will kill me again.

The late afternoons were bad, but mornings were bad, too. She felt so terribly alone when she first awoke and thought of the day before her. Yet when she looked outside and saw the day, she felt better. Still, unremembered memories of bad dreams in the night left her shaking. She was nervous, disturbed and unable to eat or to begin to move. Her stomach was a quivering mass of acid. Nevertheless, she would get up, drink some tea with honey and get dressed.

She noticed that, even though she had lost a lot of weight since she had come to New York, she was losing more now. Many of the women in her family were thin, but she had never been one of them. It was different being thin, a contrast to the problems of being fat. She had bruises on her buttocks from sitting down too hard and hitting bone. She still thought of herself as being fat, but saw a very thin woman in a mirror or store window she passed. Her image of herself was changing. She still overestimated her size when she looked at clothes, but she knew intellectually that she had lost five sizes and was at the weight the charts had always said she should be for her height.

After school on Friday, she went back to the boat and ate supper by herself. She was relieved to notice Vince was not around. It was nice to do whatever she wanted without worrying about him. At 7:30 the phone rang. It was Paul. She had almost forgotten, or rather had tried to forget about him. He told her he was on his way to her boat and would be there in 45 minutes. He was in SoHo, hanging a show, was almost finished and had time to drop by and see her. He talked so fast and furiously and seemed so confident and determined that she hardly had time to speak. She had no opportunity to say the things she had planned to say to him, about not seeing him tonight, or about her resolution to not date him or anyone else for a long time, during his entire monologue. Yet, after he hung up she was glad he insisted on coming over.

She cleaned up the boat and looked at herself in the mirror, fixing her makeup a little. At 8:30 the phone rang again. It was Paul at the gate to the boat basin, waiting to be let in. She walked out to the gate to meet him. Somehow it was nice to have someone coming to see her.

He was standing outside the chain link fence, a neat-looking man in a huge overcoat. He looked good. His collar was turned up and his hair carefully cut and combed in the latest style. His beautiful blue eyes pierced hers when she opened the gate, taking in the surroundings, analyzing, measuring. She greeted him with a kiss on the cheek as he expected, and pointed out the various kinds of boats to him on the way back to hers.

"I apologize for being late," he said, as they neared it.

"Have you eaten supper?" she asked.

"No, haven't had time. Didn't even think about it," he admitted. But he said, before they went inside, that he wanted to walk down to the end of the dock and see the river. So they did that before returning to her boat.

Inside the warm cabin, Camille took his coat and made him a little supper of fresh fish, rice, green salad and bread, with tea. She drank tea with him and they talked. She rose and got him some color copies of her work, as they were discussing it, and he seemed very interested.

"You never know what another artist does until you see it." he said, "And sometimes it is a happy surprise." He complimented her; something that meant a lot to her, as she respected his opinion.

Then she asked him questions about himself. He seemed to be pretty much on top of the art world, but avoided talking about his private life. He also seemed to sense things had been rough for her lately and turned the conversation back to her, very gently, watching her kindly as she talked. He didn't probe into the particulars, for which she was grateful, but he did ask her one thing.

"Are you free of any commitments?"

"Well, yes," she said, thinking of nothing but her present state of mind. Then she added, correcting herself, "I'm trying to get out of one relationship I've been in too long."

She felt bad even talking about it. She had to let him know how she felt about him, though, and this seemed to be a good time to do that.

"It was pretty painful and I don't really want any new commitments right now."

"You know, pain must be experienced in order for there to be growth," he said, watching her face as he spoke, looking for any indications to stop. "But I understand how you feel about pain and not wanting to get close to anyone who could hurt you. I've felt that way myself."

She tried to read his eyes, to see how much he meant what he said. His face was sensitive and when she looked into his blue, heavily lashed eyes, she felt a fleeting urge to confide in him. He made her feel better. Yet it made her nervous to realize how much he looked like John. She had to keep reminding herself that he was different.

"Didn't you just have a birthday?" she asked him. She had heard Hal mention that Paul had just turned 37. He was a couple of years older than she was and exactly the same age as John. They might have been twins, only John was heavier. "You have your whole life ahead of you. You can afford to take chances. You've got a long time to recover," she said, optimistically.

"Unlike you?" he was laughing at her a little, a smile in one corner of his chiseled lips. "Why do I feel like I'm the wise old man when I'm around you?" He looked at her seriously and intently and, though he did not move, she felt him coming closer to her. She countered this thought with the fact that he was very much like a baby. She felt older than he. She looked at his eyes, and what she saw made her look down, for he was looking at her with such longing. He looked as if he was about to say something very important, but said nothing.

"Tonight I'm going to be here with you," he said instead. "We have a lot to talk about." She looked up at him again, now that he was safe. He continued. "When I first saw you I felt very attracted to you. It is impossible to describe. . . . You seemed out of reach, yet the little smiles you gave me, the glances you made in my direction were excuses to come near you, encouragements. I felt like being around you, caring for you, giving you what you needed, being a gentleman for you, even though usually I'm not a gentleman around women I'm attracted to. You seem so refined, so delicate, sensitive. . ." He broke off, realizing perhaps he had said too much. Camille was embarrassed and had made a gesture to stop him.

"We did have fun dancing," she said, trying to lighten up. He agreed, laughing a little. From then on it was easy to talk to him. He talked more than she, but he also listened to her and tried to be understanding. He told her he was unattached and was not on the rebound; as Vince was when she had first met him, she reflected.

He left at midnight, asking if he could see her again; that he would like to, if it was all right with her. She said yes and the pain she felt in her heart, as she said it, was not as big. She said she was glad he came by and almost meant it. He kissed her on the mouth when he left, with very soft lips. She stopped him after a moment, as he was holding her tighter and would have kissed her longer.

When she closed the door she felt good. He had acted honorably after all. He had been honest and was a gentleman; not at all what she was afraid he would be. She turned and began to run the water into the sink to wash the dishes. The phone rang. It was Vince. Her heart sank. She had not known he was at home.

"Hi. I just got back." he said.

"Hi," she said, hoping to goodness he had not seen Paul.

"What did you do today?" he asked. It was an inopportune time for him to call, just as Paul had left. She quickly told him she had painted at school and found out about credit transfers. She did not say anything about Paul, but he brought it up.

"Did you see Paul today? He said he was going to see you today when he left the party the other night . . . as I recall."

"Yes," she admitted. "I saw Paul." He waited for her to go on, but she was silent.

"Well?" he said. "What else?"

"Nothing," she said, searching for some other event to report to him. "Did you eat supper?"

"Yes." he did not explain. She could tell he was upset under his cheerfulness, but she was still under the influence of Paul's calm presence and did not want to spoil it by a long discussion.

"Can I see you tomorrow and give you your Christmas present?" she asked, hoping he would want to end the conversation.

"I don't think so. I want to sleep tomorrow. I worked hard today taking pictures. I'm going to stay up all night tonight and develop film."

"Call me when you get up. That way I won't bother you," she said.

"Okay. Good night."

"Good night."

Camille washed the dishes while she watched a Fu Manchu movie on the old black-and white TV she had bought at a yard sale for $10.00.

The next day John called to ask her what time she would be arriving at the airport so he could meet her.

"He couldn't even wait until after you left, huh?" said Hal. He put his arm around Camille's shoulder as they walked to Chinatown through Little Italy with Ann walking closely behind them, trying to overhear their conversation. It was already dark at 5:30 and the brightly lit storefronts in Little Italy seemed to be open late. The restaurants on Mulberry Street were busy and the sidewalks were crowded with shoppers. Ann, however, strained to hear what the latest was on Vince, Camille and Grace.

"I moved back into my own boat, though, and I'm glad. Vince can talk as much as he wants and go out with as many women as he wants and I don't have to hear it. I don't think Grace will get back with Vince, but he sure wants her to," continued Camille. "The only problem is, I am still attached emotionally to Vince. It is hard to get over this attachment! It's amazing what can happen in the course of a few days. And yet not much seems to happen. I never would have believed our relationship could have changed so much so fast. I don't know what I did."

Hal was silent, his balding brow wrinkled in thought. Camille wished he could speak some words of wisdom, tell her what to do. Anything that would solve all her problems. But his face was bent down to the street as they walked across Canal Street, now lit with bright street lamps, the border between Little Italy and Chinatown. As they passed into the dark streets of Chinatown with its curious stores and signs all in Chinese, his kindly face with the collar turned up around it was thrown into a study of contrasts and shadows.

"I don't know, Camille." he said, finally. "All I can say is to pursue your own course. Your own career. That's what is important, being happy with yourself." He was silent for awhile, then spoke again.

"I should talk," he said, "My life is not exactly an example of discipline." He briefly traced the course of his life. He had lived a rough one, living all over the world, married, had children which were now almost grown, had been a notorious girl-chaser at one point and finally settled down with one very young woman. But this young woman was strong enough to motivate him to stop his heavy drinking and put energy into his business, which now was doing very well. Camille admired him, considering all he had been through and the fact that he had devoted many years of his life to helping young artists in the gallery.

"It's all fate, isn't it?" Camille asked Hal. "I believe it was fate that brought me to you. In this big city you helped me out by believing in my art and showing it. I wonder what my future will be like. I can't imagine."

"You want to know your fate? Look around you," said Hal, as breath puffed from their mouths along the dark, wet streets, avoiding an occasional person and tailed by silent, listening Ann.

"Look around me? What does that have to do with my future?" asked Camille.

"Look around you. Like old cars rust and salt eats out their undersides, you know your car will some day look the same, especially if you live here in the Northeast, where they put salt on the streets. If you want a car to last, go to the desert where it never rains or snows."

"What do you mean?" Camille was completely puzzled by Hal's parable.

"You know. Look at these cars we are passing. You know your car will some day look the same at that age if you drive it around here a long time. A twenty-year-old car is rusted out and falling apart. Some day your car will look like that. It's the same with you. Look at the people who are older than you. Someday you will be like them. Look at the people around you; what are their habits and their illnesses? If you stick around them, yours will be the same. It's not hard to know your fate. Look around you. Most likely you'll end up like them."

Camille felt a little depressed. She had not looked around. But if she looked at Hal, he was older and had turned out all right. She did not know about the illnesses he had mentioned, but he looked very healthy now. He had started running and now ran in the New York Marathon every year. He devoted most of his time to the gallery. His young girlfriend with her child lived far away, but he supported her. He definitely knew where he was going and what he was doing and seemed to be enjoying it. Maybe she would turn out like him.

After dinner in Chinatown, Hal left to go home and Ann and Camille took the subway to Brooklyn to the student party. On the way, with Ann's encouragement, Camille chatted mindlessly about Vince, making small talk. Believing Ann thought she and Vince were still going together, she began the story of how, last week she had taken Vince to a party and he had tried to pick up another girl. Ann twisted her lips in a grimace and said, "He's an asshole." After that Camille did not tell her any more about Vince.

As soon as they arrived at the big, noisy house where the party was, Philip met them at the door and immediately asked Camille to dance. A fast disco record was on the stereo, "You Can Ring My Bell," a 45-minute long record. The dancing and the music had a hypnotic effect on Camille, making her feel much better. She danced without stopping for about two hours and felt like she could have danced all night. Whenever she stopped, someone else asked her to dance and she started again. Once, Camille noticed Ann dancing a slow dance with Philip and it struck her that they would make a perfect couple, both being fairly short and shy in their own ways. She decided to encourage them. Ann looked sweet with her strawberry-colored hair and pale face and Philip serious, as he held Ann and leaned over her shoulder with his bangs hanging over his half-closed eyes. She guessed that everyone there was about the same age, about ten years younger than she.

Eventually she found herself dancing most of the dances with an Iranian student named Saud, who was a little taller than she, and whose skin was dark, with narrow eyes and olive skin. He had a solid face with a square jaw and a handsome Roman nose. His strong body was well-shaped, as he was an athlete. The overall effect was attractive, as he was well aware. He intruded into Camille's distracted state with flattery. He pressed her to him, whispering "your breath is like honey, you have the face of an angel." He was enjoying the contact of their bodies during the slow dance too much, and tried to hold her even closer. But Camille pulled away slowly, smiling to be polite and looking directly into his face, trying to keep him at a distance.

But when he saw her smile, he smiled back, put his head down and pushed his cheek against hers and pressed his body even harder into hers. The slow dance seemed endless and Camille was aching from the tension of trying to stand up straight, with a body leaning forward over hers.

When the dance finally ended, she heard the sound of the steady disco beat again. Saud was fun to dance with on the fast dances, since he was such a good dancer. This time he was doing the Lindy and soon he was trying to make her flip over his arm. Camille had kept up with him, laughing with the sheer energy of the dance, until that point. She considered herself a dancer, but she was not skilled at lifts and drops. When he tried to swing her between his legs and back again she doubted she could keep up with him. The next time he tried to throw her over his shoulder she felt it coming and did a twirl, instead. He only smiled evilly and threw her between his legs again. Dancers around them had to move back to avoid being hit. Now she was trying not to get thrown into other people, but found herself stepping on some toes anyway. Meanwhile, the music was getting louder and faster and the room was growing hot. Some people stood on the sidelines and watched them dance, but most of the couples were still dancing intently to the fast music under the dim lights.

Finally, the song was over. With a thank you to Saud and a sigh of relief, Camille turned to go into the kitchen and find something to drink. Saud was suddenly at her side again, taking her elbow and forcing her to walk her into a dark corner of the hall. He pressed his body full against hers until she could not move, with her back against the wall. Since she could not get away without wiggling, she decided to remain rigid and still.

"I want to give you a big kees," he breathed urgently into her ear. "Won't you come home with me and I will give you such a beautiful, big kees." His stormy breath was whistling like a steam engine and the heat from his body against hers made her feel like she was burning up. He pressed her against the wall, trying to overpower her. She began to sweat and struggle. "How crude," was all she could think. She knew what he was talking about and she had no desire to "kiss" him.

She pulled her head back as far as she could from his and tried to look sternly into his face, to maintain some dignity in her present, undignified state. Saud's eyes seemed crossed, he was so close. He pushed his face over to try to kiss her on the cheek, but Camille took advantage of his moving to duck under his arm and get out into the middle of the hall. There she stood and faced him, keeping distance between them whenever he moved toward her.

"I am here with my girlfriend, thank you. We have to go back to Manhattan together soon. I certainly cannot abandon her here. She doesn't know anyone here in Brooklyn and she can't travel alone." Then she turned and quickly went into the big, lighted room where everyone was dancing. When she looked back from the center of the room, Saud was standing in the door, the picture of 2wrejection, his face pouting and pleading, his arms stretching out to her. If she had not felt so intimidated by him, Camille might have laughed. But what happened had scared her and she did not want to make him angry.

She looked everywhere for Ann, to see if she was ready to go home. Once she found her, she stayed next to her and began to relax. Saud was not pursuing her any more. He seemed to have disappeared. She had found Ann in the kitchen, mixing drinks and sipping a drink with a straw.

"Great party!" she said.

"Yes, and don't you love Philip? He is so popular." She said to Ann, fishing to find out if Ann liked him.

"Oh yeah, he's wonderful, but I don't know him very well at this point," said Ann. She was so shy that even if she liked him, Philip would never know.

"I enjoyed the Christmas party at the gallery," said Camille, to change the subject. This got Ann's attention and she looked up at Camille with a knowing smile.

"Paul Frank sure seems to like you," she said. "I'll bet that made Vince jealous." Camille felt her heart thud at the mention of Paul's name.

"What makes you think he likes me?" said Camille, almost closing her eyes recalling what Paul had said the other night on her boat. Did he really like her or was he just putting on an act? He was famous, he was good looking and the because of these two things, she doubted he could like her.

"He made it so obvious. Kissing you. And right in front of Vince!"

But maybe he did that to other women, too, thought Camille, looking at Ann, wondering what Ann wanted to hear. Should she respond to this? Did she like Paul enough to worry about it? Did she really want to encourage him at this point? There were too many things to get in the way. He looked so much like John that she wanted to avoid him as much as she wanted to like him. And her feelings for Vince got in the way all the time.

"I wonder if he knows Vince and I went together?"

"Of course; everyone knew."

"And he still likes me?"

"You're a challenge to him, Camille, and Paul Frank loves challenges." After a moment Camille realized Ann spoke with a bit of sarcasm. "He can see you're breaking up with Vince."

"But I mean. . . he is too popular. He always has those pretty girls on his arm. I can't compete with them."

"Of course you can," said Ann, a mischievous look glinting in her green eyes. Maybe Ann knows more than I, thought Camille. Maybe Ann had talked with him. He hung around the gallery a lot. Maybe he had discussed her with Ann.

Ann continued. "He likes having them around, but he doesn't seem to like any one of them for more than a friend. They are good for his image. I think they are just friends."

"Why doesn't he like them?" asked Camille. She could not for the life of her imagine how Paul Frank could like her more than them, in spite of his words.

"I don't know. Maybe he senses they hang around him just to

be with a celebrity. You know, like groupies. Maybe they are shallow. Look how he took to you right away. Everyone was surprised."

"Surprised you, huh?" Camille said, a little irony in her voice.

"I didn't mean it that way," said Ann, looking down, her face blushing behind her freckles, as she did when she laughed.

"Well, I'm surprised, too." admitted Camille. "I think he is very nice, but I don't' know him well enough yet."

"Maybe you'll be good for each other. But watch out. As far as I can tell, all men are dangerous."

"Except Philip," mused Camille out loud. "I'm getting tired. Why don't we go on home? I don't really want to run into Saud again."

When she got home, Vince had friends visiting at his boat. Camille heard music, and from the window by her bed, could see Vince moving around behind the closed blinds with other shadows. She could not tell who was there, and dropped off to sleep, after assuring herself they were just smoking buddies.

DANGEROUS MEN

Next day, Camille went down to SoHo to meet Hal at the gallery without calling Vince. She felt good about becoming so independent and hoped he realized he had lost her. Hal had asked her to come to talk with him about a commission.

At the gallery, Hal said a woman had come in to see some of her work and wanted her to paint something for her. She was talking about it with Hal in the office, when the door opened at the far end of the gallery and Paul Frank walked in. Camille found herself breathing a little faster, but pretended not to notice him and kept her mind on what Hal was saying. Hal looked up and saw Paul and hesitated, but by then Paul had walked up to some paintings on the wall and was studying them, so Hal turned his attention back to Camille. Camille sensed, rather than saw, Paul turning his head to watch her while she conversed with Hal. After a few excruciating minutes, he walked up to join them.

He stood close to Camille, listening to Hal tell Camille what the woman had said. "She wants something with that line in it, those colors. But, you know, she wants a different subject. Do you have something with horses or cows in it?"

"Horses and cows? It's been a long time since I painted a cow."

Camille soon found herself joking with Hal and Paul, listening to herself talk with surprise. A whole separate part of her brain had taken over and she was saying things that were apropos and humorous, while the rest of her brain was shouting that Paul was standing beside her, moving his arm so it touched her, was leaning closer to hear better, even breathing words in her direction, that his eyes were caressing her mouth as she spoke.

Hal sensed he was a fifth wheel and after confirming an appointment with Camille, made an excuse to leave. So both Camille and Paul said good bye to him as he went downstairs and they found themselves alone. It seemed natural to turn to each other as if they had planned to meet this way. Yet Camille was saying to herself, "No, this isn't right. I don't like this at all. Let me out of here."

"I still feel you are a stranger," Paul said. "I don't really know anything about you, no matter how much you have told me. The other day, actually, I did most of the talking. I'm sorry. I didn't give you a chance." His eyes were more intense than his words, and Camille found herself speechless, as if the fountain of verbiage she had discovered a few minutes before had just gone dry.

"He is only a man after all, she said to herself, even if he does seem to have a strange effect on me." Surely his big name can't mean that much to him. But it did to her and she wondered how he could possibly like her. After all, she was rather independent. Often men seemed to be attracted to her, yet it always surprised her. Some day she would be his equal, she thought, and would be able to say to him "Forget you. You're not my type." But right now, almost against her will, she found herself courting him, asking him what she could tell him that he didn't already know, insinuating he could ask her certain things that she could not name. He laughed a low, pleased laugh.

"Well," he hesitated, looking at her teasingly from the corner of his eye, then straightened his gaze and asked "Where are you from?"

"The Midwest," she said, "but it's a long story and you couldn't possibly have enough time to listen to it now."

"I've got time for a cup of coffee. Would you join me on such a cold day, at Cup of Joe's, around the corner?"

"I'd like that very much." So they walked down the shining length of the gallery and out into the cold December day. The air seemed more invigorating than usual. Camille found herself feeling extremely happy. Paul walked beside her in the quiet, confident way that made people who approached them look at them with admiration. They talked only a little as they walked.

From their discussion the other night, she knew Paul was not involved with anyone now. Paul now told her he had once been married, but had been divorced for ten years. He asked her if she had ever been married.

Camille told him, yes, but she was separated and was not involved with anyone now, either. With that one sentence she realized she had severed her relationships with both John and Vince.

Something about Paul bothered her and, as they talked in the little diner, she began to sort out what it was about him that she liked and disliked. The similarities to John she had first noticed were actually superficial. His look in the face, the way he was raised and his age were the same as John's. But now she realized there was something else about in his personality that was like John's, too. She could not put her finger on just what it was. The larger, remaining areas she was finding seemed vastly different from John's. The feeling that she had at first, that she already knew him, was dissolving, and she began to realize that she did not know this man at all.

As long as she had felt she knew him she could control her actions and what she said. But now she had to be careful of what she said. He was somewhat like John in that there were land mines about to explode if she said the wrong things. She sensed that in him. She wondered if she was afraid to become involved with him because of this danger; afraid to know him better, afraid of finding those explosive places. Or was she afraid because she did not really want to become involved with anyone?

Perhaps his ego was big like John's, who knew he was important and had always known it. His general demeanor was like John's, quiet, almost cold, courting only the ones he wanted to favor him. But unlike John, he was obviously sexually active. He bent over backward to impress her with the fact that he cared about her, something John would never do. He seemed to want to possess her, to get close to her. John had never been like that. John did not care to be close to anyone, and never had. He had just chosen her, told her he had chosen her and had taken it for granted she would go with him and she had.

After brunch, when they came out onto the cold, bright street again, Paul invited her to see his new loft, nearby. They walked down the cold, iron-laced streets of SoHo to an impressive brownstone building. Big and elegant, it had an elaborate cast iron front which was much more ornate than those about it.

The doorman saluted Paul as they entered. Inside the lobby there were mirrors, etched glass, more wrought iron, and fancy grillwork revealed in the interior elevator doors when the polished wooden ones opened. Once in the cage, Paul pushed a polished brass button marked "6E." The elevator hummed and they watched the floors slowly slip past until they reached the top. Paul pushed the accordion grating open. They stepped into a tiny, paneled hall with a door at each end; one had a shiny brass plate reading "Paul Frank Studio." Paul fitted a key into the ornate lock. Everything was designed to impress.

Stepping inside the loft, Camille had to catch her breath, for immediately before them was a huge glass window with only a narrow balcony outside, overlooking roof gardens, water tanks and the varied skyline of SoHo. She gave an exclamation of surprise. Paul led her up to the sliding glass doors and pointed out landmarks around them. To the right she could see the 420 Building, with its six floors of galleries, and to the left up West Broadway to Houston Street. Turning around, she saw a collection of Paul's paintings, most of them neatly stored in built-in racks. Some paintings hung on the walls and some were on low easels, in the process of being painted. On this end of the studio was a bright red rug along the wall, in the center of which was a fireplace. Comfortable leather chairs and a big couch covered with cushions were gathered around it.

Paul took her coat, scarf and gloves, led her to the fireplace, started a fire, and told her to make herself comfortable. He stepped behind an oriental screen where Camille had glimpsed a desk and she could hear the little voices of people on his telephone answering machine. She waited, without knowing for what she waited, gazing out of the window or at the fire from her cozy coign in the middle of a big, round chair and almost hoped he would never return. She wondered what he intended to do with her now. He seemed tense, here at his place, but he wanted her to feel comfortable.

When he emerged from his office area, he waved his arm, including his studio, the living area, and the view and asked "Well, how do you like It?"

"Beautiful! I'm very impressed." She smiled approvingly at him. He seemed to relax a little. But Camille looked at her watch and jumped up, saying it was almost 1:00 and she was supposed to have a meeting at 2:00, so she had to hurry off. He did not seem relieved or distressed; he just acquiesced and said he would walk her down and help her get a taxi.

She objected, as she planned take a subway, and could not afford a taxi, but he insisted on accompanying her, and as they walked out onto the street together, walking toward Houston Street, she told him how much she appreciated being in New York now, having the cultural advantages of the city, how wonderful it was, compared to the small town she was from. He agreed and began expounding on the theater and music available. He, too, had grown up in a small town.

Of course, she said to herself bitterly, he can afford to pay for ballet and theater tickets. She was referring to the free sights and music available in the Village, at the Village Gate and the entertainers in the parks who performed for passers-by while he was referring to high-priced restaurants and Broadway plays and concerts.

"Won't you have dinner with me later this week?" Paul asked as they reached the corner. Camille did not hide her delight that he had asked her and said yes. So he said he would call her tonight and they would set a time. He gave her a little good-bye kiss and they parted. Camille walked toward the subway station feeling a new excitement. Perhaps some day this city would also be hers.

Vince must have been trying to call her all day from New Jersey, because the phone rang the moment she stepped into her boat. He abruptly asked her where she had been and she answered "in SoHo." They chatted a few moments. It seemed he just wanted to be in touch with her. He was calling from his parents' house, from his room. He said he was coming back to the boat basin soon and would see her when he got back.

Philip arrived at 2:00, as he had said he would when he called to ask her if he could come over, as he had something to discuss with her. His breath was coming in puffs, as if he had run down the hill, and his blond hair blew around his young, round face. He wore the usual jeans and plaid shirt under a down jacket. He was so happy that he made her feel happy, too. He was always helpful and cheerful and never asked anything of her. She showed him what she had been working on in her boat and accepted his praise and criticism seriously, as he was a fellow student and an excellent artist. They sat for awhile over her pictures, drinking tea.

Philip then told her he hoped to become wealthy from his plans to open an art store, once he got a little capital together. He was ambitious, but very poor. Camille smiled at his boundless hope, hoping he would be able to do exactly what he planned. He mentioned that, as part of his plan, he would get married. He discussed, hypothetically, the possibility of his marrying her, once she got her divorce. This was the first time Camille had heard this plan, but she politely refused to entertain the idea and carefully turned his thoughts to Ann. She knew Ann would be much better suited to him than she. Ann was young and cute, unattached and wanted to get married. Philip now seemed nervous and anxious to show her how much he was going to do during his life. They were still talking about his plans, both of them trying to act nonchalant, when Camille heard Vince return.

Philip kept chattering on, oblivious of the fact that Camille was growing more and more nervous. She told herself how ridiculous it was to be afraid Vince would come over to her boat and find Philip there. She had every right to have a friend over. But Vince had been in a good mood earlier and finding Philip on her boat would, at the very least, irritate him.

After a few minutes, Philip noticed Camille was not participating in the conversation any more and stood up to make his departure. He tried to be polite, but said he had overstayed his welcome. She protested and walked him to the door, where he stood, absentmindedly dawdling and obviously wanting to say something. Then he turned as if to go, took a couple of steps out the door and stood outside, still talking, in the cold wind, thinking of more things to say, delaying his departure. Once he even turned and innocently glanced into Vince's open door. Camille almost fainted, thinking Vince might see him do that, or might hear them talking, outside.

Vince had obviously left his door open so she would see he was home and come over. Camille stepped outside, wrapping her sweater around her, took Philip's arm and strolled as quickly as she could without seeming to be rude, with him toward the gate.

"What's wrong?" he asked, when they got to the gate. He was looking at her with distress.

"Nothing," said Camille, pretending to be puzzled.

"Come on, Camille. You're giving me the bum's rush. Why?"

"I'll tell you, Philip," she said, able to talk, now they were out of earshot of Vince's boat," I'm not really trying to get rid of you, but Vince lives in that boat right next to me and he left his door open. I didn't want to talk with Vince listening."

"He lives right next door to you? That's hilarious," said Philip; but he was only a little amused, now that he understood. "No wonder you're a nervous wreck. I saw you jump when I looked in his door. Gosh, I wouldn't live next door to an ex-girlfriend for anything. But I shouldn't make you stand out in this cold." He kissed her good-bye and left, chuckling to himself.

When Camille got back to her boat she felt ashamed. Why should she apologize to Vince for having Philip over? Vince really had nothing to say about what she did. She could do as she wished and he could not do anything, really. She went in her boat, leaving the door open, intending to get a warm coat on before she went to Vince's, since she was chilled. But Vince stuck his head in and said "come on over and watch some color TV." He must have been watching her all the time.

Camille stayed a couple of hours, watching TV and talking with Vince that evening. Grace came by for a few minutes and she and Camille talked amiably. The two women had been planning an outing together at her cabin in January and discussed it a little in front of Vince. Grace left and Vince turned to Camille, jealously.

"What are you being so friendly with Grace for? You're assuming a lot, aren't you? She wants to be left alone at her cabin, you know. That's why she rented it."

"Vince, Grace and I have talked about this many times. You don't even know what she and I have been discussing." Camille was hurt at his censure. Perhaps he felt she was intruding on him, but Grace had been her friend even before she met Vince. He was intruding on hers and Grace's friendship now, she thought. Perhaps Grace had intruded on hers and Vince's relationship in September, but it was hard to determine all intrusions when they were all so close.

"I'm just mad because you busted in on my conversation with her about my going to her cabin. She had just said it was okay for me to come out there when you stuck your two bits in." he said.

"Well, I'm sorry," Camille said, standing. "Do you want more coffee?" She was trying to avoid talking about it.

He sensed this, answered yes and let it drop.

"April is going to take care of Fidel for me while I'm gone for

Christmas," she said, when she brought the coffee back. "She's putting him in with her goldfish, in her big tank. He'll have a good time. He'll think it's a Christmas party."

"I thought you wanted me to feed him while you were gone."

"Now you won't have to. Besides, I thought you said you might go to Miami."

Camille went home late. She wondered if she had gotten a call from Paul, confirming their dinner. If he had called while she was at Vince's, she would not have known about it, but he probably had not called. Or perhaps he was having second thoughts, too.

Her mind dwelled on the budding relationship with Paul as she prepared to go to bed. It would be better if she did not see him until after she got back from Christmas vacation anyway, until after she had told John she was divorcing him. She could not pin any hopes on Paul. She really should forget him for the time being. He probably was the sort that would back out of a relationship that got too intense, like Vince did. The fact that he had not called to confirm dinner tomorrow night was an indication of that.

Perhaps she should not become involved with him at all. Something about him bothered her. Maybe because he was too much like John, she thought, as she fell asleep that night, or perhaps, because relationships hurt too much when they end, she should not have relationships. She ought to just be happy with a few good friends.

NO HOPE CAN HAVE NO FEAR

The last session of Camille's New Forms class was over. That morning she had put on her everyday blue jeans, a paint-spotted t-shirt and dirty tennis shoes practically falling apart from walking. There was at least one paint drip on everything she owned, even though she always wore her paint smock when she painted. The smock had so many paint smudges on front of it the original fabric was hardly visible.

She had completed the painting of the nude in the window, with eyes turned toward the light, cheeks flushed from her morning bath and body warm and full. Light brown hair flowed down her back and the drape fell from her hand to the floor in one long line. The woman had revealed herself to the sun and basked in it. Flowers bloomed outside, while the interior was elegant and soft with velvet rugs and plain, sun-bathed walls. Lacy curtains hung at the window, through which one caught glimpses of a clear blue sky. The subject matter and style was completely different than anything she had ever done.

In the afternoon, Camille emerged from her last Humanities class, searching her jacket pockets for money. There was just enough to celebrate by buying herself lunch. Standing in line in the cafeteria with a tray, she suddenly remembered she had not heard from Paul and tonight was the night he had invited her to come to his loft for dinner. She thought she should not go without talking to him first; as she wasn't sure he would be there. Perhaps he had changed his mind and did not want to have her over.

As she stood in line, she listened to the talk around her. Some students behind her were discussing a recent newspaper story about graffiti, wondering what the big deal was. She agreed with them. The artists had to be some artistic kids or maybe even adults who liked to decorate subway cars. She liked some of the graffiti on the subway cars, as it was beautiful. The two boys in front of her were talking about a lecture they had just heard on landscape painting.

"Oh, by the way," said one of the boys. "You know Saud, in our class?"

"Yes," said the other. Camille's ears perked up, was this the Saud she knew? How could it be any other?

"Well, he told me he's going back to Arabia – he's getting married. His parents chose a wife for him. He's never seen her. And when he comes back he'll be a married man."

Camille pondered the ramifications of Saud's actions with her at the party. He had known he was going to get married and still he was going after the girls! Maybe he wanted one more fling before going home to marry this woman.

After eating a sandwich and a coke, a rare treat, Camille went back to her studio to pick up books and go to her Romantic Literature class. The paper on Gauguin and the poems she had turned in had been graded and were returned during class. She received two 'A's and that made her happy. She had written the Gauguin paper sitting up all night, after doing two weeks of research in the library. She wrote it straight from her notes, and could not remember what she had written in the dead of night, after she handed it in. Now that she had it back in her hands, she read it over, enjoying it and agreeing with her findings.

Camille trudged through the melting snow, which seeped through her fabric tennis shoes, toward the tall building where her last class, New Forms, was held. Today, Alfred and Bob acted polite to her, rather than teasing her when she came in the big room and sat next to them, since it was the last day. She only smiled at them, as class was beginning. She would be able to stand around and talked with them after class. As they left the room, both Alfred and Bob gave her a kiss since they would not be seeing her until after the holidays, and she hugged them back. Their sentiment touched her. She had not told anyone what she was doing or where she was going for the holidays. She did not even want to think about it herself.

Sherry, one of the women in the class, was behind her and stopped her as she went down the stairs. "Would you like to share the rent and expenses on a loft next year? Sherry asked. She told Camille she would not be staying in the city all the time, as she was married and had to drive in from upstate New York four times a week. She would be going to school part time for a long time and wanted a place to stay in the city. Her children were grown up and gone. It sounded like a good idea to Camille and she promised she would talk to her about it next semester, if she returned. They exchanged phone numbers. One never knew what the situation might be in the future.

As she trudged through the snow and ice to the subway, Camille thought about how women, when they reach the age when their children are grown, become restless and want to do other things. But by then they have grown used to their restrictive circumstances, and, even though they may be sad and uncomfortable with their husbands, they have become so dependent upon them and on the physical things around them that they cannot leave and do the things they once dreamed they would do when their children left.

"Perhaps I can be an exception," she thought. But it struck her once again her marriage was no longer a marriage. She should not afraid to leave it because it was not there.

As James Thomson had so aptly put it in the poem she had read last night, *The City of Dreadful Night*, "No hope could have no fear."

After finally arriving home, Camille remembered once again, with a sigh of relief, that she had not heard from Paul. She looked at the clock over her bed. It was 4:00 p.m.; perhaps he did not expect her to come over. But just then the phone rang. It was Paul. First he apologized, saying he had lost her telephone number and had just found it, and then said he was expecting her at 7:30 tonight. Camille lay down on the bed and immediately fell asleep. When she awoke at 6:00 it was dark. She picked up the phone out of habit and dialed Vince's number to say hello, since she had not talked to him all day. He sounded like he was in a good mood and asked her if she would have dinner with him tomorrow night. She said yes and immediately dialed April, because she had invited April over tomorrow, and asked her if she minded coming to dinner later on in the week.

Camille took a shower, washed her hair and put on make-up, making plans in her head. She would wear her dark blue velvet slacks with two little sailor zippers on the front and a fuzzy white sweater, under a dark blue wool jacket. As she blow-dried her short, dark hair into a neat style, she began to feel a nervous excitement. She was going on a real date with someone to whom she was attracted. Suddenly she was conscious of preparing to go on a date in her own private place with her own personal things around her. She noticed her fish, Fidel, and fed him. She felt elated for some reason, happy, purposeful and appreciated. She was also starting to feel excited. She would soon be seeing Paul after all, just when she had thought she would not see him tonight.

The phone rang. It was Vince again.

"I think you are going out tonight. Am I right?"

"You're right," she admitted, slipping her arm into her fuzzy white sweater and picking a string of crystal beads out of the jewelry case at the same time, holding the phone between her ear and shoulder. She had a feeling that could best be described as smug. He didn't really believe she was dating?

"What are you going to eat?"

"Eat? I don't know."

"What do you mean you don't know? What restaurant are you going to?"

"Well, if I get a choice, I'll choose fish." She said, avoiding his last question, holding bobby pins in her teeth while she tried pulled her hair up on the sides. She had to take the bobby pins out of her mouth to talk, but she did not tell Vince she was going to eat at Paul's apartment. She was in a hurry, so she had to cut the conversation short. She decided to let her hair go loose.

"I've got to go. I'm still not dressed. See you later?" She was hoping he would not try to delay her;-she knew he hated saying good-bye.

"Sure," he said.

"Bye."

"Bye."

The phone rang again almost immediately, after she hung up. She picked it up, saying "hello," angrily. It was John, calling long distance. Her heart sank. Oh no, not now, she thought. But he only said a letter had been sent to him from the bank, requesting information about their bank account. She had applied for a separate account and he said it asked if they were getting a divorce. The letter had disturbed him, he said in a deliberate and strained voice; he was calling just to hear what she had to say.

Camille said nothing. He repeated that he was worried, and to please answer him. She told him not to worry, she would be seeing him soon and they could talk then. But after she hung up she realized she did not have to explain why she opened a separate account a couple of months ago to anyone. Besides, why would a bank ask her husband such a private question? She doubted he was telling the truth. Anyone could open a separate account.

Now, because of John's call she was running late and had to hurry. She put her jacket and wrapped a fuzzy green scarf around her neck, grabbed her big black leather handbag and gloves and ran up the hill to Broadway, stopping for a minute in a liquor store to buy a bottle of white wine.

The doorman let Camille in with a smile and showed her into the elevator. She knocked on the half-open door and heard Paul yell for her to come in. She pushed the door open and crept in. Paul was in the living room, talking on a wireless phone, and kissed her without removing it from his ear. The phone was to ring several times during the course of the evening.

"How does it feel to be in such demand?" she asked him a little sarcastically the third time it rang and he walked over and clicked the answering machine on.

"It's what I want. I'm controlling my life." he said.

Finally, they were sitting at a glass table by the window overlooking Broadway in the big room, watching the lights of the city and the cars moving below them as they ate. Dinner, which he had cooked himself, consisted of spaghetti and a big green salad. It all tasted good. There was also garlic bread and her white wine, a gelato and cappuccino from his cappuccino-maker for dessert.

After they ate, he showed her his work. The small pieces consisted mostly of sketches. Among the abstracts he was known for were portraits of people he knew, done in a highly realistic manner. At her request he brought a couple of them to the sitting area and propped them against the wall where they could be the subject of contemplation.

Camille settled into the couch in front of the fireplace while Paul lit kindling and added a big log to burn. When he turned back to her, he knelt before her and slipped off her boots before sitting down beside her. She wiggled her toes into the thick, red rug before pulling them up under her. Lights were low and the newly-made fire lit the room dimly from below. Paul was talking about what he wanted to do with his life. He wanted to travel and do exciting things all over the world, he said, to sail a boat or fly his own plane between working on special exhibitions. Camille tried to pay attention. It was important for her to remember what he said, but her mind was not on Paul, it seemed. She didn't know where her mind was.

He talked awhile, and then asked her, "What about you?

What do you want out of life?"

"Oh." Camille said, then stopped and tried to think beyond the Christmas holidays. She did not know what would happen after that. Would she even survive them and return to New York? She did not know. But she had to answer. So she opened her mouth and some words fell out.

"All I want right now is understanding from other human beings."

She realized he might consider this odd and quickly explained, "I've been having a pretty hard time lately, what with my just having moved to New York and I've met people I don't know how to deal with. I need something to show me I'm understood, for some comfort and relief from the confusion."

"I understand about the needing comfort." He said as he fell back onto the couch, stretched his arms along the back on both sides, and quietly gazed into the flames. They remained silent, letting the city fill in the gap in their conversation with sounds. Its constant hum, honks and distant sirens were noticeable in the silence. The windows were black and city lights peeped through. Camille snuggled deeper into the couch, and stretched her feet out toward the fire. Paul put his arm around her, pulling her close to him. It was an unconscious, friendly gesture, but Camille realized it was also an invitation, if she wanted to take it that way. Whatever it was, it felt good and she leaned her head back on his shoulder, deciding to enjoy it. All her life she had been warned about the dangers of being alone in a man's apartment and momentarily felt some fear, then chided herself. "No need to feel apprehensive," she thought, "Vince is probably the most dangerous man I know."

"Do you . . . Have you looked for another relationship?" asked Paul, still staring into the fire and keeping his eyes averted when she glanced at him, trying read the intent of the question. He was probably referring to her separation from her husband.

"Yes," she said, actually thinking of Vince without saying it.

Paul was silent for awhile.

"How would you feel about us just holding each other?" he said. "Would that feel good to you?" She looked into his eyes, which were searching hers. His eyes were a beautiful, pure, light blue. She knew it would feel good to be held. His reminding her of John was an illusion that made her feel like she knew him. But just because he looked like John did not mean he would be like John in other ways. Right now he was different — John would never have wanted to sit quietly in front of the fire and hold her. If they had ever sat in front of their fireplace at home, he would have either been sitting stiffly beside her without touching, or they would be having sex, nothing in between.

"I have considered getting into another relationship," she said to him, "but I don't feel like getting too close to anyone, right now."

"Just holding each other wouldn't be considered being a relationship," he replied, "though I believe we do feel attracted to each other."

"Yes," she admitted. "I just don't want to get hurt any more."

"That's why I'm being open with you." He spoke deliberately, as if reasoning with a child. But then, perhaps she was childlike. She had very little experience with this. A sophisticated woman probably would not need this explanation.

"I want you to know where I'm coming from," he continued. He was pulling her closer to him as he spoke. But Camille sat up, stopping him from bringing her any closer. He might know where he was coming from, but she did not understand him yet. She had no idea from where a man like he would be coming. His hand, which was still curled around her shoulder tightly, squeezed her and then released her.

Camille admitted to herself, once freed, that his touch had felt good and that she was hungry for a gentle touch. He seemed to be warm and confident and not wanting to overpower her. He leaned back again, watching the fire, so she relaxed and leaned back into the pillows, as well.

"I've been going through some internally explosive months, myself," he said, almost self-consciously.

Camille waited. Maybe he would explain. The flames flickered and crackled in the dark room while the portrait faces peering at them from the pictures leaning against the wall. The flames crept along the side of a big log, licking it up. They watched it burn in silence, feeling the ghosts of eternal ancestors who had also watched a fire at night in the wilderness. She had loved to watch her fireplace in the winter in Texas. She loved building a fire and watching the logs burn and crumble into ash and ruby red coals.

In the long silent watch, Camille felt herself sinking back toward Paul, yearning for more of his touch. His arm, along the back of the couch went around her again, gently pulling her against him. He seemed to be seeking comfort, too. Camille gradually leaned her head against his shoulder and felt his hand moving along her arm and eventually up to her breast, stroking the soft angora sweater absent-mindedly, as if it was a kitten. Then, with his arm and hand still around her, he began talking about his past in general terms. She grasped her wine glass with one hand, sipping it as she listened.

He talked in abstract, about theories of relationships, about being open and honest with people, of how he had been trying hard to be that way, to reach out to others. He had once been self-contained, alone. He kept on talking and she listened while he talked, turning her head to watch his chiseled face and his lips moving. But all the time his hands were stroking her, stroking her legs, which she had curled under her and finally ,falling silent, both of them warm with wine, his body leaning over hers, he was pushing her down among the pillows and she was succumbing to his murmurs, and he was saying endearing phrases, like "Little darling. Sweet baby."

She felt the tender emotions of desire creep into her heart like the flames along the log, and begin to surge through her, as if they had been waiting for him to arouse them. He murmured affectionate words, his face coming closer and closer to hers, talking until his lips were touching hers with the words, "I want to know you," and she watched as the light of the fire glowed on the side of his face, turning his skin and his blue eyes gold.

The flames roared on the big log, leaping up yellow and hot. Camille was aware of Paul's hand moving up somewhere inside her sweater, flowing down over the silky skin of her stomach, moving up to her breasts, delicately molding them into ripe fruits to bite gently, then down to the two little zippers, which were slowly unzipped, until her velvet slacks were falling on the floor. She remembered pushing his hands away with her hands, even while her body was pressing against his in pure pleasure. And then, later, somehow she saw him naked and hanging over her in the pillows, a dark shelter, with the four pillars of his legs and arms, with the central member slowly descending deep into her.

They made love slowly. It was warming flames, not fireworks. He was skillful and sensitive all the long while the log burned, was consumed and fell into hot embers. She knew she felt good to him and she knew she pleased him as much as he was pleasing her. He was so excited he was panting when he finished and threw himself to the side, to lie close by her. They lay together, his arm under her head, both gazing at the ceiling. She drifted off. Then, after awhile, he rolled back onto her to come again. When they finally pulled apart, totally exhausted, she realized two hours had passed. Camille cried in soft sobs, because it had taken so long and felt so good.

She cried, because the things she had feared in the beginning were good in the end. She did not ask anything of him and he did not ask anything of her. They had a silent understanding and gave as much as they could of all the good things their bodies knew.

"I feel like crying, too," he said, leaning beside her as she wept, propped on one elbow and gently wiping the tears from her cheeks, "because all the good feelings are leaving, draining from me. How do you feel now?"

It was hard to talk about and to analyze her feelings so soon, but she made the effort.

"I feel good," she said, trying to find a reason for all the emotions running pell-mell through her. "And happy. I feel loved." He fell silent at that, his smile fading away and his face becoming stiff and expressionless. Perhaps she had said something wrong.

"It must be nice to feel loved," he said, a little bitterly.

"I feel love toward you," she explained, sorry he had not felt it. Surely he had felt love toward her. Hadn't he? But his body was pulling away and she knew she had said something wrong this time She dropped her eyes unhappily, laying still and silent, and in a while he began to relax again. Whatever they had was ended.

"I really should go home," she said. Perhaps if she said she was leaving, he would come back to her in his mind. "What time is it? It must be very late. I don't want to be out on the streets too late."

"You're right," he said, rolling away to reach for his watch. Her heart sank. He didn't want her to stay any longer.

She used the shiny new bathroom to wash and dress. She felt comfortable in his loft; it was so well-planned, so large and roomy.

She was sorry she had to leave. For some reason she felt hurt he had not asked her to stay, even though that was not what she had intended to do. But, she told herself, tomorrow she had to be back at school early, and she presumed he had a similar schedule.

When she came out of the bathroom, he was waiting for her in the dimly lighted living room, standing in his bathrobe by the dark fireplace in which black embers still glowed red around the edges. He took her in his arms for a hug and then sat her down on the couch.

"I feel a tugging at my heart," he said, pulling Camille down onto the couch to lay with him a few minutes longer. Camille speculated that now he was feeling guilty for making her go home. Perhaps he was afraid she did not want to stay with him and she was the one who had wanted to leave first. Whatever the reason, he was being nice now. "What is it that I feel?" he asked her.

"You like me," she said hopefully. "That's what it is." She was careful not to use the word "love," but felt she had to tell him somehow that was what he felt. But she was not feeling relaxed any more. She was not used to men who wanted to hold her a long time. Perhaps she could get used to it, but she was beginning to feel uncomfortable. It was her turn to feel awkward and stiff. He was throwing her out, but was trying to not make it quite so bad. He could tell she was uncomfortable, though he held her and kissed her for a moment longer.

He sat up and let her go.

"When we see each other again, we'll remember we shared something nice."

"Yes," said Camille, a little sadly, wondering what it would be like to go to the gallery and see him there, both awkwardly remembering the night they made love. On the other hand, she might not even return from Texas. "I may never see you again." she speculated, and saw a quick look of hurt on his face, so quickly said, "Still, I have to go back to the gallery. If you're there, I'll remember."

As they stood, he said, "Don't you think this is romantic? Here we are, two strangers, two artists, who met and felt attracted to each other. We planned a rendezvous and made love in an artist's loft in SoHo." Camille glanced at him to see if he was laughing at her, but he appeared to be deadly serious. It had not occurred to her to look at themselves in such an objective way, to see that this was what was happening, though maybe some day in the distant future, she would think of it that way.

"I'll call you before you leave for Christmas vacation," he promised. At these words, the image of her husband arose when she looked up at him. It was uncanny, the similarities in their looks.

"I don't know if I should mention this, but you look a lot like my husband," she blurted out, hastening to add, "But you're not at all like him in other ways." There was an empty moment while he took this in.

"I meet people like my ex-wife all the time," he said coldly. "Fortunately, you're not at all like her. You wouldn't be here if you were."

He put on some sweat pants, some shoes and a sweatshirt and saw her down to the street, standing out in the street to wave down a taxi. He pressed cab money into her hand as he opened the door and she climbed in. She felt as if she should say something more, but did not know what else to say. He did not want to hear she loved him. Was she intruding on him somehow, by saying it? Did she remind him of someone else? But by now he was smiling graciously, stepping back into the shadows of the doorway, as if he was afraid others would see him with her. "Thank you," she said as the door closed.

"Good bye, take care," she heard him say. He turned to go in, disappearing through the door as they drove away.

She had time to think, as the taxi drove toward the river, realizing that she did like him. She could admit that to herself. Why should he feel bad about her liking him? After all, would she have made love to him if she didn't? She liked him, not because he made love to her, but because he had accepted her and had been open and honest with her, as one would be with a friend. They had made no promises to each other, except to talk, had made no plans for the future.

"If you are there, I'll remember," she had said to him. She could have no expectations of him after this, she told herself. She had failed somehow to let him know she really did like him and wanted to continue their relationship. Or, if he understood this, he did not want it. Yet she did feel a bond between them. Perhaps it would disappear in time. She had admired how successful he was; but he was also charming and exciting. In her confusion, she did not even know why she liked him, except he had convinced her to make love to him tonight with his gentleness. They had shared one experience. Only time would tell if there would be more than this, this one intense evening.

Maybe he is like John, she thought. He is objective, does not want to be loved, he looks like John and is successful in is field, like John. But he also represented all the things John could be, all the things she wanted John to be: gentle, sensitive, caring, artistic, sociable and popular. In spite of this, it was possible his similarity to John made her reject him, as she had rejected everything else having to do with John. The similarities made her feel objective and cold, while Paul's openness, his attempt to feel emotions like love, represented everything she longed for in her new life.

Vince must have been watching for her, because the phone rang soon after she got home, even though it was after midnight. He said they would have to put their dinner off tonight, but did not say much else. She hung up feeling annoyed. He had been rude and silent on the phone, but did not ask her any questions. She could hear Bessie Smith singing in the background, musical blues in the silences between his words. How immature, she thought. He acts spoiled and gets irritated over the slightest thing. He could have waited for morning to call her. After Paul's cool maturity, Vince's childishness did not contrast well. Surely Paul would not have acted like Vince, in similar circumstances.

The next day at school there were conferences with her teachers, and she decided where she would intern. She narrowed it down to a Junior Drawing course. It took most of the afternoon to make appointments and talk to the people she needed to consult in order to arrange the internship, but it all worked out as she wanted.

She got back to her painting studio in the late afternoon and did some touching up on four small paintings. Hal had told her to call a woman who was interested in her work, so she did and arranged to meet her at the gallery.

All day she moved in a happy cloud, carried along on a wave of euphoria, remembering the warmth and love of the night before. Her body was wrapped in the sensations which still swept over her. It seemed like a very realistic wave, however, as all was done with mutual sharing. She had no illusions that things would go easily for her, but at least she knew there were some mature and rational people with whom she could have a relationship. She could even have sex with them and not feel used. Sex did not have to be a weapon.

She felt good until that night, when she began to come down off her cloud. Once back in the boat, as it grew dark, she began to feel teary-eyed and alone. She knew she could not expect someone to hold her hand all the time, but she wished there was someone there to talk to, to tell about feeling insecure and sad. She wished the bad feelings would leave and she could keep the good, secure feelings she used to have. There were times these days when she felt uplifted, but right now she felt down.

As she lay in bed with the lights off at last, she thought of Paul. Perhaps he felt lonely too. Maybe he wanted to feel loved. When she had said she felt love toward him he said "it must be nice to feel loved." But when she had said the word "love" and said she loved him, why could he not accept it? The thought of his handsome, yearning face visibly turning tense embarrassed her. What was he thinking? Did he think she was not being honest with him? Perhaps he did not want her to love him. Perhaps there was someone else that he wanted to love him and she had just happened to be there. He said he thought it was romantic. He must have enjoyed it. Every word he had said was in her head to stay forever. He dreamed of adventure and travel, now that he was a successful artist, and she dreamed of becoming a great artist. They had much in common. They both loved art, traveling and being with people. One might say they were destined to meet.

But she recalled that the last time she had told herself that fate had brought her and someone else together and had trusted God that everything was right, that God had led her to the right man. She had married him and it turned out to be wrong. "God does not plan things to turn out wrong, so you can't blame God," she thought, "I'm making wrong guesses about what God wants. I had better be careful. I really don't know what God is leading me to do."

She didn't like Paul because he was like John. But what was wrong with John, why didn't she like him any more? She tried to think. It was important. She had to think about John. He was not like Paul in many ways. Paul treated her with respect, as another artist. Now that she could compare them, she felt John treated her like a child, made her dependent on him, then despised her because she was dependent, and feared her art, because she could use it to be successful like he was. Paul liked her art, felt she had promise and believed she was equal to him. Perhaps she was a threat to John, who then withdrew from her emotionally, yet wanted her to be dependent on him, all at the same time.

Paul respected her while John demeaned her and never told her she did something well. She almost come to believe him. She had tried to ignore his criticism of her abilities and her every opinion, but finally, after so long, it had begun to affect her. The year before she left she was starting to believe she was worthless. She kept on telling herself she had to think of herself being as good as he and as worthy of his respect. She would rather die than admit she was inferior. Dying was the only alternative, or going away. She knew she was better than he was, in the end. She could never have put anyone down as he had. Perhaps that was why it was so important that she go to graduate school and earn a graduate degree, just as he had. Perhaps she was trying to earn his respect.

Yes, she was attracted to Paul; he looked like the man she had married, the man she had loved. His handsome face, his slim body,

the memory of his beautiful eyes, the way he wanted to touch her—
he really desired her—and wanted her to desire him, too. She had told
herself to beware of her heart, to trust her mind instead, but she did
not do what her mind had told her to do last night. She had done what
her body wanted to do. It had not been so bad.

She warned herself that she had better watch out. Look what
had happened with Vince. He had not even taken her out to dinner
this evening after all, telling her he had a dentist appointment
tomorrow and had to be in Jersey tonight, at his parent's house, in
order to be there first thing in the morning. His tooth was giving him
a lot of trouble.

It was hard to sleep with so much to think about.

Her drawing teacher, Mr. Min, wished her a pleasant holiday
when he saw her in the hall. She was surprised, because she had
thought he was Buddhist. He paused to talk for a moment and said to
drop him a line when anything happened. He would not be back for a
year, as he was going on sabbatical. He planned to spend the next
year in his loft in SoHo, painting. He had such a nice, cool, clean,
oriental way about him, she thought. She would miss him. Things
seemed to be ending.

It was still early afternoon. On her way home from school,
Camille felt so alone that she wanted to cry. She found an old tissue
in her purse, dried her eyes and told herself to "buck up," as her father
used to say when she was sad. She would not cry. People would
notice. But even in these depressed moments, she recognized that she
did not feel the deep agony she felt two weeks ago. She hoped she
would never feel those terrible feelings again.

Her friends at school had talked with her and smiled when
they passed. Phillip even took her hand and held it silently for a
minute when she told him she was going back to Texas and would
ask her husband for a divorce in a couple of days. What a way to
spend Christmas! The couple of friends she had told said they
supported her in what she intended to do.

It came down to the fact she was going to start a new life. It
was painful to begin, and she did not know what would be good and
what would be bad, in her future. It was a beginning. All she could do
was try to plan. She was fairly certain that getting her degree would

lead to better things. If nothing else, she would be spending her time among well-educated, thinking people for a couple of years. If she remained among this kind of people, life would be interesting, at least.

But how to cope with the men? Cope with their demands for sex and still like them? Most of the men she knew respected her. At least they asked before they kissed her. To most of them she said no. But as for the ones she liked, she really wanted them to kiss her, and why should she say no? Yet she did not want to be a "loose woman," as others had called women who gave away their bodies. She regretted having given in so easily to Vince and to Paul. But so far, all her friends still liked her and seemed to respect her.

Something like this was a source of confusion to her, as she had always heard that having sex was evil, outside of marriage. While in her recent experience, it had been good, she knew it could not be continued and that she would have to rein in her emotions and not give in so easily. Look what had happened with Vince. She became involved with him so quickly and it was both good and terrible now, but mostly terrible, since he was pulling away.

Once, at the gallery, she had asked Ann what she thought of Vince. Ann had turned to Camille with a nasty face and said a dirty word. She said he was the lowest kind of bum, and a low-down flirt with the lowest of morals. Camille was shocked and then felt hurt. Vince had a bad reputation. Even Hal had told her he was always after someone. She had always known this about him, but it did not matter enough. He had a big heart and that was what mattered to her at the time.

She decided she needed new friends. But when she was hurt she withdrew into her shell. She could decide not to withdraw, even though it would be easy to do. She decided to make friends with other students if she had the opportunity. She already had some good friends among the students, though most of them were younger than she.

In the evening things began to get better. Vince and Grace were coming back from Christmas shopping when she got back. She stood and talked with them on the sidewalk. Then Vince invited them both to come into his boat and they could order Chinese dinner to be delivered. He said he would make up for his not taking her out to dinner as he had promised. Aboard the boat, he played Bessie Smith records and when the huge meal arrived, served it hot on white china. It was very pleasant, almost like a restaurant.

Vince usually was in a terrible mood after he and Grace had been together, especially if they had been shopping. But if he was annoyed today, Camille could not detect it. She felt good, and relaxed and joked with them. They seemed to enjoy her attitude as well, especially when she started telling them stories about what happened at the Institute. They both had attended Pratt and her stories reminded them of their school days there.

She told them about the student in her drawing class, Geri, a woman who made abstract drawings on enormous rolls of white paper, which she tore into six-foot pieces and laid on the floor. Yesterday was the last day of class and Camille and one other woman, named Geri, were the only ones who showed up. Geri had decided she wanted to order the model to come and model for them anyway. When the male model arrived he looked around for the students, but there were only two, Camille and Geri. He reluctantly asked if they still wanted him to model and Geri insisted he stay, so he undressed.

Two women and a naked man. It was odd, but Camille began drawing intently. She and Geri untiringly drew that poor, cold, naked man for three hours. Geri was very demanding of the model, telling him to stand still, and he endured, doing only two poses for the entire time. Normally the model would change poses often for quick drawings, until the last pose, which would be longer. Camille was able to complete one finely finished drawing and to make several more of him, using various styles and techniques, as he stood in the same pose.

At the end of the three hours she went over to see what Geri had done that had been so demanding of the model. But all she had drawn were three thick black lines. Three straight, totally disconnected lines made of graphite and charcoal were smudged onto the six-foot long piece of white paper on the floor.

The model, who was standing on the platform where he could not see her drawing, came over and looked down at the white paper with the three lines for a long time. He did not speak. You could almost see him wondering why he had been forced to stand there, naked, in a cold, empty room when all Geri did was make three straight lines.

Grace and Vince, as well as Camille, were laughing uncontrollably by the time Camille finished her story. For the first time in a long time Camille felt completely happy with them. She even felt good toward Vince, since he was leaving for the holidays later that night. He was responding positively to her for a change, his usually sullen face lighting up when she cracked a joke or talked about something he could relate to at school. Camille found herself talking a lot and he seemed to enjoy listening.

They ate and cleaned up. Camille said good night to both of them and left to go home. She was very tired. She was still awake and dressed a short time later, when she heard Grace leave, even though she was not listening for it. She realized she felt no jealousy toward Grace now. She felt no animosity toward Vince and no sexual attraction either. He was simply a good friend to her.

The phone rang. It was Vince. He wanted to talk and he talked for a long time. At last, at midnight, she told him she had to go to sleep. He said he would call her later; he wanted to see her about something. He said she could go to sleep or not, but he would call her later to come over. So she did not change into her nightgown; she washed her face and wrapped some little presents she had bought to take with her to Texas. Vince had said he was leaving to go to his parent's house for the holidays. He probably wanted to share a last cup of coffee with her, or maybe to give her a Christmas present.

At one o'clock she finally lay down on her bed, drowsing off, but thinking. Paul had not called her this evening as he had said he would. Having had sex being only point at which Paul and she could relate to each other or communicate with each other was not enough for her.

She moved around in the cold covers, uncomfortable. Sex and nothing else made for a very shallow relationship. Sex was only a small part of what she could offer a man, though it might be a necessary part. She also needed to feel loved and respected. These were more important than sex.

Finally, Camille got up to get a drink of water. She looked at herself, blurred, in the bathroom mirror. The attraction one person felt for another at the beginning was based on sex, perhaps, but she wished people would like her for her art work, for her personality or her brains first. That would be rare if it happened. She had to admit she was first attracted to a man who looked good and the next to his intelligence and charm, or charisma or whatever one might call it. It was obvious the first time she talked with him. The visual impact, the words, the looks, the movements, were important.

At 1:40 she was falling asleep. She called Vince to tell him, but his line was busy. She waited and called him a few minutes later. This time he answered.

"Camille!" he sounded happy to hear her. "Come on over." It was more a command than a question.

So she stepped over the finger dock to his boat, wondering what he wanted. Surely he would not give her a present. He had told her he had stopped giving things to girls that were not "putting out" for him.

She entered his unlocked door. Only one light was on, the spotlight over the bed. Vince was sitting on the couch, talking on the phone. Camille could tell he was talking with his friend Chino, arranging for a shipment from Miami. The fact that Vince was a dealer disturbed her, now she knew what it meant. When she first came to New York it was so far outside her experience it meant nothing to her. In the beginning, she did not know anything about it, except as something interesting. Now she realized, from his conversations recently, which he didn't bother to hide, that it meant lots of danger and dealing with criminals, as well as the mob. Vince continued to talk, motioning for her to sit, but she did not. A blues song was playing on the stereo and the TV was on mute. The faces on the late night movie moved in strangely disparate coordination with the song that played.

Camille walked to the windows and watched the slow progress of a freighter going up-river, outlined with lights burning brightly, its silhouetted bulk blacking out the backdrop of lights on the Jersey shore. She thought again of the first time she had entered Vince's boat, how impressed and excited she had been. It was with a sense of foreboding that she entered it now, never knowing what to expect. Yet sweet memories lingered here, as well.

When he finished his call, Vince came up close behind Camille, who stood with her back to him, though he did not come close enough to touch her. They stood at the window like that for awhile, he smoking, and both of them commenting on the boats which moved majestically past them in the darkness. Anticipating his touch, which did not come, Camille began to long for it. Her skin tingled in expectation of that gentle touch. She wanted to feel his arms around her once more, moving as they once did, as smooth as warm water engulfing her. But he remained a few inches from her, and whenever she moved he moved just as far away.

At last he turned and sat back down on the couch in the semi-darkness and patted the seat next to him. She went over and sat with him while he put his arm on the back of the couch. Camille stared at the work table across the room in silence, seeing the familiar shapes of the light box for sorting slides and negatives, at the tall silver poles with lights on top and cables hanging from them. The music reminded her of other evenings they had spent, inducing reminiscent stirrings in her body. Finally he will touch me, she thought. Now, when everything is hopeless. Now, when it is too late and my feelings for him are ebbing. Suddenly she felt very sad. She stood up to leave. She could never make love to him again. She had made love with Paul and her mind and body were leaving Vince.

"I thought we would make love," said Vince, in a loud, cold voice. The abruptness gave Camille a chill. Vince never said anything like this so openly. He was not himself tonight. She thought of how he had treated her lately: rudely, coldly, even worse. But she did not say the words. He has a lot of nerve, she thought to herself, to think we would make love after what has happened recently. Finally she spoke, making her voice polite and a little surprised,

"I thought we were through."

When he did not answer she watched his face, searching for expression. He was looking straight ahead, through the smoke, his eyes inscrutable and half-closed, avoiding her eyes.

"At least I had the very strong impression we were." she spoke again, less sure this time.

Still he did not speak. He had no expression of anger; he had no reaction at all. Camille turned, hesitating a moment to tuck her blouse in. Vince stood up and crushed out the end of his smoke.

"Come on, Camille," he said, standing straight and holding out his hand. She looked at him.

A little, knowing smile was on his face. She smiled back, but did not like the look on his face; his smile was lasting too long. It was late and she was tired. She needed to go home. She walked toward the door. But he was walking behind her and she felt his hand catch hers. She stopped, this time feeling a little scared and a bit disgusted with him and his coldness. She turned around and faced him calmly.

"Let me go," she said. "I need to go home and get some sleep."

But he still stood with his hand holding her wrist firmly and unmoving.

"You said we were through, right? I'm not your girlfriend any more," she said distinctly.

He turned his head a little to the side and looked at her out of the corner of his eye while he blew the last of the smoke through his lips. His face was still set in the little smile – disarming, yet a little threatening. Camille was becoming aware of how large his body was, as she was standing close to him, and of how overpowering he seemed. For the first time since she had known him she felt afraid. She squelched the feeling, remembering he had never hurt her. He had no reason to hurt her. They understood each other. She was not afraid of him.

"Come on, be a good girl," he said in a low, vibrant voice, moving his body against her, pushing her with his body and pulling her by the wrist toward the bedroom.

Camille did not want to go. She drew back, starting to pull away firmly, determinedly. But he only held her wrist tighter. She had a hard time believing he was actually forcing her to go. If he was playing a game it would be all right. She laughed a little and said she was sorry, but she had to go now. He did not stop, but reached down and caught her other hand.

"Please, Vince," she spoke in a tight voice. This could not be happening. He had to let her go. She backed toward the door, but when she began to pull back he pulled her up to him with no effort, turning her arm so it twisted behind her and holding her wrist, he held her against him.

She laughed nervously and turned her head away from his

kiss.

"Be good to me, Camille. It will feel good."

Now she did not think this was funny any more and felt a little afraid. He had no right to scare her this way. She was beginning to feel angry.

"No!" she said, successfully jerking her body away from him. He smiled, taken off guard by this parlay. Surely he would let her go now, she thought and turned away from him twisting her wrists, to remove them. But he simply lifted them up above her head now and held them both in one hand over her head. Camille felt like a rag doll. Her efforts were as futile as a frail bird's in his iron grip. She had never suspected he had so much strength, though he had told her he had kept up practicing his Tai Chi so his body would stay strong.

In the months Camille had known him intimately, she had never felt his full strength because he had never had to use it. They had played "mugging" at times; and she had struggled playfully while making love. Though this reminded her of those times, playing had given her a false sense of confidence, as he had never used force with her. Now she felt foolish. How had she not guessed? Why hadn't she stayed home? How had she gotten into this situation?

All this passed through her mind the moment she was using all of her strength into getting even one hand free of his and could not, and the thought itself was a blow. She gasped in disbelief and stopped struggling. What would he do to her?

She spoke, trying to keep her strained voice even and calm, yet firm, "Let me go."

He only smiled. She stopped struggling and tried to be more serious. She demanded he free her. But now he was going up the stairs, with one arm around her waist, lifting her. Even stepping backwards, her feet barely touched the steps and she hoped she would not stumble.

"That's a good girl," he said over and over. He moved on into the bedroom, speaking as if to a child that did not quite understand.

"Please, Vince. Please, Vince. Vince, stop it!" She was trying to keep her head and not panic. It would do no good with him. Was this really the Vince she knew? He seemed not at all angry; he was even clear-headed and calm and determined. It was not his usual manner.

"Relax, you'll enjoy it more," he said.

"What are you doing? Vince?" she said, but she was falling backward slowly, onto the bed and he was holding her up with his free arm as they slowly sank onto the top of the quilt she had once given him. With his free arm around her waist, he pulled her close to him in the loving gesture he had often used. But this time, as she was afraid and unwilling, it was frightening to be so close. She felt as if she might swoon, but she did not dare. For a long time now she had wanted him to hold her close, but now that he was doing it this way, it was a nightmare. Desire had flown from her mind and in its place fluttered panic and fear. He could not force her love out of her.

The body she had once desired and cherished was now hard as steel, and moving terribly, slowly against her, bending her back, pulling on her sore wrists which he held as if in a vise. She could not believe she could not free at least one of her hands. She tried jerking her hands apart, but could not move them from their fixed position above her head. She struggled again to get away from his body, which was lying on top of her, and realized that was useless. He was heavy and she must succumb. He was too strong.

It was humiliating. The shame was that she had always thought she was strong enough to get away from any man if she really, truly wanted to, and to her horror, she could not. She had had no idea any man was strong enough to do this to her. The confidence once gained from winning and half-winning fights with boys she had grown up with, boys her age, had disappeared in the last few minutes and in its place was the horrible truth: A woman was weaker than a man. So much for the myth of keeping one's legs crossed to keep from being raped. She had no control of them and could not cross them if she tried, as he was lying on them. Her weak muscles were no match for his, no matter how strongly she resisted or determined she was to resist.

He tried to kiss her, but she turned her face away. So he held her face with his free hand and kissed her on the lips. She closed her eyes tight and abhorred that kiss.

"Come on, behave, little Pet. Be good. You know you love it. Don't you feel it? Be good to me." He was pleading with her now as he rolled over and lay beside her. He threw one leg over both her legs and they lay facing each other on the bed. He rolled her over on her back and his body inched over hers. His thighs ground against hers and though both of them were encased in jeans, she could feel his hard cock rubbing against her stomach. Now his free hand was unbuttoning her blouse.

"No!" she said in disbelief. He would really do this? She turned her head away from seeing his relentless undressing her. But words were meaningless to him. His hand was now pressing against the flesh inside the blouse, rubbing inside her brassiere, pulling her breast out so he could reach down and lick and gently bite it. His body was beginning to move with passion and her body unwillingly responded with movements she recognized but did not want.

He suddenly jerked his hand and broke the strap of her brassiere. She smelled the familiar, sweet smell of his hair against her cheek as he bent his head again. His hand went to the other breast and pulled the bra down so the breast popped out and he grabbed it in his lips. His free hand was pulling the blouse out of her jeans and moving to the belt, which he removed and then unzipped the zipper to her jeans. She could not believe it, but he was skillfully removing her jeans, pulling them down slowly on one side and then the other, pulling at her little panties, jerking them down below her hips so he could touch her crotch. The jeans bound her legs now so she could not kick. He had been careful not to allow her legs to be free, always holding them down with his own. His fingers were moving between the lips of her private places, through the stiff hairs and finding her creamy inside.

She was shocked. Her own body was betraying her. She wanted to cry; it was feeling so intensely good in spite of her emotions. Yet she did not want it to be happening. Not like this. The conflict was confusing. Her mind was screaming and her body was laughing at her. His fingers rolled in her depths and moved up and down through the wet, swollen folds.

Her mind was in turmoil. Not like this. Every fantasy she had ever had about being raped or being forced to have sex suddenly disappeared. The reality of the event made the fantasy a weak, sick dream. Reality hurt. It hurt her body and it hurt her mind. The fact that she was weak, the insufficient respecting of her needs and desires, forcing her to make her body subject to his, insulted her. She had been a fool, worse than a fool. She had been a stupid and naive fool, believing she was as strong as he. She struggled again, yelling out of anger. But no-one could hear.

Yet, by continuing his ministrations for some minutes, his slow, persistent caresses were overcoming her. The feelings he stirred up in her with his body against hers, his intense pleasure-making, the little nips at her breasts, his kisses on her cheek awakened her body, if not her will. She heard herself groan and realized she was writhing against him in the motions of love-making.

"Ah," she heard him say, "My little one is coming around. Come, Camille. Come." His voice was gentle. Passion and memory were guiding him. He knew her body and his body was relaxing; whatever anger he had felt toward her was ebbing. Perhaps she could free herself now. She jerked her left hand loose, surprising herself and him. But he stopped it and caught it before she could reach his face to push him away. He thought she was going to scratch him!

"Oh, no you don't!" he said angrily. His face showed rage, close up, against her face. He was lightning fast. Now he moved more forcibly, making her do what he wanted, lifting her by the waist as if she were a paper doll. With both hands pinned in his right fist against the bed above her head, she felt hot and angry, but stopped struggling and waited for it to be over. Her vagina was throbbing in angry contractions, even hurting. She turned her body, but he threw his leg over hers again, after removing his own jeans with his free hand. He now pulled her jeans down past her knees and pulled them off with his foot, even though she was trying to hold her legs tightly together. Nothing she did had any effect.

He pinned her flat against the bed with his body, his hips moving in a wave to bring himself down and between her legs. She could not believe she could not stop him, but he entered her and they both struggled, their bodies hot and sweating. The feeling was so intense she could not deny her body desired his and in the middle of all this humiliation and pain, the fire from his loins burned a bright, hot, hole in her. She had never been so angry and the anger surged through her pumping body. She thought she might bite him, but he sensed this and avoided her mouth, keeping his arms and face away. She felt so helpless, so ineffective and so angry at herself in her powerlessness.

Finally, in the midst of the passion, she began to cry and

when she did they both stopped struggling. She went limp and flaccid. He lay on top of her, still moving in little bursts until he was finished, and she wept. She felt his hand release one of hers and slide down her dead arm, caressing her. His hands stroked her and calmed her. Soft words were coming out of his mouth and he was suddenly so gentle.

She struggled no longer. It was over. She had been defeated. He had had his way with her and that was all he wanted. Her anger had dissipated in the heat of emotion and defeat had made her helpless, worthless. She felt him pleading with her and she numbly and obediently held him, hearing herself crying and her crying turning into soft, defeated moans, her will resisting still as he stroked and kissed her, his body still lying flat upon her. He felt her relaxing. She put one arm around his neck and felt him snuggle into her again. After all, he had been her lover.

Now she was caught up in the rhythm of his body, which was still pulsating, becoming the familiar rhythm of two bodies who knew each other's sensations and responses well. Her body was flowing into his and somehow the terrible anger she had felt slipped into the waves of pulsations which he was bringing to a peak.

Finally he released her other hand and held her under him tightly with his arms down by her sides, his sweat sweet and wet between them, his breath coming hard and hot and his face intent on what was happening again. The rocking of his body came more rapidly, and she gasped as the sensations thrust through her swollen flesh, the excitement of the moment increasing and emotions taking over. Camille clawed at his back with her nails while both angry and loving words spewed out from between clenched teeth. She was beginning to fly away. She no longer had a body or mind. Only the beating wings of his body against and upon and in hers, pounding and heaving and beating her into the final paroxysms of climax.

And her soul was a little bird flying away into the empty sky and finding peace in nothingness. She was utterly and completely spent; utterly and completely defeated, dumb and numb, in some far, quiet corner of space.

At last his body slowed and ceased and he lay heavy and still upon her. Her mouth open, she was breathing rapidly, coming back to herself and was surprised to find her heart beating again, hard and fast. Together still, they lay as if dead in each other's grip, their legs hanging off the edge of the bed.

It was over and she could go. She struggled beneath him a little and he reached up to hold her again, weakly, as if she was escaping. A wave of sadness came over her. She felt the tears still in her eyes, through closed eyelids, now slowly rolling down her cheeks into her ears. Her sobs were silent and deep. She wept for what he had just done to her and for all the good and bad things she had known with him. She clutched at his heavy body, lying like a dead weight on hers and held him closer.

"Camille," he muttered tiredly, half-awake, "I love you. I missed you." He lifted his head at this and looked at her. She opened her eyes to see his sweat-glazed face, emotions now fully exposed in the tired lines around his mouth, where the little corners turned up naturally, around his heavily-lashed eyes, watching her with hope and fear. Will you hurt me now? His eyes were asking.

"Oh, Vince," she murmured and closed her eyes against this question. She could not look at him any longer. "I have good reason to love and hate you."

"You hate me, huh? Didn't you enjoy that?"

"What?"

"What we just did."

She could not answer; she was silent and still afraid, remembering what he had done.

"I'm tired right now. I can't think," she answered weakly. She could never trust him again. As long as he lived he would be circling the fringes of her mind, an outlaw in the outbacks of civilized life. Living or dead, he would be standing somewhere in the background: dangerous, generous, perverse, unpredictable impossible to live with, knowing her inside and out, calling to her, taking her will away, the memory of his love being her first and maybe last, real love.

"I'm going back," she said.

"You're going back to your husband," he finished for her in a dead, bitter voice.

"No," she returned, laughing a little at what he had said, revealing though it might be. "I'm going back to him, but to tell him I want a divorce. Then I'm going to my mother's for the holidays, in New Mexico. I don't know what I can afford from now on. John probably won't let me have anything."

"You'll just have to live like an artist, then. That will be cute," Vince mused, now slowly sitting up on the side of the bed and reaching for his pants. He pulled a cigarette out of the pocket and lighted it. It was almost like old times, their conversations after lovemaking. She watched the shining scratch marks on his back she had put there, gleaming red against the gold and black of his skin in the spotlight. They made an arc across the vast curve, like two roads. She reached over and touched one. He flinched and turned toward her.

"You got me after all, you bitch. Are you okay? Did I hurt you?" He was serious. Did he have any idea what he had done? His voice was the old, soothing voice he had always used, but it sounded demeaning to her now. She started to move away, assuring him she was all right, though her wrists ached. He took her hands in his own and gently kissed her wrists. "I'm sorry. They'll be sore tomorrow." Then he examined her body all over, looking for bruises. "I was trying not to hurt you."

Through all this she was silent, lost in thought and confusion, her clothes hanging half off and half on. She began to pull them back on, reaching for her panties, pulling the arm of her blouse back on.

Memories from the weeks past were throbbing wounds in her mind. For a moment she was safe, but she would never again want to make love to him. She knew tomorrow she would feel forgotten again, when she could not talk with him. But she also knew she would never be completely out of his thoughts, as she probably was already out of Paul's. Vince would always either boil with anger or weep at her memory. He would remember her even when he was making love to another woman. Even when he was with Grace. She had her own strings on him now.

"I've got to get some sleep," she said. She was feeling shaky and tired and eager to get back into her own safe haven.

"Well, I'm going to take a shower. I'm going to Jersey tonight. My brother just came in from Italy—I was talking on the phone with him earlier. They're expecting me at Mom's. I won't be here to see you off to Texas."

"You're leaving now? At this hour? It must be 2:00 in the morning."

"Two-thirty, almost," he said. "They're up late because he came in. They're waiting on me." But he did not move. He just sat there looking at her.

Camille sat there, feeling embarrassed, feeling it was her fault he was late.

"Well, I guess I had better go," she said, sitting up straight, feeling her muscles turning sore and pulling her blouse back on, tucking it into her jeans. She knew she looked completely rumpled. She pushed at her hair self-consciously as Vince continued to gaze at her with no expression. He put out his cigarette.

"You are beautiful," he said, leaning over and taking her face between his two hands and kissing her tenderly once more. "Let me help you find your shoes." He leaned over and looked under the bed.

"I'm still mad at you," she reminded him, afraid to tell him how angry she really felt and yet wanting him to know she was not able to forgive him just because he kissed her.

"You are?" He sounded surprised. "Even when I've loved you so good?"

She shook her head in total disbelief and tried to concentrate on putting on the shoes he handed her. He was saying he did it for her? That was hard to believe.

"You didn't ask me if you could."

"You wouldn't have let me if I had."

"You're right." She stood up and zipped the zipper of her jeans. "But then again, maybe I would have. We'll never know now."

"I know. I'm impossible," he said proudly as he walked into the bathroom and turned on the shower.

"Aren't you even going to say good-bye?" she shouted over the roar of the water.

"You'll be back," he shouted. "And even if you don't come back, you'll call me some day from San Francisco and say 'Vince, I need you, come on out,' and I'll fly out or down or to wherever you are and fuck you until you're tired of me again. Don't worry. I'll see you again."

Camille stood at the bathroom door while he showered, watching his beautiful body through the rippled glass. At last the water turned off and he came out, walking as tall and easily as a big cat, unself-consciously wiping only his face with a towel. His body was that of a young god's, his wide shoulders and strong torso tapering to narrow hips and long legs. He moved smoothly on bare feet, smooth gracefulness masking his strength. Camille moved out of his way as he started out of the bathroom, but he was not going out; he came to her and pulled her, fully clothed, against his wet, naked, clean-smelling body.

"My little Camille. I'm sorry I can't see you off to the airport. But you'll do all right. Just call a taxi and the driver can carry your bags." He crooned to her as if she was an idiot, his arms wrapped completely around her, pulling back only to purse his lips and croon the words.

"I'm not 'your little Camille,' and my bags are not that heavy," she protested, trying to pull away.

"All right, you win, but let him carry them anyway," he said, he went over to his wallet and handed her fifty dollars, "This is to pay for the taxi to the airport. And I'll see you when you get back." He stuffed the money into her jeans pocket.

"I hope you have a nice Christmas," she said, relenting and putting her arms around him to give him a good-bye hug.

"I won't. I hate Christmas," he said. And she knew he meant it.

"Good-bye." Camille turned and went to the door. He went with her and she let him kiss her good-bye. It was a long, soulful kiss that surprised Camille. It went straight to her heart. But she shook her head afterward. She was not fooled.

She went back to her boat feeling relieved to be in her own place. She showered really well and went to bed. She fell asleep immediately and did not even hear Vince leave.

In the morning, Camille called her lawyer friend in Texas and was reassured she would not be left penniless, no matter what. Now she could talk with John about getting a divorce when she arrived.

VIOLETS FOR REMEMBRANCE

A cold draft from the big windows drifted across her neck and hands as she painted in her Brooklyn studio. Tomorrow she would leave New York. She did not know how to express the peace she felt right now, except through her brushstrokes. Peace reigned in her mind. The sweep of her brushes against the canvas was the sound she heard. The colors in the painting of the nude gazing out of the window, which she was finishing today, were bright and cheerful. They reflected the optimism she felt, and the lines expressed her freedom.

She wore a couple of sweaters, with the painting smock over them, to keep warm. She stopped and looked around. Paintings were sitting around everywhere and the odor of turpentine was mixed in with the smoke from someone's pipe who had passed by in the hall. There was the distant sound of someone practicing on their horn in the basement, bringing back memories of happy days in the studio. The distance made the music sound thin and tinny, yet unmistakably a song she knew. She felt utterly at ease, with the day of working and painting over with. She would leave the studio in a few minutes, locking the door behind her for the last time this year. A few more strokes and the painting would be finished. She signed her name in the lower right hand corner.

She cleaned her brushes, gazing at the scratched surface of the door which had protected her from the outside world for the past four months whenever she needed privacy to cry or sleep. It had held her in a place she could work, absorbed in the exhilaration of the effort, creating something new out of old, concentrating on the canvas, creating out of the emotions of her mind, allowing her to eke them out into broad lines and brilliant colors.

She had worked hard in this place, painting and trying to absorb all new ideas that were important to know, trying to make new friends, to find fellow artists. It had been four months she would never have known if she had stayed in Texas. She knew she was not dreaming any more. She did not have to. What was happening and would continue to happen was real. It was Camille's life and no one else's; it was what she was.

"This is the real world, Camille. Welcome to it," she finally said aloud as she looked around at her studio and at the canvases she had painted.

Downstairs the trumpet player practiced scales. The clock in the tower tolled four times. The early-setting winter sun was already turning the walls orange and bringing images on the canvases all around her to life. She had painted a lot of images. The big one of a young woman facing a door was not yet finished. She could not get the man's figure in the doorway quite right. But two other paintings, one of a reclining figure and one of a standing figure in a garden were finished. They seemed to glow and move on their own in the hazy evening light. Camille gazed at them, unconscious of time passing.

The quiet was uninterrupted by passing footsteps. Everyone had gone home and the footsteps reminded her she was alone. Unwillingly she roused herself. She took off her smock. Her arms sought the sleeves of her winter coat. She looked around for her purse and keys. This was the last time she would be here this year, but it could be hers for the next two years if she wanted. How could she give it up? There was peace here, a life she had created for herself away from turmoil. This was her retreat. She wanted to stay here. She did not want to leave. But she had to do one last thing today. She had to take two paintings to the gallery for a client to look at.

She also considered trying to bring more supplies back to the boat, in case something happened and she did not return after Christmas. But she gave up on that idea when she saw how much she would have to carry if she did. So she only picked up the two paintings, each about two feet by three feet to take to the gallery. They were large and would be hard enough to handle on the subway.

The day was cold and the wind ferocious. Maneuvering the paintings was like sailing a boat. Once outside, they threatened to carry her off when the wind caught them the wrong way.

She stopped at the coffee shop for a cup of hot coffee, propping her paintings against a table and remembering the good times with friends she had shared here. She realized she was tired and sore from the night before and pulled back her sweater cuffs, examining the bruises hidden on her wrists. She had almost forgotten Vince, except when she stopped like this and felt the soreness. When she finished her hot coffee, picked up the paintings and stepped outside she almost collided with Alfred, standing talking to a blond woman on the corner. The woman stood stiffly in the cold, hands in her pockets, biting her lips as she listened. Camille looked at her sharply, trying to determine her relationship to Alfred, but they seemed to just be talking. She really didn't want to have to stop and hoped Alfred would just greet her and let her pass.

"Hello, Alfred," Camille said briefly as she passed. Alfred took a second look and recognized her behind the paintings. His face lighted up. He touched her arm and held up a finger to keep her from walking away, asking if she was heading for the subway. Camille said yes, so he said good-bye to the woman, who turned and ran across the street, obviously freezing.

"Let me take the paintings," said Alfred. Camille allowed him, gratefully. He seemed more capable than she, since he was over six feet tall and looked even more enormous than usual in a heavy wool coat with his thick red beard sticking out of the collar. Camille felt the cold more, now that she was not protected by the paintings, but was soon distracted by Alfred's lively conversation as they hurried along. Once seated on the train, she warmed up and listened to Alfred talk, mostly about himself, his favorite topic. He talked about what he had done, the grants he was applying for and the grants he had gotten in the past for art work. It did not matter, as long as he was talking. Camille felt happy.

Camille stood up when they got to the Spring Street stop and said good-bye. Alfred gave her a parting kiss and asked where she was going. She explained she was going to the gallery and he said he would carry the paintings there for her, so he went with her and looked around the gallery while Camille told Ann about the paintings. Alfred came wandering back to her and she apologized for making him wait, but she now had to stay and talk to Hal and probably would not be leaving any time soon. The gallery was closing and Ann was leaving, so Alfred said he would walk Ann home, as she was going his direction. Before he left, however, he leaned over and kissed Camille on the lips again.

"There, I got to kiss you good-bye twice. I'll see you in January, I hope." He smiled and winked as he left.

Hal was in the storage room. He looked at Camille with sad

eyes and she could not tell what he was thinking. He was aware of her estrangement from Vince now, her involvement (at least suspected involvement) with Paul, and of her coming ordeal in Texas. She had told him she was going home for the holidays, but did not expect it to be very merry. It was a Christmas that would certainly be lost. But instead of talking, he started pulling her paintings down off the shelves and asking Camille which ones she wanted to show.

While she put new slides into a file in the office, Renee mentioned some part-time jobs that might be available in January. The feeling of hope that arose in Camille as she began to think there might be an opportunity for a regular paycheck was a new one. She had not worked for money for years. So, when Renee gave her the telephone numbers, she called them right then and made appointments. She told Renee if she got a job she would give her a finder's fee. She found tears unexpectedly stinging her eyes as she hugged Hal and Renee good-bye and wished them a happy holiday.

The freezing wind pushed against her as she walked alone the long, dark blocks from subway to river. It blew newspapers caught in the doorways in circles. Puddles of water were ringed with icy shards and every step hurt because her feet were so cold in her thin tennis shoes. She closed her eyes to the wind, which blew up the front of her coat and through her sweater. She could think of nothing but the cold wind. It had the power to make her think of nothing else but getting rid of the pain it inflicted. It annoyed her by unwrapping her scarf and pulling on her purse. It made her eyes water, her lips freeze and her nose run. It would not be ignored.

April called and was eager to come see her, so she told her to come over while she dressed to go to Grace's for dinner. April chattered away while Camille dressed. She was auditioning for modeling jobs while she worked in a travel agency, which she hated. It was too much work for too little pay. The laws for divorce in New York were archaic, she complained; she was having a hard time trying to get custody of her oldest child. And to top it off she had just found out she was pregnant again.

At this, Camille stopped and looked at April, trying to imagine her tiny waist swollen with child. She won't even be twenty-one when she has her third baby, she thought. She sympathized and gave April a hug, as April's swollen eyes filled with tears again. They would miss each other. Life was not easy, but at least April had her man to protect her now. She told April she would give her the fish in the morning, to keep for a few days. April smiled a little and said good-bye.

Camille arrived at Grace's late. Grace led her up the narrow steps to the dining room. They found themselves discussing women's issues, something Grace was very involved in and Camille was interested in. They discussed the mid-life crisis, a term made popular by the book Passages, which Camille had read last year. Grace said it seemed nature had designed things in the correct order for women, with their hormones or glands or whatever it was that made them more aggressive, beginning to come alive in their bodies later than in the man's. Because when women are young they seem to be more dependent on men and men's strength, being weaker and pregnant and having children hanging all over them. Then, when the children are old enough to be out on their own, when the woman is about 35, she becomes more aggressive and actually wants to become independent and live a free life. The age of 35 is the natural time to have a mid-life crisis, she said, if having a mid-life crisis means you want to strike out on your own.

Camille guessed Grace brought this up because she wanted to talk to her about divorce. Together they looked at the facts and decided women had three choices, like in the prayer, when it became necessary to make changes in life:

"Say things were bad in your marriage. First, if you didn't even try to change yourself or the circumstances, if you accept your fate eventually you feel hopeless and helpless and unhappy. Second, you try to change only the alterable circumstances, realizing there are some things which are inalterable which you have to accept and you are still a little unhappy. Third, if you have already tried changing yourself and the circumstances which were changeable and the second choice still did not make you happy, you have to accept yourself and the circumstances and be content knowing you tried. Or you can change yourself and change the circumstances and change everything so that it makes you happy."

In this discussion Grace's choice of the word "circumstances" sounded an awful like "husband," to Camille. She stayed with Grace until 11:30, discussing this and many more things, eating and drinking coffee. In spite of the closeness she felt with Grace, she was beginning to realize there were still some things she could not talk with her about – namely Vince.

It was midnight when she let herself back in her boat, tired and ready to fall into bed. The phone rang as soon as she stepped inside, startling her in the black silence. She turned on the single light by the phone and picked up the receiver. It was Paul! Her heart jumped. She was happy to hear his voice and realized her voice showed it. He said he had called to say "hello" and "good-bye." He was going to East Hampton for the holidays in the morning. She said she hoped he would have good weather.

"My classes are over," she said, "I'm very relieved. I think I did all right. I'm still packing my bags and trying to find room for the presents I got for friends and relatives." She glanced at the bed where she had laid out everything she planned to pack.

"I enjoyed being with you the other evening," he said. It the first time he had called since then and she thought he must not have enjoyed it as much as she had or he would have called earlier.

"I enjoyed it, too," she said, feeling her enthusiasm drop. "I thought I would regret it the next day, but I didn't. I felt like I had been given a gift." She had memorized these words to say to him after mulling over various phrases to find a way of thanking him so he would not feel overwhelmed, but would know she was happy with him. Still, in saying the words she had chosen to say, they became false to her. Did they sound false to him, too?

"I'm glad," he said quietly and thoughtfully. "I felt that way, too." There was a little, awkward silence. "I'll send you a Christmas card from the Island."

"I'll look for it."

"I'll see you next year."

"I'll be thinking of you enjoying the Hamptons while I'm suffering with my relatives in Texas," she said. He did not know how much she would be suffering.

"The Hamptons are not pleasant in the winter, but that's where my family is," he said and added, "My uncle and aunt live there year round." They exchanged a few words about unimportant things, a little stiffly, as if they were strangers, then he said "Well, good-bye."

"Bye, Paul, have a Merry Christmas," said Camille as she hung up. It had been a short call, but at least he had called her. She felt a little better toward him, happy he had thought of her, realizing he had not been negative in any way. Though they had only been together once, they shared a good experience. Paul's notoriety could have made her feel a little self-conscious around him, but she kept on telling herself he was just another man and not to take everything so seriously, to try to appreciate him for what he gave her personally.

She was packing her bags as she mulled over the conversation. Finally she put her bags on the floor, climbed into bed and tried to sleep. She hoped she would survive the next week and return to tell about it.

The next morning when she woke up at 8:45, it was snowing. Big flakes fell on the gray water and disappeared, becoming the mirror they melted into. She stood at the window in the dull light blurred by swiftly falling snow and thought of Paul again, trying to go out to the Hamptons in this weather. It had been wrong of her to wish him good weather. It had brought bad luck. But even as she watched, the snow stopped and the sun began to come through the clouds, glistening on the fresh snow. Perhaps the day would not be so bad.

She ate, put on some old clothes and cleaned up the boat. She called April and Grace. April came across the dock in her housecoat to talk, bringing her baby, who played on the floor. She left with a bag of eggs, butter, potatoes, onions, a lemon and Fidel in a glass. Fidel would visit April's fish for the holidays.

Grace arrived later and got the rest of the fresh fruit and vegetables that would spoil while Camille was gone. She left, giving Camille a hug at the door and said she would see her next year. Camille knew she not only appreciated her as a friend, but appreciated getting rent for her boat. So she felt she was helping Grace, after all, and not just receiving from her.

At noon, Camille called a taxi to come to the boat basin, found her purse, put her plane ticket in it, picked up her bags and set them on the dock outside the door. She went back inside to take one more look around before locking the door, to see if she had forgotten anything. She reached a hand out for the bunch of dry violets that had sat by the telephone all those months. She intended to throw them out, but now that she was about to do so, she relented. Though they had dried, they had not faded or fallen apart, but sat, as purple as ever, inside their little paper lace collar. So she left them right where they were.

View from the back of the boat